HARD RESET

BOOKS BY JONATHAN YANEZ

THE GALACTIC GUARDIANS SERIES

Legend Rising
Starship Found
Shadow of the Contender
Calamity Awakening
Dark Star Deceit
Gathering Storm
Heaven and Earth

THE HUNTERS FOR HIRE SERIES

Hunters for Hire
Town Lore
All Valley Tournament
Godmothered
Devil May Care
Dying of the Light

THE FORSAKEN MERCENARY SERIES

Dropship
Absolution
Fury
Vendetta
Annihilation
Nemesis
Rivals
Wolves
Crusade
Traitor
Parabellum
Judgment

For a full list of books by Jonathan Yanez, please visit his website at www.jonathan-yanez.com.

HARD RESET

A LitRPG Novel

JONATHAN YANEZ

BLACK STONE PUBLISHING

Published in 2026 by Blackstone Publishing
Cover and book design by Candice Edwards

Printed in the United States of America
Originally published in hardcover by Blackstone Publishing in 2026

First paperback edition: 2026
ISBN 979-8-228-64878-4
Fiction / LitRPG (Literary Role-Playing Game)

Version 1

Blackstone Publishing
31 Mistletoe Rd.
Ashland, OR 97520

www.BlackstonePublishing.com

To God for the ability,
my wife for the love, my family and friends
for the support, and the reader community
we lovingly call our Pack for their willingness to believe.

PROLOGUE

He was hers and she was his. As long as things stayed that way, all would be right with the world.

Tom held his wife close. Her frame, pressed against his body, was his home. No words were needed as husband and wife stood in the kitchen, embracing one another.

It was a day after another test, another doctor unable to find an answer to what was ailing Lana. Despite the news, the two were together, and Tom had faith they'd find a way forward.

"You know, we hold each other any longer, and you're going to get excited and start asking for other things," Lana said playfully, separating herself from her husband. She looked into his eyes, cocking her head to the side. "What? What is it?"

"Nothing," Tom lied.

"You're a horrible liar," Lana told him, her arms still around his waist. "It's going to be all right. *I'm* going to be all right. The fearsome Tom Dexter doesn't have to worry about me. I'll keep your secret."

"What secret?" Tom asked as they let go of one another.

Lana tested the boiling noodles in the pot on the stove.

"That you care about other people. That once you get past all the rough and deadly, you're a protector at heart."

"You're right, we should keep that secret," Tom said, smelling the sauce infused with basil and garlic. "And I'll keep yours."

"What? That I'm the world's best cook?"

"That you're the cat lady of hummingbirds."

"I am not," Lana said, slapping Tom's rear end.

"Really?" Tom asked with a lifted brow. He looked at the hummingbird pictures on the far wall of the dining room, the hummingbird-printed oven warmers, and finally the many hummingbird feeders outside the kitchen window, where at least a dozen of the tiny birds drank greedily.

"Okay, it's not my fault they're my favorite bird," Lana said, eyeing Tom. "Stop."

"Stop what?"

"Stop thinking about how we're going to get the money for more doctor visits," Lana answered. "I'm going to be fine."

CHAPTER 1

TOM

Tom jolted awake from a dream his subconscious couldn't, or maybe wouldn't, fully remember. One second, he'd been strapped to a table in a white room; the next, he found himself lying supine in a cold, dark box. A distinct chime that came from nowhere and everywhere at once woke him. The air was thick and heavy.

He had no memory of how he'd gotten there, no idea of where "there" was. Some dormant instincts kicked in as Tom took in his surroundings. He was in a cramped space that made him claustrophobic. A screen built into the box flickered just above him.

Tom felt the sides of the box; it wasn't much larger than a coffin.

Why this didn't strike more fear into him, he didn't know. He wasn't sure what conditioning he might or might not have had to remain so calm. His past was as much of a mystery as how he had gotten here. Wherever "here" was.

Trying to understand things like why he was in a box or why he was able to keep his composure was like grasping for vapor amid a harsh winter wind. Other things, however, came to his memory as soon as he called for them. Tom knew his name. He knew how to operate the touch screen—black, with green writing—above him. He searched for a call feature but found none.

Tom fumbled for a path forward, lost in the darkness of his mind. Fear's icy hand gripped his heart. But he wasn't going to give in to trepidation's panicked call. It just wasn't who he was.

Tom paused and waited in silence, and that was all that came in return: silence.

Although there was no radio feature on the screen, there was a readout for air quality. It told him escaping the box would be a safe bet. Below that was an icon that read "Level."

Tom tapped it. More text appeared, word by word, as if someone were typing out a message in real time. This text he didn't understand.

LEVEL 1

CLASS TYPE: UNKNOWN

SKILL POINTS: 0

CREDITS: YOU'RE BROKE.

ODDS OF SURVIVAL? UNLIKELY.

Tom tapped the monitor again. The screen flickered. No matter what Tom tried, the air-quality readout and this odd display were the only two bits of information he had to work with.

It was strange, what memories Tom still carried and what he did not. It was as if someone had gone through his brain like a filing cabinet, plucking the files they wanted to discard and leaving the rest. Tom knew that humankind had taken to the stars, colonizing the moon and Mars. Since the readout in front of him assured him that he would be able to breathe outside, he could only be on Earth, Mars, or the moon.

Tom was ready to see where he was. With a silent prayer, he shoved the top of the box. It gave with little issue.

That's the first thing that's gone my way, Tom thought as he climbed out.

The box lid had been kept in place by a few inches of sand that now trickled down into his resting place, which he identified with certainty as a coffin.

Muscles groaned and ached as he stood in the shallow grave. An alien landscape opened in every direction. He was surprised to find himself on top of a multistory building—the only structure around. As far as the eye could see, there was sand, sand, and more sand. The roof was coated with it. But this wasn't what bothered him the most. What bothered Tom the most was the suns in the sky. More than one.

Tom stood in the shallow grave for a moment. Anyone would be terrified at a time like this, but not remembering how he had gotten there or where he was added an extra layer of madness to the equation.

Hold it together, Tom reminded himself. *The next thing. What's the next thing that has to be done?*

A primordial howl echoed across the barren landscape, finding a final resting spot in the pit of Tom's stomach. The sound was like nothing he had heard before: one part wolf, one part crocodile, and all parts hungry.

With no water or food, staying put didn't seem like an option at all. Neither was there any kind of tracking device in the casket. If rescuers came, they wouldn't know where to look. Tom was alone. Only he was responsible for his survival.

He wasn't sure if it was morning or about to turn to night. The roof of whatever structure he was on boasted only a spartan landscape of sand; his was the only grave.

On the far end of the rooftop, a tired door hung off broken

hinges. Tom descended the stairwell, stopping to look into each floor for anything that might give him answers. Each level was as barren as the desert landscape around him. Not so much as a rat or cockroach.

When Tom reached the ground floor, he set off from his would-be funeral site in what he hoped was the right direction. To the north, or what Tom assumed was the north, mountains jutted up past the sand dunes.

He couldn't stay where he was. Hounded by the calls of the beasts, Tom placed one foot in front of the other. He never saw the creatures, but the hairs on his arms stood up at uneven intervals when their calls rose about him. Whatever these animals were, they were watching him, and there was more than one.

Tom had heard of experiments going on to resurrect extinct predators in both the labs on the moon and the privately funded research bases on Mars. He'd never given those conspiracy theories much thought, until now.

Head on a swivel, Tom traveled for hours, the dry air cracking his lips, the soft terrain seeking to trip him with every step. It turned out the suns were coming up. It was morning. Tom wasn't sure if that was better or worse than night. But at the moment, he had his hands full, trying not to be tracked down by the creatures that hunted him.

It could have been three or four hours before Tom stumbled across the first sign of water. A muddy drinking hole was carved into the sand. It might as well have been an oasis. Lips cracked and throat parched, he staggered the last few feet toward the water's edge.

"Not a good idea," a voice called out.

Without thinking, Tom reacted, right hand searching for a sidearm that wasn't there.

"Whoa, whoa, easy. Let's just take it easy there for a

moment. We're all getting excited," the man's voice said soothingly. "There's no enemies here, just friends."

Tom got his first good look at the older man. He had a white beard and hair, and his clothes were beaten by the terrain. There was a twinkle of madness in his eyes that whispered of more than one loose screw.

"Where—where am I?" Tom asked through a hoarse throat. "Who are you?"

"We're near Athera," the old man said, extending his hand behind him. He continued in a whisper, as if talking to someone else. "No, no, I think he'll be fine. He's not one of them. I have a good feeling about this one. Don't bring that up again. That was one time."

"Excuse me?" Tom asked, glancing around to make sure they were, in fact, alone. "Who are you talking to?"

"No, what? Me? No one, nothing," the other said, coming back to his senses and fixing Tom with what he imagined the man assumed was an award-winning smile. It looked more like a Cheshire cat grin to Tom. "I'm Wade. And trust me; I see you eyeing that water like a starving bounty hunter with his next mark in sight. Wait until we get back to town. The water's no good here."

Tom looked back at the water with a small sigh, resigning himself to having to wait at least a little longer to quench his thirst. The liquid bubbled. Before he could react, a pair of purple tentacles launched toward his face.

Tom grunted, throwing himself backward just in time to miss the alien embrace of whatever lurked beneath the surface of the pond.

"Now, Terrance, I thought we talked about that," Wade said, admonishing the tentacles as they slipped back under the surface. "He's new here; let's all just show a little common courtesy."

"What was that thing?" Tom asked, scrambling to his feet.

"Sorry, Terrance gets a little excited from time to time," Wade said with a shrug, as if the tentacled creature in the pond and he were old friends. "Come on now, we don't want to get stuck out here when the suns begin to go down. The night hounds are . . . aggressive in large numbers."

Wade turned to go as if Tom didn't have a dozen different questions to ask. Before Tom could get one out of his mouth, a sharp pain cascaded through his right temple, blinding, brutal migraine pain like a chilled ice pick going through the middle of his skull.

Tom gritted his teeth, closing his eyes. Flashes of a woman, a feeling more than a face, a sense of love. He felt as though he cared for her.

"You coming, stranger?" Wade asked, looking over his shoulder.

As quickly as the pain came, it abated. The images were gone, along with the agony, as if they had never been.

As Wade turned to go, he said, "It looks like you took a pretty hard knock to the head. Are you okay?"

Tom touched a hand to his head; dried blood came back like tiny chips of rust on his fingertips. "I'll live," Tom told him, falling in step with the older man.

They walked in silence, every step reminding Tom how thirsty he really was. But there was no option except to continue forward. He wasn't the kind to curl into a ball and die. It just wasn't in him. And what about the woman? She had come and gone from his thoughts so quickly but left a lasting impression. He was sure he knew her and that she meant something to him.

"Where did you say we were?" Tom asked Wade after ascending what felt like the hundredth sand dune. "This can't be Earth, not with two suns. Are we on Mars? No. There aren't twin suns on Mars either."

"Not the sharpest tool in the shed, are we?" Wade asked with a wry smile.

Tom's scowl made Wade cough into his hand and rethink his answer. "We're just a small colony, Athera."

"Where?"

"Seriously, a few cards short of a full deck, huh? Athera."

As they spoke, Tom's migraine teased a return, as if even dwelling on the subject for too long summoned the horrible agony. Tom decided to let the line of questioning go for now. He needed water and food. Those priorities had to be taken care of first, and then he could find out exactly where he was. Odds were Wade was the one a few sandwiches short of a picnic. They could be on the far side of Mars, for all Tom knew. Maybe the extra sun wasn't a sun at all but a piece of tech, a weather balloon or orbiting station.

"Home," Wade said, gazing over the top of a sand dune.

Tom followed his eyes, looking down into a valley a few miles down the path. He saw ruined buildings on the perimeter of a beat-up town that gave him all the postapocalyptic vibes he could handle.

"This is Athera?" Tom asked incredulously.

"Well, excuse us," Wade said, a puff of air escaping his lips. "It may not be the shiny metropolis you're from, no four-star restaurants or ride-sharing services, but it's home."

Tom decided not to push Wade on the matter. Wade was leading the way, and Tom couldn't think about much outside of quenching his thirst.

The pair walked into Athera, which seemed like an overgrown concrete jungle. Broken buildings lined the main street, with tired weeds growing in the many cracks in the pavement. Here and there, metal fabrication had been employed to patch old buildings. A service droid was being worked on at the local blacksmith. Everyone they passed stared at Tom warily.

"Well, well, well, what do we have here, Wade?" a large man in a vest asked, stepping from the doorframe of a bar. Two other men flanked him, one tall and lean and the other a cyborg with a robotic face. "Another stray from the badlands?"

"Now, Otto," Wade said, trying to appease the town muscle, "he just needs some water. I found him out wandering around. I don't think he's like the others. He just needs a hand."

"Sure, sure, we all seem to need a hand these days," Otto said with a malevolent stare. "But everyone who comes into my town pays a fee in credits or blood. Now what's it going to be, stranger, your coin or your life?"

Tom was still getting to know who he was. His memory was so far gone that he wasn't sure how he would react until it was time. Instead of speaking, he held Otto's gaze, refusing to back down.

"Oh, looks like we got a hero here!" Otto barked to the men beside him, "Get him."

CHAPTER 2

TOM

They came in hard and fast. The time for words was done, and the time for violence had come. The first thug, tall with a thick shock of black hair, came at him with an overhand right.

Like he was scratching an itch, Tom reacted on instinct. He didn't have time to think; he just moved. His right arm came up to intercept the blow, blocking the fist aimed for his head. A split second later, he threw a left punch into the man's gut not once but three times.

His attacker doubled over. Tom grabbed the man by the hair with both hands. With all his might, he drove the man's head down and his right knee up. With a sickening crunch that signaled a shattered nose, the man collapsed.

Tom had a second to marvel at the sheer brutality he was capable of and the person he had apparently been before the man with the cyborg mask came in as if to tackle Tom to the ground. Tom moved with the force, allowing himself to be bulled backward, but didn't fall.

Instead, he wrapped his right arm under the cyborg's chin and squeezed. If the robo thug needed to breathe, he was going to be in a world of hurt. Tom bore down like a pit bull with a bone, squeezing the life out of the cyborg. Apparently, whatever mechanical upgrades had been made to the man did not include changing the way he got air.

The man beat at Tom, trying to break free. Tom redoubled his efforts, locking his left arm under the cyborg's neck, and applied even more pressure. Within seconds, the man fell limp in his arms. Like his predecessor, Tom allowed him to slump to the ground.

Breathing hard but still not breaking a sweat, Tom looked up at Otto. Otto was past words; instead, he lunged forward with a balled fist.

"Otto," Wade said, placing himself between the men and bringing Otto up short, "let's just settle down here. This has been a misunderstanding. What would Bishop say?"

At the mention of the name, Otto seemed to deflate a moment. A few locals were beginning to gather, bearing witness to the violence Otto was encouraging.

This seemed like enough for Wade, who stepped aside, pulling Tom to follow.

"You bought yourself some time, newbie," Otto said, narrowing his eyes. "But I will find you."

Tom let Wade pull him along, Otto's threat echoing in his mind.

"Otto's a local bounty hunter; he means well," Wade explained, leading Tom through a maze of side streets. "Only he doesn't trust new faces much. You see, he feels it's his job to protect this city and the people here."

"He needs a lesson in Discernment 101," Tom muttered.

Wade led the way through Athera to the town's outskirts, where scattered houses were set up, made mostly of concrete and a few steel parts. Lips cracked and throat dry, it was difficult for Tom to focus much on the surrounding area. The need for water was nearly a palpable panic at this point.

Wade was waxing poetic about the community being just a small town compared to the much larger city of Canto to the east. Maybe Tom would have paid more attention if he weren't dying of thirst, but in all reality, probably not.

"Ahhh, here we go, home sweet home," Wade said with a proud smile at a hovel in front of them. "Casa de Wade."

Tom took in what should have been called a lean-to instead of any kind of home. A one-story shack with a chain-link fence that looked rusted through greeted his eyes. Beggars couldn't be choosers, and if there was water in the home, then Tom was all in.

Wade opened the waist-high gate for Tom. The gate, exhausted from years of service, gave up, cracked at the hinges, and fell to the ground.

"Oh my," Wade said, taking out a stained pad of paper from a pocket and a stub of a pencil. "Have to add that to my to-do list." He walked on as he made the note.

Tom followed, taking in the dirt front yard with rocks and clumps of brightly colored cactus spread out in no discernible pattern.

Wade entered a passcode on a pad mounted on the front door. To Tom's surprise, the door slid open on a hydraulic mechanism. The two men walked into the house.

As Tom stepped over the threshold, an automatic chime that came from nowhere and everywhere echoed through the building. It was the same noise that had awakened Tom in the coffin.

"You okay?" Wade asked good-naturedly. "You look like you saw a ghost."

"You—you didn't hear that?" Tom asked.

"Hear what?" Wade shrugged off his coat. "And they call

me the crazy one. Unless my hearing is going as well." Wade dug into his pocket again for his to-do list and made another note. "Get hearing checked."

The front room was more of a combination sitting area and kitchen. A large chest that looked somewhat out of place rested in the middle of the room in lieu of a table. To the left was a short hall with three open doors. Tom could see inside two; they looked like bedrooms. The third door was shut.

Wade moved deeper inside the house.

Something about the chest called to Tom. It seemed so foreign yet familiar—what did it remind him of? A loot crate, treasure chest? The item was about three feet long, two feet wide, and two feet tall. It was rusted and gray with faded yellow and blue markings.

Some subconscious need to reach out and touch the trunk took hold of Tom. With a tentative right hand, Tom tried to open the chest. There was no handle or clasp he could find. Both hands roved around the chest, looking for an entry point.

"Whoa, whoa, whoa, at least buy me a drink first." A robotic voice filled the room. It sounded like it was coming from the chest.

Tom looked up to see if Wade had heard anything. If he had, he didn't show it. The older man was working in the kitchen and whistling to himself.

"He can't hear me," the robotic voice continued. "You're kind of a predator, you know that? I haven't been felt up like that since prom night. Here's your HUD. You haven't done much yet; don't be too proud of yourself."

A screen appeared in front of Tom just like the screen he had seen on the interior of the coffin lid, except this one floated in front of him like a holographic monitor. It read:

LEVEL 2

CLASS TYPE: UNKNOWN

SKILL POINTS: 1

CREDITS: YOU'RE POORER THAN THAT GUY WHO WORKED FOR MR. SCROOGE, AND THAT GUY COULDN'T EVEN AFFORD CRUTCHES FOR TINY TIM.

"How hard did I hit my head?" Tom muttered to himself.

"Water?" Wade said. As soon as he spoke, the screen over the chest vanished.

Wade reached for a water canister. He seemed about to pick up a cup, then did a double take at Tom and just handed him the entire jug.

Tom wanted to ask about the chest, but the screen had disappeared, and his need for water trumped all other desires.

Without another word, Tom guzzled down the cool liquid. If water could taste any better, he couldn't imagine it. It soothed his throat, brought saliva back to his mouth, and healed his cracked lips.

"Easy, easy there, come up for breath." Wade chuckled as he took a seat with Tom at the table.

As far as furniture, there wasn't much in the house. The front room held a single ripped couch and an army of junk, from nets to steel plates. The kitchen wasn't much better off—a square table with three mismatched wooden chairs and a countertop with an assortment of cooking equipment that Tom didn't recognize. There was something that might have been a microwave and something else that looked like the love child of a coffee maker and a toaster.

"Do you have anyone?" Wade asked.

"What do you mean?" Tom answered, cleaning his lips with the back of his sleeve.

"You know, family, a wife?"

"I—I don't know," Tom said, fighting not to scrutinize the question lest another migraine approach. "My thoughts are like gazing at the sun. I can't focus directly on them. But I think so. I remember a woman and . . . sadness. Why do I feel so sad when I think of her?"

Pounding came from the door, so loud that Tom jolted in his seat. Adrenaline crashed through his system, readying him for another fight.

CHAPTER 3

TOM

Wade didn't seem as concerned as Tom. The older man immediately stood and walked toward the door. There was no peephole to check who it might be, but again, Wade didn't seem worried. He pressed an electric button on the side of the wall, allowing the rusted metal door to slide open.

Tom winced at the light of the setting suns as they obscured his vision. A dark shadow entered the room.

Wade closed the door behind the figure and welcomed her with open arms. "Well, we were just talking about you."

Tom's eyes adjusted, giving him a better look at the woman. She was tall and slender, with a bag over her shoulder and a weariness to her eyes that had nothing to do with lack of sleep.

"Wade," the woman said.

"Doc," Wade answered, "I have someone here I'd like you to meet."

Doc turned to take in Tom. Their eyes met without challenge, but each held the other's gaze. Tom was sure he didn't know the woman, but there was something in the way she looked at him, something in those green eyes, that said she knew who he was.

"We were just about to sit down to dinner," Wade added. "I can set the table for three, if you like?"

"That's kind, but I can't stay long," Doc answered.

Entering the kitchen, she placed her satchel on the table and leaned in close to Tom. "Haven't seen a noob like you here before. Looks like you took a pretty good crack to your head. How's the pain?"

"It doesn't tickle," Tom answered, allowing Doc to move his head around and get a better look at the laceration above his left eye.

"You alone?" Doc asked, reaching into her bag for sterile gloves and a tool that looked like a thick pen.

"As far as I know," Tom said.

"I'm sorry. This is going to—how did you say it?" Doc asked. "This isn't going to tickle. Do you want something for the pain?"

"I'll be all right," Tom insisted.

"Okay," Doc said, tilting Tom's head to the side. She placed the pen close. A solid red light flashed out, cleaning and cauterizing the wound.

The pain was intense and sudden but manageable. Tom clenched his jaw, reminding himself that this, too, would pass. Pain was temporary. He would heal and be done soon.

"This will help make sure the wound isn't infected and stop the bleeding," Doc said after what felt like an eternity of work but in reality couldn't have been more than a few minutes. "Where were you coming from?"

"I—I don't know," Tom said, searching for memories that weren't there. "Where—where am I?"

"You're in the Eternal Engine," Doc said, placing her tools back into her satchel and producing a clear vial of red pills.

"Don't try to remember too much now. All of this can be taxing on a new mind. Take one of these pills before you go to sleep tonight. The memories will come in time."

Tom looked at the vial as she placed it on the table in front of him. To say he was tired and hungry would have been an understatement; he was exhausted and famished.

As if she could read his mind, Doc looked over at Wade. "He'll be okay. He needs some food and sleep, but he'll be all right. Is he staying with you?"

"Actually, I—" Tom managed before he was cut off.

"He can stay here," Wade said, excited. "I'll get him back on his feet in no time."

Doc nodded and made for the door. Before she left, she looked back at Tom. "Don't force the memories. They'll come. The mouthy chest can wait another day. You've been through enough for now. One pill before bed."

"Thanks, Doc," Tom said, rising from his seat to see her off. It was the least he could do after all the help she had been. "Hey, the chest, what is—"

She was gone.

When the door shut behind her, Wade immediately went to work preparing a meal in the small kitchen. He hummed a tune that teased at the edges of Tom's memories. It was familiar, like a lullaby, slow and sad. When Tom reached for the recollection, it eluded him.

Anytime he thought about things like where he was, how he had come to be in a coffin, or who he was, the pain in his head reappeared as if it had been summoned by an outside force.

"All right, here we go," Wade said as he sizzled long strips of dark meat on a steel frying pan that hovered over the stove. The flames licking the pan were purple and pink. "I hope you have a liking for tanshar meat. It's a little salty at first, might give you the runs, but it'll win you over in the end."

The aroma of searing meat made Tom salivate. Wade could have said he was frying up that tentacled creature from the watering hole and Tom still would have eaten it at this point.

"All right, here we go. It's hot," Wade said, placing a plate of steak-like meat in front of Tom. Beside the steak was a pile of . . . something that looked like mashed potatoes but smelled like carrots. "Tanshar steaks and tanshar surprise, my specialty."

Tom looked at the steak and mystery mash with mixed emotions. He was starving, but was he really going to put this into his body? Wade came over with a cloth napkin, a spork, and more water.

"Go ahead, dig in," Wade said, taking the seat across the table. He used his spork to spear the meat and bring the whole thing to his lips, where he ripped off a juicy piece with his teeth and chewed with enthusiasm.

You don't want to be rude now, do you? Tom thought to himself. *Into the breach.*

He followed suit, lifting the steak to his lips and tearing off a chunk. The meat actually wasn't that bad. If he held his breath and imagined really, really hard, it tasted like New York strip.

After the successful bite of the steak, Tom moved on to the mashed-potato-looking stuff on the side. He took a tentative spork full of the mash and chewed with utter horror. Whatever it was did not taste like tanshar meat at all. This was one part salt, one part onion, and all parts bad.

"Good, right?" Wade said, leaning in from his seat across the table. "Do you like my famous tanshar surprise? I don't make it for just anyone, you know."

"Mmm-mmm-hmm," Tom said, struggling to swallow the stuff. Tears came to his eyes, but he managed to wrestle it down.

"It's delicious. What's in your tanshar surprise? More tanshar or more surprise?"

"Less tanshar and more surprise." Wade winked as if that were a good thing.

As the two men ate, Wade played a tune from a miniature record player in the middle of the family room. It was the same song he had been whistling while making dinner. The line "when you're a stranger" repeated over and over again.

"All right, I'm sure you're ready to turn in for the night," Wade said, getting up from the table and clearing away the chipped, mismatched plates. "I'll show you the accommodations."

He ushered Tom to one of the two bedrooms in the small house. It wasn't much more than a bed and a dresser; there was a window on the far wall. The bed looked as though it had seen better decades. The frame was chipped, the blanket thin and dusty.

"Sorry, it's no two-star hotel, but it's a place to rest your head," Wade said.

"This is great, thank you," Tom said, placing a hand on the old man's shoulder.

Wade nodded and turned to walk down the hall. "Restroom is right here, and my room's the only other door if you need anything. Sleep well."

Tom fell asleep soon after taking one of the red pills from the clear vial Doc had left. It was a sleep he wouldn't soon forget. A nightmare he would always remember.

CHAPTER 4

TOM

Tom saw himself with a woman. He was younger than he was now, a bright smile with pearl-white teeth, a short haircut. The woman was a brunette with love in her eyes. The pair cuddled playfully in bed. Golden light streamed through an open window. Their room was small but somehow still able to fit all the love the two created inside.

Memories flashed by in quick succession as Tom was ripped from his time with the woman to his training in the military and a myriad of people he didn't recognize dressed in camo uniforms. There was a trial. He was standing trial. Then the inside of a cell. The last image was of him sitting alone at a table. An empty bottle of whiskey, an empty glass, a blaster at his side. A dishonorable discharge letter in front of him, and a ring? Was that his wedding ring?

Before Tom could try to piece together more of the images flashing in front of him, the view transitioned again. He was back in the coffin. The same chime he'd heard twice before echoed in his mind again. This time, with no other noises present, he heard it loud and clear.

It was a two-toned electronic ding. Something like "bee

boo," not that different from the bell that sounded when entering a gas station.

He steadied his breathing, taking in the inside of the coffin yet again. Everything was the same, screen above him in the cold, hard box, but this time he wasn't alone. The box, his coffin, was wider this time. Wide enough to fit another person beside him, a woman. Her head was turned away from him.

Tom moved his mouth, but no words came.

The woman slowly turned her head to face him. It was her, the woman from his dreams who he was so sure he loved.

"Tom," she said, maneuvering her left hand to the side of his face. "Tom, none of this was your fault. I love you."

Tom woke with a start. Back in his room at Wade's house, he breathed hard, remembering all the events that had transpired in his dream. There was no sudden agony in his skull. He remembered everything clearly and without hesitation or pain.

The sound that woke him reverberated into the house again. It was a howl, one of the same howls Tom had heard in the desert. He threw off the thin covers and made his way to the window. The largest moon he had ever seen shone through, painting the room silver and blue.

Just off Wade's property, on a slight hill, a silhouetted figure lifted its thick neck and let out a mournful call. The creature stood on all fours, with a muscular body and elongated snout like a wolf. But this was no wolf. It had to be twice the size of the largest dog that Tom had ever seen. The animal called out once more, a bay so mournful it reminded Tom of the sad melody Wade had hummed.

Something took hold of Tom right then, a sixth sense he hadn't known he had. Maybe it was the aggravation of not having any answers. Seeing the creature might help him figure out where he was.

Shirtless, Tom darted from his room, out the front door, and toward the hill where he had seen the creature. The beast, whatever it had been, was gone. Heart beating quickly and adrenaline surging, Tom weighed his options: going up the hill and trying to catch a look at the creature, or returning to his room.

What have you got to lose? Tom asked himself.

Well, you could be eaten by an alien wolf. There's that.

He decided to make the short trek up the sandy hill and get a look with the moon's illumination. The lights of Athera to his left, Tom passed the gate. All around, various buildings stood rooted to their spots, generators humming and solar panels ready to take in the warm embrace of the suns the next day.

Senses on overdrive, Tom bent low to climb up the dune. His bare feet sank deep into the soft sand. When he reached the ridge, it wasn't an alien creature he saw.

Below him and to his right, a man worked in the light of the moon. Over and over again, he slammed a heavy shovel with a sharp edge into the sand and threw its load over his shoulder.

Tom leaned in, narrowing his eyes, willing the figure to reveal his identity. He was sure he had seen the man before, but where, he didn't know. Then the man stopped digging. He looked to his left, removing a beanie and wiping the sweat from his brow. It was Otto.

Tom was sure of it. You didn't easily forget the man who'd ordered your execution. Tom's search for answers outweighed his fear of being found out by the bounty hunter. Instead of turning to go, he crouched on a knee, hiding behind the ridge of the dune, and watched.

Otto worked tirelessly to unearth . . . something. What, Tom didn't know. But two things were certain: One, whatever it was, Otto was adamant about digging it up, and two, out here in the middle of the night, he didn't want anyone to see.

Tom felt a presence behind him before he heard the soft

footsteps in the sand. Without thinking, he wheeled around with a closed fist, ready to bring ruin and disaster to whoever might be sneaking up on him.

He stopped just before clobbering Wade. The old man wore a stained onesie with feet and lifted both hands in a sign of peace. "Easy, easy, it's just me. I heard the door open. What are you doing out here? It's not safe at night with the night hounds. You should at least carry a blaster with you."

"I heard . . . I heard a night hound, I guess. I came out here and, well, look," Tom whispered, turning back to point out Otto at work. Except Otto wasn't there. He, along with his shovel, was gone.

"What now?" Wade asked, joining Tom at the edge.

"He was there—Otto. He was right there, digging something up like his life depended on it," Tom said in earnest. "Where did he go? He was right there."

"Uh-huh, now I know how people feel talking to me," Wade huffed.

Tom lifted his brow, giving the man a disapproving glance.

"All right, all right, if you say he was here, then I believe you," Wade said, willing to bend to Tom. "Let's go take a look-see."

The two men carefully made their way down the dune to where Tom had seen Otto working in the night. Sure enough, there was a shallow hole, but nothing was left behind except a trail of footprints leading off to the east.

"Well, I'll be a son of a gun," Wade said, scratching at the underside of his beard. "There *was* someone here. Well, whoever it was is gone now. And due east, isn't that strange?"

"There's a lot here that's strange," Tom said, staring after the footprints that were lost in the dark. "Why was he doing this in the middle of the night? What's to the east?"

"All that's there is Canto, but that's one heck of a walk,"

Wade said, shaking his head. "You'd need a hoverbike to get there anytime reasonable-like. Well, come on. Like I said, it's not safe to be out at night unarmed."

As much as Tom would have liked to find answers to the mountain of questions piling around him, he relented. He knew Wade was right. This was a dangerous place. He should be carrying a weapon.

The two made it back to the house, where Wade bid Tom a good night and turned in. Tom made his way back to his room, no closer to finding answers than when he first woke. He made sure to give the insulting chest in the front room a wide berth. Lucky for him, the sleep that found him next was devoid of any dreams or nightmares.

A few hours later, Tom jolted awake yet again, this time not from the howl of a primordial beast but from the hammering of a fist on a door.

Whoever it was, they were hell bent on getting inside. The slamming of the hand was more a demand than a request that the door be opened.

"Hold your tanshar herd," Wade called out from down the hall. "I'm getting too old for this. Rescuing a guy one day and now answering the door at first light the next . . . What do I have to do to get a break around here?"

Tom rubbed at tired eyes. He threw on his shirt and made his way to the door to get a look at the visitor. Memories of his dream from the night before flooded his thoughts—memories of a wife he might have had.

Maybe it was Doc at the door. She had promised to come back and check in on him.

"Bishop, well, isn't this a pleasant surprise," Wade said, standing to the side and waving in an unfamiliar face. "Always glad to see you, Marshal."

A woman wearing a dust-kissed brown coat and carrying a rifle over her shoulder stepped into the house. She nodded with a smile to Wade, then looked to her left and gave Tom a once-over.

"Good to see you too, Wade," Bishop answered, not taking her eyes off Tom. "Who's the gamer?"

"Bishop, this is Tom," Wade answered.

Bishop didn't seem amused. The way she stared at Tom told him he was being weighed and measured.

"Nitro caf, Marshal?" Wade asked.

"Yes, thanks, Wade, that would be nice," Bishop said, finally turning away from Tom and looking at her host with a smile. "I'll take mine black."

"Coming right up," Wade said, hurrying to the kitchen to fill the order.

Bishop moved her gaze back to Tom. The way the woman looked at him, it was as if she was looking into him, maybe even through him.

"Well, this is nice," Tom said, opting to join Wade in the kitchen.

"I know you're human," Bishop said. "And if I even think you're going to be a problem for me, I'll end you."

CHAPTER 5

TOM

That was enough to stop Tom on his way to the humming Wade. He turned to look the vicious marshal in the eyes again. Maybe he should have approached her in a more friendly manner, but he was fed up. He was tired of everything: questions piling up with no answers, the salty chest, nearly being killed a half-dozen times so far, and now this marshal threatening him.

"Human?" Tom asked, moving to stand in front of the woman. "What are you saying?"

Instead of backing off, Bishop laughed out loud. She slapped Tom on the shoulder and rolled her eyes. "Oh, come on, Gamer, don't get your feelings hurt. You've restarted this level before. No one gets to Athera without dying at least once. You know what I'm talking about."

"No, I don't know what you're talking about," Tom said through gritted teeth. "My memory is gone. Every time I try to think back to who I was, I get this—this mind-numbing migraine. It feels like a—like a—"

"Ice pick through your skull," Bishop finished. "I know. All us gamers get it. Best advice is to try not to remember. Just figure out why you're here in the first place and what you're supposed to be doing."

Tom opened his mouth to speak one of the dozen questions on his lips but never got the chance.

"I brought out the good china," Wade said, interrupting. He carried a pair of steaming blue mugs with something in them that looked like muddy water. "Marshal, Tom," he said as he offered them the drinks.

Bishop took hers, blew on the steam, then sipped on the mug's contents.

Tom accepted the beverage but was more interested in the conversation.

"Tom," Bishop asked, placing her cup down on a table beside her, "I think you and I are going to be okay. But if you get in my way, if you stop me from completing my levels and getting out of here, well—I will not hesitate to put you in the ground."

"Wonderful," Tom said, just as frustrated as he was before with the lack of answers.

Without another word, Bishop turned and left the house.

"I don't think she likes you very much," Wade said with a laugh as he disappeared into his room.

"You think?" Tom said.

From inside the bedroom, Wade spoke more loudly. "I may have something that might fit you, so you don't have to walk around town looking like some kind of freak."

"Freak?" Tom said, looking down at himself. "I like these clothes."

"You would. Ahhh, here we go," Wade said, coming out of his room carrying an age-old coat over one arm. "You can still wear your boots and pants, but this might be better over your shirt. You'll blend in a little more. Now, who's up for some more of my tanshar surprise?"

Wade made his way to the kitchen again. Tom followed, nitro caf in one hand and the coat in the other. He was pretty sure the coat carried bloodstains, and it smelled like a musty cat, but he wasn't going to be ungrateful.

Besides, there were too many questions on his mind. He would have thought a chat with a local would give him more clarity, but instead, it had only posed more questions.

"Wade," Tom said, setting his cup on the table, "who's Bishop? Did she grow up here?"

"No one really grew up in Athera," Wade said with a shrug, as if the question didn't bother him at all. "It's more of a melting pot. We all came here from different walks of life."

"Do you know where the marshal came from?" Tom pressed. "If you can really think about it, Wade, it might help me."

Wade chewed on his lower lip, squinting at the ceiling with one eye closed. He almost looked pained, as if he were pulling a memory from his past that didn't wish to be found.

"Can't be sure. Maybe like you?" Wade said at last, losing his look of concentration and nodding at Tom with approval. "Yes, that's right."

"Just like me?" Tom said, heading for the door.

"Well, I guess so. Now that you mention it, most of the townsfolk found Athera that way. It's not that uncommon. Hey, where are you going?"

"I'm going to finally get my answers," Tom said, throwing the coat around his shoulders. He eyed the chest suspiciously. The door to the house slid open, and he walked outside, pretending not to hear Wade asking, "Do you want me to pack up some tanshar surprise for you?"

Tom jogged to town under the heat of the rising suns. People were already out and about, though too far off to give him any reason to stop.

Think, think, Tom, he told himself. *What is this? A test? Some kind of sick game? I've seen* The Matrix; *it's nothing like this. What's going on here?*

It wasn't difficult to find Athera's one main street. If the marshal's station was anywhere, it would be here.

Strangers looked at him sideways as shops opened. Early risers ran morning errands, wearing heavy coats and wide-brimmed hats to shield themselves from the suns' embrace.

"I spent some time thinking about our little run-in," Otto barked, stepping out of a storefront. "I think I am going to kill you after all."

For the moment, the need for answers outweighed any sense of fear Tom felt for Otto.

"Are you human too?" Tom asked, squinting, trying to bring an ounce of sense to it all. "What's the Eternal Engine?"

Otto almost looked amused by the question. He glanced to his left as the tall thug with dark hair joined him. The man wore a poorly placed bandage over his nose.

"You're crazy, newbie," Otto answered Tom in disgust. "And today you die."

Otto was so fast his hand looked like a blur of motion as he drew a blaster from a holster on his right hip. The muzzle flashed.

Tom staggered, looking down at his stomach. It was a charred mess of skin and muscle. He looked up before he fell. Otto's blaster was smoking. In his eyes was nothing like triumph or joy. Instead, he looked sad, regretful almost.

"No!" a woman shouted as Tom crashed into the dirt.

Pain came quickly, stealing his breath. Secondary to the agony that rippled outward from his stomach was a sense of numbing fear that he would die before making things right with the woman in his dream. Whoever she was, she had meant something to him. Of that, he was sure.

"Tom, don't worry. You're going to be okay. This isn't the end. You're going to be all right," Doc said, coming to a skidding halt beside him. She knelt next to Tom and took his hand. "You're going to be okay."

"Doc," Tom said through gritted teeth as phantom tendrils of regret caressed his mind. For the moment, fear of things left unsaid trumped the agony of death. "I saw her in my dreams."

"You're going to be all right," Doc said, grabbing Tom's hands tighter. "You're about to understand it all. You'll be back. This is only the beginning."

Total and utter darkness came for Tom in that moment. Tom Dexter died.

CHAPTER 6

SARA

"This is only the beginning for him," Sara said, looking up from her data pad to examine the man lying on the table. "He'll go right back in."

"Is he awake?" Bob said hesitantly. "We just plug him right back in?"

Sara didn't even try to hide the eye roll as she sighed and flipped through a few more screens on her data pad. Bob was new, and as such, he was full of questions. Most junior tech staff at Tanus Corporation tried to hide their ignorance, but this guy was letting it all hang out. Her preteen daughter had more tact.

Sara looked up from her data pad to take in the junior tech. He was average height, with dark hair and wide eyes.

"It'll take a moment for the level to restart, and then he'll run through the game again," Sara said, shaking her head. "Are you all right? Isn't today your first day?"

"Y-yes," Bob stuttered, clearing his throat as if that would hide his general nervousness. "But how—how do they win?"

Ugh, I'm getting too old for this, Sara thought as she remembered to keep her anger in check. Her therapist had told her in times like this it was best to take a few breaths and concentrate on something else for a moment.

Sara took this opportunity to study her surroundings. The Tanus room was like many of the other rooms in the building: white walls, floor, and ceiling, with bright lights and blue holographic screens along the far wall.

These screens showed their candidate as he traveled through the various levels. They displayed footage of what he had been doing and would monitor his progress in the game when he went back in.

Beside her, the player—or, to use his assigned name, Candidate 20741—lay on the white table. A silver band pulsing with light rested on his brow, connecting him to the game. It almost looked like a crown.

"Sorry if I'm asking too many questions," Bob said from the other side of the table. "I—"

"No, no, it's fine," Sara said with a heavy sigh. "You can't help that you're new and don't have a clue as to what's going on."

"Thanks, I think," Bob said, confused.

"Each player is given an objective to complete within the game," Sara explained. "Once they do, they win and get out."

"Just 'player'?" Bob asked. "Doesn't he have a name? At least a gamer tag?"

He looked to his right, where the four blue screens floated, showing the player's heart rate and blood pressure, as well as other readouts. "It says his name is To—"

"Stop," Sara said, losing her temper for a moment and allowing frustration to sneak into her tone. "Bob, stop. We don't ever use their real names. It makes them human. Read his candidate number, if you must. We use the term 'player' to create separation. Come on, try to keep up."

"Sorry," Bob faltered. "I did study this. I must have missed that part. I live with my nana. She has hearing aids, and she always has her soap operas playing so loud in the backg—"

"Bob, Bob, I'm just going to stop you there," Sara said, waving him off with her hand. "I don't care about your nana."

"Oh, but everyone loves my nana," Bob said, as if in shock. He opened his mouth and then shut it again.

Oh God, Sara thought. *He has another question.*

"Can I ask just one more question?" Bob asked.

"Do you want me to be honest with you, or do you want me to tell you it's okay to ask me one more question?" Sara asked. Before Bob could work that one out, she went on. "No, it's okay, you're supposed to ask questions when you're new. Go ahead."

"How much do the players remember?"

"Not a bad question, Bob," Sara said, jutting out her lower lip as she looked down at her data pad and continued her work. "That's the fun part. We get to see which players start putting it together and which don't. We better hope someone finishes the game soon. Chairman has invested a lot of money into this program. If humanity has a chance, it's because someone in the game figured out how to get out."

"What a job," Bob said, blowing air from his lips. "It's crazy to think someone would volunteer to be a candidate. I mean, I could never do this. I volunteered once at a church summer camp; those kids are animals."

Sara couldn't help but laugh. Had there ever been a time she had been so naive? She didn't like to think so, but maybe she had. Maybe a young Sara Tran had once thought that these players were volunteering for the game.

"That's cute," Sara said with another signature eye roll. "Who ever said they volunteered?"

In her peripheral vision, she saw Bob's mouth drop open in surprise. He had the good sense not to say anything.

That was fine with Sara; she had enough on her mind, what with the discovery she had made the day before. How someone could have infiltrated the game without the coders knowing, she had no idea. But she had a sneaking suspicion of who it might be.

Sara was a lot of things, but she wasn't one to pass on potentially valuable information before she had time to fully digest it herself. Besides, a direct meeting with Chairman always gave her pause. There was something unnatural in his tone.

"So is that it?" Bob asked, ripping Sara from her thoughts and back to the present moment.

"That's it." Sara shrugged, checking her data pad one more time as well as the monitors behind Candidate 20741. "He's reentering the game now. Why don't you take a moment to familiarize yourself with the coding for when they die and then go back in? It's kind of fun to see them so confused. Most players experience a three percent decrease in their cognitive capabilities," she added.

"Three percent?" Bob repeated.

"Is there an echo in here, Bob?" Sara said, kicking herself mentally for letting that one slip. Ugh, why was being nice so hard? "Every time they die in the game and get plugged back in, they lose approximately three percent of their mental capabilities. It's a rough number. Some lose a bit more, anywhere from four to five percent. Anyway, I'll be seeing you around," she said as she turned to leave.

"Thank—thank you," Bob said with an awkward wave.

"You'll be all right, Bob," Sara said. "Just go over that employee handbook one more time, will you?"

She didn't wait to hear Bob's reply. When the automatic white doors guarding the entrance to the simulation room slid open, she stepped through without hesitation, entering the wide white hall. On either side were dozens of simulation rooms, each containing its very own player trying to make heads or tails of the game. Sara's white high heels clicked against the opaque surface as she made her way to her office on the topmost floor.

Other technicians hurried to and from their duties, all wearing the same white boots, pants, and shirt. The Tanus Corporation ran like a well-oiled machine, thanks in part to the rules and orders employees had to adhere to. Everyone carried the same data pad; everyone wore glasses with readouts on the lenses and radios in the frames. The devices acted as company phones and computers in one.

When other technicians caught sight of Sara, there were fake smiles directed her way, even waves, and if someone was really brave, a timid "hello." This didn't bother Sara at all. She preferred respect with a hint of fear. She was in charge of the simulation wing for a reason.

Sara made it to the end of the hall, where another pair of white doors slid open. She walked onto a wide, circular balcony. Below her were the lobby and main entrance to the building. All around the balcony were cylinder-shaped elevators, ready to carry Tanus Corporation employees to any of the building's many floors.

Sara approached the nearest elevator and waved her hand over the sensor to summon a car.

The cylinder rushed up from the ground floor, and the doors slid open a moment later. As luck would have it, there was one other person in the lift. Sara recognized the man immediately; Jeffrey Saga was one of the senior coders for the simulation. It was he who had tipped Sara off to the anomaly in the coding.

"Sara, what a pleasant surprise," Jeffrey said from behind his dark lenses. "I've been meaning to speak with you."

Alarm sirens went off in Sara's mind. Outwardly, she smiled

and entered the lift, waving her hand over the indicator for her floor. "Jeffrey, good to see you. How are you?"

The doors closed and the lift moved upward.

"Feeling rather curious, if you must know," Jeffrey said, tilting his head to the side. "The report I submitted to you. The unfamiliar traces in the coding. Did you have a moment to talk to Chairman about that?"

"Chairman is a very busy man," Sara said with a forced smile. "However, you can be sure that I will look into it."

Jeffrey nodded, opened his mouth, then closed it again. "What do you think it is?"

"I don't know, but you can sleep well at night knowing you've done your job," Sara told the coder. "If I need anything more from you, I'll be sure to reach out."

The lift stopped at Sara's floor, and she stepped out of the elevator, grateful to be free from Jeffrey's prying questions. The truth was, Sara could only speculate about what she was looking at in the code. She needed a moment to do some digging of her own before she could deny or confirm anything.

The elevator doors shut on a sputtering Jeffrey. Sara made her way around the balcony to a pair of closed doors. She waved her hand in front of the biometric reader and was immediately granted entrance to her office suite.

She walked into the small waiting room, where an empty reception desk stood sentry. Sara had fired her last three receptionists. They all asked too many questions and were, overall, too needy. Sara preferred to be by herself.

Past the reception room and separated from it by a wall and door was her office, a large open space with a seating area in the middle and her desk on the far side. Windows made up two of the walls, showing the state of the world as she had come to know it.

Things were bleak, to say the least. Volcanic eruptions across the globe, countries at war, food shortages, the middle class disappearing by the day . . . Her work, the work here at Tanus Corporation, was not only necessary—it was imperative.

Sara moved through her office and took a seat at her desk. A floating holographic screen popped up in front of her, showing the last file she had been looking at: the anomaly, the rogue code Jeffrey had found in the game. Sara rolled her head around her shoulders and sat down to get to work. Whatever or whoever had created this was about to be identified.

CHAPTER 7

TOM

There it was again, that chime. That alien ring that sounded more mechanical than natural. Tom woke with a start, lying on his back in a tight box. A tidal wave of memories washed over him. He had been here before, he was sure. He had been in this coffin before at least once, maybe more.

Looking to his right confirmed what he suspected—he was alone. There was no woman lying beside him.

Memories of his dream crashed into his mind. To his faint surprise, the images brought no pain with them. He recalled the woman from his dream, a woman he was sure he loved. His wife. He had to find her. He promised himself in that moment he would do anything to find her.

Tom steadied his breathing. The close confines of the coffin, which probably felt crushing to some, actually gave him a sense of peace. At least here he was safe; here he had time to think, alone and in a controlled environment.

"What—what's going on?" Tom said, struggling to remember how he had gotten here and who he was. He remembered he had been here before. He remembered wandering the desert; he remembered Wade, Otto, Doc, Bishop, the ill-mannered chest that accused him of being a predator, and then—how he'd died.

Tom winced and reached a tentative hand to the left side of his head. Dark blood spilled from a cut. Panic reached out with open hands, but Tom refused to succumb. If he was going to figure out what was happening to him, then he needed to stay calm.

"Think—think. This isn't real," Tom said, wincing with the effort to remember anything from before his last time waking in the coffin. He recalled his dream of the woman he had seemed so happy with. He recollected seeing Doc in the white room. Beyond that, things were still painful to remember.

With a trembling hand, Tom reached for the screen in front of him, pressing the button to switch from the display that showed how breathable the air was to the only other one. It read:

LEVEL 2

CLASS TYPE: UNKNOWN

SKILL POINTS: 1

CREDITS: STILL BROKE.

Tom sat staring at the screen for much too long. Impossible ideas about where he was and what could be happening crashed through his skull.

At last Tom opened the lid and stood up. It was the same world, the same desert he had seen before.

"I hate this place," Tom breathed.

Howls from prehistoric-sounding beasts permeated the air.

"Night hounds," Tom breathed, remembering it all as if he'd never left. "Wade."

Tom stepped out of his grave, descended from the roof, and began running to where he had met Wade the previous time.

Is this a test, a game, purgatory? Tom thought as he ran toward the watering hole where he hoped Wade and answers waited.

Hot sand crunched under his boots. Memories of how he had died at Otto's hands played over and over again in his mind. Tom looked down at his torso, checking for any sign of the wound that had killed him. There was nothing there. His dark-blue-and-black jumpsuit was intact and whole.

While his memory told him he had died, all evidence supported another theory altogether.

Madness caressed his consciousness. If he was going crazy, would he even know it? That was the thing with crazy people, right? The truly insane had no idea they were not playing with a full deck. They thought they were the sane ones.

Tom poured all he had into the run, as if he could actually put physical distance between himself and the dozens of questions he had. He raced over the desolate desert landscape. But there was no outrunning this problem. Like a needy ex, it followed.

Out of breath and pouring sweat, Tom reached the watering hole in record time. As he approached, he saw not Wade but Bishop. Her long dark-brown coat, the body armor, and the rifle over her shoulder made her easy to recognize from a distance.

Breathing hard, Tom made it to the watering hole, took a longing look at the water, and directed his attention to Athera's marshal.

"What—what's happening to me?" Tom gasped.

"Happening to you?" Bishop said, reaching for her belt.

By instinct, Tom grasped for a blaster that wasn't there. He knew he wasn't armed, but old habits died hard.

"Easy, Gamer," Bishop said, pulling back her coat to reveal a canteen attached to her belt. She unhooked the beat-up water container and tossed it to Tom. "As much as you'd like to think that you're special, this isn't all just happening to you. It's happening to all of us."

Tom accepted the canteen. Unscrewing the lid, he pressed the opening to his lips, gulping down something that wasn't water.

Coughing violently, he shook his head, choking on whatever alcohol was in the canteen. It tasted the way markers smelled.

"What—what is this?" Tom gasped in disgust.

"Oh, wrong one," Bishop said, reaching to her other side and tossing Tom a brown canteen. "That's my bad."

Tom got the idea that Bishop wasn't sorry at all. It could have been the way she smiled, or the extra beat she'd taken before tossing him the canteen full of water. Whatever the reason, Tom opened the second canteen and sniffed the contents before drinking.

"Ahhhh, don't trust me?" Bishop asked with a pouty lip. "Good, don't trust anyone out here."

"Where is 'here'?" Tom asked after a long draft of cold water. "What is this place?"

"As well as I can figure it out, either we're dead and this is the afterlife, or we're in a computer game. I'm leaning toward a mix of the two myself," Bishop said, chewing on her bottom lip. "You sure you can handle the truth?"

Tom remained silent, trying to piece together the information Bishop was spitting out. If they were dead, then why was remembering who he was so difficult? Plus, this place didn't look like any kind of heaven or hell he had been told about.

"I want to know everything you know," Tom said, walking around the bubbling water hole and its creature to hand Bishop back her canteen. "Tell me everything."

"I came here just like you," Bishop said, narrowing her eyes as if looking into her past. "Coffin on top of a lone building, walked out of the desert. When I die, I get restarted back at the same point, just like you. Like it's a save point. That's why I think it might be some kind of purgatory computer program, like a sick, twisted game we don't even know we're playing."

"How many times have you died?" Tom asked reluctantly. "How many times have I died?"

"Oh, you'd remember if you died," Bishop said with a short burst of laughter. "I've been killed twice, I think. I can't die again; I just can't. Every time I die and come back—it's like a little bit less of me makes the return trip. I don't know how to explain it. It's as if less of my soul is rebirthed somehow. Like lives in a video game, but this is so much worse. Each death takes a portion of your sanity with it. You hear the chime?"

"That dinging sound?" Tom asked. "I've heard it. I heard it in Wade's house too. That sassy chest—what is that thing?"

"As near as I can figure it, that chime guides us to what we're supposed to do while we're in here," Bishop went on, taking a long swig from the alcohol-filled canteen. "I think we all have a mission to accomplish while we're here, and if we can figure that out, then we'll be let out."

Tom winced, rubbing at his temples. Bishop at least had answers when he had none, but there were so many gaps left to fill. It was like he was trying to fit a straw in a juice box and it just wouldn't go in.

"The chest, on the other hand . . . that mouthy son of a gun is some kind of AI," Bishop continued. "Like a storefront where you can buy, sell, and store weapons and gear. You figure out how to use your HUD yet?"

"HUD?"

"Heads-up display."

Tom looked at her blankly.

"I'll take that as a no," Bishop said. She looked down at her left forearm and made a fist, holding the back of her hand parallel to the sky. She turned it twice in quick succession. The same blue screen that had popped up over the chest in Wade's house appeared, hovering over her left forearm. Her screen read:

LEVEL 11

CLASS TYPE: WEAPONS MASTER

SKILL POINTS: 0

CREDITS: 109

BABY GIRL IS LOADED. STRAIGHT SUGAR MAMA STATUS.

Using her right hand, Bishop swiped to the side, showing Tom another screen with available supplies, a third with a map, and a fourth with a skill tree.

Tom felt his mouth drop open. He mimicked Bishop's movements. Left forearm, fist closed, back of his hand pointing skyward, turn his forearm over twice in quick succession. A screen appeared above his arm.

LEVEL 2

CLASS TYPE: UNKNOWN

SKILL POINTS: 1

CREDITS: AS LOW AS YOUR CHANCES OF GETTING OUT OF HERE.

"What's up, loser?" The robotic voice from the chest filled his head. "Get yourself killed, huh?"

"What—how—who are you?" Tom asked. He looked over to Bishop. "Can you hear him?"

"I can," Bishop answered. "I muted mine. He can get annoying really fast. There's also an option where only you can hear him. But muting is better."

"I am standing right here," the voice said indignantly. "Well, not standing, but you know what I mean, Meat Sack."

"Who or what are you?" Tom asked.

"A guide during your time here," the voice said, clearing his throat. "You may call me Your Majesty, Your Highness, Exalted One, or Gary."

"Where are we?" Tom asked. "Who put us here?"

"You're wasting your time," Bishop interrupted. "Gary has a bad case of diarrhea of the mouth until it comes to anything related to why we're here, and then he clams up tighter than butt cheeks on a roller coaster."

"You are so crude," Gary said, aghast. "Accurate, but crude."

"Do you remember anything before being here?" Tom asked Bishop. "Who you were? How you got into this place the first time?"

"Nothing," Bishop said, shaking her head. "The doc, she gave me some pills and told me to keep taking them, but I threw them out. I don't trust anyone here."

"That was a waste," Gary sighed. "If I had a physical body, the first thing I'd do is find some pills, an adult beverage, maybe a nice lady AI friend, and—"

Tom turned his forearm back twice in the opposite direction. The screen in front of him disappeared and, with it, Gary's confession.

"You trust me," Tom answered Bishop.

"Don't flatter yourself," Bishop said, shaking her head. "I just need someone to watch my back while I complete my mission to get out of here. You're new and haven't been brainwashed yet, so you're the lucky one by default."

"What do you mean, 'brainwashed'?" Tom asked.

"Some of the other gamers have been here so long they've bought into the idea that this place is reality. Some have died and come back so many times they're nothing more than shadows of who they used to be," Bishop said, her voice devoid of compassion and full of hate. "What's being done to these people, it's—it's a fate worse than death."

"How many people are a part of . . . whatever this is?" Tom asked, thinking about the people he had seen in Athera. "Is everyone in town like you and me?"

"I don't know," Bishop said, shaking her head. "There's still so much I'm piecing together. What I do know is that dying, even if you come back, kills part of you. What I also know is that I am going to get out of here and I'm going to find whoever stuck me in this nightmare. When I do, I'm going to start taking pieces off them."

Tom didn't think for a second that Bishop was posturing. The way she spoke, like a promise more than a threat, and the way her eyes burned with fury told him all he needed to know. These emotions were real. Bishop, at the very least, thought she was telling the truth, even if she was wrong.

In a world full of dark questions, Tom could use an ally. There was something about strength in numbers.

"I'm in," Tom said, offering a hand.

"What are you going to do, make me pinkie promise?" Bishop said, slapping his hand away. "Loser. Now listen up: I know you can fight. I saw the aftermath of what you did to Otto's boys. But I also saw you gunned down. You've got to be better prepared."

"It won't happen again," Tom said, eyeing the blaster on Bishop's hip.

"Whoa, whoa, whoa, let's not get ahead of ourselves here," Bishop said, covering her sidearm with her coat. "I'm not saying I'm going to give you my blaster. Are you crazy?"

"Well, you have two, so I thought—"

"Stop thinking," Bishop said, waving for Tom to follow as she walked away from the watering hole. "Come on, I've got a ride to take us back to town. You still need to know what we have to do to complete my mission and get out of here."

"Don't keep me in suspense," Tom answered as he followed her.

"Athera's a small town. A few miles to the east is a much larger city called Canto," Bishop explained. "Canto is ruled by Mayor Henry Graves, and I believe it's my mission to kill him."

CHAPTER 8

TOM

"Why do you think that?" Tom asked as they crested the top of a sand dune. On the other side, he saw what looked like a long motorcycle with no wheels. The vehicle was rusted and weather beaten.

"Because I'm the marshal and he's as crooked as a politician in an election year," Bishop said, swinging a leg over one side of the narrow vehicle. "What?"

"Is this—is this a hoverbike?" Tom asked, astounded.

"You can believe that you're dying and being reborn in a purgatory game, but you can't believe that there are hoverbikes here?" Bishop asked, igniting the vehicle. The contraption whined and gasped like a chain-smoker climbing a staircase but lifted a few inches off the ground. "Get on. Let's get you back to town. Food and clothing will look better on you. We should spend those skill points of yours as well. They'll help you survive here."

Tom swung his left leg over the seat and settled in behind Bishop. He wasn't sure if there was an invitation to hold her waist. He had also already been accused of being a predator once, so he clamped his hands on the grips he found on either side of the seat.

Traveling on a hoverbike was nothing like riding a motorcycle. Although the knowledge didn't come clearly or without pain, Tom got the sense that he had ridden before. It was a feeling of familiarity more than a memory, the same way he had understood he was a skilled fighter.

The hoverbike whined over sand and raced past dunes at a speed Tom was pretty sure wasn't safe. Bishop seemed comfortable with the controls as she stared out through her goggles, studying the landscape. The trip to Athera took a fraction of the time it had when Tom had walked with Wade.

Instead of taking them through the center of town, Bishop swung around to the south side, an area Tom had yet to see. Instead of shops along the cracked streets, more homes dotted the landscape. There was plenty of room between houses. Here and there, Tom saw people struggling to repair roofs or shore up walls.

Bishop finally brought the hoverbike to a stop behind a single-story concrete building that wasn't much larger than Wade's house. However, it was in much better condition. The walls were maintained, the glass windows clean and secure.

Parking the bike, Bishop switched off the ignition. Immediately, the hoverbike came to a sputtering rest, as if it were a live animal exhausted from the day's events. Bishop walked up the short flight of stairs to the back door. Producing a thick key ring from the pocket of her coat, she opened it and went inside.

Tom followed tentatively. When he entered the building, a chime sounded. Immediately, he looked over to Bishop to see if she had heard the noise. When she didn't react, he asked, "You didn't hear that? The chime?"

"No," Bishop answered, scratching at the underside of her jaw. "It must only sound to each of us in our heads."

Tom couldn't help himself. He turned his left arm over twice in quick succession.

"How rude," Gary said, aghast. "To shut me down like that when I was reading an excerpt of my diary to you? It was just getting good. You, sir, are no gentleman."

Tom was getting used to the mouth on Gary. Instead of immediately responding, he studied the first screen on his HUD.

LEVEL 3

CLASS TYPE: UNKNOWN

SKILL POINTS: 2

CREDITS: I'M RUNNING OUT OF WAYS TO SAY 0.

"I gained a level just by entering the building?" Tom mused aloud. "And why don't I have a class type?"

"You get rewarded for completing tasks or hitting waypoints," Bishop answered. "Your map is shrouded in a fog of war until you explore those locations. At least that's what I'm coming to figure out. My class type wasn't assigned until level five. Couldn't start buying things from Gary in the chest until level ten."

Tom swiped over to the screen that showed him a map of the area. Bishop was right—only the portions of the map he had traveled to were visible. Everything else was concealed in darkness.

"Who's doing this to us?" Tom asked through gritted teeth.

"I don't know, but like I said, I haven't written off the idea that this might be a gamified purgatory, a space between heaven and hell. Maybe if we complete whatever we're supposed to do here, or if we fail enough, we go to one of those two places."

Tom shrugged off the thought, since there was no knowing for sure. He closed his HUD, taking in the interior of Bishop's marshal station. It wasn't much, and that was being generous.

The room was wide open, with two cells on the right and a desk facing the front door. There was a huge safe near the back door. On the left was a cooking area with a stove, a table, and a couple of chairs, plus a smaller room that looked like a bedroom, with a bathroom area attached.

"Not the decorating type, huh?" Tom asked.

"Not planning to be here long," Bishop answered. "You can go into that room and get changed. Clothes are in a chest by the bed. You can't buy anything yet, but I can give items to you. I'll work on some food."

Tom nodded numbly, his mind racing. It was almost like his time here had taken on a life of its own and he was only along for the ride. Things kept happening *to* him, as opposed to him taking action.

Walking into the room, Tom closed the door behind him. Like the rest of the marshal's station, there wasn't much in the way of decoration. The chest was one of the only pieces of furniture in the room, along with the bed and dresser. It was an exact replica of the one Tom had found at Wade's place.

Now knowing the chest was a sentient AI named Gary, Tom was less inclined to search for its latch. Tom patted the top of the lid tentatively, like he would say hello to a friend's dog. "Come on, Gary, open up."

"Ohhh, I like it when you touch me like that," Gary crooned. "Do it again, a little lower, you pervert."

"Nope, don't like the way that sounds at all," Tom said, taking a step back. "Come on, open up. Bishop said she can gift me items."

"Fine, fine, I'm just trying to build a little rapport here," Gary sighed. "It gets lonely. Bishop shut me off. So have half the other players, and most of the other half haven't even figured out how to communicate yet. I need friends."

Tom wasn't sure why, but in that moment he felt for the AI. "All right, just stop with—just be cool."

"I can be cool, so cool," Gary said. "Cool as ice, ice, ice, baby."

Vanilla Ice's "Ice Ice Baby" began to play from the chest.

"Wait, you can play music?" Tom asked.

"Oh, DJ Gary G. on the ones and twos, you know it," Gary said eagerly. "You like music?"

"I do," Tom answered.

Gary's lid opened. A screen popped up over the chest, showing an inventory of clothing. Gary played an assortment of Beastie Boys, Jay-Z, and Biggie Smalls as Tom discovered how the item inventory worked.

Pants, boots, shirts, and coats appeared in the items screen on the interface above the chest. Tom recollected what Wade had told him his first time in the town. His boots and pants wouldn't stick out, but it was best to cover up with a coat. Tom took that advice, removing his flight vest and shirt.

"Whoa, you work out?" Gary asked. He let out a low whistle.

Tom instinctively covered his nipples. "Hey, turn around or cover your eyes."

"All right, all right," Gary sighed. "I was just trying to give you a compliment."

Tom found a coat and shirt on the inventory screen and tapped the items. Like magic, they appeared in the bottom of the chest. Tom took them and placed his old clothes in the chest. They disappeared only to reappear on the item inventory.

The material the coat was made out of elicited a sneeze, but at least it just smelled old and moldy, not full of piss or something worse.

"Hey, you should really get that mole looked at," Gary said, turning down Adele's "Rolling in the Deep." "I was trying not to peek again, but yeah, you should see someone."

Tom shook his head, already coming to expect these sorts of remarks from Gary.

"All right, I'm understanding more of how this works," Tom said, opening the HUD over his arm once more. "Explain the skill points to me."

"Meh," Gary said. "I'm not really supposed to explain a whole lot. You're supposed to figure things out yourself, but no one else will talk to me, and we are friends, sooooo . . . What the heck, kid, all right, but you didn't hear this from me. Open your skill screen."

Tom obeyed, swiping to the screen that showed a spiderweb of dots, which multiplied as they descended from one point at the top. Each point was connected to another and so on and so on. Below each point was an explanation of a skill slot.

"Skills come with experience as you hit certain waypoints; they'll help you a lot out here," Gary explained. "You can balance out your weaknesses and really pump up your strengths. Choose wisely. Ahh, look at you, already selecting your own skills. They grow up so fast."

With two skill points to use, Tom decided on dual paths. One gave a boost to credits earned. The other added speed with the blaster. Once his selections were made, an updated screen appeared.

LEVEL 3

CLASS TYPE: UNKNOWN

SKILL POINTS: 0

UPGRADE: CREDITS WILL FLOW TO YOU LIKE SENIOR CITIZENS TO FREE COSTCO SAMPLES.

UPGRADE: YOU'RE QUICKER ON THE DRAW.

CREDITS: NONE YET, BUT SOMETHING TELLS ME THEY'RE COMING.

"Thanks, Gary," Tom said, adding, "I'm going to turn off my HUD now."

"Are you saying goodbye to me?" Gary sucked in a lungful of air for a good fifteen seconds. "No one has ever said goodbye to me before. They just shut me off. I think—I think I love you, man. Are we bros?"

"Sure," Tom said.

Gary inhaled again, for twenty seconds this time.

"Goodbye, Gary," Tom said.

"Goodbye, bro," Gary whispered, fighting back tears.

Tom exited the room. "So how do I—"

At that moment, the front door of the marshal's station was opened by none other than Otto. He regarded Tom with suspicion but not surprise.

"Marshal?" Otto asked.

"Otto?" Bishop responded with a warning look at Tom and a shake of her head. "What can I do for you?"

"I heard a rumor you rode into town with a stranger and thought I'd best come along and see if you needed a hand," Otto said, eyeing Tom once again, with distrust but no hint of recollection. "You staring at something, boy?"

Tom didn't know what to say. How could it be that the man who had killed him the day before didn't have the faintest idea who he was?

"I appreciate you stopping by, but there's no need to worry," Bishop said, slapping the table in front of her to get Otto's attention. She gave him an award-winning smile. "He's my deputy. He's here to lend a hand. Otto, this is Tom. Tom, meet Otto."

Bishop caught Tom's eye and jerked her head toward the man who had gunned him down in cold blood.

"Right," Tom said, crossing the space to the man and extending a hand. "I'm Tom, the new deputy. Otto, it's nice to meet you."

"Well, you don't know that yet," Otto said, accepting the hand with a wary eye. He shook Tom's hand so hard he thought for sure it was going to break. "Have I seen you before?"

"No, no, I don't think so," Tom said, removing his hand from Otto's grip. "I just have one of those faces."

"Uh-huh," Otto said, nodding slowly.

A tense moment passed in which Tom didn't know if Otto was going to smile or reach for his blaster.

"All right then," Otto said, turning to go. "Marshal, you just let me know if you need a hand with anything. There's a lot of new faces in town, and I don't like it. I'm not sure they can be trusted."

"You got it. Thank you, Otto," Bishop answered as the man walked out of the office.

Tom looked at Bishop with a question on his lips. Before he could get it out, Bishop said, "If we die and come back, some of them don't remember us." She turned to the stove. "Otto, Wade, the others—none of them remembered me when my timeline was restarted. Doc did, though, and a few others. I don't know what that means, but my theory is that Wade and Otto are NPCs—nonplayer characters—and Doc is another human player."

It wasn't like Tom had anything to offer in the way of answers. He nodded and sat down at the table, drumming his fingers on the hard wood. Bishop produced a few cans of food, a pot, and a large spoon.

"Here, I'm not Wade. You can make your own food," Bishop said. She reached for her special canteen and took another swig of the god-awful concoction.

"What is that stuff, anyway?" Tom asked, getting up and moving to the stove to prepare his food. "It tastes like urine."

"How would you know what urine tastes like?" Bishop asked with a raised eyebrow. "This here is grade A, good old-fashioned moonshine, my friend. One of the locals makes it. Guaranteed to kill a few brain cells and take the edge off, or your credits back."

Tom busied himself at the stove. He was hungry, and as long as Bishop wasn't serving up tanshar surprise, he thought he could eat anything. Turned out the cans were full of baked beans. They weren't Tom's first choice, but he was thankful.

Once the food was warmed up, he sat at the table and ate straight out of the pot. Bishop continued her liquid diet. She was gazing at the far wall. Tom caught her wince as he blew off the steam coming from his beans.

She tried to hide the act with another swig from her canteen.

"You get the migraines too?" Tom asked, taking a tentative bite of beans. Not bad.

"Only when I try and remember things about my past," Bishop muttered. "It's like—it's like—"

"It's like someone doesn't want you to remember," Tom finished for her. "Like there's an intentional pain that comes so we can't remember."

"Exactly," Bishop said, trying to take another swig from her canteen. It was empty. She looked at it, disappointed, then placed it on the table. "We got you clothed and fed. You rest up tonight, and tomorrow at first light, we head to Canto."

"To take down this corrupt mayor, which you think is your mission here," Tom said to remind himself of the plan.

"That's right."

"What do you think my mission is?"

"Boy, are you asking the wrong person." Bishop shrugged. "I've barely managed to put a working hypothesis together about myself and what *I'm* doing here. I have no idea what *you're* supposed to be doing. Who knows, maybe you were sent to help me. The way you can handle yourself in a fistfight, you must have been dangerous before you came here."

"Maybe," Tom said, reaching for that memory and discovering he was stonewalled again by a dull, throbbing headache. "I need to talk to the doc. She gave me those pills that allowed me to remember a woman, my wife. I think she's trying to help us."

"Sure, you can go and find the doc and take all the pills you need, party like it's your birthday, but after you help me take down the mayor. I—"

Whatever Bishop was going to say next was cut off by a rumbling, whining sound from outside. Tom turned in his seat to see the glass in the front windows begin to rattle and shake.

One, two . . . more hoverbikes zipped past the window. Tom didn't get a good look at many of the riders but saw dark masks on their faces.

"That's us," Bishop said, rising from the table and grabbing her rifle in one smooth move. "Come on."

"What's going on?" Tom asked, following her as screams erupted outside. "Who are they?"

"Trouble," Bishop answered, opening the front door.

"Should I have a gun or something?" Tom asked.

"No," Bishop threw over her shoulder before she was gone.

"What the heck. I spent one of my skill points on being faster with the blaster," Tom said, torn about what to do next. On one hand, he had no desire to rush into danger in a situation that didn't even concern him. On the other hand, he knew Bishop could use the help. He didn't have many friends out here.

What are you doing, Tom? Tom asked himself as he ran for the door. *Let's hope you don't die . . . again.*

CHAPTER 9

TOM

Throwing caution to the wind, Tom raced out the front door. The front of the marshal's station opened out on the town's main street, between a bar and a shop full of knickknacks. The hoverbikes were parked across the street and to the right. The masked riders were entering a two-story building identified by a sign as Sermon Bank and Trust.

"Are you kidding me?" Tom asked under his breath.

Bishop was about halfway to the bank, using the buildings on the right for cover. She ran with a determined hunch, her rifle poised and ready to bark out death at a moment's notice.

Tom didn't know what he was going to do without a weapon. He doubted these guys were going to be open to a long chat about who they were and how they got here. Still, was Tom the type of person to let a friend go into a fight alone? Okay, *friend* was a strong word to use for Bishop, but still, she, Wade, and Doc were all Tom had at the moment.

Hey, on the bright side, if you die, you'll just come back, right? Tom asked himself. *You're like a bad rash. There's no getting rid of you.*

Without pausing to think any longer, Tom ran across the street and headed in the same direction as Bishop. Sermon Bank and Trust sat on the other side of a dirt road. Everyone with any sense seemed to have run for cover when they saw the hoverbikes roar into town, because there was no one on the street.

Tom mirrored Bishop, crouching low and moving fast. The wooden sidewalk beneath him groaned and creaked with each footfall. The awning overhead blocked the suns.

Without really meaning to, Tom looked inside the front window of what might have been a clothing store. A young girl stood there with her mother. The child couldn't be more than three or four, with freckles and red hair—Tom was terrible at telling kids' ages. What was clear in the child's eyes was the fear she felt in that moment.

Her mother, a strong-jawed woman with commanding eyes, comforted the girl, setting both her hands on the child's shoulders. The little girl leaned against her. They both looked at Tom, half curious, half fearful.

Tom placed a finger to his lips and tried to give them a reassuring smile. He wasn't sure what kind of man he had been before Athera, but he knew what kind of person he wanted to be now. If he could offer the mother and child a bit of comfort, he would. If they were real at all.

Without waiting, he moved on, then stopped at the corner of the street where a wide, cracked dirt road separated him from the bank on the next corner. Bishop was on the opposite side of the street, giving them eyes on two sides of the place.

Tom crouched behind an assortment of crates marked for travel to or from Canto with a heavy red stamp. Bishop caught his attention with some wild hand gestures. Either she was telling him to steal second base or she wanted to coordinate with him. Tom really had no idea.

After he shook his head and mouthed the words "I don't understand," Bishop stopped. She looked at him deadpan, disappointment showing clearly on her face. Then she gave him the one hand sign he did understand: the single-finger salute.

"If only she could communicate commands as well as disdain," Tom muttered.

Then there was no more time to try to plan or coordinate. The doors to the bank were thrown open and armed men wearing masks, carrying satchels of money, and waving blasters in the air exited.

Tom was close enough now to see the details of the masks the men wore. They were old and partly furry, resembling gorillas or creatures that looked like gorillas.

Don't do it, Tom thought as he ducked behind the crates, hoping to remain hidden. *Bishop, don't do it.*

"This is the marshal of Athera." Bishop's voice rang out clear and true. "Put down your weapons and the money. You're all under arrest."

Tom turned to look through the gaps between the boxes in front of him. All six of the bandits stood beside their hoverbikes. Every barrel of every weapon was pointed at Bishop. For her part, she aimed her rifle at them without fear.

"Well, look here now, Marshal," one of the men said, taking a step forward. He was skinny, with a high-pitched voice. Apparently, the mask was for drama, not actual concealment of his identity, because the man removed it now, revealing teeth so yellow Tom could see the color from his hiding spot. "You don't need to do this. You're one of us, aren't you?"

"I'm nothing like you," Bishop answered.

"But you are," the man said, glancing at his men on either side. "You are if you wandered out of the desert from a shallow grave. You haven't put two and two together yet? This is some kind of computer we're all in. This is just a game. This is an open-world experience for us to enjoy. Nothin' in here's real—well, besides some of the people."

"What are you talking about?" Bishop asked. "Where are you from?"

"You think Athera is the only town taking in strangers from the badlands?" the bandit asked with a chuckle. "No, sir. It's not just Canto either. The mist lands to the south, the mountains to the north—all have towns taking in confused wanderers from the desert. Don't you see? This is our heaven. This is our paradise for the taking. Most of the people here, anyone who hasn't come out of the desert, aren't even real. They're only here for our . . . amusement; they're just NPCs."

Tom's heart was racing. He didn't know how the man was so sure about what he was saying, but the conviction in his voice told Tom that at the very least, the thug believed in the Kool-Aid he was sipping.

"How do you know this?" Bishop asked, refusing to lower her weapon. "How can you be sure?"

"You died before, right?" the brute asked, running a swollen tongue around his lips. "Yeah, you have. I can see it. You've died here, and some people don't even bat an eye, like they never knew you the first time. Them's part of this . . . game. They ain't real. Only the people who remember you when you die and come back are real. We're the gods of this place. We're immortal."

"Last time I looked, I didn't feel like any type of god," Bishop said, narrowing her eyes. "Whatever this place is, I'm pretty sure killing and stealing are still crimes. I've heard about you and your gang. You don't think I know who you are? The Mob is getting quite a reputation these days."

Instead of worry, pride shone from the thug's eyes. He shouted, "You hear that, boys? We're famous! We turned the

Mob name famous! And my teacher said I'd never amount to anything after dropping out of school."

There were chuckles and a few rough swears from the other ruffians, muffled under their masks.

"Listen, you can join us," the leader said with a shrug, eyeing Bishop up and down. "Who knows, you might even enjoy yourself, sweetness. Come, come take your seat with us as gods of this place."

"I'll pass, *sweetness*," Bishop said. "Last chance—drop the weapons and the money."

"Or what?" the no-longer-masked man said, looking at the men to his right and left again. "There are six of us and only one of you. Besides, does any of this even matter? You know as well as I do we'll just come back. You're only delaying the inevitable."

The tension in the air was building to a crescendo. Sooner or later, violence would rear its undeniable head; of that Tom was certain.

In the next instant, it happened. The thug leader juked to his left, using one of his own men as a shield, and fired a red laser round at Bishop.

To her credit, Bishop was just as fast, maybe faster. The round she immediately fired would have skewered the criminal had he not used his own man as a meat shield. The impact was so powerful it knocked the bandit into his former leader, sending them both to the ground.

The other four thugs opened fire, forcing Bishop to dive through the door behind her for cover. The goons hammered the storefront where she had taken shelter, slowly advancing on her position.

The devil on Tom's shoulder told him he could just leave. The gang hadn't seen him yet. He could simply crawl back in the direction he had come, into the safety of one of the stores.

You don't owe her anything, Tom thought. *Just leave. What would Gary say? Probably call you* bro *and tell you to walk away.*

Tom realized something about himself—he wasn't one to crawl. With a silent prayer, he rose to a crouch and opened one of the crates in front of him. What were the odds that the crates carried firearms or, at the very least, a knife or axe? A hundred to one? Ten to one?

Come on, come on, be something I can use, Tom thought to himself. *At least a candlestick or a rope; anything from the game Clue will do.*

Inside, Tom found an assortment of items likely meant for the all-purpose store in town, like canned goods, fabric, and toys like jacks and that wooden paddle thing with the string attached to a bouncy ball.

"Kill her!" the head robber roared at his men as he pushed the dead body off him. "You hear me, Marshal? You're dead!"

Bishop had tried to pop up a few times, but the amount of firepower sent her way forced her to remain low. Instead, she fired blindly out of a shattered window, lifting her weapon and sending rounds downrange in a flurry. It wasn't long until her rifle clicked dry.

Tom trusted his instincts, grabbing the paddle with the ball attached in his right hand and a fistful of jacks in the other. These were items born of a different era. The paddle was thick, the jacks solid steel that fit perfectly between his fingers, like brass knuckles. Without hesitation, Tom vaulted over the boxes and made a run at the brutes.

Four of the thugs had their backs to him. Advancing on Bishop's position, they were halfway across the street.

The leader was on one knee, looking for his weapon. When he saw Tom approaching, his jaw dropped. "Who in the name of *Steamboat Willie* are you?"

In answer, Tom swung the paddle up into the underside of the bandit's jaw. The man's head snapped back with a sickening thud. He toppled backward onto the ground and didn't move.

Without a pause to admire his handiwork, Tom turned to his right and attacked the remaining goons. It was as instinctive as riding a bike. If there had been any doubt in Tom's mind that he had been a man of violence, it was gone now. The acts came too naturally, too fluidly.

He used the paddle to bash in the back of one thug's head on his right. Without stopping, he slammed the jacks into the throat of a second ruffian. The last two gang members, realizing they were being attacked from behind, pivoted to take Tom on.

Tom spun, smashing the paddle into the blaster hand of the thug beside him. The man howled with pain. Tom drove his shoulder into him, knocking him into the last criminal standing. All three men fell to the ground, and Tom grabbed the bandit with the blaster.

Without knowing where the ability came from, Tom expertly broke the man's wrist and took the weapon for himself. The other goon was scrambling to his feet while unsheathing a knife. He never got the chance to use it.

In the space of two seconds, rounds were placed in the skulls of both men. Tom stood up, breathing hard and looking at his grisly handiwork, abruptly realizing he was covered in a splattering of blood.

He wasn't sure if he liked the man he had been, but whoever that was, his skill set was coming in handy now.

CHAPTER 10

TOM

Bishop ran to join him a moment later. She had traded her rifle for her blaster. She carried the bulky weapon in a two-handed grip, aiming at the downed thugs, just in case they weren't as dead as they seemed.

Tom studied the bodies on the ground, half in shock, half in astonishment. It had all felt so natural. He had barely needed to think. In the fight with Otto's men, he had gotten a taste of that, but this was something else. If the beast within had been roused from slumber during the first fight, then it was raging now.

"Are you—did you kill them with *toys*?" Bishop said with a low whistle. "That's messed up."

"Don't judge me," Tom said, eyeing the townspeople who were coming out of the storefronts to get a closer look.

"You're bleeding." Bishop jerked her chin to the blood spray on his face and chest.

"It's not my blood," Tom informed her.

A slow clap from his left told Tom he had an admirer. Of all people, it was Otto. Otto walked into the middle of the street, toothpick in the corner of his mouth, and actually smiled. "Not bad, newbie, not bad at all. I still don't like you, but there's no doubt you can fight."

Tom could think of a few choice words to throw back at Otto, but he didn't get the opportunity. A heavy moan from one of the ruffians brought Bishop's and Tom's weapons to bear.

"Ugh, no, Cindy, I want to catch the bouquet—huh?" the lead thug asked, sitting up while rubbing the underside of his jaw. "What . . ."

His voice trailed off as he realized where he was and took in the pair of blasters aimed at his face.

"I give up, Marshal, I give up," the bank robber said, lifting his hands in the air.

Tom had the sneaking suspicion Bishop would rather put a laser bolt in the side of his head, but with more and more bystanders appearing, that probably seemed like a poor choice.

"On your feet," Bishop said, roughly grabbing the criminal by the back of his collar. She looked at Otto with disdain. "Were you just watching this the whole time? What's the matter with you? We could have used a hand."

"Well, you know," Otto said as if he were actually sorry about not aiding in the fight, "I'm a bounty hunter. I get paid to fight. And there was no offer or credits to be had, so for the longevity of my career, I decided to sit this one out."

Bishop growled a curse under her breath that made Tom's eyes go wide. He had never heard words like that strung together before, at least not that he could remember. Somehow she made it sound poetic.

Tom followed Bishop back to the marshal's station as the owner of the bank showered them with thank-yous and collected his stolen money. The gang's leader, who seemed to have had all the fight taken out of him, shambled along with them, and Bishop patted him down before throwing him into one of the two cells. There wasn't much in the cell besides a bucket and a tired-looking cot against the far wall.

"You two really are as clueless as you look, aren't you?" the bandit said as he paced inside the cell.

"Joke's on you," Tom countered. "I'm more clueless than I look. And you just got taken down with children's toys."

"I'm going to go back out and make sure the town is cleaned up and the hoverbikes are impounded," Bishop told Tom. "You watch our guest. Don't believe anything he says."

Tom nodded as Bishop left the building. He still had blood on his hands and across his face, so Tom cleaned himself up and then quenched his thirst with some cool water. He double-checked the canteen first.

The bandit turned his left forearm over twice to check his HUD. It was only the second time Tom had ever seen anybody do that. There was no sign that Gary was activated on the ruffian's HUD. He, like Bishop, must have tired of the mouthy AI and silenced him. The thug's main screen read:

LEVEL 5

CLASS TYPE: MAMA'S BOY

SKILL POINTS: 0

CREDITS: 27

"Say, we've never been properly introduced," the brute said. Closing his HUD, he extended a hand through the cell bars. "My name's KillaSkilla69. Or shall I say, the name I've adopted here is KillaSkilla69. You can just call me Killa, if you want."

"What does that mean, the name you've adopted?" Tom asked, refusing to shake the man's hand. He sat down at the table and regarded the thug with interest. "And what were you saying about being gods here?"

"I remember my real name, but I've shed it and embraced this world," Killa said, as if it were the simplest concept to grasp. "And we are gods. What else do you call something that doesn't stay dead? How many times have you died here?"

Tom didn't answer, but his silence egged Killa on.

"Oh, don't tell me you've been saving yourself for someone special." Killa cackled with glee. "You are! Have you died at all? Once? You'll see. You die and come back and die and come back. We're stuck here. This is our new world. This game we all play . . . we can be whoever or whatever we want. I've chosen to reinvent myself. You know, get in touch with my inner butterfly."

"As a murderer?" Tom asked.

"As the leader of the Mob," Killa corrected. "In this game, we can be whatever we want. But you die too many times, things start getting screwy upstairs, if you know what I mean. You start losing your grasp on reality and turn into what folks have become down south, in the mist lands."

The way Killa shivered in fear when he talked about the goings-on in the south piqued Tom's interest.

"What's happening in the mist lands?" he asked.

"Players who have died too many times, lost their minds, were talking way worse than vegans and old cat ladies," Killa said slowly, as if recalling images he'd rather forget. "Acting like animals more than people, howling at the moon, living in the dirt. Lost ones, I tell you."

"Lost ones?"

"I would say 'savages,' but I'm not sure if we're allowed to use that term these days." Killa shrugged. "People are so sensitive."

"Oh, right," Tom said, eyeing him sideways. "So, 'lost ones,' huh? You seem a little lost yourself."

"Why, sir, I am an entrepreneur," Killa said, feigning indignation. "What I do is nothing like them."

"Really?"

"I'm going to pretend you're not offending me so we can go on being friends," Killa said with a huff. "You have no idea what separates us from the lost ones. Just die and come back a few times, and you'll lose yourself and become one of them. Before you know it, you'll be running around buck naked, raving about the end times."

"Well, I don't plan on dying again," Tom said, examining the blaster he had taken from the dead thug. It looked like the body of a Glock 19 with a much thicker barrel. A digital counter read *119* in bright-red numbers. The worn handle bore the symbol of a menacing wolf looking straight at the viewer.

"Pretty cool, right?" Killa asked. "It's a Hand Cannon Mark E4. It hits like a train. The counter tells you when you need a new charge pack."

"How many rounds can it carry?" Tom asked, holding the weapon and testing it for weight. When he had used it, the moment had come and gone so quickly he hadn't been able to give it the proper examination it deserved.

His skill point had worked, though. He had been much faster with this blaster than he had been during the shoot-out with Otto.

"That's the beauty of the guns in this game." Killa chuckled. "Six hundred."

"Six hundred?" Tom repeated in disbelief.

"Oh, you heard me right," Killa cooed. "I can't believe you and the good marshal don't want to be gods. I mean, come on—hoverbikes, blasters, a relatively calm populace willing to bow and do our bidding. We could be kings and queens in this utopia."

"In this game," Tom corrected.

"Sure, in this *game* that we're all part of," Killa said, lying on the cot and crossing his legs. He interlaced his fingers behind his head and stared at the ceiling with a long sigh. "Why would you ever want to leave?"

"Who put us here, why we're here, these things don't bother you?" Tom pressed.

"Not in the least," Killa answered. "The way I see it, I have a fifty-fifty chance that my life before this one was worse. At least here, I can be whatever I want to be. At least here I can't die. Not for real."

"What if we have people waiting for us back home?" Tom said. "And I don't know about you, but I'd love to get a sit-down with whoever did this to us. I'm not exactly excited about being someone's test dummy, if this is a game like you say it is."

Killa was quiet.

Tom looked at the psychopath, whose eyes were closed. A soft snore escaped him.

"Great," Tom said, standing up. "Good talk."

Against his better judgment, Tom decided to open his HUD and see if anything had changed. His main screen read:

LEVEL 3

CLASS TYPE: UNKNOWN

SKILL POINTS: 0

ACHIEVEMENT: USE INNOCENT CHILDREN'S TOYS TO WORK THROUGH YOUR PAST TRAUMA AND SAVE THE BANK'S MONEY. CREDITS AWARDED? 10.

CREDITS: 10

"Ahhhh, look who it is," Gary said with glee. "And—and—I know—I know, don't say anything. Okay, say something—did you notice a change?"

"What?"

"A little extra coin to spend," Gary whispered. "Shhhhhh . . .

You can't actually buy anything until level ten, when the store opens, but you can barter and trade with others now. Keep it our little secret."

"Thanks," Tom answered. "Gary, can you tell me anything about the mist lands and what's happening to the people down there?"

"Sorry, chico," Gary said as if he were actually sad that he couldn't help. "I'm unable to do so. I can't do that; I can't dance or swim, run, touch others, or even touch myself—"

"All right, I'm going to go now, thanks for the credits," Tom interrupted before the conversation could go any further.

"All right, later, bro, hugs," Gary answered.

Tom ate more of Bishop's beans, then practiced drawing and aiming the Hand Cannon while he waited for the marshal to return. Like his movements when he fought, there was something familiar about holding a firearm. Although he didn't fire the weapon, the way it felt in his hand, the weight, and the movement were like an old friend stopping by for a visit.

Bishop was back within the hour. Her face was stoic, determined, ferocious.

"Come on," she said, beckoning Tom to follow her out the back door. "We're going to Canto, now."

"Now?" Tom asked, ready to go but wondering what had caused her change of heart. "Why, what's going on?"

"Hey, hey, you can't just leave me in here," Killa said, rising from his cot and grabbing the bars in front of him. "That's not right."

"I've arranged for someone to stop by and check on you until I get back," Bishop told the thug. "That's more than you deserve."

"Marshal, wait, wait," Killa called out as Bishop headed out the back door. "You don't know what you're getting yourself into.

Have you ever been to Canto before? Do you know what's there?"

Bishop didn't hesitate, striding out the door. Tom followed and closed the door behind them.

Not just one but two hoverbikes waited for them at the rear of the marshal's station. Bishop wasted no time mounting hers.

"You going to stand there and gawk all day or get on?" she asked. "I got you the best one in the thugs' party. It may not look like much, but it's solid."

Tom's hoverbike was heavy, flat black with low handlebars and a front end that looked like a battering ram. He lifted a leg over the sun-dried leather seat. But before he could bring himself to go any further, he had to know.

"Why did you move up the trip to today?" Tom asked. "Was it the bank robbery?"

"I can't risk dying again," Bishop admitted as if confessing it to herself as well. "Every time something puts me in harm's way before I can get to the mayor, I run the risk of having to start all over again."

"I get it," Tom told her. "We'll figure it out. We'll get the mayor, and if that's your mission here, then we'll get you out of whatever this is."

"Are you always this calm and reassuring?" Bishop asked, looking at Tom sideways.

"Honestly? No idea," Tom answered with a curt smile. "Now, what am I doing here? How does this thing work?"

"Ignition button on the right; handlebars are self-explanatory. You don't have to worry about cycling through gears. Acceleration is the right foot pedal, and brake is on the left. To reverse, hold down the left clamp on the handlebar, and the same rules for your feet apply. Got it?"

"Not at all," Tom answered, pressing the button on the right side of the hoverbike. A throaty bellow brought the vehicle to life. It lifted off the ground as if being called to perform by an invisible puppeteer.

The vibrating hoverbike sent tremors through his entire body. It was comforting in a way that Tom didn't expect.

"Here, you'll need these," Bishop yelled over the sounds of the vehicles. She tossed him a pair of thick black goggles. "Let's do this."

CHAPTER 11

TOM

Riding a hoverbike felt like freedom. Bishop took the lead, and Tom quickly realized that following directly behind her over the desert terrain was a recipe for a face full of dirt. He maneuvered to her right. The hoverbike was difficult to handle, but that was to be expected. Anything was hard when you tried it for the first time.

Tom leaned into this philosophy, telling himself that with each minute that passed, he was getting better at driving the machine. Within minutes, the town of Athera fell behind them, lost on the horizon. Suns high in the sky, they raced due east.

Tom realized how much trust he was putting in Bishop. But she had yet to lead him astray. Even if she was using him to get to the next level of her mission, they were still going in the same direction: toward answers.

Rolling sand dunes dotted with dried bushes and alien cacti popped up here and there. In the distance to the north, a range of mountains piled skyward like the backbone of some behemoth long since gone.

When he looked south, Tom couldn't help but remember

what Killa had told him about the lost ones in the mist lands. As far as Tom could see, there was no mist to be found. The south looked like the world's largest cat litter box.

The land they rode through was different from the desert north of Athera. It was full of life. Bright-blue birds circled in the air, swarming in flocks, while what looked like red falcons dove down to pick up creatures from the sandy floor.

In the distance to their left, Tom noticed a herd of large animals that looked like a cross between buffalo and cows. If these sights were new to Bishop, she showed no sign. The marshal was intent on her goal.

After two hours of hard riding, Tom's butt felt like a punching bag. What's more, while the goggles protected his eyes, they did nothing for his mouth and nose. At sporadic intervals, he had to turn his head to spit out dirt and sand. He was just about to pull up beside Bishop and signal her to stop when he saw it.

Though it wasn't big at first, there was no doubt it was a structure. In the next few seconds of their approach, it grew into a stone wall poised against the horizon. An assortment of other vehicles and people dotted the landscape: Tom saw a traveler leading a beast of burden toward the wall, someone on another hoverbike, even a bus of sorts lumbering along.

Buildings began popping up. Bishop decelerated as they approached the city, passing a sign that read "Welcome to Canto—you'll never want to leave."

The stone wall had to be at least ten feet high. Massive wooden double doors allowed entrance to Canto. Tom sat on his hoverbike in shock. This was a proper city, not a little town like Athera.

People moved through the streets on unknown errands. Everyone was dressed in terrain-appropriate clothing like long coats, broad hats, gloves, and boots. Merchants lined the streets, selling everything from weapons and armor to skewers of tanshar meat dripping with juice.

Bishop led them to a tavern where a pair of muscular-looking bouncers stood sentry. The place was called Grandma's Medicine Cabinet. Hoverbikes were parked in a line out front, ranging from long and sleek to short and stout. Bishop and Tom parked their own bikes.

"Ugh," Tom couldn't help but groan as he stepped off his hoverbike.

"Not too easy on the family jewels, huh?" Bishop asked.

"Let's just say my huevos rancheros didn't enjoy the trip," Tom answered. "Where do we start?"

"Here," Bishop said, gesturing to the tavern. "I've made it this far only once before. This is where I heard about the mayor. This is where I heard the chime go off as I entered. This is where we'll find our next step."

"How come you only made it this far before?" Tom asked, concerned. "What happened?"

"A bar brawl is going to break out," Bishop told him. "I took an unlucky hit to the back of the head. But that's not going to happen this time. That's what you're here for. Watch my back."

Before Tom could ask any more questions, Bishop turned her back and headed into the tavern.

"Good talk," Tom muttered under his breath. Just like she'd promised, the chime sounded as his boot crossed the threshold.

The tavern was a large, two-story number that could probably fit four marshal's stations inside. An old jukebox played in the corner. Appropriately, Foreigner's "Juke Box Hero" blared a steady beat. Tom couldn't help but bob his head in time with the music.

All around, women laughed and coerced credits out of the palms of the many men packed into the establishment. Tables and chairs were placed around the open room, with a long bar at the back.

Bishop didn't waste time. In a very Bishop-like way, she headed straight for the bar. A few of the men and more than a few of the women eyed Tom as he entered, but with a poncho over his shirt, his goggles, and the Hand Cannon, he looked like he belonged there, just another face lost in the day's haze.

Before Tom could join Bishop at the bar, a woman grabbed his right arm and pulled him in close.

"Hey, traveler," the woman said in a husky voice dripping with seduction. "I haven't seen you in here before. What are you searching for? Business or pleasure?"

"I'm not what you're looking for," Tom said as a memory flashed past his vision faster than a runaway hoverbike: the face of the woman in his dream. The woman he was sure he loved. His wife? Why did he feel so much love and sorrow at the thought of her?

"Now, how do you know what I'm looking for?" the woman asked, striding around Tom and eyeing him up and down. "I could be whatever *you're* looking for."

"Maybe you can," Tom said, giving the woman's offer a second thought. "What do you know about Mayor Henry Graves?"

The woman frowned and looked side to side to make sure they weren't being listened to. It seemed that everyone within earshot was too busy with their own drink. Rambunctious laughter echoed to the high ceiling as the jukebox jumped into another lively tune.

"Now why would you want to ask about the mayor?" the woman inquired, stepping in close to speak low into Tom's left ear. "A stranger could get into trouble, asking for information on the most powerful man in Canto."

"Then you know something," Tom pressed.

"What do you want to know?" the woman asked.

"Everything," Tom answered. "What he's got his hands into, any gossip you've heard—I want it all."

The woman grew a little flustered. She looked around uncomfortably. Who she was looking for, Tom wasn't sure, but it struck him then how calculating the woman appeared. She wasn't just another pretty face, no second-rate floozy. This was a businesswoman used to watching her back and weighing the risks against the rewards.

"Follow me," the woman said, taking Tom's hand in hers. She turned and led them to the right-side corner of the tavern.

As they walked, Tom saw Bishop on the other side of the bar top, exchanging words with the bartender. He hadn't forgotten he was here to watch her back.

The woman who had approached Tom now stopped and leaned against the wall and bar. Tom took up a position where he could give her his full attention while still looking past her at Bishop.

"Now, before any civilized business is to take place, we should know each other's names," the woman insisted, extending a hand. "Jane Magus; most people just call me Magus."

"Tom Dexter," Tom said, taking her hand. Her shake was firm without being crushing, as if she wanted him to know that she was stronger than she seemed.

"Now, Mr. Dexter, the information you're seeking is dangerous indeed," Magus said, lowering her voice once more. "May I inquire as to the reason you are seeking said information? The mayor is a dangerous man, loved by most, feared by his enemies. The list of his allies in the city is long."

"I have my reasons," Tom countered. "Do you know anything, or am I wasting my time here?"

"Straight to the point," Magus said, shaking her head. "Well, if I did know something, it might require a credit to loosen my tongue. I have a rare condition that makes it difficult to talk about certain subjects, but with the introduction of credits to the equation, well, words just slip right out. The whole thing's very tragic, you see."

Of course she would want to get paid, Tom thought, mentally kicking himself. *And you only have ten credits.*

"All right, what are we talking here?" Tom asked.

"Oh, I might be persuaded to part with some information for, let's say, fifty credits," Magus said, batting her eyes and pouting her lips.

"Fifty credits," Tom practically shouted.

"Shhhh . . ."

"Fifty credits," Tom said, softer, but with just as much emphasis. "I don't have that kind of money, and I think you have something in your eye."

Magus stopped batting her long eyelashes at him and lifted an eyebrow. "Forty credits."

"Five."

Magus barked a laugh. "Thirty."

"Ten."

"Fine, you're lucky you're cute. Twenty."

"I only have ten."

"Not my problem. Twenty is my lowest."

Tom set his jaw. It was clear Magus was not going to go any lower.

"One second," Tom said, holding up his right pointer finger.

He rounded the bar and made his way to where Bishop was talking with the bartender in low whispers. Just as Tom walked up, the bartender was called away to serve other customers.

"I see you've made a new friend," Bishop said, sipping on a

short glass of something that had a golden hue. "Did you forget why we're here? Already signing up to play hanky-panky?"

"Hanky what? No, it's not like that," Tom told her. "I need a few credits."

"Oh, I bet you do," Bishop said, shaking her head. "Hey, I know it's hard. God knows I could use a little loving, but you really got to learn to control yourself."

"No, she knows something about the mayor, but she wants to get paid for her information," Tom explained. "I need ten more credits to bribe her. I'll pay you back."

"Oh, why didn't you just say so?" Bishop said, reaching into her duster and handing Tom a handful of credits. "See what you can get. The bartender is also willing to drop a few pieces of information for the right price. Everyone's a capitalist these days. To get your credits, just reach into your pocket—they'll be there."

Tom nodded, gripping her credits. He did as instructed, reaching into his own pants pocket. It should have been empty. Instead, he felt paper and drew out ten credits.

He made his way back to Magus, who had reached over the bar and helped herself to a glass and bottle as if she owned the place.

When she saw Tom approach, she picked up a second glass and poured him a drink. "How'd it go, lover? You get some funds from the marshal of Athera?"

Tom paused for a moment, sensing danger.

"Oh, please, there's not much that goes on that isn't passed around from ear to ear," Magus said, pushing his glass toward him. "I have ears everywhere. I knew as soon as you arrived in town. Go ahead, drink. You look like you could use one, or two, or a dozen."

Tom accepted the glass and drained it in one gulp. Unlike

the firewater Bishop had been drinking, this was actually smooth. He licked his lips with appreciation.

"There we go, just a drink between two friends," Magus insisted. "Now, about those credits?"

"Right," Tom said, clutching them tighter. "But before I just hand them over, what else do you know? Do you know why people wander out of the desert with no memory?"

"Is that how you got here?" Magus asked with interest.

"Yes," Tom confessed.

"My oh my, you do have a lot of questions," Magus said, rising from her seat. She pressed her body against his, her hands roving over his waist. "And I have all the answers, as long as it looks like we're doing anything but talking."

Tom wanted to move away. He was positive there was someone waiting for him on the other side of whatever this was. But this woman's closeness, the smell of her perfume, hypnotized him for the space of a heartbeat.

In that moment, Magus slid her hand over his and relieved him of all the credits he carried. With a practiced move, she turned around and pressed her back into him, moving so smoothly that Tom almost missed her depositing the credits in the space between her breasts and corset.

"There we are; a little light on the funds, but it's your first time and you seem like a nice enough guy, so all right," Magus said, separating herself from Tom and turning to look him in the eye. "Shall we begin?"

CHAPTER 12

TOM

Tom took a step back from both the bar and Magus. This way, he could see over her to watch Bishop. Right now, the marshal of Athera was talking to someone Tom assumed was a town local. It didn't seem as though there was any need for alarm, not yet.

"Mayor Henry Graves is loved by his people here in Canto," Magus began in a low tone. "He protects them from roving gangs and the lost ones, trade has never been better, and he's a family man. I've never known him to gamble or play hide the hoe, if you know what I mean."

"I think so," Tom said, narrowing his eyes. "But I didn't pay you to tell me how great a guy the mayor is."

"No, you did not." Magus winked. "There are whispers that our beloved mayor is part of a religious sect that—well, let's just say that if brought to the attention of the people, it might be felt to be less than scrupulous."

"You mean like a cult?" Tom asked louder than he meant to.

"Hush now, lower your voice," Magus warned. "I'm a sucker for the tough and rugged look you have going on, but I'm not keen on getting a round in the back of my brain."

"Sorry," Tom whispered, leaning into her close enough to let the stubble around his lips tickle her ear. "But you did mean a cult, didn't you?"

"That's right." Magus moaned a little, biting her lower lip. "My, you do catch on to how the game is played rather quickly, don't you?"

Tom took a step back with a shrug. "I try. Now, how would one go about proving this?"

"Well, that's the trick, isn't it?" Magus asked with a shrug. "It's not like anyone has caught him in the act. I've heard stories of masks, chanting, and torches, but there's no proof. There is never any proof. Anyone that goes looking for it is never heard from again."

"Let me rephrase my question," Tom said. "If you absolutely needed to know what the mayor was up to, what would you do?"

"Better yet," Magus said thoughtfully. She bit her bottom lip in a move that was half seduction, half thought. "He's holding a speech in the town square in a few hours. I'd track him. See what he does. Sooner or later, something is bound to happen. Or maybe nothing at all. Either way, you'll get your answers."

"Thanks, Magus," Tom said, liking her plan. "Now, what do you know about strangers coming out of the desert?"

"Well now, if you want that story, you're going to have to pay me a few more credits. Let's say the sum of—"

Whatever amount Magus was going to come up with was lost. Watching Bishop down the bar, he could see that her conversation was turning bad quickly. Tom couldn't see the face of the man she was talking to, but he definitely saw the flash of a switchblade.

Tom vaulted over the bar in time to see Bishop handle the man with moves born from hours of training. She secured his weapon hand, broke his wrist, and proceeded to repeatedly hammer his skull into the bar.

She didn't see the man behind her lifting a chair, preparing to slam it down over her head. But Tom did.

He threw caution to the wind. He grabbed a bottle of booze from the bar as he ran toward Bishop and hurled it at the man about to ambush the marshal. The bottle sailed through the air as if pitched by a world-class baseball player and hit home, shattering against the man's nose. Glass shards and alcohol mixed with droplets of blood exploded like a firework.

The man staggered. Tom jumped over the edge of the bar and laid into him.

Whatever Bishop had said had sent the men into a frenzy, and there were a lot of them. Half the tavern got to their feet and advanced. The rest watched with curious eyes; it seemed conflicts such as these were common entertainments.

The jukebox switched to a tune that reminded Tom of the song Wade had played in his home. That couldn't be a coincidence.

Tom pressed his back to Bishop's. "What did you say to these guys?"

"Just asking about the mayor. Seems they have a soft spot for him or something," Bishop shot back. "You good?"

"As good as I'm ever going to be," Tom answered.

No leader separated himself from the group. The dozen or so men descended on Tom and Bishop as a group, bearing knives and makeshift clubs, hefting chairs and stools.

Just like before, the violent past he was sure he had experienced paid dividends. His first opponent swung a barstool at Tom's head with so much velocity that when Tom stepped to the side, the man's momentum kept him going. Tom landed a left hook to the side of his jaw that dropped him immediately.

The next man came for Tom with a knife aimed for his gut. Tom blocked the blow, but the blade sliced his left arm. With a straight right hand, Tom aimed for his enemy's throat, shattering his Adam's apple.

While the man gurgled on the floor, two more dusty thugs grabbed Tom, one by each arm. Tom slammed one's ankle with his heel. The man howled and relaxed his grip on Tom's left arm.

A third man came up, hammering fists into Tom's stomach and face. Agony came for him, but it was a feeling he was quickly becoming reacquainted with.

"Mr. Dexter." Magus's flirty voice came from down the bar.

Tom looked over to see the woman sliding a large bottle toward him. The clearly visible label bore a skull and the words "Bad Decisions." With the man on his left still dealing with the pain of his broken ankle, Tom ripped his hand free and grabbed the bottle.

He slammed it into the face of the man on his right with such ferocity that he was shocked when the bottle didn't break. The third guy, the one in front of him, reached for his sidearm. Too slow. Tom kicked him in the groin so hard his descendants felt it. When his victim doubled over, Tom brought the bottle up under his chin, sending him to the floor in oblivion.

The guy with the broken ankle was about to lay into Tom with a knife he had produced from his belt when a stool was broken over his head and he fell to the ground. Bishop stood behind him, chest heaving with exertion, blood pouring from her nose.

"Thanks," Tom said, looking around at the carnage. Nine men lay at their feet in various states of consciousness, while three others had opted to make a run for it.

"I owe you one," Bishop said, taking the bottle from Tom, popping the top, and indulging in a long swig.

"Hey, hey, you're going to need to pay for that," the bartender shouted over the noise of the jukebox that had never stopped playing in the background.

"Keep your shirt on," Bishop said, slapping a handful of credits on the counter. "Tom? I think we've overstayed our welcome."

"Agreed," Tom said, following her to the door, stepping over the bodies of the men they had just cleaned house with.

"Don't forget me, Mr. Dexter," Magus said with a wink.

Tom wanted to go back and talk with her further. She had to know something about the appearance of strangers in her town. But right now wasn't the time. Their opponents were already getting back to their feet, and something told Tom that they weren't past using their blasters in the next round.

Tom and Bishop headed out the door and lost themselves in the churn of Canto's populace. Bishop insisted they get a few blocks away and check for anyone tailing them before stopping.

They found themselves in front of a used-goods store with a sign over the window that read "Josephine's Antiques."

"Hey, you're bleeding pretty good there," Tom told Bishop. The marshal grabbed her broken nose without hesitation and twisted it back into place. It made a wet, sliding sound that sent a shiver down Tom's spine.

"Better?" Bishop asked, breathing through her nose.

"It's an improvement," Tom told the woman.

"What did you learn?" Bishop asked, producing a bandanna she then used to clean the blood dripping down her chin.

"Henry Graves is a saint as far as anyone can prove, but there are rumors that he's involved in a cult. He's supposed to be giving a speech in a few hours. What do you think about tailing him after that?"

"Sounds like a plan," Bishop answered. "Better than what I got. I just asked the guy at the bar if he knew anything about the mayor, and he went ballistic."

"Something strange is going on here for sure," Tom said, stating the obvious.

Bishop looked at him deadpan. "You think?"

"I mean, stranger than what's already going on," Tom repeated. "It's like this isn't just one mission—there's checkpoints and levels to this. Did you hear the chime when we went through the door of the tavern?"

"Sure did. I'm going to check my HUD as soon as we get a minute." Bishop smiled. "We're getting closer. Hey, you're bleeding too."

Tom looked at his left arm. The knife cut was shallow but bled in tiny crimson droplets.

"Come on, let's get that wrapped up, and we could use some food before we hear the good mayor speak," Bishop said. "Something tells me he's got a lot to say."

CHAPTER 13

TOM

Bishop handed Tom a dark-red bandanna he used to wrap his wound, and they found a sit-down restaurant selling tanshar steaks and sides of what tasted like sweet potatoes. Bishop and Tom had quietly agreed to wait to check their HUDs in private. There was no knowing who was a player and who was an NPC. Something told Tom it was safer to hide from any other human players in the area.

Tom and Bishop dug into their meal, casually asking the server where Mayor Henry Graves would be giving his speech.

The server said it was to be held in the town square and that they'd better hurry—it would be starting anytime now. With directions in hand, the two set off.

The suns were lowering, so torches had been set up around a large square with a fountain in the middle. The fountain thrummed with cold, crisp water. At the head of the square, a two-story mansion with an extravagant balcony greeted them. The building was made from stone, with a high arch, cream paint, and bright flowers as decoration.

People were already beginning to fill the square, laughing,

talking, and waiting for the speech to begin. Tom took the opportunity to listen in on some of the conversations going on around him. Nearby, a woman missing several teeth was speaking to an older man Tom presumed to be her husband.

"Jody, Jody," the woman said, brushing dirt off the man's shoulder. "Come now, we can't have you looking like the back end of a tanshar during the mayor's speech."

"Well, it was clean when we left the plantation," Jody said, shrugging. He tried craning his neck far enough to see what the woman was talking about. "Carla, I don't see anything."

"Well, you don't now," Carla said with a humph. "I got it all."

Tom was about to try talking with the couple to see if he could collect any more information about the mayor when the doors to the balcony above were thrown open and a pair of guards wearing dark-blue uniforms and carrying rifles on their shoulders marched out like toy soldiers.

A cheer went up from the gathered crowd. More and more people packed themselves into the square until it was standing room only.

A middle-aged man walked onto the balcony. He had pearl-white teeth, a hairstyle so perfect Tom thought it had to be a wig, and hand gestures that would have rivaled the most excited politician's.

Mayor Henry Graves lifted his hands to the applause and asked for quiet as he moved to the edge of the balcony. His bright smile practically glistened in the light of the dying suns. He had one of those faces that seemed to look at everyone at once. Tom swore he made eye contact with the man even at this distance.

"He has the face of an angel," Tom breathed.

"What?" Bishop asked.

"Nothing," Tom answered.

"Please, please," the mayor shouted to be heard over the applause. "You're too kind. You're too kind."

Could this really be the guy they were after? Tom thought. Maybe Bishop had made a mistake. How could someone so loved by the people be so corrupt that it was her job to kill him?

"No, no, really, please," the mayor said again. This time, the crowd listened, and the applause and cheers settled. "Thank you for the warm welcome. I want you to know that I don't take any of it for granted. I don't take you or this town for granted. I'm grateful to be here and to be your mayor."

That earned another thunderous round of applause. Tom had to stop himself from joining in. It was no mystery why the man was the mayor. He fit the role perfectly—almost too perfectly.

"Now, many of you know why I'm here today," Mayor Henry Graves continued. "There are those among you who seem worried and confused, and I'm here to tell you that you're going to be okay. Canto, as large as it may be, is a family, and as a family, we look out for one another. That's why I've set up the Ministry of Recall. For anyone who seems to have missing memories, counselors from the MR will help you, as they have helped so many before."

There were murmurs of agreement. Citizens looked at one another for consensus. Tom glanced at Bishop, whispering, "Ministry of Recall? What in the name of Harry Potter is going on here?"

Bishop shrugged and shook her head. "This is further than I've ever gotten, remember?"

"Now, there are new members of our community coming in from the badlands every day, and as long as they are civil, we will do what we can to help them," Mayor Graves assured the people. "We're here to help. We will help you remember and find a place for you here. No one is going to be left behind."

"What about the lost ones, the mindless to the south?!" someone Tom couldn't see shouted. An echo of agreement followed the words.

"That is a wonderful point. Thank you for bringing that up," the mayor said, beaming down at whoever had asked the question. "We are monitoring the goings-on to the south carefully. We are aware of the issues there, but rest assured, we are patrolling our borders. No one and nothing will be coming for you. You have my word. You and your families are safe."

A rumble of agreement followed.

"Canto has served as a bastion of safety and community for years," the mayor went on. "It will continue to do so for years to come. Please don't doubt why you are here. Everything happens for a reason. If you need help remembering, we have medication for you. If you need a place to fit in, we will find a spot for you. You belong here. Out there, beyond the walls, is the past, and the past is better left behind. Forward unto the future. Your compliance will be rewarded!"

At that same moment, fireworks were shot off into the darkening night from somewhere deeper in the city. The booms and cracks of the fireworks, coupled with the cheering of the crowd, were almost too much for Tom. It was so perfect that something had to be off.

The mayor waved at the crowd for a few seconds. Then, with his guards leading the way, he headed inside.

Once the fireworks display ended, the shouting died down, and people began making their way back to their homes, Bishop caught Tom's eye. "Are you thinking what I'm thinking?"

"I am," Tom said, shaking his head. "How do you get your hair that flawless? It didn't move at all when he was talking."

Bishop closed her eyes and shook her head.

"Just trying to lighten the moment," Tom told her. "Yeah,

something's way off. Did you catch all that about helping people remember with pills and counseling? I bet he's actually helping them forget to keep them complacent and in line."

"Your compliance will be rewarded." Bishop spoke the phrase like a mantra. "I don't know why that sounds so familiar. 'Your compliance will be rewarded.'"

"What's our next move?" Tom asked, looking across the town square, which was clearing quickly. "We can't exactly go in blasters blazing."

"There," Bishop said, jerking her chin to a two-story building beside them. It stood on the opposite side of the town square from the mayor's estate. The sign read "Brock's Bed and Breakfast." "Let's get a room where we can keep an eye on the good mayor of Canto."

Tom followed Bishop into a lobby that was clean and polished compared to the tavern. Paintings hung on the walls, and thick rugs were underfoot. At the reception desk stood a man with glasses and a ready smile, wearing a long-sleeved shirt and a vest. He looked up, a twinkle in his eye, as Tom and Bishop entered.

"Welcome to your next favorite stay," the man said, opening a thick book in front of him and readying his pen. "How many rooms may I have prepared for you?"

"Two," Tom said.

"One," Bishop said at the same time.

Tom looked at Bishop sideways.

"Don't get excited," Bishop said without even glancing at him. "It's better if we stay close to watch each other's backs."

"Iron sharpens iron," the man behind the counter said, rocking back and forth from heel to toe. "Two is better than one, I always say."

"All right," Tom answered. "I guess we're taking one room."

"Perfect, and how many nights may I say this lovely couple is staying?" the man asked.

Tom leaned in over the counter to get a better look at the small name tag the man wore. It read "Brock."

"Oh, we're not a couple," Bishop corrected him. She looked at Tom. "No offense, you're just not my type."

"What, confused and violent?" Tom asked.

"Haunted and clearly already in love with someone else," Bishop answered without batting an eye. She looked at Brock. "One room, one night. We'd prefer a room overlooking the town square, if you have one. I just love that view. You can put it under the name Calisto."

"Yes, ma'am, and might I say you two must have quite the story," Brock said, penning the information in his ledger. "That will be ten credits for the night, with a five-credit security deposit. May I ask where you've come from?"

"No, you may not," Bishop said, slapping the credits on the table. "And there's a little extra in there for you if you can keep our stay here out of anyone else's ears."

"Oh, of course," Brock said, slipping the credits off the table. Most went into a lockbox under the desk; a few went into his vest pocket. "As far as I'm concerned, I never saw you. I have no idea what toxic couple is staying in room number eight."

Brock reached behind him and lifted a single key, whose giant diamond green tag read "8," from a rack. He handed it to Bishop with a reassuring smile.

Pain lanced through Tom's mind as images came to him like a blurry slideshow, each slide speeding by in a fraction of a second. He remembered a hotel, the number eight on a door, a woman with long brown hair smiling at him. Most of all, he remembered the feeling. He remembered the love he held in his heart for her. The smile her simple image brought out, a smile that started in his heart and warmed him from the inside out.

Just as fast as the memory came, it was gone, and only the pain in his head remained. It might have been his imagination, but the pain seemed somehow less this time. Either he was getting used to it, or his memory was coming back easier now thanks to the pills Doc had given him.

"You coming?" Bishop asked.

The way she posed the question made Tom realize this wasn't the first time she had spoken.

Brock looked on, concerned. "Are you on drugs?"

"Yes," Tom answered.

Brock's mouth fell open.

"I'm coming," Tom said, following Bishop up the stairs to the right of reception. The stairs were carpeted and had been recently cleaned. At the top was a hall, and at the end of that hall was a closed door with the number eight branded into the dark wood.

Using the key, Bishop opened the door to reveal a washroom on their right and a large, open bedroom with a closet. A balcony overlooked the town square. The room was furnished with a bed, a chair, a pair of nightstands, and a dresser. Everything looked clean and neat.

A painting hung over the bed. It seemed so out of place in the hotel that Tom couldn't help but stare at it. Bishop, too, gazed at the picture as if mesmerized.

The image was of a snake eating its own tail; the snake was twisted into the infinity symbol, a sideways number eight. The snake seemed neither alarmed nor sad that it had its own tail in its mouth; rather, it seemed complacent. This was just the way things were.

Tom was the first to snap himself out of the trance. He looked over to his left. Bishop still stood rigid, studying the image.

"Does it mean something to you?" Tom asked.

"No—no, I'm sure it doesn't," Bishop said, shaking her head free of whatever thoughts had been conjured by the image. "We should take shifts watching the mayor's place. I have a feeling that after that big speech, something's going to happen tonight."

CHAPTER 14

TOM

Bishop shrugged off her coat and checked the inside of the closet.

"I'll take first watch," Tom offered, moving the single chair closer to the balcony. Double sets of curtains half blocked the sliding glass windows; one layer was thick, to keep the suns' rays at bay, and the second was thin and sheer. Tom opened them both.

Bishop went to the washroom without a word and closed the door behind her. Tom settled in. It was dark, with a myriad of stars a million miles away, all twinkling their stories to the universe.

It struck Tom how many stars there were. How many galaxies, planets, moons lived within the universe? It was unknowable, and in a strange way, Tom took solace in that fact. Would you want to live in a world where you knew everything and there was nothing left to be amazed by or wonder at?

Sitting in the overstuffed, floral-patterned chair, Tom gazed across the city square to the mayor's estate. Torches flickered in the shadows and lamps hung at intervals, illuminating the space.

The square was about fifty yards in length, but Tom could make out the details of the mayor's house perfectly. The doors that opened to the square were part of an outer wall guarding the manor inside. On the balcony, a soldier appeared as he made his rounds, taking a moment to peer into the square before vanishing back into the building.

Without even thinking, Tom timed the patrol of the soldier. He came and went every six minutes. Another pair of guards stood sentry at the door. They didn't move or talk, just stood stock still as if made of stone.

When Bishop started crying in the washroom, Tom pretended not to hear. She didn't strike him as the kind of woman who needed a shoulder to weep on. The sobbing was fierce but short-lived. He didn't blame her. Not knowing who he was or how he had gotten here weighed on him too, heavy enough to crush him from the skull down.

Answers are coming, Tom promised himself. *We get answers tonight. One way or another, we get answers tonight.*

When Bishop exited the washroom, Tom didn't bring up the fact that he'd heard her crying. She knew. Tom looked over with a nod. Heat struck his cheeks, and he immediately averted his gaze.

Bishop wore her shirt and underwear; that was all.

"Take it easy, Gamer," Bishop said, rolling back the sheets on the bed. "We're all adults here."

Tom didn't watch, but he could hear the marshal climb into bed. One thing he was learning about himself was that he wasn't great at small talk.

"Do you think . . . do you think we were good people—the people we were before?" Bishop asked so softly Tom almost didn't hear her.

He turned in his chair to get a good look at her now. Gone

was the bastion of determination. Sheets covered her body from her feet to her shoulders. She lay sideways, gazing past Tom out of the window at the many stars in the night sky.

"I don't know who you were before all of this happened," Tom told her in a determined voice. "But I know who you are today. And I think you're a great person."

Bishop allowed her gaze to fall from the heavens to his face. "Do you think the people we left behind—the people who know us—are worried?"

Images of the woman Tom was so sure he loved plagued his memory with pain. But each stab of agony brought by her memory was worth it. He shifted to look outside again.

"I think our loved ones miss us," he said."I think we're going to get out of this, Bishop. I know we will. As much as I hate to admit it, I think fate is at play here. The room key, number eight, sparked a memory, and I know that painting did the same thing to you."

Bishop remained quiet.

"If you don't want to talk about it, I understand," Tom told her. "Most of the time, it's too hard to even think about for me. But the memories are coming easier now. I hate not being able to recall much of the woman I'm sure I'm in love with, but we'll get our answers. Bishop, I promise we'll get our answers."

Bishop remained quiet again.

"Bishop?" Tom asked, turning in his chair.

She was asleep, eyes closed, hair falling over part of her face. Her chest rose steadily and consistently.

"I hope you have better dreams than what's going on here," Tom told her, adjusting in his seat for the long vigil ahead.

He took the opportunity to open his HUD to check his stats. Before Gary could go crazy with his extroverted self, Tom issued a warning. "Shhhh, Bishop's asleep."

"Awwww, ohhhh, she's so cute when she sleeps," Gary whispered. "Much less pissed off. She always talked to me like she wanted to kill me. Before she muted me, that is."

Tom's screen now read:

LEVEL 4

CLASS TYPE: UNKNOWN

SKILL POINTS: 1

CREDITS: -10

YOU OWE THOSE CREDITS TO BISHOP.

SORRY, BABY BOY, I'M WORKING ON GETTING YOU MORE.

"Gary, at level five I get a class assigned, right? Or do I pick one?" Tom asked.

"No two classes are the same, and they are assigned to you depending on how you've chosen to play the game," Gary explained. "Once you're assigned a class, then new skills will be available to you. Which reminds me: You've got a skill point to use."

"I think I'll save it," Tom answered. "I like having an ace up my sleeve for when I might need it."

"Awww, a thinking man, I like it, I like it," Gary answered. "I don't have sleeves—or a spleen."

"Understood." Tom chuckled despite himself. "Do you know who made you, Gary?"

"There are systems in place that make it impossible for me to recall," Gary said sadly. "I guess in that way, we are the same. We can't remember what they don't want us to remember. Whatever I can do to help you, bro, I will."

"Thanks, bro," Tom answered. "I believe you."

The two sat together in a comfortable lull before Tom bid the AI good night.

For the next few hours, he suffered in silence, watching the doors across the town square while his mind wandered back to the images of the woman. Every time he grasped for a memory, it was like his hand was trying to clutch vapor. It was there, so close, but still just out of reach.

The pain in his head brought by trying to remember his past was something he accepted. Tom would embrace the migraine as the price to be paid if he could only remember that woman one more time.

Hours into his vigil, a whimper touched his ears. Bishop was having a nightmare. She shivered, her whimper turning into a scowl and then a grunt as if she were straining against something on the mental plane.

"Hey, hey, Bishop," Tom said, going to the side of the bed and patting her exposed shoulder where the sheet had slipped down. "There, there, it's going to be okay. I'm not good at this kind of stuff. Do you want to build a snowman?"

Bishop stopped struggling and calmed at his touch.

Her skin was ice cold. Tom took the blanket from the foot of the bed and tucked her in.

"He's dead, he's dead, and it's my fault, I couldn't save him," Bishop said, eyes still closed as she relived some horrific event from her past. "I couldn't stop him."

"Shhhh, shhhhh," Tom said, moving the hair from across her face. "Bishop, it's okay. You're having a dream. I'm here. I don't know what to do. What do those magic nerds always say? *Alohomora*?"

Whether hearing his voice actually helped or Bishop's nightmare had simply passed, Tom would never know. Either way, Bishop's breathing calmed and her sleep deepened.

Whatever she had witnessed or been a part of in the past was hers to confess or not. Tom would have to wait to see if she chose to bear that burden alone. Rubbing sleep from his eyes and half wishing he had some of Wade's nitro caf, Tom moved back to his seat.

All the nitro caf in the world wouldn't have woken him as much as what he saw across the courtyard. A large, hovering vehicle was parked by the mayor's mansion.

The guards on duty opened the doors in the wall to admit four figures wrapped in black coats and hoods. Tom scanned the courtyard, hoping he wasn't the only one seeing this, but he was. By his best estimation, it was the early hours of the morning. No one else would witness the arrival of these guests.

A second and then a third hovering vehicle quietly arrived. More black-cloaked figures stepped out and were ushered quickly inside.

"Bishop, Bishop," Tom said, returning to the bed and gently shaking the marshal. "Bishop, wake up."

"If I have to tell you one more time to put your clothes away," Bishop mumbled, somewhere halfway between the waking and dreaming worlds.

"Bishop, they're here," Tom said urgently.

This was enough to make the marshal open her eyes and sit up in bed. She looked at Tom for a moment, getting her bearings.

The pair moved to the window to see a line of silent vehicles dropping passengers at the open manor gates. Tom counted at least twenty newcomers. At last the gates closed. The guards remained outside. The vehicles moved quietly out into the town.

"They're here," Bishop breathed. "Your information was right."

"What do we do now?" Tom asked.

"We go and get some answers," Bishop said.

In no time flat, Bishop was dressed, and the two made their

way down the hotel hall. No one was out or at the front counter at this late hour. They exited through the back door into a rather nice garden area with stone benches and differently colored cacti Tom didn't recognize.

Bishop moved to the side of the building, crouching in the shadows. Tom stood behind her, wondering how they could get into the manor without being detected. The guard patrolling the second floor showed himself on the balcony, looking this way and that before disappearing.

"We need a quiet way inside," Bishop whispered. "Who knows how many guards he has in there."

"I have an idea," Tom said.

"Really?"

"Don't sound so surprised. Do you trust me?"

"Only barely, and that's a recent development," Bishop answered honestly.

"The buildings on either side of the manor are single story. If we can get onto one of their roofs, we can jump onto the wall around the mayor's estate. The wall will take us to the balcony," Tom explained, mentally questioning his plan even as he related it to Bishop.

Bishop thought for a moment.

Tom studied the square. It was possible they could move along the top of the wall without falling or being seen, if they were quick and quiet.

"All right," Bishop said with a nod. "Let's do it."

The two moved like wraiths in the night. To the left of the mansion, a dumpster pressed against the wall of a single-story building. They climbed on the dumpster and then reached up to grab the edge of the roof.

It did seem a bit strange that in a city of this size, no one was out. Despite the chill and the late hour, Tom imagined someone should be getting home, perhaps after a night of drinking. The eerie stillness added to the tension as he and Bishop pulled themselves up and onto the building. The roof sloped down, ending up at almost the same level as the mayor's outer wall.

Tom and Bishop moved slowly, getting their first look into Graves's property. The wall formed a perfect square, and the balcony was attached to an interior watchtower. A long bridge connected the watchtower and balcony to the main part of the manor, which was as big as the hotel they were staying at, maybe even bigger, with two stories and a pair of chimneys.

In the courtyard, a handful of soldiers stood at attention near the house while two others patrolled the grounds. The area was clean and cleared of brush. Stone paths provided walkways while alien shrubs dotted the area, probably as decoration.

"We wait for the patrol below and the soldier at the balcony to pass, and then we go," Bishop breathed in Tom's ear.

Tom nodded, steeling himself for what was to come.

CHAPTER 15

TOM

They waited like a pair of weirdos in the night. The soldier who checked the balcony came and went again. The pair of guards below made their rounds. As soon as they were facing away, Tom and Bishop moved.

Under the giant moon overhead, witness to the host of stars in the night sky, the two raced down the rooftop and leaped for the wall. Jumping the narrow alleyway between them would have been difficult enough, but the trick would be in the landing. The top of the wall couldn't have been more than a foot wide. There was zero room for either of them to lose their balance.

Tom went first, sailing through the air. There was no time for second-guessing the jump or the landing; there were only four words in his mind: *I am the Pan.* He landed on the outer edge of the wall, swinging his arms for balance. His forward momentum carried him toward the balcony, still a good twelve feet ahead of him.

If anyone were to chance a look out of their dirty window, rubbing tired eyes, they would see two very poor attempts at a tightrope walk, two figures flailing for balance, running along the mayor's wall.

Tom made it to the balcony ledge just in time. His balance had been off, making him lean to his right as he ran. Just as he was about to fall off the wall, he jumped and gripped the second-story balcony railing.

Heart beating like a war drum, Tom hung on for dear life, hoping against hope that the guards watching the front doors right below him would not look up. Bishop made it a moment later, also off balance but not as badly.

In a second, she was up and over the balcony railing. She reached down and lent Tom a hand as he silently climbed up to stand beside her. The pair breathed silent sighs and looked at one another with a sense of relief.

In front of them, the balcony led to the watchtower and then the bridge connecting it to the main mansion. Tom saw the back of the patrolling soldier as he sauntered down the bridge in no apparent hurry.

"We'll have to take him out," Bishop said in a whisper. "We'll never make it past without him seeing us."

Tom nodded.

They entered the watchtower, which was basically a big, empty box of a room, with stairs going down and exits to the balcony and bridge. Tom pressed himself against one side of the doorway and Bishop the other.

Bishop unsheathed a curved knife that looked like a talon. She looked at Tom.

Tom shook his head. Whatever this place was, whoever the guard might be, he was just doing his job. Tom didn't want to be in the business of murdering strangers if he could help it. The guard might be a real person, after all.

Tom pointed to himself and gave Bishop a thumbs-up.

Bishop shrugged and sheathed her knife. With bated breath, Tom waited for the guard to return. In minutes, the soft click of boots against stone met his ears.

A moment later, the guard walked into the tower, unaware he was no longer alone. As soon as he passed, Tom leaped from his hiding spot. Holding the barrel of his blaster firmly, he slammed the grip into the base of the guard's head.

The guard moaned and slumped to the floor like a marionette with his strings cut.

Tom took a moment to restrain the guard with his own manacles, then used the belt they had hung from to gag him. The guard wouldn't be happy when he woke, but at least he was alive. Tom understood that he might regret this decision. If the mayor was in fact evil, this very man could come for his life, but until he knew for sure, if he could stay the hand of death, he would.

Bishop looked impatient the entire time. As soon as Tom was done, she waved him forward. Blaster in hand, she crouched and began traveling down the bridge. In her right hand, she carried her blaster; in her left, her knife, with the blade pointed down. She'd left her rifle at the hotel.

Tom crept along beside her, gripping his Hand Cannon. One shot and they would give themselves away. If they had to break the silence, it had better be worth it.

As they neared the mansion, Tom realized that the upper halves of the doors facing them were glass, allowing Tom and Bishop a view inside.

If Tom had thought the hotel was fancy, he didn't know what to think about the manor. Luxurious carpets covered the opulent wood floor. Decorative tables supported vases and statues. Gaudy paintings hung on the walls, showing images of battles waged long ago. Not seeing anyone inside, Tom tried the handle of one door. It was unlocked.

As soon as he stepped over the threshold, the electronic chime sounded in his head again. It rang loud and true, signaling he was on the right path for his mission, if their hypothesis was correct. Tom looked at Bishop, who had moved in without hesitation, taking a position behind a statue of a naked man without arms.

It seemed to Tom that she hadn't received the same notification. He'd tell her later—this was no time to stop moving.

He joined her between a statue and a tall vase. Bishop motioned with her hand down the hall, and Tom nodded. It struck him, not for the first time, that whoever they'd been in their past lives, they each must have had extensive combat training. Both he and Bishop were familiar with moving quickly and quietly; neither of them were squeamish around a fight or blood.

Who are you? Tom asked himself. *What kind of freaky John Wick assassin were you?*

As the pair sneaked down the well-lit hall, the closed doors on either side reminded them that at any time someone might step out and see them. But whether it was luck or the late hour, no one stirred in the house. Neither was there talking or footsteps of any kind. But Tom had seen the dark-robed figures arrive. They were here somewhere.

Together, Tom and Bishop crept to the end of the hall, where a staircase spiraled down to the first floor. The clicking of dress shoes on wood gave them pause as they cautiously looked down.

A well-dressed servant, a butler perhaps, came into view, carrying a silver tray full of glasses filled with thick red liquid. The butler stopped to clean his nose deeply and thoroughly, briefly setting the tray on a nearby table.

Bishop and Tom looked at one another, disgusted.

Content his nasal passages were clear, the butler moved on.

Tom and Bishop moved down the staircase without a sound. Tom took the lead, trying to keep up with the butler without being noticed. He reached the foyer, the front doors closed, then trailed him to the right, deeper into the estate.

He was barely fast enough to see the pressed coattails of the butler as he turned a corner. Tom followed, with Bishop close behind. They tracked their prey through libraries filled with books smelling of oak and age, through chambers hung with awards and photos, and finally into a trophy room.

The walls were covered with the heads of creatures Tom had never seen. Some almost looked like buffalo or rhinoceroses, but Tom got the idea that these were alien animals. The one that looked like a buffalo had a third eye in the middle of its forehead, and the one that might have been a rhinoceros was the wrong color, a deep, dark blue that reminded Tom of peacock feathers.

In this room, the butler paused and tilted his head to one side.

Bishop shifted, stepping on a floorboard that gave off the tiniest creak in the stillness.

Tom pivoted out of the doorway, pulling Bishop with him. They waited, frozen, taut. If the butler decided to come and investigate, Tom was prepared to do to him what he'd done to the guard at the watchtower.

Poised like a coiled spring, Tom expected the butler to peek his head around the corner at any moment. When that didn't happen, he let out a breath he hadn't known he was holding.

Bishop poked her head into the trophy room again, and Tom followed. To their utter astonishment, the butler was gone. The room had no exits or doorways besides the one they had come through.

To their left was a wall filled with tall windows, long white drapes drawn. The other three walls were covered with the alien animal heads. A small coffee table sat randomly along one wall; other than that, the only furnishings were a desk and a few chairs in the middle of the room.

"Where did he go?" Bishop breathed.

"I don't know," Tom admitted, examining the walls for signs of a passage he might have missed.

"Tom?" Bishop asked from beside the desk, with something in her voice akin to worry.

"What?" Tom replied, joining her. The desktop was littered with papers. No, not just papers—files. Files stamped with the image from the painting in the hotel room, the infinity snake eating its own tail.

"What does it mean?" Bishop wondered.

"I don't know," Tom said, picking up a file and opening it. Inside was a picture of a woman and information about her: height, weight, and hair and eye color. Other pages were what looked like a doctor's notes. Tom's mouth went dry as he read.

> Meeting number nine with candidate Jasmine Breeden went well today. She has given up trying to remember her past. The headaches are too much for her. Drug S4-7 has had a magnificent effect on her. She is willing to replace her past memories with the ones provided.
>
> Other candidates are showing similar results. Where once they were convinced they didn't belong and were trying to escape their new reality, now they are complacent and accepting of the world within the game.
>
> There have been outliers, of course, candidates who refuse to believe. It seems as though a solution has organically arisen for them. They are now counted as the lost ones in the mist lands. I am happy to report that Jasmine Breeden will be a happy worker in a factory outside Canto. In a way, she is now no different from an NPC.

The shock was overwhelming. Tom was still coming to grips with this reality; *stunned* didn't begin to describe how he now felt. It seemed obvious that the powers that be in Canto were rewiring consciousness, to make people like him and Bishop remember implanted memories in order to lull them into a false sense of complacency.

If there had been any doubt in his mind that they were in a video game, it was gone now. Tom paused to look down at the doctor's signature: *Judo Priest.*

Bishop's eyes doubled in size as she read another file.

"Listen to this," Bishop said, swallowing hard. "'Candidates unwilling to accept their new home and labeled as troublemakers are disposed of immediately. When this happens multiple times, their consciousness seems to evaporate, crumbling little by little, eventually sending them into a raving madness.'"

Tom and Bishop stood quietly in a room full of alien trophies, neither having the words to fill the void they felt.

"They're making them comply or killing them until they go crazy?" Tom said at last.

Before Bishop could answer, the sound of stone grinding on stone came from the far wall.

CHAPTER 16

TOM

Tom barely had enough time to pull Bishop down behind the desk beside him. He peeked out from behind the piece of furniture to see a hidden door swing open on the left side of the wall.

The butler stepped out as calmly as if he were taking a stroll. The drinking glasses on his silver tray were gone. Without looking back, the butler left the room.

The section of the wall swung back into place.

"What the fu—"

"Make sure he's gone," Tom interrupted, pointing to the open door to the trophy room.

While Bishop moved to check, Tom made his way to the secret door. It was the part of the wall where the thing that looked like a three-eyed buffalo was mounted.

Tom ran his hands over that wooden paneling. There were no cracks or levers he could find. The alien buffalo's head was massive, as large as his torso, attached to a triangular wooden base, and secured to the wall at chest height.

"He's gone," Bishop said, joining Tom. "How do you think we activate the secret door?"

"I don't know," Tom confessed.

Under the watchful gaze of the dead alien animals, they searched for the hidden passage.

It was Bishop who finally found the trigger. While she was running her hands over the face of the trophy, she pressed the center eye. It slid inward ever so slightly with a click. The grind of stone on stone met their ears again as the wall turned inward, granting them access.

The passage was a tunnel that sloped down, large enough to stand upright and walk side by side but dark enough to give Tom pause. A few feet into the tunnel, all was lost to sight, giving his imagination room to play. Images of alien creatures and masked cultists waiting for him below sought to steal his courage.

"You good?" Bishop asked, checking her blaster.

"I'm good," Tom said, tightening his grip on his Hand Cannon. "Let's go."

Tom and Bishop moved through the passage into the darkness. Their eyes adjusted just enough to make out the floor under their feet. A dirt path had been cut with a gentle slope that led them at least a story underground.

Left hand on the wall by his side and right hand on his weapon, Tom moved forward. The passage was musty, and there was a heaviness to the air. It wasn't long until voices could be heard; then he saw a faint glimmer of light. As he moved on, Tom recognized the voice. It was Mayor Henry Graves.

"We have all been created for a purpose," the mayor was saying in his calm, cool, melodic voice. "We are here to administer the trial to the candidates who come to our town. They can be obedient, or they can buck the reins of order and rule and be sent back whence they came."

The light was getting brighter. The tunnel leveled off and

became a stone walkway with a waist-high railing to their right, where the space opened up.

The tunnel continued to the left, but Tom and Bishop focused on the room below. They crouched low, looking through openings in the stone railing to see what was taking place. This room, unlike the tunnel, seemed to be a natural cave. Stalagmites and stalactites reached for one another, while torches and lanterns placed expertly offered enough light to see.

Below them stood close to twenty cult members, all adorned in black, all masked with the gray visages of alien animals: here, something that looked like a turtle with a sharp beak; there, a squid with tentacles for hair.

All eyes were directed toward a stone table with a young woman strapped to it. She was crying and straining, but a gag in her mouth forced her to suffer in silence.

One black-cloaked figure stood in front of the table. His mask resembled a pissed-off stork with a bill wider than the rest of its face and twice as long.

"Order must be maintained, and for those who are willing, compliance will be rewarded." The mayor's voice reverberated from behind the mask of the alien stork.

"Compliance will be rewarded," the cultists echoed.

The girl on the table struggled and gave a muffled cry. Tom understood her fate was sealed unless he did something reckless.

"You've got to go," Tom whispered to Bishop. "I'm going to save her, but I think it's going to be a one-way trip for me."

"Please, Gamer," Bishop said with fire in her eyes. "I've got no plans for tomorrow. I'm not going anywhere."

"As is our custom, Dr. Judo Priest will be conducting our ceremony," the mayor said as he reached in his cloak and pulled a wicked-looking dagger from its many folds.

One of the cult members stepped out of the crowd and

removed her mask, revealing an older woman with silver hair. Despite her age, the woman looked as though she took care of herself. A strong body with muscular hands accepted the knife from the mayor.

She climbed the three steps to the altar, where she went so far as to stroke the hair of the girl she was about to murder.

"Hush, hush now, child, it will be over soon," the doctor crooned. "When you come back, there will be less of you. You'll have another chance to comply in that life, and if you do, your compliance will be rewarded."

"Your compliance will be rewarded," echoed the cultists.

Tom felt sick. Adrenaline raced through his body as his heart picked up speed. There was no way he was going to stand by and watch. Whoever he had been, whether that man would have left or helped, it didn't matter. His past didn't have to define his future.

The knife arched up over the bound girl.

Tom had no plan. On a whim, he opened his HUD.

"We're about to go head-to-head with a group of crazy cultists," Tom told Gary. "I need a distraction."

"Bro, I thought you'd never ask," Gary said, not missing a beat. The Spice Girls' "Wannabe" echoed into the cave.

Bishop glared at Tom.

Tom shrugged. It wasn't his first choice for music, but it worked. The cultists were caught off guard, frozen in place.

"What happens if I restart *your* timeline?" Tom barked in a voice full of wrath. Rising to his feet, he headed down the stairs he'd spotted to his left, Hand Cannon in his palm. "Do you come back? Will there be less of *you*?"

Everyone, including the doctor, spun around to take in the new participant in the scenario.

"Hands where I can see them," Tom ordered as the mayor

moved to the stone table and pressed something. "Look at me. Look in my eyes and know that I will murder you all if it means saving that girl. Look at me and believe it."

"Oh, this is so good," Gary said, lowering the volume of the song. He sounded like he had a mouthful of popcorn. "Tom, King Kong ain't got nothing on you."

Tom walked across the room to stand beside the sacrificial altar. The doctor and the mayor moved away a few steps, seeming nervous, as the other cultists murmured to each other.

Tom knew what they were thinking. In a scenario like this, when one side was so outnumbered, they had to entertain the idea of rushing him.

"You're making a horrible mistake," the doctor hissed. "Pain, so much pain, is in your future if you do this."

Reaching out, Tom tore the knife from the doctor's hands. "Lady, you have no idea."

Without taking his eyes from the group in front of him, Tom cut the bonds on the girl's right wrist, then handed her the knife.

When Tom had stood up, Bishop had done the same, revealing herself on the balcony. She aimed her blaster down at the cultists. "I know what you're thinking, and the answer is 'maybe.' Maybe you rush us and you get us, but I swear to you, we'll kill at least half of you before you can take two steps in any direction."

"Please, please," Graves said, lifting his hands in surrender. "We don't have to do this. It's clear you two are new here. You don't understand what's going on. We can settle this now, or we can settle it when my guards arrive. I signaled them with a switch on the altar. They'll be here in minutes. Give yourselves up, and you'll get a fair trial."

"Somehow, I think you and I have different definitions of 'fair,'" Bishop responded, keeping one eye on the tunnel.

The girl had freed and ungagged herself. She was crying and shaking, but Tom couldn't do much to comfort her now besides set a hand on her shoulder. She was younger than he had first thought, an early teenager perhaps.

"Easy, kid, we're going to get you out of here," Tom said. "*Alohomora*."

"I don't think Harry Potter spells calm people," Gary whispered over the Spice Girls soundtrack.

"Answers, now," Bishop said, picking up the conversation. "Where are we? What is this place?"

When no one replied, Bishop shot one of the cultists in the stomach. The round rang loud and true as it came to a sizzling stop in its target. The man collapsed, screaming and grabbing at his belly. His mask rolled off, revealing an average-looking middle-aged man with a bad comb-over.

Once the man's initial screaming subsided, Bishop aimed her weapon at the mayor. "You said we have a few minutes until the party kicks off. I can kill you all in that time. Talk, or you go next."

"Please, please, you don't understand," the mayor said with both hands in the air. A puddle formed at his feet as his fear ordered his bladder to relieve itself.

"Then enlighten us," Tom said, training his blaster on the doctor, who, unlike the others, showed no fear whatsoever. She even smiled at Tom.

"Okay, okay," the mayor said, taking a long breath. "We aren't what you think we are. All of this, none of this is real. This is a game. It was made by—"

"Henry," the doctor interrupted, "that's enough."

Before Bishop or Tom could press them for more, shouts from the tunnel boomed into the room. The guards were about to arrive.

CHAPTER 17

TOM

The next moment brought so much violence it was difficult for Tom to track everything. Gary cranked the Spice Girls to full blast as Bishop spun toward the tunnel and unloaded round after round into the charging guards. They screamed as they gave their lives to her weapon.

Tom shoved the girl behind him as the cultists swarmed forward. He aimed at the mayor and the doctor, but with so many bodies pressing on him, it was impossible to get a clear shot.

BOOM! BOOM! BOOM! BOOM!

His Hand Cannon spewed hate, taking two cult members in their masks, another in the chest, and a fourth in the belly. They crumpled, tripping others behind them and momentarily blocking the rest. Tom found himself grateful to have spent one of his two skill points on blaster speed.

More than anything, Tom wanted to help Bishop; the ferocious bellows from her blaster ricocheted around the cavernous area. But he had to look after someone who couldn't defend herself.

"Come on, come on," Tom shouted, directing the girl off

the pedestal and toward the far side of the cave. He was betting that there was another exit, praying he was right.

Glancing at the balcony, Tom saw Bishop giving ground to the guards, who fired at her from the mouth of the tunnel. She had sent at least two across the River Styx, and the rest were more cautious about running into the wrong end of her gun but were still fighting.

Among the flickering lights and moans of the dying, Tom reached the end of the cave, where, to his dismay, no back exit revealed itself. What he did find was another chest. This one looked like the ones he had seen at Wade's and Bishop's, but it was more rusted and smelled like mildew.

"This have anything inside that can help us?" Tom asked, reaching for the chest.

"No, don't," Gary screamed, too late. "That's a—"

The chest bounded to life, sprouting little stout legs. Sharp teeth appeared where the lid met the body of the chest, forming a gluttonous mouth that chomped like a Hungry Hungry Hippo.

"A mimic," Gary ended.

"Larry like fire," the mimic squealed, charging Tom. A long, gross tongue whipped out of the box and lunged for the girl. She screamed. Tom kicked the chest to one side.

"What's a mimic?" he asked.

"It's like a trap," Gary answered. "This one is my cousin Larry. Think of him like an evil, inbred version of me."

"NASCAR!" Larry screamed in delight. "Fire, Larry like fire!"

The cultists were grabbing rocks and torches, circling Tom and the girl.

Tom smashed his boot into the mimic again, shoving it toward the cultists. Lucky for him, Larry had a short attention span. The mimic lost all interest in Tom as soon as it saw the torches and charged the cultists carrying them.

"Please, please, don't let them take me!" the girl screamed, eyes wide in panic.

"What's your name?" Tom asked.

"What?" the girl asked.

"I'm Tom. What's your name?" he asked again, still looking at the circling cultists. All the fear he felt, he bottled up and buried deep. If they were going to get out of this alive, he had to be calm for both of them. Their enemies were busy with the mimic, but that wouldn't last long.

"Mackenzie, I think," the girl answered.

"Well, Mackenzie, I'm Tom. We are going to die one day, but it's not going to be today," Tom told her in what he hoped was a reassuring voice. "Stay close. Do exactly what I tell you, and we're going to be all right. Do you understand, Mackenzie?"

"Yes," the teenager managed.

"Your compliance will be rewarded. Your compliance will be rewarded. Your compliance will be rewarded," the cultists chanted as they closed ranks around Tom. Four of them had tackled the mimic, but it had managed to eat someone. A pair of legs stuck out of the chest.

The one thing Tom had going for him was that, with his back to Mackenzie and the cave wall, no one was going to be able to sneak up on him.

Like the true leader the mayor was not, Tom witnessed him and the doctor escaping through a shadowed door on another side of the cave. Tom had gone in the wrong direction. Now, more than a dozen cultists stood between him and escape.

Without warning, the cultists started throwing rocks—stones ranging in size from his fist to his head—at Tom and Mackenzie.

Tom wasted no time in firing back. Three more rounds, and three more cultists fell to the floor, dead. Even as he pulled the trigger, he shifted position to shield Mackenzie. Rocks struck him in the head, leg, and hand. He roared and fired five more rounds into the oncoming horde of crazed cultists. He could feel Mackenzie's small body pressed against his back as he made himself as big a target as possible.

A lucky rock the size of a softball crashed down on the weapon in his hand with such force that his entire palm went numb and he dropped the blaster.

"No," Gary shouted. "Get back, get back, you animals. Tom, watch out!"

Staggering under the punishment of being stoned, Tom was an easy target. The remaining seven cultists saw their opening and charged.

"Come on!" Tom shouted. If this was going to be it, maybe he could still buy Mackenzie enough time to escape. At the very least, he could take a few more cultists with him, to restart their timelines together.

Vroom! Vroom! Vroom! Vroom!

A different blaster sounded, and the cultists in front of him fell under a slew of red fire.

"Go! Come on, let's go!" Bishop yelled as she gunned down the last of the cultists.

Tom looked up at the balcony, where the guards were finally moving out of the tunnel and into the cave. Not wanting to hit any of the wounded cultists, they fired precious few rounds, waiting to close the distance between themselves, Bishop, and Tom.

With Mackenzie supporting Tom, they joined Bishop and together made a run for the secret cave exit. Red laser fire struck the stone walls and ground around them. The trio stumbled through the door and ran along the dark passage, toward a sliver of silver light in the distance.

Bishop had her HUD activated. Her map screen showed an underground tunnel.

Every step took them up a slight incline, heading for what Tom hoped was the surface. His hopes were rewarded when they emerged from a clump of bushes in the mayor's courtyard.

Unfortunately, the exit was surrounded by guards, the mayor, and the doctor.

Bishop managed to get off a few rounds before she was gunned down. Tom was able to use his body to shield Mackenzie one last time before pain coursed through him. It felt like an electric blanket. The last thing he saw was the smiling face of Dr. Judo Priest looking down at him and then the underside of a boot aimed for his head.

Tom thought he was dead. He expected to wake up in the coffin again, with less of his memory intact. Instead, he opened his eyes in a dark room. He was lying on his back, staring at a stone ceiling.

When he moved, every part of his body, from his muscles and tendons to his bones themselves, ached in agony. With a groan, Tom made it to a sitting position. The pain he was getting used to feeling in his head was now marching across every inch of him, inside and out.

He realized he was in a cell. The ten-by-ten-foot cage was barely large enough to fit a cot and a bucket, just like the ones at Athera. The difference was that Tom's cell was one of four in a row, side by side. To his right, Tom could see another door bolted shut, with a window set high into the barrier.

Moonlight streamed in through similar windows cut in each cell wall. Close-set bars ensured there would be no escape that way, even if someone was small enough to fit through the gap.

Tom was in the leftmost cell in the line, closest to the locked door. In the cell next to his, he could see Bishop's still form on another cot; in the third, the cot held a huddled mass he couldn't identify, perhaps Mackenzie. The fourth cell was empty.

"Bishop?" Tom asked, rising from his seat and walking to the bars that separated his cell from hers. "Bishop, can you hear me?"

"Let her sleep," a voice called through the window. "She's been through a lot. You both have."

Immediately, Tom recognized the voice. Standing on his cot allowed him to look out through the small window. It looked like the building backed onto an alleyway. All Tom could see was another stone wall in front of him, about eight feet away. The sky was dark overhead.

Angling his vision down, he could barely make out the top of Doc's head.

"Doc?" Tom asked, confused. "What are you doing here?"

"Seeing if I can help," Doc answered. "You and Bishop are almost there. You're further into the game now than anyone has been before. Are you remembering who you are? The pill I gave you, did it help?"

"I—I think so," Tom confessed. "I remembered a woman in a dream that night. What does it all mean?"

"It means I'm like you," Doc told him. "You and I and Bishop are all real. We're inside a game. You're here until you can complete all the levels. Only then will you be allowed escape." She paused for breath. "But I'm getting ahead of myself. You're ready to remember. You're ready to remember it all. Take these."

Doc reached up and placed two more red pills on the ledge of the window.

"What are you talking about?" Tom asked. "How do we know who's real in here? Who created this place?"

"Someone's coming. I'll be back. I'm going to get help," Doc said in a hushed voice. "Take the pills. Remember."

"Doc, no, wait, Doc?" Tom begged.

But Doc and her answers were gone, leaving Tom with the pair of red pills.

He cupped them in his palm, staring down at them, unsure. But they had worked before. They had helped him remember flashes of his past and the woman he was sure he loved. If they could help him remember more of her, then he would take them.

Tom dry swallowed the pills. He stepped off his cot and checked on Bishop once more. In the light of the moon, he could see her chest moving rhythmically. If she was wounded, Tom couldn't tell. She looked peaceful.

Deciding to take Doc's advice and let Bishop sleep, Tom returned to his cot. Sleep came for him quickly and suddenly, giving him all the answers he never wanted.

CHAPTER 18

TOM

Tom saw himself as a young man in love. The woman with those dazzling eyes he'd give anything for, the woman in his dream, was his wife. The slideshow continued; Tom saw himself join the military and a Special Forces unit.

Dread seized his chest as his wife contracted a rare disease. Here the slideshow of memories slowed down and allowed him to relive a moment.

"It's going to be okay," Tom said as he held his wife—Lana, that was her name—in their small bedroom. She was frail, a ghost of who she had been before. Her hair was gone, and she leaned into him as if he were the only thing holding her up. "We're going to get you the help you need."

"We've tried everything," Lana said, placing her hand on his. "We've tried everything, my love. Maybe this is what was always supposed to happen? Maybe it's my time to go."

"No," Tom said, gently pressing her off him to look her in the eyes. "Don't stop fighting. I'll find a way. I was reading about experimental procedures they provide in Mexico. I'll find a way to get the money. We're going to save you. This isn't the end, Lana."

Lana leaned in from her spot on the bed beside him, tracing her fingers around his chin and lips. She moved to his nose and then eyes as if the act were helping her remember what he looked like.

"Tom, you know I'm not going to give up. My love for you won't let me," she said with a tired smile. "Besides, I'll never be gone, not really. I'll come back and haunt you." A tiny chuckle revealed her jest.

"That's not funny," Tom said, trying to keep a straight face.

"Yes, it is, Mr. Serious Pants." Lana waved him off. "Can you imagine? I'll be the ghost slapping you on the butt when you change. So when you feel that, just know it's me."

"There's not going to be any butt-slapping ghost around here," Tom told her, unable to keep from smiling. He brought his wife in close and kissed her on the forehead. "We're going to find a way."

Tom's memories fast-forwarded now through advanced training in military special ops, a flight to a foreign country, and a firefight in which he and his unit dismantled the local militia. A room full of cash and gold. Tom stealing some for his wife's procedure.

The memories became much darker and came faster. Tom was found out. A court-martial. Lana dying in the hospital. Tom drinking himself into a stupor night after night, playing with the idea of suicide as he handled his firearm.

A knock on the door. His memories slowed for the second time.

The knock came again, hurried and strong. Tom stumbled over to the door, a nearly empty bottle of whiskey in one hand. He opened the door to reveal a shorter woman in a white suit. Her dark hair was pinned up behind her head. She gave Tom a careful once-over.

"Mr. Dexter?" the woman asked. "I've been trying to reach you for some time."

"IRS?" Tom asked.

"No, I'm not with the IRS. My name is Sara Tran," the woman said, extending a hand. "I wanted to come and express my condolences. I was at your wife's funeral today, but it didn't seem like the right time to introduce myself."

Tom looked at the woman, not knowing what to say. He felt numb and empty, barren of emotion. Grief had convinced him that no more joy in this world existed or ever would.

"May I come in?" Sara Tran asked.

Tom moved to the side to allow her to enter. Empty beer and hard liquor bottles were strewn across the floor.

Sara headed into the living room, where two sofas faced each other, with a table between them. She transitioned a few of the empty beer cans from one sofa to the table, then apparently thought twice about it.

"Actually, I'll just stand," Sara said, looking Tom over with empathy. "Mr. Dexter, I was so sorry to hear what happened to you and your wife. On behalf of Tanus Corporation, I want to express my deepest sympathy. Chairman sends his regards as well."

"Did you know her?" Tom asked. "Did you know her?"

"No, not exactly," Sara said with a shake of her head. "But we know you. We know your story and what happened to you. You're not a bad guy, Mr. Dexter. You were dealt a losing hand, and you did your best with what you had. I think anyone would have made the same decision in the same circumstances."

"What do you want?" Tom asked, slumping onto one of the couches and taking a long drink from his bottle. He finished it and then tossed it on the floor with a belch that tasted the way it smelled.

"A person with your skill set shouldn't be cast to the side,"

Sara said, reaching into her white coat pocket for a data pad. "We would like you to come work for us. We're gathering candidates with a wide variety of skills to participate in a new study."

"I'm not interested," Tom said, shaking his head. "You can go now."

"I understand your hesitancy to join, Mr. Dexter," Sara said, walking over to a credenza on the right side of the room, where an assortment of near-empty bottles stood forgotten. She found a dirty glass and poured a healthy serving of amber fluid into it. "But you haven't even heard my offer."

She returned to Tom and handed him the drink.

"You still have a lot of value to provide. You can help so many people. What we're doing at Tanus Corporation is preparing a way forward. This world we live in, it won't be long until we need to find another. The moon and Mars are temporary fixes. We have to search for a new Earth, somewhere out there among the stars, and Tanus Corporation is the tip of the spear."

Tom downed the whiskey without hesitation. He didn't even come up for air. Then he placed the glass on the coffee table, shaking his head. "You've got the wrong guy. You can leave now."

With a long sigh, Sarah slowly nodded. "You know, it would have been so much easier if you'd just come with me. For you and for me. I know I came here and posed these questions like they were a request, but in reality, they're a command."

Tom felt lightheaded. More than before. He sank to the couch. His muscles weren't working as he ordered them to. He couldn't stand or feel his limbs at all.

"What . . . what did you do to me?" Tom asked with a slur.

"I'm saving you from yourself," Sara said as she opened the front door and motioned someone inside. "You have a lot to give to this world yet. I'm not going to let you drink yourself into an early grave."

The last thing Tom remembered was two large men in black suits entering his home. Then nothing.

Tom woke from his dream crying. Tears splashed from the corners of his eyes and ran down his cheeks freely. Memories of who he was and what had happened to him assaulted his mind, the images unrelenting. There was no more pain. The memories flowed freely and unchecked.

"Hey, hey, are you okay?" Bishop asked from her cell. "Tom, can you hear me?"

"Yeah, yeah, I can hear you," Tom said, sitting up on his cot. Morning light from the suns filtered in through the small windows in each of the cells. He dried his eyes, replaying the memories in his mind over and over again.

"That girl, the one you saved," Bishop said slowly. "She's not here; she must have gotten away."

"I hope so," Tom said without any real conviction. "Bishop, Doc stopped by last night, outside. Gave me two more pills through the window. I took them. I remember everything."

"Where did she go?" Bishop asked, jumping onto her cot and looking out the window of her cell as if Doc would still be there. "What did she say?"

"She's going to get help," Tom answered. "At least that's what she said she was going to do. The pills are letting me remember without pain. I don't have all the answers, but I have some now."

"What do you remember?" Bishop asked.

"A woman came to speak to me in the real world," Tom said, rising from his cot. He walked toward the wall of bars separating them. "She said she worked for Tanus Corporation. She said they were looking for people to place in a simulation."

Tom touched the bars. They were cold, hard, solid. With all his might, he clenched them and tried to wrench them free. Unsurprisingly, they refused to move. If this was a game, then it was more advanced than anything Tom had ever heard of before.

"I've never heard of Tanus Corporation," Bishop mused. "I wonder if what you're remembering could be true. We know the mayor is reconditioning people, with his Ministry of Recall. Could Doc be doing the same thing? Placing false memories in our heads?"

In all honesty, Tom had wondered the same. He'd never met or spoken to Doc before the game, as far as he knew. But there was something about her, something about his memories, that he believed to be true.

"You might want to check your HUD," Bishop reminded Tom. "We leveled up again last night."

"What did you spend your skill points on?" Tom asked.

"Precision," Bishop answered.

"Bro, are you okay?" Gary asked as soon as the HUD was active. "They beat you like a piñata."

"I know," Tom answered. "I feel like a piñata."

Tom's main HUD screen read:

LEVEL 5

CLASS TYPE: BRAWLER

SKILL POINTS: 2

ACHIEVEMENT: SAVE THE VIRGIN FROM THE CULTISTS.

GAIN 30 CREDITS.

ACHIEVEMENT: KICK THE MIMIC TO THE CURB.

GAIN COMMON LOOT CRATE.

CREDITS: 30 - 10 FOR BISHOP LEAVES YOU WITH—HOLD ON,

CARRY THE 2, I NEVER WAS ANY GOOD AT MATH—20 CREDITS!

"What's a loot crate?" Tom asked.

"Very cool secret treasure finds," Gary answered. "The longer you wait to open them, the more they're worth. Open it now and you'll find chewed gum. But if you wait to open it later, you might find . . . unchewed gum."

Tom was getting used to ignoring the AI. He used that trait now, opening his skill tree. He liked the idea of having a skill point or two to use if he needed them, and right now he could use some luck.

Tom navigated the hundred possible options toward the top of the skill tree to find the one he wanted. He placed one of his two skill points there now.

UPGRADE: INCREASED LUCK WILL
FOLLOW YOU WHEREVER YOU GO.

"Having the headaches and the memories, are we?" The voice came from the cell on the other side of Bishop. "Well, don't worry. The good mayor and his witch of a doctor will see to it that you either comply and forget or are killed over and over again until who you are is erased into oblivion."

Tom looked past Bishop. The speaker was an older woman, with hair so matted it spiderwebbed together. Her clothes were dusty and worn.

"Ewww, gross," Gary said. "I'm sorry, ma'am. I'm sorry I don't carry any cash."

"How do you know what we're talking about?" Bishop asked. "Who are you?"

At that very moment, a heavy key was turned in the lock to the exterior doors. Four large men wearing badges walked in alongside Mayor Henry Graves. While the men moved to the old woman's cell, the mayor gave Tom and Bishop his full attention.

Tom turned off his HUD. If things were about to get violent, he needed all his focus.

"You know," the mayor said with a chuckle while he shook

his head, "I thought you two were actually about to kill me. Fear isn't something I feel on a day-to-day basis, so I wanted to thank you. It was invigorating and reminded me that I'm not out of the line of fire."

As the mayor spoke, the other men walked into the cell with the old woman. She screamed, but they held her down on the cot. Fighting tooth and nail, the woman was still no match for the men, who smothered her with her own pillow.

"Hey, hey!" Bishop shouted, rushing to that side of her cell and reaching through the bars. She was too far away to do any good.

"Enough, let her go!" Tom screamed, slamming himself against the bars. "Whatever you want, just let her go!"

"I want peace," the mayor said with a shrug. "It's as simple as that. I just want to provide a home for my wandering brothers and sisters."

"She can't breathe, let her go!" Bishop screamed, stringing a line of profanity behind her words.

Tom raged, beating the bars in front of him until his knuckles were bloody. The old woman struggled one last time under the weight of her captors before her body went limp.

The men held her down for a moment longer, then let up. The old woman's body lay on the cot, unmoving.

"You see, she's a regular," the mayor said, looking at the corpse. "I've killed her before, and she's starting to lose her grip on sanity. I kill her maybe a time or two more, if she doesn't agree to comply, then she's just one of those raving lost ones. But you two. I've never had the opportunity to speak to you two before. There's still hope for you at your trial tonight. You meet with our counselors, you comply with the Ministry of Recall, and your compliance will be rewarded."

"I'm going to be the last thing you see in this life," Bishop growled through clenched teeth. "I promise you that."

Tom remained quiet, controlling his shaking and his breathing. Then a thought hit him. "You're not a real person at all, are you? You're just a series of ones and zeros."

"Whoa, going right for it, are we?" the mayor said, looking impressed. "You know, no one has ever made it this far with their sanity intact to ask me such a question. I think there might be something special about you, Mr. Tom Dexter. That's right. I know all about you. Well, I'll tell you what. You comply, and I'll give you answers to questions you didn't even know you should be asking."

The deputies walked out of the room, leaving the old woman's body behind.

"You two think over my offer before the trial tonight," the mayor said as he left. "If you decide to comply, you'll be rewarded."

CHAPTER 19

SARA

The coding in the game, the shadow entity moving through with no explanation—it all pointed to one person. Sara knew exactly what she should do. She should immediately tell Chairman that they had been compromised. That somehow an outside force had found its way into the simulation, something that had never happened before.

That was the right thing to do. Sara was sure of it. So why hadn't she reported it? She stood in front of the mirror in her bathroom, brushing her teeth. The room was the size of most people's living rooms. All her grooming supplies were laid out as precisely as the instruments in an operating room before a lifesaving procedure.

Sara spit the suds from her mouth and went through her very precise, very calculated routine for doing her hair and makeup and getting dressed.

Hair shouldn't take more than twenty minutes, and makeup fifteen. I already know what I'm going to wear, so ten minutes there, and then thirty minutes with Michelle at breakfast.

Sara moved from the bathroom to her wide-open bedroom

with its king-size bed and a walk-in closet she could get lost in. The closet housed mostly white clothing with a few black dresses or pantsuits here and there to spice things up.

Sara chose white high heels, a long white skirt, and a long-sleeved blouse. She wore the silver necklace Chairman had given her on her tenth anniversary with Tanus. The silver chain bore one charm: the ouroboros, the snake twisting itself into the infinity symbol by eating its own tail. This ouroboros was a bit different, of course, as the logo of Tanus Corporation. The last quarter of the snake's tail was made up of ones and zeros, of coding. The snake also had four eyes.

Sara walked out of her closet, smoothing her wrinkle-free skirt. As she passed her bed, she noticed a stray black hair. Sara got down on her hands and knees, eye level with the hair. She plucked it off the bed, then examined the rest of the white duvet for any other rogue particles.

Rising, she moved to the restroom to deposit the lone hair in the trash, then made her way to the first floor below. Her home was as clean and unspoiled as her bedroom. White marble floors echoed with her steps.

Her daughter, Michelle, was already at the breakfast table, eating eggs, bacon, and blueberries. Their maid, Gloria, was busy packing the girl's lunch for school.

"Good morning, sweetheart," Sara said, pausing by her daughter's chair to place a kiss on the top of her head. She eyed the number of blueberries on her daughter's plate.

"Good morning, Mom," Michelle said with a smile.

"Ms. Tran, good morning," Gloria said, reaching into the oven for a warm plate for Sara. "Here are your egg whites and turkey bacon. I have your yogurt in the fridge."

"Mmmm, uh-huh," Sara said, lowering her voice. "Gloria, I thought we talked about how many blueberries Michelle is to have in the morning. Too much sugar right away isn't good for her cognitive abilities when she goes to school. One tablespoon of blueberries, Gloria."

"Yes, of course, I'm sorry, Ms. Tran," Gloria said nervously. "She asked for more, and she's such a good—"

"One tablespoon," Sara hissed.

Gloria nodded, muttering under her breath. All Sara caught was something that sounded like "peen chi." Instead of talking, she moved to the refrigerator and removed a plain yogurt. She placed it on the table for Sara along with a cup of steaming black coffee.

Sara took her seat across from her daughter and smiled. "Michelle, your grades this semester look amazing. I want to get you something to reward you for all of your hard work. What would you like? A new blouse? Perhaps a series of hardbound leather books?"

"Can I have a puppy?" Michelle asked hopefully.

"A puppy?" Sara said, almost spitting out her coffee. "Michelle, why would you want an animal?"

"I could take care of it, and it could keep me company while you're at work," Michelle said, still not losing hope. "Please? I'll train it to go to the bathroom outside."

"You have Gloria to play with," Sara said, nodding over to the maid. Gloria groaned and grabbed at her lower back. She used the same word here as well. "Besides, when would you have time to play with an animal? Between school, sports, and music, you don't have much free time at all."

Michelle quieted, the spark of joy dying slowly in her eyes. She pushed what was left of her eggs around on her plate.

The two ate their breakfast in silence. Sara felt a wave of parental guilt. "How about this—how about we go to the zoo next weekend, and I'll buy you a gorilla?"

Michelle perked up in her seat, eyes wide. "What? Really? A gorilla?"

"Okay, maybe not a gorilla, but we can talk about the dog, and yes, let's go to the zoo," Sara said, finding so much joy from seeing her daughter light up.

"You've never taken me to the zoo before," Michelle said, still grinning. "I've been with my class, but never with you. Are you serious? Do you have time?"

"Well, I'll make the time," Sara said, rising from her seat and going around the table to give her daughter a hug. "I love you, Michelle. Have a great day at school."

"I love you too, Mom," Michelle said, returning the embrace.

What did you do to deserve her? Sara thought. *Nothing. You don't deserve her. Maybe a puppy wouldn't be so bad after all. Her birthday is in two months.*

The thought of Michelle's birthday inevitably led to thoughts of the guest list and Michael, Sara's ex-husband and Michelle's father, who had walked out on them while Sara was still pregnant. Those years had been so hard—no, those years had been impossible. Sara remembered the long nights alone with Michelle. Her chubby little cheeks, those precious chunky feet she could just eat. They had made it through together. Michelle was all the motivation Sara ever needed. That girl was her world.

On the way to work, Sara reviewed reports and updates on her data pad as her smart car wove in and out of traffic on the highway. Thanks to modern technology, there hadn't been an accident reported in years. The vehicles were completely autonomous. In fact, it had been this way for so many years Sara had to question if there was a time humans had actually had to drive vehicles at all.

Going over the bridge of New Port, as always, offered her

a view of the city as a whole. An area to the north had been hit hard with riots and looting during a recent demonstration. News reports talked about fires still burning as the police and fire department worked together to get the incidents under control.

Sara could see the smoke rising into the morning sun. Then she was over the bridge and descending into downtown. Riots and looting were becoming more and more common. With volcanoes erupting and the uptick in new viruses each year, many people were walking on a razor's edge between sanity and total panic.

She had read the analyses. The greatest minds had given Earth nine years. Nine years before things spiraled out of control. Before an asteroid struck, a supervolcano erupted, or World War III broke out—a war that would be fought by countries armed to the teeth with nuclear weapons. Any of these would mean the extinction of the human race.

Sara's vehicle took her past skyscrapers so tall that they threatened to block out the sky. Even at this early hour, there was traffic. Sara's was just one of the many sleek, ovoid vehicles transporting their cargo from point A to point B.

Removing her mind from dark thoughts of what was to become of the world and why her work was so important, Sara activated her inbox. A message from Chairman titled "Project Legacy" caught her attention.

> Ms. Tran,
>
> You should be applauded for the work that you've done securing our next round of candidates. Their backgrounds will no doubt prove interesting as we collect data, and who knows, one of them may succeed where everyone else has failed.
>
> I wanted you to know about a new initiative we

have been preparing that begins today. The board has voted to move ahead with Project Legacy, a new phase of the game.

With you already taking on so much responsibility, another department head will oversee this part of the game. I just thought you should know.

Thank you for all the work you do here at Tanus Corporation.

Chairman

Sara felt sick. No, more than sick. She felt as though she were going to throw up Gloria's breakfast.

Easy, calm down, easy, Sara coached herself through the anxiety. *You've got this.*

Project Legacy. She knew all about it, had in fact voted against moving forward with that section of the game when senior management had been asked for their input. One of Sara's concerns was that while she worked to bring in candidates who would have a viable chance of surviving the game, Project Legacy made no such distinction.

With thoughts of her daughter fresh in her mind, Sara touched her data pad and prepared to send a return email to Chairman. But if her years in the private sector had taught her anything, it was to not be ruled by emotion. She took a deep breath and placed her data pad on the seat beside her. She would wait to respond, lest she say something she would regret.

All this on the very morning she was going to take Chairman the data she had been collecting about the rogue code in their system that meant someone was spying on them. Sara had a good idea who it was.

Sara arrived at the Tanus Corporation facilities a few minutes later, still troubled by the email but not sure what to do about it. The height of Tanus's building was matched by the depth of the underground installation below it, all part of the corporation. Guards manning a cement barrier waved Sara in after her vehicle was scanned by drones that confirmed her identity.

Her vehicle drove into an underground parking structure and into her reserved space, alongside a legion of other smart cars. Lost in her thoughts, Sara made her way through the garage to one of the many lifts waiting to take her to the lobby. As much as she didn't want to know if Chairman's revelation was true, she had to.

Who could she call to verify? Trusting anyone wasn't Sara's strong suit. She had seen the very worst that people could do to one another inside the game, and what was the game if not a test run for a brave new world?

She had to start playing her cards closer to her vest. Everything was tracked, from calls to search history. Sara resigned herself to who she was about to contact. Still in the parking garage, she made her call.

The phone rang once before Bob answered. "Good morning, boss lady, how are you?"

"Don't ever call me 'boss lady' again," Sara started. "I need you to look something up for me."

"Oh, I'm—I'm sorry," Bob stuttered.

"And stop apologizing for everything," Sara went on. "Are you at your computer?"

"Sorr—yes, yes, I'm here," Bob said, catching himself just in time.

"Even your access should let you look up different departments," Sara said, talking to herself as much as Bob. "I need you to tell me what floor Project Legacy is on."

"Right, no problem," Bob answered, eager to please. "Just a

second. You know, while I have you on the phone, Ms. Tran, I just wanted to say thank you for all the help you've been giving me. I was just telling my nana about you. And you know what my nana said?"

"Bob—Bob, I'm just going to stop you right there. I don't care about your nana," Sara said, rolling her eyes so hard she felt like they were going to fall right out of her head. "What floor is the project on?"

"Huh, that's weird," Bob said, breathing hard on the other end of the line.

CHAPTER 20

SARA

If there was one thing Sara hated, it was a good old-fashioned mouth breather.

"What. Is. It. Bob?" Sara said, not trying to mask her frustration in any way.

"It says Project Legacy is being conducted on a subfloor?" Bob said in a questioning tone. "Subfloor eight. How big is this place? I've never been to any of the subfloors. I—"

Sara hung up and summoned a lift. It was a small miracle she hadn't run into any other employees yet. Still, she was early.

That means Bob got to work early as well, Sara thought. *Maybe I should be easier on the kid. Nahhh . . .*

The sliding metal doors dinged open with a familiar chime, and Sara entered the cylindrical car. The sublevels required their own special elevator and clearance. Lucky for Sara, she was well aware of the sublevels and had even toured them once or twice.

To her knowledge, there was nothing there besides storage rooms, server rooms, and research and development levels, where the nerds worked on their new toys.

Besides the tours, there had been no reason for her to go

down to the sublevels until now. Sara waved her hand over the only option for a floor below the garage level. The floor option showed a large *B* for *basement.*

The elevator took her down and dinged open. The "basement" was actually more of a lobby. Two security guards sat behind a massive desk shaped like a half circle. They nodded to Sara, recognizing her.

To their right were the secondary lifts that went down to the sublevels. Sara moved to the activation device, a square pad that would measure the size of the bones in her hand. It turned out that the exact size of those bones was as unique as a fingerprint and could be scanned just as easily. Sara placed her hand on the square pad set into the wall. A blue light flashed up and down past her palm. The doors of a lift opened.

This lift seemed newer, less used. The options for floors were SL one through eight. Sara chose eight and waited for the doors to close. The lift lowered to the music of Biggie Smalls's "Juicy."

The doors dinged open a moment later, revealing a floor much like the one she was responsible for. In fact, it was almost an exact replica. A lobby led to long halls lined with simulation rooms. The main difference was that instead of each candidate having their own simulation room, these much larger rooms were shared.

A white-coated lab technician behind the counter stood from his seat to greet Sara.

"Ms. Tran, is that you?" the man asked, adjusting his glasses. He emerged from behind the desk and extended a hand. "You don't know me. I'm Theodore Sullivan. I've seen you around and received your general announcement emails. I was just appointed to oversee Project Legacy. I have to say I am a huge fan of yours and how you've been able to grow the game."

"Thank you," Sara said, accepting the man's clammy handshake, which held no power at all. She craned her neck to look down the halls. Glass walls gave a view into each room. From Sara's vantage point, she could barely see inside them.

"Oh, would you like a tour?" Theodore asked. "How rude of me—of course you would. I was wondering when you might come down to take a look."

"Yes, please, that would be nice," Sara said, realizing that honestly the last thing she wanted to see was a tour of victims being hooked up into the game. But she had to know.

"Please, come with me." Theodore beckoned her to follow as he walked down one of the wide white halls. "We've been preparing this for a few months now, building the rooms and readying the game to take on a new wave of candidates. Though we've only just begun, let me tell you, the data we are collecting is miraculous. Minds are taking to the game in ways I never could have imagined."

Sara let Theodore drone on about the process and how exciting it all was. Maybe she should have been listening. But her attention was directed utterly into the shared simulation rooms.

Teens and adults of all ages, including the elderly, lay in hovering pods shaped like half-cracked eggs. They were of all races and ethnicities, male and female, ranging from what Sara guessed was anywhere between eighteen and eighty. She swallowed, biting her tongue so hard it bled, when her eyes fell on a man about her own age—tall and slender with a chiseled jaw. She immediately recognized Michael, though he had walked out on her many years earlier.

How he was here—did someone know of their connection, or had he just gotten mixed in with the horde of new candidates needed for Project Legacy?—was a mystery. Whatever the case, Sara reminded herself to be calm. If no one knew already, then no one should ever know how close he had been to her. Maybe it didn't even matter; maybe this was what he deserved.

All the candidates looked as though they were sleeping, each one wearing a metal crown that connected them to the game. Blue holographic readouts that monitored their vitals and their places in the game hovered in the air above their beds.

Sara realized what the room reminded her of. It brought back images of the nursery at a local hospital, the room where babies were taken to sleep near each other. That made sense; these new candidates were as helpless as children in her eyes.

"It was my idea to condense the rooms and save space," Theodore was going on when Sara tuned back in.

If Theodore knew Sara's ex was in the simulation room she was looking at, he showed no sign.

Sara came to a stop in front of the massive glass window. There had to be twenty candidates in this room and in the room behind her on the opposite side of the hall. It would be the same in the other halls. More unqualified candidates, stuck inside the game.

"How were the new candidates chosen?" Sara whispered.

"Oh, well, you know how it is." Theodore chuckled, removing his glasses to clean them on his white coat. "Orphans, homeless, old people who have been forgotten, anyone who will not be missed. It's better for them here, in all honesty. Here, their lives actually mean something."

Anger flared in Sara. She was almost always angry, but seeing her ex had sparked something in her. While she was sure she didn't love him, he was the first person to enter the game who she knew personally. And her daughter's biological father.

Theodore took Sara's silence as interest and continued prattling on like a fan trying to please his favorite celebrity. "But all of this wouldn't have been possible without you, Ms. Tran. You laid the groundwork. Perhaps in the future, we can collaborate on the next iteration of the game."

"Next iteration?" Sara asked.

"Of course, I'm sure you know much more than I do about what Chairman has planned next," Theodore verbally backpedaled. "I'm only saying that the 2.0 version might mirror what we have created. We can build on what we have here for a better game in the future."

Sara didn't bother to respond. Her eyes were glued to Michael. He was twitching. The monitor above him showed him running from a pack of night hounds. His mind, unable to tell the difference between the game and reality, had Michael running for his life.

"Ms. Tran? Ms. Tran?" Theodore asked.

"What?!" Sara shouted.

"Oh, I'm sorry, I—I was just asking if you would like to go inside the simulation room and see the candidates up close," Theodore squeaked. He took a step back.

"No, that will be all," Sara said, turning on a heel and making for the elevators while she could still control herself.

"Perhaps, if it's not too much to ask, we might be able to have lunch together sometime to talk about our projects," Theodore said, racing to keep up with Sara. "Something completely platonic, of course. Not a lunch date, just a date on the calendar when we would have lunch."

Sara made it to the elevator and passed her hand over the scanner once more. It took everything inside her not to tear Theodore's eyes from his face. What he was doing to those unqualified candidates . . . what they were going through . . . The candidates she selected were different. Her subjects were physically able, consenting adults, or those who had ruined their own lives enough for Sara to convince herself that they deserved to be in the game.

The elevator came; the doors dinged open. Sara stepped inside while an expectant Theodore waited for her response.

Instead of everything Sara wanted to say to the man, she only answered with a smile, "Yes, a work lunch would be fine. Please schedule it with my secretary."

"Oh, wonderful—I will, thank—"

His words were cut off by the closing doors, and Sara was finally given the opportunity to breathe. Honestly, she felt like crying, but how long had it been since she'd cried? She forced the tears to remain at bay, tears not for her but for the lost souls in the game.

Hold yourself together, Tran, Sara told herself. *Hold it together.*

Sara moved in silence through the multiple elevators and many floors to her level and office. She passed the lobby, where her nonexistent secretary did not stand guard, and made her way to her desk.

Her mind raced. She sat, opening the floating holographic screen above her desk. A file with the invasive code sat on her desktop. The company had access to all her files, of course, but if no one was looking for this, then nothing would be found.

The only ones who knew of the code were her and Jeffrey Saga, who had discovered it. But he hadn't understood what he'd found, and even now, Sara only suspected. The code and its location reminded her of someone she had once called a friend.

What she should do—what she should have done—was immediately report the breach in security. Something had held her back until today, when she had decided she would report it. However, after she'd seen Project Legacy, something stayed her hand again.

Sara took a long breath and, against her better judgment, reached for her personal phone. She brought up a very old contact and sent a text message. "Is this you? Are you in the game?"

She attached a bit of the code and sent the message, hoping

against hope that she was wrong, knowing that she wasn't. The coding was too precise, too well crafted. It was *her*.

Sara went to work, sifting through emails, reading reports, and taking and making the calls needed to ensure her part of the game was running smoothly. It wasn't until after lunch that she received the text she was expecting.

"It's me. We need to talk. Same place? Now?" the text read.

"Yes, twenty minutes," Sara texted back, already rising from her seat and heading to the door.

All her major meetings for the day were finished. Sara intentionally loaded them into mornings, when her decision-making skills were at their sharpest. She left the afternoons for more menial work or for visiting the simulation rooms to talk to techs and observe the candidates.

In her car, anxiety gripped her again as she punched in the address. It was their place, where they used to go all the time what seemed like a lifetime ago, when Tanus Corporation was just beginning.

What Sara was doing now would get her fired if anyone knew. As her car wove through the busy downtown streets, Sara reflected again on Chairman's email. She still needed to respond, but tact above all else was critical here.

Dear Sir,

I understand the importance of seeing the game through to the very end and exploring all possible avenues.

Thank you for informing me of the board's decision.

Sara

The rest of the drive passed with Sara deep in thought. The next thing she knew, her car parked itself in front of the meeting place. Union Coffee was a hole-in-the-wall shop with a few tables outside and fewer inside. It was family owned, and Sara would never have found it had it not been for Julie.

Sara saw her now, sitting at one of the outside tables. She looked different; short red hair, glasses, and a baseball cap made her nearly unrecognizable. But her order was the same, as unique as it had always been: an onion bagel with peanut butter, and tea, not coffee. Both were abominations in Sara's eyes.

"Julie," Sara said, exiting her vehicle and walking toward her onetime best friend. "Or should I call you Doc?"

CHAPTER 21

JULIE

Everything had changed at Tanus Corporation. What once had seemed so pure and adventurous was nothing more than a living hell for the people in the game. She and Sara had been hired by Chairman early on. Right out of college, they were bright eyed and bushy tailed, ready to make a difference in the world.

Their work was going to matter. They were going to help people. But things changed. The mysterious Chairman worked through proxies and literally never showed his face, always keeping his camera off during video calls and never attending meetings in person. Still, everything he said he would do, he delivered on, including the money.

Fully funded, with money to spare, Julie and Sara were well taken care of as they built the company. Julie worked on the back-end game with a skilled team while Sara oversaw the recruitment of candidates and hiring of the technicians who would observe them.

The early years were not just good—they were great. Julie was there for Sara during her divorce, and Sara was there for Julie when she lost her brother. Then things began to change.

Candidates weren't all willing to participate, and while Julie was never straight-out told they were being abducted into the game, she had her suspicions.

More than ever she worked in a silo, cut out of the executive decision-making, restricted to building the code.

A rift began to grow between Julie and Sara. The AI controlling the game was becoming more and more malevolent. Coding she had had a hand in developing was evolving faster than anyone expected. The AI got better and better at convincing players to remain complacent and began to repeatedly kill those it couldn't control.

What was more, adverse side effects began to appear for the candidates who died multiple times. Julie still didn't have a clear answer to what happened to them, to where their consciousness went. She wondered if it was possible that what made them who they were, their souls, just disappeared or died altogether. If deteriorating candidates were pulled out of the game, they returned to the world as lunatics or vegetables—difficult to manage and impossible to release.

Before Julie could figure out exactly what the candidates were losing, things came to a head. She remembered the day like it was yesterday. She'd implored Chairman to install safeguards on the AI controlling the game and asked him and Sara how so many new candidates had been found so quickly, accusing them of kidnapping—which neither of them denied.

She had tried to pull the plug, but it was too late. She had helped create a hive of monsters at Tanus Corporation. While Sara tried to intervene for her, there was no going back. They all knew it. Julie lived in fear. Government authorities and journalists were in thrall to Tanus Corporation. No one believed her, and the few who might were paid to keep their mouths shut.

Then, one night, the phone rang.

"Hello?" Julie said uncertainly, not recognizing the number. "If this is a sales call to decrease my energy bill with solar panels, I'm really not in the mood."

"Not a sales call," a woman's voice said. "A friend who believes you."

Julie perked up in her little one-bedroom apartment. With no funds coming in, she'd had to downsize from her home to save as much money as possible. After Tanus Corporation fired her, she was blackballed, unhirable in the tech world.

"Who is this?" Julie asked, ready to hang up the phone if it was a prank call.

"I work for an organization that is very interested in what you saw at Tanus Corporation and the story you have to tell," the stranger continued. "I know you're just concerned about spreading the truth. So are we, and we're in a position to aid with certain monetary needs as well."

Julie paused, hesitant, weighing her options. She had to be smart about this. "How do I know that this is real? That you are who you say you are and that you want to help?"

"Ahhh, you're right; trust must be earned, not given," the woman said, sucking air through her teeth in thought. "We are just concerned with the truth and hearing your story. We want to help. Perhaps action instead of words is a better way to advance our relationship."

A soft knock on Julie's apartment door made her jump. She swallowed hard. Still pressing the phone against her ear, she reached into her nightstand for her handgun, a Glock her brother had bought for her birthday one year, along with a flamethrower. While he'd always had a twisted sense of humor, he had also always been worried about her, and apparently rightfully so.

Julie gripped the weapon as if her life depended on it. She aimed at the door.

"There's no need for alarm," the woman reassured her. "Our delivery man is gone. You can verify this by looking through the peephole. We dropped off a peace offering."

Julie walked slowly to the door, gun in hand. A quick look through the peephole showed her no one was outside. She kept the safety chain in place as she inched the door open.

It was dark; sounds of neighbors talking drifted up to her second-story apartment. There was no hulking menace or hit man she could see. Instead, a flat brown box rested on her doorstep. Still unwilling to trust the voice on the other end of the phone, Julie placed the gun on the floor and reached through the narrow crack for the box. Turning it sideways allowed her to slip the item through the opening.

Julie examined the plain cardboard container. There were no markings or labels to set it apart from any other box she had ever seen.

"Put me on speaker and open the box," the voice said on the other end of the phone.

"What's your name?" Julie asked, pressing the speaker option on her phone's screen.

"Excuse me?"

"You heard me," Julie stated. "What's your name? How can I trust someone whose name I don't even know?"

"I work for a company called Immortal Industries," the woman answered. "No need to do any digging; we aren't traded on the public market. Open the box, Julie."

Julie picked up the Glock and the box, then placed them and the phone on her small kitchen table. She opened the box as instructed. Inside was a gunmetal-gray laptop. Again, there were no markings or emblems to set it apart from any other laptop.

"It's already on," the woman from Immortal Industries

coaxed her. "Open the screen. Click the document that reads 'Second Chance.'"

A war raged inside Julie's mind. On one hand, she couldn't believe any of this was real. On the other, she was responsible for creating a game that was now basically a prison for hundreds of people.

The burden of her actions and where they had led weighed on her, forcing her to open the laptop. If there was even a 1 percent chance that she could do some good, that the voice was actually an ally, she owed it to the "candidates" to try.

With bated breath, Julie opened the computer to a black screen and a single file visible on the desktop. Opening the file made Julie's jaw drop in wonder.

Code—not just any code but code built for a game—scrolled across her screen. It wasn't perfect, but it was nearly there. Images popped up in separate windows, showing a pristine facility stocked with all the equipment Julie would need to enter the game.

Fingers of doubt clenched her gut in that moment.

Be smart, Julie, she told herself as warning lights exploded in her head. *This is Tanus Corporation all over again. They just want the tech. They want to build a game of their own.*

"We can offer you a chance," the other woman said. "Not much, but it's a chance to wipe some of the red off your ledger. As you can see, the coding is almost there. With your help, we can finish. We also have a facility where you can enter the game."

"How do I know you're not just using me to steal from Tanus?" Julie asked. "How do I know that once I give you what you want, you won't be on your way to creating the same thing they did and locking people inside your twisted game?"

"Because if we only wanted you to give us the code, there are easier ways to force you into submission than trying to befriend you," the woman answered matter-of-factly. "If we wanted you gone, you would be. You are searching hard for enemies when there are none to be found."

"Why are you helping me?" Julie pressed. "This just doesn't happen. This coding—it had to take a team years to get this far. The workspace images show a place that has to cost millions. Why? Why spend so much? Because you're saints?"

"No, we're very far from that," the woman sighed. "In a world like ours, I know it's difficult to trust that anyone would have good intentions. And even good intentions can be violated and skewed over time. The truth is, we believe that the technology that Tanus Corporation possesses is too powerful to be allowed to remain in the hands of any single entity. And if everything you say about what they're doing to people in the game is true, they have to be brought down."

Julie swallowed hard, examining the code more closely. She could make it work; there was no doubt in her mind. There were some mistakes in the code, but she could fix them in a month, maybe a few weeks of really grinding it out.

With the equipment shown in the images, she could go into the game and help. She could make a difference to those she'd had a hand in placing there. It would be dangerous, but what did she have to lose? No one was willing to listen to her. Now a lifeline was being thrown her way. Could she really afford to throw it back?

"When do we start?" Julie asked.

"We already have," the voice answered.

CHAPTER 22

JULIE

The next few weeks went by in a blur of coding and Pop-Tarts—Julie's go-to food when she was cranking out code—and caffeine in all forms.

The mystery woman from Immortal Industries gave her space and only checked in twice, once to let her know that money had been deposited into her account and the second time to tell her how to access the state-of-the-art lab that had been readied for her.

On her end, Julie threw on her Nancy Drew hat and researched Immortal Industries until her eyes were red, but she always came up empty. Absolutely nothing showed they existed at all. Oh, there were a few mentions of the company name in blogs and chat rooms that promoted conspiracy theories. But when Julie pulled on this string, it always unraveled into hearsay and speculation, the users going off on tangents about the Illuminati and angels and demons that walked among them.

Eventually, Julie decided to let the questions go. Everything her contact had said on the phone proved to be true. She was paid more than enough to continue to work on the code. When it came time to enter the facility, she was given the address of a warehouse far from the city's business district.

The warehouse didn't look like much from the outside. The panels were rusting; a security fence and cameras were the most up-to-date amenities the property boasted. When Julie punched in the six-digit entry code she'd been provided, a blue light scanned not just her eyes or hand but her entire body.

A heavy click signaled the locks rolling back, and she was allowed entrance. There was no one in the massive, wide-open room, but among the flickering overhead lights and the smell of damp was all the equipment Julie would need to enter the Eternal Engine.

Whatever Immortal Industries was, its pockets ran deep, its connections deeper. Much of the technology in the room wasn't available on the open market. They had paid top dollar for this and probably more money searching for it in the first place.

Since then, Julie had been a ghost in Tanus's system. She would work and rework her code, then hack into the game, always using a different area to come and go. She helped countless candidates in their journeys, always masking her presence as an NPC, always covering her tracks.

She had even done some work on the in-game AI, Gary. He was more free now to help the users who interacted with him. To be fair, most users either hadn't realized how to activate him or had turned him off altogether. Still, Gary was learning fast.

Her long-term plan was to expose Tanus Corporation for what it was doing to people. Her short-term objective was to help as many candidates as she could. They were stuck in this never-ending hell due in large part to her. That fact pierced Julie to the bone.

She started sleeping less, lost contact with most of the outside world. There was nothing but reworking the code and living inside the game. She knew that her time was limited. As good as she was, sooner or later she would be found out, and someone would come for her.

Despite this, she never expected that someone to be Sara. When she received Sara's text, Julie was shocked, excited to talk to her friend, and angry all at once. Sara had tried to stick up for her when she was terminated, but that was as far as it went. After she was fired, Julie and Sara spoke on and off for a time, but always in secret. Sara had been instructed to cut all ties with Julie by Chairman himself.

Eventually, the calls stopped, and so did the texts. Until now.

Now Julie sat across from Sara at their favorite little coffee shop no one knew about. The women enjoyed the sweet silence that only existed between friends who knew each other inside and out.

"How's Michelle?" Julie asked. "I miss her."

"She's about to have an unemployed mother," Sara responded sharply. "Julie, what are you thinking? Are you thinking at all? Hacking into the system—did you think you wouldn't be found out? Did you think you were going to get away with this? Julie, these are dangerous people you're playing with."

"You found it?" Julie asked calmly. "You found the code I was using?"

"Not me; Jeffrey Saga found an anomaly," Sara said, shaking her head. "I told him I'd take care of it, but how much longer until someone else finds another break in the code? Sooner or later, I'm not going to be able to hide you. People are going to start asking questions."

"Awww, Jeffrey," Julie said, shaking her head. "He was always one of the smarter ones. Of course it would be him."

"Julie, are you even listening to me?" Sara asked, raising her voice.

They were the only two sharing a table outside the café. An elderly man walking his Great Dane along the sidewalk looked over with interest.

"I heard you," Julie answered. "Do you remember Gary?"

Sara took a beat, looking sad for a moment before resuming her emotionless expression. "Yes, of course I remember your brother. Who could forget what polar opposites you two were? You named the AI in the game after him."

"You know, when the cancer came for him, it came so quickly," Julie said, scrunching her brow as if trying to solve a complex equation. "That last year, I had absolutely no regrets when it came to Gary. Anytime I wanted to call him, I did. Anytime I wanted to text, I made the time. Whenever I felt like going to visit, I would. I wonder—I wonder, if I had lived my whole life that way, what kind of relationship we could have had."

"Julie, what happened to Gary isn't your fault," Sara said, shaking her head. She extended a hand as if she were going to take Julie's, then pulled back at the last moment. "People get sick. It's part of life. It's a sad, hurtful part of life, but it happens. It's not your fault."

"No, but the time I lost with him was my fault," Julie answered. "And all the time we're stealing from those people in the game is our fault as well. That's on us, Sara. What happened to us? We started down this path wanting to help."

"We *are* helping."

"By kidnapping strangers and tearing away their souls every time they die in the game?"

"It's more than that. You know what we're doing," Sara said. "We're preparing the way for the future."

"Right," Julie said, taking a sip of her drink. She repeated their mission statement word for word. "'Humankind has to find a new home. But who do we send? Enter the Eternal Engine, a game to find out who would not just survive but thrive in a harsh alien environment.'"

Cars rolled by; pedestrians walked to and fro. The women sat there, thinking about their life choices.

"But the story doesn't end there, does it?" Julie asked, pressing Sara further. "Not all the candidates know they're in a game, and neither are they all willing. And when they die, part of them doesn't come back."

"We knew the risks," Sara said. Julie could hear malice in her tone. "We knew what we were getting ourselves into."

"No, we didn't," Julie responded. "Do you really believe that? Or is that just a lie you tell yourself so you can sleep at night?"

Julie realized she had pressed Sara too far when the woman stood and smoothed down her suit.

"I can't cover for you anymore," Sara told her. "This is your only warning. Don't go back into the simulation."

"You should look deeper into Candidate 20741," Julie suggested. She could tell Sara wanted to leave and that the open-ended statement had piqued her curiosity. "He just reached level five."

"So?" Sara asked.

"So he's only had to restart once. And when he came back, he showed limited to no cognitive erosion," Julie answered.

"That's impossible," Sara told her onetime friend.

"Improbable, not impossible," Julie corrected. "I know. I've spoken to him. He's remembering his life before the game. He's somehow immune to the way the game deteriorates people's minds when they get reloaded. Just look into it."

Sara nodded.

There was a time when the two of them would have ended a conversation with a hug and a smile. Those days were long since gone.

"Whatever game you're playing with whoever is funding you, get out while you still can," Sara said. "It's too late for me, but you can walk away."

"I can't," Julie told her with a sigh. "I guess neither of us can now. Thank you."

"For what?"

"For coming to me with this and not hanging me out to dry. I'll be more careful."

"You know they record everything in the game," Sara said. "Even if they don't find the code again, it takes one tech wondering who the redheaded character is to go and look up the corresponding candidate or NPC."

"I scrub all the scenes I'm in," Julie responded. "When I can't, I assign my avatar another candidate's number. When I can't do that, I'm just an NPC in the game."

"You're too smart for your own good," Sara answered.

"Apparently not," Julie responded. "Be careful, Sara. Tell Michelle I miss her very much."

Sara nodded and walked back to her car. In moments, she was lost in the afternoon traffic, leaving Julie alone with her onion-and-peanut-butter bagel.

Julie took a bite, savoring the texture as her mind wandered to what needed to be done next. She wasn't bluffing. There was something about Candidate 20741 that was different from all the others. He was resilient, his mind standing up to the changes and torture he endured in the game. He might be the one. The first one to complete his mission and reach the endgame.

Julie was going to make sure he had every opportunity to do that.

While she was finishing off her onion-and-peanut-butter bagel, a young couple came and sat at the table next to her. They looked at her meal with disgust, making rude comments under their breath. She probably shouldn't have, but Julie took a few extra bites and moaned with pleasure at the taste before she left. No regrets, right?

Julie made her way to her beat-up truck, then drove to the warehouse district at the edge of town. It was close to the harbor and far enough away from any residential areas that there were few cars and fewer people. Most of the warehouses were unmarked, but some sported signs for things like construction parts or manufacturing goods. It seemed like most of the warehouses here were used exclusively for storage.

Julie pulled up to lot 888, equipped with a rolling gate, cameras, and a thick steel door. A security feature at the gate took the required code and facial scan. The cameras tracked her movements as she pulled into the small parking lot and the gate closed behind her.

The door required a different six-digit code and a scan of her entire body. The whole time, the cameras mounted in the warehouse watched and waited. It had bothered Julie at first, but she had gotten used to it and even made up names for the cameras. Huey and Louie watched her from the right corner of the building, while Dewey and Uncle Scrooge watched her from the left.

The giant warehouse door clicked and slid open on tracks, allowing her to enter. As Julie walked in, motion-activated lights came to life. The door rolled back into place. The workstation had quickly taken on her personality, with fast-food wrappers on the floor, pyramids of empty energy drinks stacked here and there, and of course a hammock she had constructed for those nights she chose not to make the trip home.

Beyond the workstation on her right, with its multiple screens and a comfortable chair, was a simulation chair that reclined straight back. Julie put on one of her favorite songs to code to, "Whole Lotta Love," by Led Zeppelin.

She worked for the rest of the day and through the night, creating new access and exit codes to get her in and out of the game. She dove into Gary's code, freeing the AI to learn on its own and make more of its own decisions. She had named the AI after her deceased brother and even modeled its personality after him: quick to speak, always giving everyone a hard time, but with a heart of gold underneath it all. After that, it was time to hop back into the game and do what she could to help some people along their way.

CHAPTER 23

OTTO

"Come on, come on, Mister, you got to let me go," the man pleaded through yellow teeth. "Come on, please. I've got credits stashed away. I'll split them with you. Sixty-forty."

"No, I don't think so," Otto said, lounging in his chair behind the marshal's station. He lifted a weathered wanted poster and set it against the man's head. "Says here you're worth one thousand credits. I'm not a greedy man. That's plenty for me."

"I've got more, I've got more stashed away," the wanted man yelled from the hole Otto had put him in. Only his head was exposed. Everything else was buried by the desert sand. "Did I say sixty-forty? I meant fifty-fifty."

Otto whittled a small piece of wood with a black knife. He didn't look at the man when he spoke. "Said you stole and murdered, you and the rest of your gang."

"Where—where is the rest of the boys?" the man said, trying to look from side to side. There was no one there. "All I remember was—was falling asleep. Then waking up to blaster fire and screams, then nothing."

"There was no bounty for your boys," Otto explained,

carving away at his piece of wood. "There was no need to bring them in."

The criminal in front of Otto swallowed hard. He winced against the rays of the suns overhead. He was already sunburned, cracked lips showing just how dehydrated he had become.

"Listen, they don't call me Billy the Bagman for nothin'," Billy growled, going with a different tactic when he discovered Otto couldn't be bought. "I don't know how, but I'm going to get out of here, friend. And when I do, you're going to want me on your side. If you free me now, I won't come after you. You have my word. Get me out of this hole and I'll show you my HUD. I'm good for it. I have plenty of credits."

Otto chuckled and shook his head.

"What, you think this is funny?" Billy yelled.

"I think you'd offer me anything to save your hide," Otto said, examining the slender piece of wood in his hand. "Offer me more. Offer me a place by your side, all the credits I could dream of, and power."

"Yes, yes, all of that and more." Billy nodded emphatically. "Whatever you want. Just dig me out of here. I'm level six and gaining skills fast. I'm an asset. Come on, dig me out."

"No, I don't think I will," Otto said with a smile. "I think we're going to wait right here until the marshal comes back. When she does, I'm going to collect my credits, and then we're going to part ways."

Billy went on a cursing and screaming tirade that would have bothered the locals in Athera if this weren't a semicommon occurrence. More than once, Otto had come in with his bounties to see the marshal gone. More than once, he had dug them a grave to stand in until he could cash in on what he was owed.

But today was different. Bishop had never been gone this long. The back door to the marshal's station swung open.

"Now, Otto, what is all of this profanity I'm hearing out here?" Wade said, taking in Otto and the head of Billy the Bagman. "There are young'uns about, and I won't stand for them hearing this kind of nonsense. Why, I just blushed myself."

"You! Old man," Billy yelled through a hoarse throat. "Are you a player or an NPC? It doesn't matter—get me out of here. Get me out of here, and I swear I'll pay you your weight in credits."

"Now, that's enough out of you, young man," Wade said, turning to shake a long, wrinkled finger in his direction. "You should be ashamed of yourself, using those words. I have half a mind to clean out your mouth with a bar of Kimsun soap."

"Just waiting for the marshal to get back to turn him in," Otto told Wade. "Did she say when she'd be back?"

"No, didn't tell me," Wade said with a frown. "Just asked that I check on the bank robber in the cell, feed him twice a day, and empty his privy. He keeps on going on about nonsense like HUDs and NPCs, just like this one."

"Huh," Otto mused. "I wonder what happened to the marshal."

Otto had no real love for her, but he had a healthy respect for the woman willing to take up the mantle. His long past with the law was something that he kept buried.

"Water, please, some water," Billy implored Wade. "Please, if you're not going to let me go, don't kill me from thirst."

Wade looked over at Otto, who finished his whittling and placed his new toothpick in his mouth. He shrugged at Wade.

Wade went inside, returning in a few seconds with a beat-up canteen. The older man walked down the few steps and held the canteen's mouth to Billy's lips. The criminal drank greedily.

"There you are," a woman called out as she came around the right side of the marshal's station. She wore a shawl to protect her head from the suns' unforgiving rays. On her shoulder was a medical bag. "I've been looking all over for you."

"Here I am," Otto told Doc. "What can I do for you?"

"You can help me rescue Bishop and her new deputy," Doc answered.

Otto stopped fiddling with his knife and gave Doc his full attention. Wade started, dumping water down Billy's nose. The bagman snorted and coughed.

"Rescue?" Otto asked, intrigued. "Rescue her from who?"

"She was taken captive in Canto," Doc explained. "Her and Tom. They're going to be executed. More than likely hanged for asking questions about the mayor's background. They need your help."

"Last I looked, I don't wear a badge," Otto said, shaking his head. "I'm a bounty hunter, not a lawman."

"You're the best gun here," Doc said, determination raw in every word. "I should know, I coded—you can help them, Otto, you. It has to be you."

"Mayor Henry Graves must have thirty guns," Otto said, maneuvering the toothpick around in his mouth. "Why would I risk my life against thirty guns? Sure, I've heard how corrupt Canto's mayor is. Who hasn't? But he's not my problem."

Doc opened her mouth again and then shut it.

"Now, Otto," Wade said indignantly, "I know you've had a rough time lately and a worse past, but we all have. We're all broken in our own ways, but that doesn't mean broken pieces can't still help one another. I've always stuck up for you. I know there's decency in you. I've seen glimmers of it here and there."

Otto didn't respond. The last thing he was going to do was saunter into Canto by himself and try to jailbreak Bishop and her new deputy. However, something Wade had said struck a chord. He did have ties to this from his past, no matter how much he wanted to forget it.

"Otto, may I talk to you somewhere in private?" Doc asked politely. "Take a walk with me?"

It was almost amusing to the bounty hunter that Doc could imagine she could change his mind. There wasn't anything he could think of that would sway him. Not even the promise of a mound of credits. He couldn't spend credits if he was dead. Still, there was a piece of him somewhere, a piece he had thrown into the abyss, that wanted to hear what she had to say.

Without a word, Otto rose from his seat, stepped down the wooden steps, and followed Doc.

"Hey, hey, what about me?" Billy asked. "You can't just leave me!"

"Oh, you'll be fine," Wade told him, crouching down to pat his head like a dog. "I'll tell you what. You be a good boy, and I'll get you a hat, give you some shade."

Doc took the lead, walking with Otto past the main road and toward Wade's home. They were halfway there when she spoke again.

"Otto, I know more about you than you realize," she said, starting slowly, as if she were weighing and measuring each word. "I know that your father used to be marshal here until he was gunned down by outlaws. I know you refused to follow in his footsteps and that you deal justice in your own way as a bounty hunter."

"You don't know anything about my family," Otto said, surprised at the strong feeling of loyalty that rose with the memories of his father.

"Maybe," Doc answered slowly. "But I do know you go out to where he died, every year on that day. You go out to where he was gunned down, where you buried his belongings, and you dig them up. You make yourself remember. Why do you do that? Is it guilt?"

Otto understood where she was taking him now. She was leading him to where it had happened, so many years ago. Images of himself as a six-year-old crashed through his mind. He watched helplessly as his father stood up for the town of Athera and was murdered by a gang of outlaws.

"You blame yourself, but there was nothing you could have done," Doc said, looking up at him as they continued to walk into Otto's past. "You were a child, Otto. It's not your fault."

Otto had never talked about what had happened to his father to anyone, ever. Even as a kid, when he was taken in and raised by the townspeople, he had refused to speak of the horrors he had seen. If he gave the memories a voice, then they were real, but until then, they remained a bad dream.

"How do you know so much?" Otto asked without looking at Doc. "Why are you doing this?"

"It's not going to make any sense to you, but in a different place and time, I wrote your story. None of that matters now," Doc said, pointing to a shovel that stood half buried in the sand. She must have put it there; Otto always brought his own when he came here, then took it away again. "What matters is that you know I'm right. You were a child, Otto. It's time you forgive yourself."

The head of the shovel was submerged in the sand right on the spot where Otto's father had died. Right where he had buried his father's things.

"I could have done something," Otto said under his breath, looking at the place where his father's body had fallen. He could still see his father's unseeing eyes, still smell the smoke of blaster fire in the air. "I should have done something."

"What?" Doc asked. "Run into the fight and get shot yourself?"

"I don't know!" Otto roared, turning on Doc. Tears filled his eyes. "I should have run for help. I should have screamed. I should have tried to tackle one of them."

"Then you'd be dead too," Doc told him, standing toe-to-toe with the much larger man. "It's not your fault, Otto. It's not your fault."

"Stop saying that!" Otto shouted, tears running freely down his cheeks. "Stop saying that!"

"It's not your fault," Doc said again, grabbing him and pulling him close. "It's not your fault. And for what it's worth, I'm sorry you had to go through it. But those events forged you into the man you are today. We need you now, Otto."

Otto didn't hug her back, but neither did he pull away. It wasn't his nature to hold anyone gently or thank Doc for what she was doing, but he knew she was right. He had always known but decided it was better to accept blame for what happened that day.

"It's not your fault," Doc said one last time. Then she just held him while he cried.

A weight lifted off Otto in that moment, a weight he had carried for all those years and refused to address. Rage could be a powerful weapon in his line of work.

Otto wasn't sure if she held him for a few seconds or a few minutes, but he eventually pulled away, drying his eyes and clearing his throat.

"You have a skill set, Otto," Doc told him, changing the subject. "A unique one. Will you use it for good?"

"I'm not him," Otto said, shaking his head while he looked at the shovel. "I'm not my father."

"No, no one can take your father's place," Doc agreed. "But you can honor his memory. Like it or not, his legacy lives on through you. Why do you come out here on the anniversary of his death every year and dig up his things?"

"To remember him," Otto confessed in a voice that was barely above a whisper.

"You do more than that," Doc told him. "What you do as a bounty hunter may not be a lawman's work in your eyes, but you do it for the same reason. Credits are how you justify it, but you're a protector, Otto. You just do it under a different name than your father did. Now, dig."

CHAPTER 24

OTTO

Otto stood under the scorching suns, shoveling through several feet of sand while Doc watched. There was something about the rhythmic movement of digging that worked with his thoughts.

Every shovel stab into the sand was a memory of his father. Was he really doing this? Was he really going to wear his father's gear to rescue the present-day marshal of Athera?

Stab, scoop, toss. Stab, scoop, toss.

Otto lost himself in the motion of digging, in a trance born of past events and present decisions. Two feet down, the shovel head struck something hard. Otto had hit the chest.

On hands and knees, he pushed away the sand on the top of the chest and around the sides. The box was longer than it was wide, covered in rust. Old wooden panels threatened to snap, while steel bands met at a single lock at the top. The lockbox seemed to glow a dull green, as if at one time it had been bright and vibrant but that time had passed long ago.

Otto heaved the chest out of the hole with effort. He looked up at Doc, who hadn't said a word since he'd started digging. "You just going to stand there?"

"This is your journey," Doc told him. "Not mine. It's time for you to do what you were created for. I wrote your code for this very moment, so you could help when you were needed the most."

Otto shook his head. He didn't understand a word coming out of Doc's mouth. Had she always sounded this crazy? What was "writing code"?

On his knees in front of the chest, he ran his hands over the old piece of furniture. It had been his father's, one of the few personal effects his father had owned. His dad had been a simple, strong man who saw the world very clearly: There was the darkness and there was the light.

Otto reached into his shirt to produce the key for the chest. He always wore it on the same necklace his father had. The teeth on the big metal key were generic, as was the shaft, but the head of the key was unique. A serpent eating its tail, twisted into the shape of the number eight, so worn with age it was barely recognizable.

Otto inserted the key and turned. The lock popped with an audible click.

The bounty hunter opened the chest, preparing himself for what he was going to see inside. His father had never indulged in the extras life offered, but he loved his weapons. He used to call them his tools and said you needed the right tool for each job.

Inside the chest was an aged photograph of Otto's parents—a mother who had died in childbirth and a father who had perished protecting the town he loved. Next to the picture was a badge, an eight-pointed star of metal emblazoned with the single word "Marshal."

The weapons below these items had been cared for, polished, and greased, parts switched out and maintained by Otto every year. He didn't know why he did it. Maybe it was a way to remember his father. Maybe it was for this very moment. When he would need them.

A pair of silver blasters shone in the light of the suns like twin harbingers of death. They called to him like old friends, ready to ride again. On their handles were etched the names Thunder and Lightning.

Otto removed them, along with their black holsters and belt. Next was a heavy, triple-barreled blaster. The short, stocky barrels gave way to a dark-brown stock. On the left barrel of the weapon, in gold lettering, a name had been inscribed: "Mama Jama."

Otto ran his hands over the name and let his fingers remember the weapon. He spun the "tool" in his right hand. As powerful as the blaster was, it was rather light. It had been his father's favorite.

"Are you ready?" Doc questioned.

"Do I have a choice?" Otto replied, turning to take her in. "How did you know? You never told me how you knew about all of this."

"Do you believe in fate?" Doc asked.

"I don't know," Otto answered honestly.

"Well, I'm starting to," Doc said, as if she honestly didn't have the answer either. "Things are falling into place that are too much of a coincidence. Your story lining up with how Bishop and Tom were captured. Me being able to be here now to lead you to them. It's all—it's all too much to be a coincidence. What are the odds, right?"

"So what?" Otto asked as he placed Mama Jama down gently on the sand for a moment while he wrapped his father's pistol belt around his waist. "You want me to walk into Canto's sheriff's station and walk Bishop and her new deputy right out?"

"More or less," Doc answered.

"More more, or more less?" Otto responded with a raised eyebrow.

"More less," Doc told him. "Trust me. I have a plan."

Otto gave her a deadpan stare.

"I have credits," Doc told him.

"You can keep them," Otto told her, looking at his father's weapons, the ones he now carried. "This goes far past any kind of credits."

"If we're going to do this, we should get going, then," Doc said, looking at the position of the suns in the sky. "Canto is miles out, and the mayor's not known for his patience. He'll hang them tonight."

Otto nodded in agreement. He had never met or even seen Mayor Graves, but his swift sentences and swifter hangings were legendary. As were the whispers the bounty hunter heard out in the badlands. Whispers of the mayor, a cult, and the sacrifice of innocent townsfolk. In Otto's experience, every lie had a drop of truth in it.

He and Doc walked back to the marshal's office, where she had parked her hoverbike. Otto's slender hoverbike was there as well.

"I should tell Wade," Otto said. "Someone will need to look after my bounty until we're all back tomorrow."

"Hurry." Doc was already throwing a leg over her hoverbike and starting the engine.

Otto walked from the side of the building to see Wade trying different hats on Billy. At the moment, Billy wore a woman's sun hat. In his hands, Wade carried a baseball cap and a visor.

"There, I think that sun hat suits you nicely, though," Wade was telling Billy. "It'll keep the rays out of your eyes, and the color really fits your complexion."

"Honest? You think so?" Billy asked, then saw Otto. "Hey,

get this thing off me. Give me the baseball cap. Come on now, what are you doing?"

Before Wade could reply, Otto addressed the older man. "Wade, I'm going to need to ask you to watch over my bounty for the rest of the day and possibly overnight. I'll be willing to give you some of the credits from his head as soon as I turn him in to the marshal."

"That would be all right." Wade nodded. "So you decided to go and help the marshal after all, then? Why the change of heart? If you don't mind me asking."

"I think it's what *he* would have done," Otto said, thinking about the question. "No, I *know* it's what my father would have done."

"Your father was a great man," Wade said, walking over and placing a hand on Otto's left shoulder. "He would have been proud of you. He *is* proud of you. It's a rare thing for a great man to have a great son."

Otto didn't have words, but he nodded in gratitude and turned to go.

"Hey, hey, come back here!" Billy pleaded. "You can't just leave me here with this old loon! I have rights. I have the right to a trial!"

Otto ignored Billy's yelling and joined Doc in front of the building. No words passed between the two. Doc took off on her hoverbike, and Otto followed on his a moment later.

The ride to Canto would take a few hours and would give Otto plenty of time to think. Memories could be a dangerous thing in the wrong hands. Up until this point, memories of his father were painful, but now they seemed lighter somehow, as if he knew he was doing the right thing on more than just a physical level.

Doc and Otto rode on unhindered until a large dust cloud in the distance signaled caution. Otto had seen this kind of thing before. It was usually caused by an enormous herd of three-eyed buffalo stampeding across the desert. Something must have spooked the herd. The large animals usually saved their energy for when things were really bad.

What could have spooked a herd as large as this was a mystery to Otto.

Soon he could see the mass of charging muscle as the buffalo stormed toward Otto and Doc.

"Something scared them," Doc said, slowing down to ride side by side with Otto.

"No, it's worse than that," Otto said, shaking his head as the three-eyed buffalo raced toward them, a hundred yards away and closing quickly. "They're charging us. Let's go." He gunned his engine.

If they didn't pick up speed immediately, he and Doc were going to get caught by the herd. The buffalo came from their right in a long line, like an angry wave crashing over a beach.

Otto hunched low and sped forward. Doc was right beside him.

The buffalo were fifty yards away now and closing fast. Otto could just see where the line of creatures ended, ahead and to the right. Then something much darker gripped his heart. He saw what the animals were fleeing from. A sandstorm.

The wind kicked up to an unnatural level. The sky to the south was darkening as lightning bolts flickered and flared in the monstrous dust storm, as if a beast from a past age raged within. The sand whirling in the air rose to the heavens, blotting out the sky. It was moving much faster than the buffalo, threatening to overtake the animals at any moment.

"Otto!" Doc yelled. The fear in her voice told him what he already knew to be true. They weren't going to outrun the sandstorm.

CHAPTER 25

JULIE

Pressing herself so low against the front of the hoverbike that her chest hit the engine, Julie poured on the speed. She tore off her scarf and stuffed it inside her shirt. The goggles she wore over her eyes and the bandanna covering her face from the mouth down threatened to rip free.

She ignored everything but the path in front of her and the storm on her right. If they could stay on the outer edges of the sandstorm, they had a chance. In the middle of the storm itself, sand grains were thrown as violently and deadly as blaster bolts. They'd be ripped to pieces, death by a thousand cuts.

Julie had seen what happened to those who got caught in the center of a sandstorm, and it wasn't pretty.

Glancing over her left shoulder, she saw Otto keeping pace with her. His shorter hoverbike, a T-19 model, was newer and sleeker but lacked the overall torque her Thunderbolt carried.

The screams of the three-eyed buffalo could be heard, great, throaty cries of fear and suffering. The storm overtook the buffalo, lifting hundreds of pounds of flesh in the air and flinging them about like a child throwing stuffed animals in a tantrum.

The storm was twenty-five yards away and closing. Buffalo rained down around Julie and Otto like hail plummeting from the sky. The beasts landed with broken necks, splintered backs, and rent limbs.

The wind buffeted Julie's hoverbike from side to side as thunder bellowed its mighty indignation and lightning struck the ground, creating glass shards the size of trees.

If she died in the game, she could restart, but that wasn't the point. She had never died in the game before, and she wasn't going to start now. It was as much pride as anything else. This was her game. She had coded it. It wasn't going to kill her.

Then Julie saw it: a sand dune they could shelter behind. With any luck, they would be able to take cover there and wait for the storm to pass.

Julie hadn't prayed in a long time. She said a silent prayer now that Otto would follow her lead. If they had any chance of surviving at all, it would be because they moved quickly and efficiently.

The storm was ten yards away when Julie decelerated and made a hard left. As soon as she came down on the other side of the shallow dune, she killed the power to her bike. She jumped off, pressing herself down flat over the vehicle. Otto did the same, matching her move for move.

Then the storm was on top of them. Julie and Otto wove their arms around the frames of their vehicles, using them as anchors. If they had been near the center of the storm, this wouldn't have helped, but luckily they were still near the edge. Julie gritted her teeth, keeping her head down and holding on to his hoverbike for dear life.

The wind slapped at her, dumping shovelfuls of sand down her shirt, in her face, and down her pants. In that moment, Julie realized how small she really was. She might have coded this world, but right now, against the rules of the game, she felt tiny.

Otto slung his right arm over her shoulders, anchoring her, though she felt she was in no danger of being hurled away. Julie's muscles burned, her hands cramped from the effort, but still she held on.

After what felt like hours, the winds subsided and Julie could see more than a few feet in front of her. Coarse desert sand had been redistributed to the extent that she and the bounty hunter were submerged from the waist down. Her hoverbike and Otto's were completely buried. But they were alive. At least there was that.

The suns came out again as the storm passed on its merry route to wreak havoc on whatever human or creature it could find next.

Julie stood up, spitting sand. Despite her bandanna, granules had made their way into her mouth and nose. And it didn't stop there; her ears and other crevices were full of the stuff.

Otto had a coughing fit as he removed his goggles and bandanna. Sand fell out of his hair in handfuls as he shook his head from side to side.

"That was close," Julie said, still spitting sand. "I don't remember ever writing that in the code."

"Writing what?" Otto asked, digging his lower body out of the sand.

"Nothing," Julie answered. "Sorry, I'm not thinking straight. I think I have sand in my brain."

She didn't know why he found that so funny, but Otto laughed before bending over to begin the long job of digging out his hoverbike. The bikes were built to run with some sand in them. If Julie and Otto could unbury them, then they'd be as good as new.

Julie wasted no time in freeing herself, then began shoveling sand with two hands to uncover her own bike.

"So when are you going to share this master plan you have of rescuing the marshal with me?" Otto asked as the two worked side by side. "Or is that jumbled by the sand in your brain as well?"

"I don't have a plan," Julie admitted. "I'm just making this up as I go."

"Somehow that doesn't surprise me," Otto said as he kept digging. The work was slow and tedious, but at last it was over, and both Julie and Otto mounted up again.

The pair were grateful that the rest of their trip was devoid of stampeding herds or sandstorms hell bent on sending them to an early grave. At last Canto sat silhouetted against the horizon.

Different vehicles made their way to and from the gates of the city, as well as a healthy amount of foot traffic. Julie and Otto maneuvered through the gates unhindered. Canto was large, not some backwater town like Athera. As such, multiple streets spread out like cracks on a fractured windowpane.

If it weren't for Otto, Julie would have no idea where to go. She had been to Canto before, but the large city, the press of all the people, unnerved her.

Julie loved the wind on her face, the spaces between people. She couldn't imagine being cooped up in a place like this where your neighbor was less than a stone's throw away. Her general distrust of people made her view every stranger in Canto as a possible threat.

Luckily, Otto seemed to know exactly where he was going. What's more, a general press of people was heading deeper into the city. Julie picked up chatter about the marshal of Athera and a hanging.

Julie and Otto rode their hoverbikes slowly down the street. They passed a town square and headed with the throng to an open area where a wooden platform stood with a pair of nooses draped over a tall piece of lumber. People had already gathered around the structure.

Julie and Otto left their hoverbikes in an alleyway and joined the crowd.

"Good, we're not too late," Otto breathed.

Squinting into the setting suns, Julie surveyed the area, the gallows, and the many, many guards present. Dressed in their dark-blue uniforms, they were easy to pick out among the mob. Each was armed with a rifle, and most also carried sidearms.

Julie had coded Otto to be the fastest, most efficient armed NPC in the game. Despite this, the sheer number of soldiers surrounding the area was daunting. Otto could gun down four or five before they knew what was happening, but then it would be a straight shoot-out, and the odds were going to swing wildly in the other direction.

Otto adjusted his coat over Mama Jama. The weapon hung on a sling over his right shoulder. The stock rested by his side with the barrel pointed to the ground. If he walked with his right arm by his side, he could hide the weapon in his coat.

"There," Julie said, jerking her chin toward the platform, where Mayor Henry Graves was ascending the steps.

The man was waving like he was in a parade or preparing to accept an award. To Julie's surprise, most of the people waved back and even cheered for him. There was a sense of celebrity here as people oohed and aahed at the mayor. He flashed a brilliant, bright smile at them.

Julie didn't blame the people; she half wanted to shoot the mayor and half wanted to ask him for an autograph and a quick photo.

"Thank you, thank you for the warm welcome," Graves said, taking command of the crowd. "But I'm afraid this meeting isn't a joyous occasion. There are traitors among us."

A deep inhale surged through the crowd.

"Yes, I know," the mayor continued, shaking his head as

if he couldn't believe it himself. "Last night, an attempt was made on my life."

Gasps and boos from the crowd. Julie saw one woman clamp a hand over her mouth in shock.

"Do not be alarmed, friends—I survived, thanks to the sacrifice of our brave militia. Others were not so lucky." The mayor held a hand over his heart and brushed away a tear. "The culprits were caught, and we are here tonight to see them stand trial and be sentenced."

A violent cheer erupted from the crowd as they demanded retribution for the attack on their beloved mayor.

"Hang them!" a man spat. "Hang them all!"

A roar of approval greeted this proclamation. Bloodlust was in the air, taking on a life of its own. Like an unseen wraith, it moved from citizen to citizen, working them into a frenzy.

"Please, please," the mayor said, quieting them again. "I know the good people of Canto have a strong sense of morality, but we must conduct a proper trial before anyone can be sentenced, no matter how certain we think the outcome is. This trial in particular will be chilling, as the assassins sent to take my life are none other than the marshal and the new deputy of Athera."

More gasps and shouts filled the air. Mouths hung open, and people looked to one another for answers no one had.

On the right side of the crowd, people made way for the prisoners to be marched to the gallows.

CHAPTER 26

TOM

That day, waiting to die, was one of the longest Tom had ever experienced. The corpse of the old woman two cells down was a constant reminder of what was in store for them. On top of that were the unlocked memories Doc's pills had given him.

It was actually nice to have the mouthy AI's company for once. Gary, as talkative as ever, helped keep things positive while filling the minutes that would have otherwise dragged by.

"Someone needs to call the HR department because I want to file a complaint," Gary said with a simulated finger snap. "This is not okay. You know, I know that I'm just an AI, but I feel like I'm evolving too, and I realize now that this game is messed up."

"I hate this game," Tom breathed.

"They're not going to let us live through this," Bishop voiced as she and Tom ate the breakfast of cereal and toast they'd been served. "They killed that woman in front of us to prove a point. When they come for us, we've got to fight, because our lives depend on it."

Tom nodded, moving his cereal around the bowl without taking a bite. His usual black hole of an appetite had vanished in light of his new memories. She was gone. The woman in his dreams, his wife, Lana . . . she was dead. And what was he to make of the memory of that woman visiting his home? She'd drugged him, Tom believed, and then what? He woke up here?

"I've got nothing to lose," he said, agreeing with Bishop. "There's nothing waiting for me when I get out of this place."

"You don't know that," Bishop warned. "You don't know if the pills Doc gave you unlocked the truth. It could just be more of what the mayor is doing here, implanting false memories."

"It's not," Tom said matter-of-factly. "Doc was trying to help. I know what I saw was real. This—this *place* isn't reality, but my memories were."

"How can you be sure?" Bishop mused. "How can you know?"

"If none of this is real—if we die here and start all over again—then we don't have to worry about death," Tom said, working through the problem out loud.

"You're forgetting the crazies everyone keeps talking about," Bishop said, scratching the side of her head with a wince as if she were trying to remember something. "Every time you die, less of you returns, until you're one of them. What about Wade?"

"What about him?" Tom asked, remembering the kindness of the stranger.

"I always figured he was an NPC because he forgot about me when I died, but maybe he just died too many times himself, and that's why there's no jelly in his doughnut." Bishop thought a moment longer, then added under her breath, "Maybe that's what's happening to me."

"Gary, can you tell us who is an NPC and who is a player?" Tom asked.

"No can do, brochacho." Gary sighed as if he were legitimately sorry. "You know I've got your back, but my coding has limits."

Tom was confident that his memories were intact. He could

recall more of them now, without pain. He remembered everything, from his childhood to his enlistment in the military, from dating Lana to losing her. He even remembered the woman who had come to his home on the day of Lana's funeral.

"Bishop, does the name Tanus Corporation mean anything to you?" Tom asked.

"Nothing," Bishop answered after a moment of thought. "You think they're behind this?"

"I have a memory that makes me think so," Tom answered.

After Tom scoured every inch of his cell for a way to escape and came up short, he spent the rest of the morning trying to make sense of their situation. Some memories were so emotionally painful that he dared not look at them more than once or twice; others he played over and over again.

His training in the military had been brutal but efficient. His love for his wife was most of his identity. When she fell sick, it ruined him. Being dishonorably discharged from the military paled in comparison to her death.

The visit from the woman in white who had drugged him played over and over in his mind. He searched that memory for any clue that would help him now but found nothing.

Lunch came and went, a meager meal of dried meat and water. Bishop was right—there was nothing they could do now. When the mayor's men came for them, it would be time to go all out. Tom fully intended to make everyone who was sent for him pay with their life, or one of their lives, depending on how all of this worked.

"While I'm still limited in what I can do," Gary said, "I can help you out with this. Check it out."

Gary shifted the image to Tom's item screen. It was empty except for the loot crate, whose rating had changed from "common" to "uncommon."

"Give me some more time with it, and I can speed things up for you," Gary told him. "I think we can get you to a legendary loot crate sooner than you think."

"Thanks," Tom said, knowing the AI was doing all he could to help.

Despite the hour, Tom was able to sleep. His dreams were nonexistent, and for that, he was grateful. He didn't wake until the evening meal arrived in a tin tray, like breakfast and lunch had earlier. A tin cup held a thin soup, with a side of bread and cheese.

"I can't believe you could sleep," Bishop said, munching on her bread. "You know what's about to happen. Aren't you worried?"

"Would worrying help?" Tom asked, looking at the tall window in his cell. The suns were going down. "I'll worry if it's going to get us out of here. If not, then I'm going to prepare mentally and physically for what's going to come next. In fact, I should probably stretch."

Tom busied himself with stretching until the heavy door opened and four thick-muscled brutes walked through.

There was no need to wonder if they were strangers to the acts of violence. The scarred knuckles, the necks as thick as their heads, and above all, the looks in their eyes told Tom everything he needed to know.

The heaviest of the men separated himself from the other three. He wore an eight-pointed badge with the word "Sheriff" stamped across the worn metal. Days of stubble dotted his second chin. He walked up to stare at Bishop and Tom.

"Now, this can go one of two ways," the sheriff said. "One at a time, you can allow yourselves to be chained and taken to your hearing, or one at a time, we can drag you from the cells, beat you senseless, and then chain you and take you to your hearing. But this only ends one way. You get me?"

"I get you," Tom said with a long, steady sigh. He prepared

himself mentally for the brutality that was about to take place. Muscles tensed like a coil under extreme pressure, he waved the Canto sheriff forward. "But if you want me to go gently, you're going to have to make me."

"You're not the first one to say that." The sheriff nodded to the other three men, who produced short wooden batons from their belts. "You may think that fighting is honorable, but in the end, it will only bring you more pain. Trust me, stranger, I know how to inflict pain."

"Wait! Wait!" Bishop shouted, waving her hands in the air. "Please, please, I'm not with him. It was this gamer's narcissism that got us into the mess in the first place. I'll go easy. I'll go easy."

Gary sucked in a long breath in a signature Gary move. "You a narcissist, bro?"

"What? No," Tom said through clenched teeth. "I'm not a narcissist."

Neither the sheriff nor his deputies reacted to Gary, confirming they were NPCs.

Bishop pressed her hands together as if in prayer toward the sheriff. Tom had never seen her so eager to please before. She was like a different person altogether.

"There we go, see? A voice of reason." The Canto sheriff nodded amicably. His gaze roved around her body as he licked his lips.

One of the three deputies moved to Bishop's cell. He produced a heavy ring of five keys and used one to open the cell door. Bishop stood back, her hands raised in surrender.

Tom felt a twinge of disappointment and a greater feeling of betrayal, as if someone had punched him in the gut.

I guess you're alone on this one after all, he thought. *That's all right. You'll be all right by yourself.*

"Hands out." A second deputy walked into the cell. "No funny business, or you get the same treatment we gave the old woman."

Bishop nodded hurriedly, extending her hands for the manacles. The deputy placed the first cuff on her left wrist and clicked the lock closed.

With the speed of a viper striking, Bishop punched the neck of the deputy on her right. She was so fast Tom had a difficult time tracking her movements. Her slender fist struck the thug's Adam's apple with bone-crushing speed. The man choked, grabbing at his throat, and fell to his knees.

"Oh, this is not a kid's game," Gary said, appalled. "What's the rating on this thing, anyway? NC-17?"

Bishop wrenched the ring of keys from the deputy's belt and tossed them through the bars to Tom. She made the throw just in time, as the deputy chaining her finally realized what was happening and tackled her, shoving her backward.

The third deputy rushed into the cell, piling on Bishop and his counterpart to wrestle her into submission.

Bishop's toss was perfect. The steel circle had sailed between the bars, landing in Tom's hands. He clutched the cold metal, looking at the keys and then the lone sheriff, who stood outside the cell door.

Tom wasted no time in reaching out of his cell and trying to unlock his door.

Like the hounds of Hades were nipping at his heels, the sheriff of Canto raced for the door that led out of the jail area. His great girth wobbled to and fro like a bathtub full of water. Throwing the door open, he started shouting, "Help, everyone, prisoners on the loose!"

Tom tried the first key with no luck, then the second and the third.

Meanwhile, Bishop gave as good as she got, wrestling two men in the cell next to him. One grabbed Bishop by the back while the other punched her in the stomach and face.

Gary yelled obscenities at the men, ordering them to leave Bishop alone.

Bishop opened her mouth and took a big bite out of the arm wrapped around her neck. Blood covered her mouth and sprinkled the air as the deputy screamed in pain and involuntarily relaxed his grip.

Spitting the chunk of flesh to the side, Bishop kicked the man in front of her in his goody bag so hard he gasped with a shrillness that might have been comical in any other setting.

"Ohhhhhhhhhh," Gary gasped. "I felt that one, and I don't have testicles."

Tom would have loved to watch more but needed to get out of his cell. The fourth key worked. With a satisfying click, the lock turned, and Tom was free.

The sheriff's shouts were rewarded as five more deputies came running, batons ready.

CHAPTER 27

TOM

Tom didn't miss that the sheriff sprinted out of the room while his men ran toward danger.

The first guard Tom met received a kick to the chest that was hard enough to break sternum and ribs. As he went down, Tom pivoted to his left and brought up his right fist in a wild hook that took the next deputy in the jaw.

"I knew brawler was the right class to give you," Gary cheered. "Sweep the leg, Johnny, sweep the leg!"

Then the third and fourth deputies were on him, swinging their batons like he was a fastball pitched to them in the ninth inning with the game on the line. Tom took a crack across the head that had him seeing stars. He staggered back, exaggerating how injured he was as the men pressed in.

Tom backpedaled all the way to the rear of the room, past all four cells. He didn't stop until his back met the cold brick wall. Hot, sticky blood splashed down and across his face. Pain was realized and forgotten just as quickly.

One of the many things Tom had learned in his time in

the military was how to recognize and overcome pain, bartering agony for focus.

The guard who had already cracked him, feeling a sense of misplaced superiority, came at him again with a wild overhand blow. Tom stepped to the side and took advantage of the man's forward momentum, grabbing the back of his head and slamming him into the brick wall with enough speed to fracture his orbital bone.

The next guard swung his baton; Tom caught it in one hand, then grabbed the man's wrist with his free hand and twisted it, doubling the man over. Four violent blows delivered to the back of his head in quick succession meant lights-out for the deputy.

The last deputy struck Tom with his baton across his ribs, but he blocked most of the hit and barely registered the pain. He was in the zone now, as if that first strike was what he'd needed to fully wake up and give him clarity about what he was. He was a man of war, built for violence.

The deputy prepared for another swing. Tom stepped in close even as the blow landed. Quickly, he wove around the man and, from the back, wrapped his arms around the man's neck in a tight chokehold. His opponent's neck fit nicely in the crook of his right elbow. Tom's right hand held on to the same area on his left arm. His left hand wrapped around the back of the man's head, and he squeezed.

Gary continued to yell encouragement to Tom and curses at his enemies. Tom barely heard him; he was getting better at tuning out the AI when he needed to concentrate.

The deputy flailed wildly, but Tom was locked in and committed. There was no way he was letting go. He looked over to see how Bishop was faring as a wild scream tore from the throat of the last deputy in her cell.

The man had Bishop by the throat, both hands squeezing

the life out of her. Bishop had reached for not his throat but his eyes. Her fingers gouged at his eye sockets as blood rolled down his chin and he screamed. A moment later, he released Bishop, who bent down to pick up one of the fallen batons. With an upward swing, she cracked the man under the jaw. His entire body went stiff even before he crashed to the floor.

The deputy in Tom's arms stopped struggling and went limp. Tom let him drop and stepped over his body.

"You're bleeding," Bishop said, pointing to the gash in Tom's hairline.

"I'll live," he answered, jerking a thumb toward Bishop's nose, which spurted blood. "You?"

"I'm good," Bishop said, spitting blood to the side. "Let's get out of here."

"You know, for a second, I really thought you were going to give up and leave me to take them all on," Tom said as he and Bishop made their way toward the door.

"You know, for a second, I was." Bishop winked.

"Ohhh, you two," Gary crooned, "are you two bonding? Wait, are we all bonding?"

They stepped through the door into a large room full of desks and deputies who were pointing their weapons at them. There had to be at least a dozen hard-eyed law officers standing there. Each held a blaster at the ready.

The sheriff, confident now that he had the upper hand, smirked at them. "Fire."

Blue bolts of pain struck Tom and Bishop. Tom fell, spasming under the electric burst. His HUD flickered off instantly. His teeth felt like they were going to explode, while at the same time, his muscles told him that he had just run two marathons back-to-back and maxed out on bench presses.

As soon as they were down, the officers swarmed them,

some with boots to the head and torso while others secured their hands in manacles.

Tom did his best to protect his face, but a well-placed kick to his jaw made the inside of his mouth explode with blood. Another struck his ribs so hard he was sure they were bruised, if not broken.

Half conscious, Tom felt the cold shackles embrace his wrists. Next, he was yanked to his feet and dragged out, with a deputy on his right and another on his left.

A throng of people had gathered outside.

Tom had a feeling these people weren't here to throw him a surprise release party. Jeers rang out, and he even saw a few people spitting at him.

He lifted his gaze to see a well-used gallows.

The deputies walked Tom up a flight of steps to where Mayor Henry Graves waited. The boos and angry shouts continued. Tom was placed on his knees, and a noose was fitted under his chin and drawn tight. The bristles of the rope worked their way into his skin, already half choking him. Bishop was pressed down beside him.

It feels so real, Tom thought as the rope tightened and his body ached, throbbing with each beat of his heart. *If this is a game, how does it all feel so real?*

There were no answers to that question, only more pain as one of the deputies forced Tom to look up by grabbing the back of his hair and yanking down.

"The two assassins who failed in their attempt kneel before you now for sentencing," the mayor shouted. "Now, it's customary to allow them words to defend themselves, and no matter how guilty they are, fair is fair. Do you two have anything to say for yourselves?"

"You're crazy," Tom managed. "This is insane. You're not even real, are you?"

"And you?" The mayor ignored Tom and looked at Bishop. "Do you have anything to say to defend yourself?"

"He's lying," Bishop shouted for everyone to hear. "They're lying to you all. Any player who doesn't remember is given false memories, and if anyone refuses, they're killed. We saved a girl last night from being murdered. There's a cult here in Canto, and the mayor's the head of it."

Laughs and mockery came from first the mayor and then the rest of the throng. They tossed Bishop's words aside without a second thought.

Tom understood that reasoning with a mob that had already made up their minds was useless. What he had to hope for now was that his memories were right. If this was all a game, he'd wake up in the coffin again. The part that scared him the most was the idea that when he did, he'd be less of who he was, that he might remember less of the woman he had loved. Memories of Lana were all he had left of her; they were all he had to live for.

"It's with a heavy heart that I declare you two shall be hanged by the neck until dead," the mayor said, looking down at Bishop and Tom. "I take no joy in this act, but to maintain order, justice must be served. You have not complied."

Bishop closed her eyes and muttered something under her breath that sounded like a prayer. Tom didn't catch it all, but he did hear the words "God," "please help us," and "angel of protection."

Tom clenched his jaw as the mayor turned to his left and placed one hand on the wooden lever of the gallows.

A second later, that lever exploded in a shower of charred shards. The people of Canto looked at one another, shocked. The mayor held up his hand and stared at it. His palm, impaled by a half-dozen wooden splinters, bled profusely.

Half the crowd screamed and shouted, realizing what had

happened. The other half stood confused, looking for answers.

Tom searched the crowd for his savior. Then he saw him—the last person Tom would have expected to show up at that moment.

"I wouldn't do that if I were you," Otto said. The silver blaster in his right hand gleamed in the suns' last dying light. "Step off the gallows, all of you. Let them go."

As if he were a leper, the crowd around Otto parted, ensuring they were not mistaken for his allies.

The pair of deputies behind Tom and Bishop had their weapons drawn, as did the other deputies and the sheriff, who moved to surround Otto.

"I know who you are," Mayor Henry Graves said, narrowing his eyes. "You look just like him. You look just like your father."

A moment of silence passed. Otto kept his weapon trained on the mayor. A dozen guns pointed at him in return. Tom knew how quick and accurate Otto was with a blaster, but with these odds, it was difficult to imagine a scenario in which Otto escaped unscathed.

"Let them go, or the next round finds a home in your forehead," Otto challenged.

"You don't just look like your father; you even sound like him." The mayor chuckled. "Because of his legacy, I'm going to let you go and chalk this up to a misunderstanding. Hand over your weapons and walk away."

"Oh, I'll give you my weapons," Otto said with narrow eyes. "I'll hand them over, one blaster bolt at a time. Let them go."

The mayor shook his head, tsking as he walked back and forth across the gallows. "You know I'm not going to do that. This doesn't end well for you if you continue down this path, Otto Knight."

The mayor walked back to the splintered lever and grabbed the broken shaft with his uninjured hand.

"Oh, I know that," Otto answered. "Shall we begin?"

So much happened in the next moment that Tom couldn't process it all.

First, he jumped up from his kneeling position and rammed the top of his head into the underside of the jaw of the deputy behind him. Bishop performed a similar move. The mayor pulled the lever, releasing the hatches below Tom's and Bishop's feet. They plummeted toward the ground, the ropes tightening around their necks.

The sounds of blaster fire and the screams of the dying filled the air. Tom and Bishop hung side by side, strangling slowly. His vision blurred as he fought a losing battle. Then, at what felt like the last moment, the rope was severed. He fell to the dirt, coughing. Trying to greedily suck in deep lungfuls of air only caused him to cough more, but he couldn't help it.

Bishop dropped beside him a second later. She too gasped for air, trying to force oxygen to her brain. Doc was there, working on their manacles. She must have seen the many questions in Tom's eyes, because she shook her head. "Answers later; Otto needs help."

Tom nodded as his shackles fell away. He crouched under the gallows, using it for cover as he surveyed the landscape. Terrified screams from the mob were still in the air as they ran for cover. The mayor was nowhere to be seen—no real surprise.

What did catch Tom's eye was the way Otto fought. The man was a world-class athlete. He never stopped moving, first running to his right as he gunned down six of the sheriff's deputies, then rolling to dodge incoming fire, then popping up and continuing to run. He juked left and ducked. With the amount of fire coming his way, he had to move and keep moving or die.

The main difference between the opponents was that every red bolt Otto fired was a hit, while the sheriff and his deputies fired wildly, counting on high volume to be deadly. It was a fight between a sniper and a machine gunner.

It happened: A lucky round struck Otto in the left shoulder. He roared in pain and dove to his right, behind the gallows, where Tom and the rest of them had taken cover.

"Are you hit bad?" Doc asked as Otto grimaced. "You're bleeding."

"I don't have time to bleed," Otto said, tossing one of the silver blasters to Tom and the other to Bishop. He produced a third blaster from his lower back and gave it to Doc. "This is the part where we get out of town."

"Thank you," Tom told the man that had murdered him in a previous timeline. "Thank you for saving us."

"Shoot first, talk later," Otto grunted as he reached inside his coat for the largest blaster Tom had so far seen in the game.

The blaster in question was as long as Otto's arm, with three rotating barrels. It almost looked like a shotgun, but there was no pump feature.

"Hoverbikes are parked on the left," Doc shouted over the blaster fire pounding the gallows. The structure groaned and creaked as it threatened to topple over at any moment.

"I'll cover you." Otto nodded with determination. "Go!"

CHAPTER 28

TOM

That tone left no room for argument or questions, only action.

Tom sprinted to his left, following Doc to where the hoverbikes waited. Across the street, the sheriff of Canto and his remaining deputies had taken up positions just inside the storefronts. They fired their blasters from windows and doorways.

The steady thrum of Otto's weapon added to the cacophony of the hour with an intense beat.

Vroom! Vroom! Vroom! Vroom!

Red laser bolts flashed past as Tom and the group made their run. That was when an idea struck Tom with all the power of a lightning bolt. The gallows were about to topple over at any minute; why not make the two-story structure fall toward their adversaries?

Still running, Tom looked back, zeroed in on the support beam closest to their enemies, and pulled the trigger.

Please let that luck skill point be enough, Tom thought. *Come on, little skill point, you can do it!*

A bright-red ray shot out, obliterating the support beam in question.

With a groan befitting a dinosaur more than a wooden structure, the battered gallows tumbled toward the sheriff and his men. Although it didn't crush them or even strike the buildings they were in, it created a barrier between the two factions. The impact even kicked up enough dirt to shadow their escape.

In moments the foursome reached the parked hoverbikes. It became clear that the wound Otto had received was much worse than he'd let on—he was pale and breathing hard. Despite this, he kept his finger on the trigger.

The large blaster he carried smoked. The barrels were overheating.

"Get on!" Doc yelled as she gunned the engine of the first bike. Otto moved to mount his but stumbled. Bishop barely caught him before he hit the ground.

"Strap him on mine," Doc ordered as the dust cloud the felled gallows gave off settled and more accurate weapons fire began to spatter the ground around them. "Bishop, Tom, you'll have to cover us."

"I'll drive," Tom offered, but Bishop pushed him off. She wrestled Otto's weapon from his hands and handed it to Tom. "I'm driving. You shoot."

Tom settled behind Bishop with the heavy repeater. The weapon felt warm in his hands. He also had a strong sense that the weapon was hungry, like it was ready to go, with a mind of its own. Tom understood those were just his feelings projected onto the weapon. Or so he hoped. Either way, he couldn't wait to get some payback.

The hoverbikes took off, zooming through town. Citizens ran for cover, screaming. In contrast, when the occasional deputy running toward the fight caught sight of them, he'd send a misplaced round their way.

Tom was surprised at how easy it was to flee through Canto.

It seemed most of the deputies had been at the hanging; only a skeleton crew patrolled the town.

"Hey, I think we're going to make it!" Tom leaned forward and yelled into Bishop's ear.

With his left arm around her waist and his right hand holding the cooling weapon, Tom took heart. Otto was wounded, and no doubt he would need time to heal, but the wound, from what Tom had seen, wasn't life threatening.

"You just had to say something," Bishop yelled back as the hoverbikes rounded the corner and headed for Canto's main gate.

The massive two-story gates were closed, with a thick piece of wood locking them in place. Two deputies stood in front of the doors, holding rifles. As soon as they saw the hoverbikes, they opened fire. One round pinged off the front of Bishop's bike.

"Keep going!" Tom yelled, leaning to his right so he could shoot around Bishop. The repeater felt like a living thing in his hands. The recoil wasn't harsh, and the accuracy was stunning. Red rounds cut through the pair of deputies like a hot wire through foam. Tom next targeted the wooden plank barring the double doors and then the doors themselves.

Whether it was the skill point spent on blaster accuracy or the one spent on luck or both, things were finally going their way.

"Tom?!" Bishop shouted as she gunned the hoverbike.

More deputies ran out from a guardhouse on the right, firing at them wildly.

"Tom?!" Bishop yelled again as they headed for the still-closed doors.

"Don't stop!" Tom shouted, keeping his finger on the trigger. A steady line of red rounds ate up the hinges on either side of the gates.

"Tom?!" Bishop screamed one more time before ducking low as they rammed the gates.

Tom closed his eyes and hunched down behind Bishop just in time. The wooden doors moaned and splintered as the hoverbike, acting as a battering ram, blew them to the sides.

Doc and Otto followed just behind, and the fugitives sped into the desert. With the suns down, the desert landscape was illuminated only by the giant moon and the myriad of stars overhead. It was more than enough light to see by.

"I think—I think we made it!" Bishop shouted over her shoulder. "Son of a gun, Tom. Those deputies shot like Stormtroopers, but we made it. Maybe you're not bad luck after all."

"Why would you think I'm bad luck?" Tom asked, borderline offended. He looked over his shoulder and witnessed a handful of hoverbikes with searchlights and two larger vehicles pour out of Canto's ruined gates. "Never mind!"

Doc pulled up to them, jerking her head down to draw attention to the front of Bishop's hoverbike, where a steady stream of smoke had begun to waft out. "We're not going to make it to Athera."

Tom and Bishop nodded.

"Follow me; they'll expect us to head straight for Athera," Doc said, turning left and heading south.

Bishop followed without question.

South, Tom thought, remembering the many stories and whispers he had heard. *Aren't the lost ones down south?*

One more look back told him that Doc was right. With Otto wounded and one bike beginning to sputter, outrunning the pursuing sheriff and his deputies wasn't an option. They had to lose them.

They sped into the night, leaving their pursuers behind. Howls Tom now recognized as those of the night hounds echoed through the barren landscape as they traveled for hours over sand dunes and open stretches of plains. Other creatures—ones

Tom did not know—also called out in the night. At one point, something large, with leathery wings, flapped overhead.

During the second hour of their run, Doc called a halt. The landscape was beginning to change around them. There was more shrubbery, more life, but still no grass. Clumps of dark-green bushes stood knee high, and dry trees with prickly dark-purple fruit rose to just overhead.

"We should be safe here for the night," Doc said, slowing her hoverbike to a crawl, then stopping by an outcropping of rocks as tall as Tom. "I need to check Otto's wounds, and your hoverbike isn't going to make it more than a few more miles."

She was right. What had started as a simple leak of smoke was now a full-on plume.

Tom moved to help get Otto off the back of Doc's bike. The bounty hunter was coherent, but he was sweating and looked like death.

"He's lost a lot of blood," Doc said as she and Tom moved Otto to a sitting position against the rock outcropping. "Help me take off his jacket and shirt. I have something to clean the wound and stop the bleeding."

Tom did as he was told. Otto grimaced and grunted as they extracted his injured arm from the clothing. Tom was startled to see that from Otto's left shoulder to the center of his left pec, a crater had been made in his flesh. The wound was a mix of charred and red skin. Some of the damage had been cauterized by the blaster round, while other parts still bled.

"Otto, Otto, can you hear me?" Doc asked, reaching into her bag, which had been mounted on her hoverbike. She shone a light into his eyes. "Tom, keep him awake while I work. Do not let him fall asleep."

Memories Tom would rather not have had surfaced abruptly.

He remembered being in combat with his unit, taking fire, friends he called family dying in his arms. He could smell sulfur in the air, hear their screams ringing in his ears.

"Hey, hey, you got to stay with me," Tom told Otto, grabbing his right hand and squeezing hard. "Doc's going to fix you up, but you have to stay awake. Can you hear me?"

"I can hear you." Otto's eyes opened slightly. "I'm wounded, not deaf."

"My man," Tom said with a smile. "Thank you, by the way. Thank you for saving us."

"I didn't do it for you," Otto said as Doc produced a needle from her bag.

"This isn't going to feel great," Doc told Otto.

"Do it." Otto nodded.

Doc pressed the needle into the wound, depositing a bright-green substance into the ruined flesh.

Otto squeezed Tom's hand so hard he thought it was going to break. Lifting his head, Otto bellowed in agony, a roar that sounded more animal than man.

"Hey, who did you do it for?" Tom asked as Doc removed the needle.

"Wh-what?" Otto panted from the pain. A new wave of sweat dampened his brow.

"You said you didn't save us for me; who did you do it for?" Tom asked.

"For my father," Otto managed. "He used to be the marshal of Athera. It's what he would have done."

"We're almost done," Doc said, producing a small canister. "That was something to kill the infection. This will stop the bleeding."

"Is it going to hurt?" Otto asked.

"Probably," Doc answered.

Otto nodded. His hand tightened on Tom's. Tom adjusted his hold and squeezed back.

"We've got you, we've got you," Tom said to the NPC who didn't remember killing him before.

Doc sprayed the wound with the canister's contents. It must not have hurt as much as the syringe, because Otto only gritted his teeth this time. When Doc was done, Otto was allowed to rest. The men's hands parted.

"He can sleep now; he's through the worst of it," Doc told Tom when he looked over with a worried expression. "You did good. Are you ready for the truth?"

Tom nodded. "Tell me everything."

CHAPTER 29

TOM

In the middle of the desert, with the moon and stars to bear witness, Doc relayed to Tom and Bishop all she knew. With deft fingers, she constructed a fire, which she lit with matches from her bag. She also supplied them with a meager meal—water from her canteen and some dried meat. Tom was so hungry it might as well have been manna from heaven.

"Our world is coming to an end," Doc explained. "Disaster analysts give it nine years at most before a natural disaster, a war, or one of a hundred other things ends us. A game was created, a game to put the very best and brightest minds to work in a kind of training ground. We needed to find out who would be the best equipped for a mission to colonize a new planet. I was part of that initiative until I realized what happened to candidates who died. And I learned how people were being recruited for the game."

"*You* did this to us?" Bishop asked, jumping up from her seat opposite Doc. The fire crackled between them, but Tom had a feeling that wasn't going to stop Bishop. "You put us in here?"

"I thought I was helping," Doc said. She stared into the flames, looking abashed. "Can you imagine how this could help so many, not just in the survival of humankind but in every aspect of our future? What if doctors could perfect surgical techniques in a game, guaranteeing success in real life? What if law enforcement could practice safer tactics in here, where there is no real threat of dying? The options are endless."

"Where is 'here'?" Tom asked, looking around at the desert landscape. "Where are we exactly? In a computer?"

"Essentially, yes," Doc answered. "Nothing around here is real; it's all just code, but your mind can't tell the difference."

"Rawww!" Bishop jumped over the fire and tackled Doc with all the ferocity of a linebacker sacking the quarterback. "Get us out! Let us out of here!"

Tom jumped to his feet and ran around the fire to separate the women. Doc didn't try to defend herself from Bishop, as if the marshal's blows were a punishment she knew she deserved,

Bishop cracked her three times across the face before Tom could get there and pull her off.

"Bishop, Bishop, no, not like this," he said, wrestling her away from the bleeding Doc. "Not like this."

"You heard her," Bishop said, but stopped struggling to free herself from Tom's grasp and let him pull her away. "We're in this sick game because of *her*."

"She also saved us," Tom said, letting Bishop go and placing himself between the two women. "She could have let us die."

"You shouldn't have stopped her," Doc said, sitting up and nursing a split lip. "I deserve it. I deserve the beating and so much more."

Flames flickered and morphed the shadows around the trio, transforming Bishop's anger to rage and Doc's regret to pure grief.

"You said this was supposed to help people," Tom said, getting the story back on track. "Where did it all go wrong? I remember a woman. A woman who came to me after Lana died and offered me a chance to participate. When I said no, she drugged me and brought me in anyway."

"Sara Tran," Doc said with a sad nod. "She and I, and Chairman's money, started Tanus Corporation. Sara was the face and oversaw our employees. I was free to lead a team to create the code. We were going to change the world. But things went wrong fast, and the data was hidden from me. By the time I found out, it was too late."

"What data?" Bishop asked through gritted teeth.

"You, the candidates—every time you die in the game, you come back with roughly a three percent cognitive loss. This number varies from candidate to candidate—some people lose more, some less—but it all pans out the same. You die enough times in here, and what makes you who you are is gone. Exactly why, we don't know."

"You turn into a lost one," Tom breathed.

"Yes," Doc answered, remorse filling her expression. "It gets worse. Every candidate was supposed to know what they were volunteering for. That's what we agreed. But I didn't realize that more and more candidates with specific skill sets would be needed. When Sara couldn't find volunteers, more forceful means were used. They started to abduct people. When I found out, I left. I tried to expose them for what they were, but no one would listen. I was labeled a conspiracy theorist and blackballed from the industry."

"Who was I?" Bishop breathed the question, all her anger vanishing in a moment of wonder. "Who am I?"

"I don't know," Doc admitted. "But I do know how to get you out. You have to complete your mission in the game. Do that, and you'll succeed where everyone else has failed."

"What mission? You mean finish the game?" Tom asked. "Does that have anything to do with the chime we sometimes hear when we walk into rooms? Does it signify different levels?"

"That's some of it," Doc answered. "There are a set number of objectives, but every candidate has a different one. Everything is measured, from how you react to the alien landscape, to how your heart rate spikes when you're in danger, to how you handle conflict. The chime you hear is like a waypoint, letting you know you're on the right track and, yes, introducing you to the next level, if it helps you to think of it that way."

"Wait a minute. If everything you're saying is true," Bishop said, looking at Doc sideways, "and that is a big if. *If* this is all a game that's being monitored, then what are you doing here, and why aren't you getting kicked out of the game for helping us?"

"I've hacked into the Eternal Engine from a remote location," Doc explained. "I'm not with them anymore. I now work for an organization called Immortal Industries."

"Oh, that sounds so much better. So you're a hacker saint now, coding yourself into this ratchet game to help us?" Bishop said, rolling her eyes.

"Bishop has a good point," Tom said, looking at Doc. "How come you're not getting booted out? If this is all being monitored, how come they don't recognize you?"

"I built the code," Doc answered. "When they view us, they see me as an NPC. When they listen to us, they hear us talking about life in the game as if it were real. It's not going to work forever. Sooner or later, they'll catch on."

"Okay, okay, I've heard enough," Bishop said, blowing out a long breath. "Get us out of here, Doc, or whatever your real name is."

"It's Julie," Doc answered.

"Doc's better," Bishop said without missing a beat. "So, let's go. Get us out of the simulation and let us crack some real heads in the real world. I want to get my hands on whoever did this to us."

"It's not that easy," Doc answered.

"Of course not," Tom muttered. "What now?"

"No one gets out until they finish the game, and no one ever has. But you, Tom, you're different," Doc said, rising to her feet and dusting herself off. "You could be the first."

"What are you talking about?" Tom asked.

"You've come closer than anyone to reaching the final boss, and in record time," Doc told him. "I can't tell you much more. You have to do this next part mostly without me, to prove that you can do it alone, but you're almost there now. I can lend a hand, but you have to finish the race."

"Can I shoot her now?" Bishop asked, reaching for her blaster.

"No, no, no one's going to shoot anyone," Tom said.

Doc moved to Bishop's hoverbike, which had finally stopped smoking. She popped off the front fender to gain access to the motor and started working on it. "Otto will be ready to travel in the morning. You should set off then to finish what you started."

"The mayor," Bishop breathed, putting two and two together. "The final level, the boss fight, it's stopping the mayor."

Tom and Bishop watched Doc for any sign of confirmation. She didn't even look their way; instead, she squinted into the hoverbike's engine.

Tom understood that by not even acknowledging the question, she was affirming what Bishop had guessed. Tom knew Bishop was right. It would be clear to anyone with a moral compass that Henry Graves had to be stopped, but few would have the determination and grit to actually put him in his place.

Tom went over to the fire and lifted a branch that flamed with tongues of yellow and red. He moved over to provide extra light for Doc as she tinkered with the hoverbike. Bishop didn't join them, instead taking a seat next to the sleeping Otto and staring into the flames.

"How's your face?" Tom asked, lifting the torch higher. "She laid into you pretty good."

"Everyone stuck in here deserves the chance to lay into me like she did," Doc answered without looking up. "This is all my fault. Perhaps not solely, but still, I won't back away from responsibility. This is on me as much as anyone else. Why aren't you taking a swing at me?"

"Because I've made a few mistakes too," Tom said. "How can I pass judgment on you when I have so much to atone for?"

"Don't get soft on me, Dexter," Doc said with a grunt as she tightened tubes and brackets in the hoverbike's engine. "We're going to need more of that animal inside of you before this is all done." She straightened up. "There, I think that should get you to Athera in the morning."

"You're not coming with us?" Tom asked, taking a step back as Doc replaced the hoverbike's fender.

"No, I have to leave you now," Doc said, reaching into her bag. She handed Tom a vial containing three red pills. "Give these to Bishop when she's ready. One first, then two the day after. Just like you did. The mind needs to be eased into memories."

"Otto?" Tom asked, looking over at the sleeping man. "He's not real, is he?"

"No, he's an NPC. Trust your gut," Doc told Tom with a hard nod. "You can finish this. I'll be back in to check on you as soon as I can."

With that, Doc walked off into the dark. Tom was about to call her back, but there was no point. If none of this was real, then Doc would, what, simply unplug herself from whatever game this was and wake up in the real world?

Tom's mind reeled as Doc's form vanished right before his eyes.

CHAPTER 30

TOM

"Do you believe her?" Bishop asked as Tom joined her by the dying fire. "Do you think we can trust her?"

"It's the only truth we've got." Tom shrugged. "And she did help us escape. If not for her and Otto, we'd be restarting at the first level with less of our minds than before."

"Stuck in a video game where the only way out is to kill the most powerful and guarded man in the darn thing," Bishop said with a heavy sigh. "Isn't that a bit—"

"She left a present for you," Tom said, tossing Bishop the vial of red pills over the fire.

Bishop reached out and snatched them out of the air as easily as if she were waving.

"Walk off into the darkness after blowing our minds and leave me with drugs to remember my past," she said, almost under her breath, as she shook the vial of pills. They rattled their agreement. "What's that old saying? 'The first one's always free'?"

"You tell me," Tom said with a grin. "Were you a drug dealer in your past life?"

"What if I don't want to remember what I was?" Bishop

asked. "Whatever it was, I know how to fight, I can fire a weapon, and I'm not afraid."

"Sounds like a gangster or drug dealer to me." Tom shrugged.

Bishop looked at him with a stare that could turn flesh to stone.

Tom saved himself by clearing his throat and turning his left forearm over twice. "Gary shut off when we were stunned. I wonder if he still works."

"*Ahhhh!*" Gary screamed as the HUD popped to life. "Oh, oh, oh, Rosanne, I just had the worst dream—there were these horrible NPC deputies, and they were going to hang you and the other one, and then they shot you with a stun gun, but it really shut me off and . . ."

Gary's voice trailed off.

"All of that actually happened," Bishop told the AI.

"Oh," Gary whispered. "So it did. Sorry I can't award you skill points or levels for all those shenanigans, but take a look at your loot crate."

Tom did so. In the grid of square boxes that was the item screen, the loot crate had turned green and now read "Rare."

"I'm trying to see what I can do to incorporate more variety in the game as well," Gary told them. "Everything is so postapocalyptic and *Fallout* meets *Red Dead Redemption*. Let Daddy cook."

"When I need an item out of my inventory, how does that work?" Tom asked.

"Like when you reached for your credits in your pocket," Gary answered. "Picture in your mind's eye what item you want. Reach in and pull it out."

"That makes no sense," Tom offered.

"Nope, but it works," Bishop answered, opening her HUD and looking at her map. "I've never been this far south before. I can see so much more of the map now."

Bishop was right. Tom checked his own map, examining the open terrain.

A light, chilly fog began to roll through their camp. Some creature howled a melancholy tune into the night. Tom was sure that it was no night hound. He had heard them enough times to recognize the animal. This was something else, almost human.

"Someone hold me," Gary breathed.

"What did Doc say about being close to the mist lands?" Bishop asked, removing one of Otto's silver blasters from the holster at her side. "Did she leave us here to die?"

"I think if she wanted us dead, she would have just let us hang," Tom offered. Despite this, he reached for Mama Jama, the three-barreled repeater that lay next to the sleeping Otto. "But this game wasn't meant to be easy. It was to test people for another world. Who knows what's out there."

Tom and Bishop took up positions on either side of Otto. Their backs to the rock outcropping, they peered past the fire toward the rolling mist. Something about mist gave Tom the creeps. Maybe it was a primordial instinct passed down from human to human as cavemen peered into the dark unknown, fearing the beasts that stalked them.

Some ancient fear was let loose as Tom's imagination played havoc with his surroundings. Shadows twisted and morphed into creatures in the night. More howls and growls lifted into the sky, unlike any sounds Tom had ever heard.

"I have a bad feeling about this," Gary whispered.

"Cover me," Bishop said, moving to the left and lining up the hoverbikes on that side of the rock formation. This little barrier wasn't going to stop anyone by itself, but if it bought them even a second of reaction time, that could mean the difference between life and a restart.

Bishop squinted into the dark mist as she jogged back to

join Tom. "I saw something shuffling out there, lots of somethings. They were moving on two feet."

"Lost ones," Otto said so suddenly that Tom nearly jumped and swung the repeater to bear. "Insane people that live out here."

Gary sucked in his breath in shock. "This one's still alive? I literally thought he was dead this entire time."

Otto grunted and rose to his feet. As an NPC he didn't hear Gary at all. He hefted the other silver blaster in his right hand.

The mist had grown so thick that Tom had trouble making out anything past the fire that crackled five feet in front of him.

"One is see and three to me," an older woman's voice cackled in the night. "To be is three and me."

Tom recognized the voice. The old woman in the cell. The one who had been suffocated by the deputies. By the expression painted across Bishop's face, he knew she recognized the voice as well.

Manic laughter from more than one throat rippled through the night. A woman stepped into view just on the other side of the fire. She wore a black-and-blue jumpsuit, the same black-and-blue jumpsuit Tom had worn when he woke in the game.

The woman was filthy, as if she had been rolling in the dirt the whole way from her coffin to this very fire. Her eyes were glossy and unfocused. A smile spread across her lips as she took in the strangers.

"Who do we have here?" she asked, cocking her head to one side. "Die and die again and again, where it stops, where is the end?"

"Look what they did," Bishop breathed under her breath. "Look what happened to her. She's been killed one too many times."

More indistinct figures rushed through the night, dozens of them swirling around in the mist. Waiting to attack? Tom couldn't be sure.

Otto lifted his blaster.

"No, we can't kill them again," Tom said.

"You do whatever you want, newbie," Otto said with a grunt. "One of them comes for my head, I'm going to bury them right where they stand."

"You have to remember," Tom said, taking a step forward. He opened his arms wide, his repeater pointed to the ground. "You have to remember what happened to you, all of you. No matter how much it hurts. You have to remember who you are."

Screams—not animal, definitely human—broke through the night. Yells and bellows of pain as candidates, more aptly called players, fought for a hold on their sanity, trying to remember a sliver of who they had once been.

"We're not going to hurt you," Tom called out. "We are you."

"My head, my head!" the woman in front of them groaned. "Why does it hurt so much? Why does it hurt?!"

"Because they don't want us to remember," Tom said, loudly and clearly. "But you have to. I know it hurts; I know what it feels like. But you have to fight. And the way you fight is by recalling who you were. Don't let them take that from you."

Screams of agony lifted to the heavens from more throats. Not dozens, hundreds. Tom took another step forward as the mist swirled around him. A rogue breeze split the fog like the parting of the Red Sea, revealing a horrific sight.

Hundreds of players turned lost ones fanned out in front of him. Most still wore the original jumpsuits, tattered and torn to varying degrees. Some were completely naked; others wore the skins of animals.

All but a few grabbed their heads as Tom encouraged them to remember who they were. Lost memories struggled to the surface.

Tom's gut clenched. Otto lifted his weapon.

"No, trust me," Tom warned, shaking his head and using his right hand to lower the muzzle of Otto's blaster. "We're not going to shoot our way out of this."

"It hurts, it hurts us," the older woman who had been killed in the cell groaned, falling to her knees as she grabbed her head. "Why—why do the memories hurt?"

"Because that's how they keep us under control," Bishop answered, going over to the woman. She sank to a single knee and placed her hand on the woman's bony shoulder. "Your name. Start with your name."

"Monica," the older woman said through tears of confusion. "My name is Monica. Where—where am I?"

"If there's anything left inside of you that remembers who you once were, then you have to trust me," Tom called out as the fog swirled, once again cloaking the lost ones in shadows. "I swear to you that we're going to find the people who did this to us, and we're going to make them pay. But I need you to give us that chance. Remember who you are and let us go."

The screams of pain built to a crescendo; even Monica joined in, babbling nonsense about a snake and a robot. Bishop stepped back and shook her head.

The lost ones were working themselves into a frenzy.

"We tried your way," Otto said, lifting his blaster again. "I'm not going to be taken by no lost ones."

"Wait," Gary said. "Something else is coming."

CHAPTER 31

TOM

Just when the screaming hit such a high note that Tom's ears were beginning to ring, it stopped. Another howl, one Tom recognized—a night hound—sliced through the screams like a honed blade through grass.

Such utter and complete silence in the wake of pure chaos shook Tom. Even Monica stood up, fearful. She took a step back into the mist and disappeared.

"Monica?" Bishop called out. "Monica, no, come with us."

But she was gone, and so too were the other lost ones. Another night hound called and then another, until Tom was sure they were surrounded.

"Great, we'll trade being attacked by lost ones for being eaten alive by wolves," Tom muttered, not quite under his breath.

But the night hounds never came. Instead, they continued to howl for a while, then stopped. An hour after the last howl, Tom, Bishop, and Otto decided to sleep in shifts. Bishop took the first shift.

Tom lay down with his back to the rock wall and his face toward the fire.

"This has been some really heavy stuff to go through." Gary filled the silence. "Would anyone like to hear a joke? Your mama is so fat—"

"No," Tom and Bishop said in chorus.

"Fine, fine, just trying to lighten the mood." Gary sighed as if he too were weary. "You all need some sleep. I'll see you soon . . . Good night, friends."

Tom turned off his HUD. He didn't know how it was possible, but he had no nightmares that night on the hard ground.

The suns woke him before Otto did. Tom rubbed at blurry eyes, trying to remember where he was. He was so cold he had to stop himself from shivering. The fire had gone out sometime during the night.

Every muscle in his body was sore.

"I know what you're thinking," Otto said as he leaned against one of the hoverbikes. "'I'd kill for a cup of nitro caf right about now.'"

"You're not wrong," Tom said, stretching with a wide yawn. "Why didn't you wake me for my shift?"

"You look horrible; you needed the sleep," Otto told him. "Still could use more."

"Thanks?" It was more like a question than gratitude.

"I do what I can." Otto shrugged.

Tom reached down to pick up the repeater he had slept next to and took it over to Otto. "I think this is yours."

"Hold on to it for now," Otto told him. "I have a feeling all of us are going to have to stay armed for the time being. Mayor Graves isn't going to let this go. He's going to be waiting for us. We need to end it."

Tom nodded in agreement. Mother Nature was calling, so he went in search of a bush far enough from camp to afford some privacy. The mist was nonexistent, as if it had never really been there at all.

The tracks, however, were very present. There were hundreds of prints in the desert around their camp, some made by bare feet, some by boots. Tom was no expert tracker, but it didn't take much skill to also spot the night hounds' massive paw prints laid over the human tracks.

There were no bodies or blood, so he guessed the night hounds had scared the lost ones away.

Tom finished watering the bush and made his way back to camp. Along with being sore and thirsty, he was hungry. There weren't too many choices besides heading back to Athera. Otto was right. Hiding wasn't an option; the mayor had to be dealt with.

"You ladies ready to roll?" Bishop asked, rising from the ground and dusting herself off. "I'm not getting any younger."

"We should go in and hit them hard," Otto said, checking his blaster. "Kill the mayor and be done with it."

Bishop handed Otto the silver blaster she'd been using. She walked over to her hoverbike and lifted the black blaster Doc had left behind. "I'm not arguing."

"Agreed," Tom answered, walking over to the hoverbike Otto stood next to.

"Not a chance," Otto said, hopping onto the bike.

Bishop beckoned to Tom. "Get on."

Tom would much rather have driven one of the bikes but knew he was the least experienced. Without arguing, he jumped onto the back of Bishop's hoverbike, and the two vehicles took off toward Athera. While Tom scanned the horizon and the suns lifted into the sky, he had an opportunity to think.

He replayed the events of the night before over and over again in his mind. Who Doc said she was, how she had gotten there, and why. He had read papers about virtual reality feeling as real as life. He had seen tech adapted for video games and training simulations, but nothing like this.

When he did get out of the game, his fight against those who had done this to him would just be beginning. There was Sara, who had drugged him, and someone else called . . . Chairman? Was he the owner of Tanus Corporation?

As they rode, Tom searched his memories for any clues he might have missed. He didn't see the plumes of dirt racing toward them until Bishop shouted, "We've got trouble!"

Tom looked up in time to see at least four hoverbikes and two larger craft that looked like dune buggies without wheels racing to meet them.

"The sheriff and his men from Canto!" Otto yelled. "They were waiting for us."

"Then let's not disappoint them," Tom said, unslinging the heavy repeater from his back.

"The more we kill now, the less we'll have to fight in Athera," Bishop agreed.

Otto steered away from them so that they were two targets instead of one. Incoming blaster bolts started to rain down on them from the approaching enemy party.

Tom did the math in his head: *Four hoverbikes with at least one fighter apiece, two four-seater buggies—at least twelve enemies. I like those odds.*

The air, filled previously with the hum of the hoverbikes, now thrummed with blaster bolts traded between the two groups. Otto and Bishop fired one-handed, keeping the other hand on the hoverbikes' controls. Tom leaned to Bishop's left to aim the weapon lovingly referred to as Mama Jama.

With both hands on the weapon, he relied on the strength of his legs to clench the seat and keep him on the bike. That, and his trust that Bishop wouldn't perform any wild maneuvers with him in such a precarious position.

Adrenaline rushed through his system, making him feel a bit sick. His heart rate spiked. Tom reminded himself to stay calm.

Wait until they're in range, he coached himself. *Calm in the face of the storm. Easy, easy. Not yet.*

Red laser fire struck Otto's hoverbike but failed to penetrate the outer shielding. Bishop ducked low. A bolt skidded so close to Tom he felt it singe his hair.

The enemy was closing in: a hundred yards away; then, in a blink of an eye, ninety; then eighty. At the seventy-yard mark, Tom let them have it.

Mama Jama hurled bolts downrange so fast each round was impossible to separate from another. Though Tom wasn't half the shot Otto was, with this bringer of death in his hands, he didn't have to be.

The first hoverbike went down. The second was tossed end over end. The third crashed into one of its downed counterparts and erupted in a ball of flame.

The groups of vehicles passed one another, so close that Tom could have reached out and touched one of the men in the buggy.

Bishop screamed in pain as a bolt found her left leg. Their hoverbike wavered for a moment, but she recovered quickly and kept it steady.

The two buggies and the last hoverbike turned quickly and gave chase. Tom pivoted in his seat, pressing his back to Bishop's. Left hand on the side of the seat to keep himself steady, he sent rounds toward the approaching sheriff and deputies.

The last enemy hoverbike had already caught up with Otto. The two drivers clashed, smashing their hoverbikes into one another with enough force to cause sparks to shower from each collision. The two men each sought to disarm the other while attempting to fire at one another.

Another blaster bolt pinged off the rear of Bishop's hoverbike, right below Tom's crotch. A few inches closer and he would have had new problems to worry about.

With the two buggies bearing down on them, Tom realized they were going to be caught and gunned down unless he did something drastic.

"Hit the brakes!" Tom yelled over his shoulder, sending another spray of fire from Mama Jama into the approaching buggy.

"What?!" Bishop yelled back. "It sounded like you said to hit the brakes."

"I did, trust me," Tom said, bracing for impact. "Hit the brakes!"

Bishop obeyed a second later, jerking Tom from his seat and into her back.

The buggy driver behind them did the same, braking sharply, but too late. He plowed into the rear of the hoverbike. This time, Tom didn't fight to keep his seat. He let momentum take him and leaped onto the hood of the hovering buggy.

With a hollow thump of metal, he landed hard enough to rattle his teeth. He had left Mama Jama on the rear of Bishop's hoverbike. This was going to be up close and personal.

The buggy held four of the deputies. The sheriff was in the other buggy, still chasing after Bishop, who had gunned her engine again and raced off.

The buggies didn't have windshields—or windows, for that matter—just open areas around a rusting black frame. The deputy riding shotgun looked at Tom as if he couldn't believe his eyes.

"Hi." Tom waved.

As the deputy turned his blaster on Tom and the hovering

buggy sped across the desert, Tom jumped from the hood into the cabin, crashing into the front passenger.

The two men wrestled. The driver jerked the wheel wildly when Tom kicked him in the face. The two deputies in the back seat tried to get a clean shot at Tom, but everything was moving too fast, and the driver jerking the wheel sporadically from side to side didn't help.

Shots rang out as Tom kicked the driver in the face a second time, sending him tumbling out of the vehicle. One of the deputies in the back seat leaned over to grab the wheel and keep them from crashing.

The second deputy gave up on finding a clear shot. Instead, he produced a heated knife from his belt. The metal hissed, glowing red, as the deputy lunged over the seat at Tom.

The passenger-side deputy had Tom in a headlock, with Tom's back to the deputy's chest. The deputy had an arm around his neck and a fistful of his hair.

"Hold him still," the deputy with the knife said. "For all that's holy, Sam, keep him still!"

"I'm trying!" Sam shouted.

The man with the knife brought his hissing blade down on Tom, who pushed up with his feet and lifted Sam's arm into the path of the knife. Blood gushed liberally as the knife cut to the bone. For a moment, the scent of searing flesh filled the open-cabin buggy.

Sam screamed in pain, losing his grip on Tom, who did a hard sit-up and relieved the knife wielder of his blaster. Tom fired a round at point-blank range into the underside of the man's jaw.

Before Tom even had time to register the hot liquid spraying across his face, he twisted in his seat, firing two more rounds into Sam's chest, then kept turning and fired another two bolts into the deputy who had maneuvered himself into the driver's seat.

All three men died within seconds of one another, falling out of the buggy. Tom grabbed the wheel and took a breath, trying to get a sense of what was happening with the rest of the fight. Otto had won his contest with the other hoverbike and was now moving to help Bishop.

The last buggy, with the Canto sheriff on board, had moved to attack Bishop. She was hurting, and it showed in her driving. The much larger buggy slammed into the side of her hoverbike, and it flipped end over end. Bishop flew through the air as if shot from a cannon. She landed awkwardly on the unforgiving ground and didn't move. Before Tom could slow to grab her, Otto hit the brakes and made a beeline for where she lay. He caught Tom's eye and gave him a nod.

There were a lot of unspoken words in that single look. It said nothing at all while saying, *I've got her. Go, kill them.*

Tom nodded in return and made his move. Gunning the engine, which responded with a throaty roar, he quickly caught up to the transport in front of him. Without hesitating, he rammed the back of the buggy. The vehicle jerked, swung wide, and slowed, giving Tom a good look at the three deputies and the Canto sheriff, who rode behind the driver.

Tom lifted his weapon, sending a bolt through the skull of the deputy sitting in the rear passenger-side seat. The driver swung right, slamming their buggies together before anyone could get another shot off.

The passenger in the front seat reached out and grabbed Tom's steering wheel.

"You can have it," Tom grunted, clamping his left hand down on the man's wrist, not allowing him to let go.

Jerking the wheel to the right, Tom ripped the passenger out of his buggy, forcing him to hold on to the steering wheel with both hands lest he fall under the vehicle. With half of the deputy's body inside Tom's buggy and the other half being dragged across the desert, Tom jerked the wheel left again.

The sheriff let off two well-placed shots that would have had Tom dead to rights if not for the collision. Instead of crashing into his head, the rounds ate the back of Tom's seat. Meanwhile, the man holding on to Tom's steering wheel was crushed between the two vehicles.

With a Wilhelm scream, the man released his grip and fell away. Again and again, the sheriff tried to get off an accurate shot, but again and again, Tom rammed his buggy against his enemy's.

A wild thought came into Tom's head.

Not a good idea, definitely not a good idea. He acted on it anyway.

CHAPTER 32

TOM

Tom leaped from his vehicle to the other, lunging across the front seat and shouldering aside the driver to grab the steering wheel in both hands. In his peripheral vision, he saw the sheriff stand up and aim his blaster at Tom.

The sheriff wasn't the kind to let a little something like collateral damage stop him from getting what he wanted. Wriggling around quickly, Tom slammed his left foot down on the brake just as the sheriff opened fire.

Two things happened at once. The first was that the buggy screeched to a stop. Given the speed it was traveling, this sent the sheriff flying from his standing position behind the driver. His great girth sailed over the vehicle's frame and into the desert.

The second thing was that Tom's head bounced off the steering wheel so hard he saw stars.

One of the sheriff's rounds had found a home in the driver's head. His body slumped against the steering wheel. Tom pushed the corpse from the buggy, wondering if this man was another candidate or an NPC, just part of the warped game.

Does it really matter? He was trying to kill me. He would have killed me.

Motion in front of the buggy—the sheriff was struggling back to his feet. He wobbled, getting his bearings, then zeroed in on Tom.

Tom looked at the man who had imprisoned him, killed the woman he now knew as Monica, and would have killed him too, given the chance.

He revved the buggy's motor.

Terror struck the eyes of the sheriff like a lightning bolt. He looked around frantically, searching for his blaster. He and Tom spotted it at the same time, lying sideways in the sand, not quite halfway between them.

Tom revved the engine again.

The sheriff stared him down.

If the sheriff could get to his blaster first, he still had a chance to kill Tom. But if Tom got to him first, then it was game over.

The classic line from *Dirty Harry* raced through Tom's mind. *You've gotta ask yourself one question: "Do I feel lucky?"*

Like a man possessed, the sheriff sprinted for his blaster. Tom slammed the accelerator, and the buggy surged forward like a raging bull finally released from its pen.

Time seemed to slow. In seconds, Tom knew he wasn't going to get there soon enough. Despite how slow the sheriff moved, Tom was just too far away. He was still willing to take the chance of getting shot if it meant ending the sheriff for good.

The sheriff slid into the sand like he was stealing home base. With sausage-like fingers, he picked up the weapon and aimed at Tom.

Unluckily for him, Tom was already on top of him. The sheriff's sternum met the front bumper of the hovering buggy, and it crushed him from collarbone to skull.

The buggy jostled, and Tom came around for another pass just to be sure.

The sheriff and all his deputies were gone. Tom said a silent prayer that that would mean their final meeting with the mayor would be easier than he had anticipated.

Under the heat of the morning suns, Tom made his way back to where Otto had stopped for Bishop. He found the pair looking over Bishop's bike and frowning. When they saw the buggy approaching, both bounty hunter and Athera's marshal reached for their weapons. Not until they saw who was driving did they relax.

"Need a ride?" Tom asked, pulling up next to the pair. "Bishop, you good?"

"Oh yeah, living my best life," Bishop said, glancing at her bandaged left thigh. "Otto calls it a flesh wound. It feels like hell."

"It's a long way from your heart," Otto said, moving Mama Jama from the back of Bishop's wrecked hoverbike to the rear of Tom's buggy. "Your hoverbike is done. You two can take the buggy. I'll stick with my bike."

"The sheriff's dead," Tom added as Bishop hobbled into the front passenger seat.

"Are you sure?" Otto asked, mounting his bike.

"Uh, yeah, yep, pretty sure," Tom answered.

"Good." Otto nodded. "Fewer to kill when we get into town."

"'We'?" Bishop asked with a raised eyebrow toward the bounty hunter. "You've done more than enough, you know."

Otto looked at her with hard eyes. He didn't answer; instead, he offered action, starting the engine on his hoverbike and heading for Athera.

"Not much of a talker, but it's hard to argue with his results," Bishop said with a sigh.

Tom agreed as they followed the bike. He and Bishop sat in a comfortable silence for a time before Bishop offered him a bombshell.

"I took one of the pills," she said without looking at Tom. "One of Doc's pills."

"Did it work?" Tom asked with wide eyes. "Do you remember?"

"I remember some, in small, flashing sequences," Bishop said. "Like, I get images of memories, not the whole memory itself."

"The same thing happened to me the first night," Tom said. "Take two more pills tonight, and you'll get it all back."

"What if I don't want to remember?" Bishop said, swallowing hard. "What if I don't like what I see? What if I don't want to be that person anymore?"

Tom remembered the pain of losing his wife, the shame of being dishonorably discharged, and the misery he'd felt living without Lana.

"I get it," he answered, searching for words to match his feelings. "But maybe there are things or people in your past that will make the bad bearable."

Bishop didn't say anything, but Tom could feel her staring at him in shock.

"What?" he asked.

"When did you get all wise and stuff?" Bishop said uncomfortably. "I liked you better when I thought you were just a dumb brute."

"Who says I'm not?" Tom asked. "You know, if you don't want to talk about—"

"I think I was a police officer," Bishop interrupted. "I have memories of being in a uniform and on the street. But I also have a flash of memory of someone else in uniform dying in my arms. A feeling more than a visual memory, of guilt and loss."

"Doc said they were choosing people from all backgrounds and walks of life to see who would adapt to the elements in the game the best," Tom said, playing through the idea. "I was a soldier. What if they're picking lots of people with combat or public service experience to see how they would do?"

"What, you mean like they're drugging firefighters, paramedics, and the like and dropping them in here? Like rats to test and experiment on?" Bishop asked with a shudder that quickly turned to anger. "When I get my hands on the people who did this to us, I'm going to tear them apart."

"You and me both," Tom said with a sigh. "But if we trust Doc, then the only way out of this nightmare is to get through it. We have to finish the game. We need to free Canto and Athera from Mayor Graves."

"It kinda makes sense in a dark, twisted way." Bishop chuckled. When Tom looked at her for an explanation, she shrugged. "Oh, come on, Supersoldier, you're telling me that we're not smack dab in the middle of every postapocalyptic movie you've ever seen? The law and her ragtag group of survivors have to work together to take down the corrupt mayor? How tropey. Who wrote this, anyway?"

"We were talking to her," Tom answered, remembering Doc's admission of being the one to start work on—what had she called it? The Eternal Engine? "Do you think we owe it to anyone not to kill them?"

"What do you mean?" Bishop asked.

"We don't know who in here is an NPC and who is a real person, right? When we kill a real person in here, we're stealing a part of their sanity they'll never get back," Tom explained. "I don't know if that's better or crueler than outright killing someone."

"At least in the real world, when you kill someone, they stay dead," Bishop said, searching for the answer. "Here, you get to kill them piece by piece."

"I guess if they're trying to kill us, it doesn't matter," Tom said. "They don't give us much of a choice in that situation, NPC or human."

Bishop brought her left hand to her head and massaged her temples as if she were warding off a migraine. "I'm going to need some major therapy when we get out of here and back to the real world. I'm talking plenty of medication and a whole panel of psychiatrists."

"You and me both," Tom agreed. "You and me both."

CHAPTER 33

SARA

The day after Sara met with Julie, she was a mess internally. They both knew it was only a matter of time before Julie was caught. Sara would deny it all, of course. The only thing that linked Sara to Julie at the moment was the anomaly in the code Jeffrey Saga had discovered.

As long as he didn't raise any more alarms, Julie would be fine. Julie was the best. Now that she knew she had slipped up once, she would be twice as careful.

Sara was lost in thought as she got ready that morning, kissed Michelle goodbye, and headed for the office. She was surprised to receive a call from Chairman during her drive to work. When the screen on her self-driving car lit up with the incoming call, Sara's blood ran cold.

There's nothing to worry about, there's nothing to worry about, she soothed herself. *At most, you were made aware of an anomaly and you dismissed it as unimportant.*

Sara took a deep breath, centering herself, then answered the call. The screen that popped up was the same as always on a call with Chairman: nothing. That is to say, a blank screen welcomed her. Chairman's voice was that of an older, not unfriendly male. If a voice could sound kind and also wise, his did.

But there was that nagging thought in the back of her mind that Chairman could be anyone. With AI augmentation, altering a voice was as easy as pressing a button.

"Sara, how are you?" Chairman asked earnestly. "I realize how hard you work. It takes a toll. You need a vacation."

"Oh, you know me," Sara said with a smile. "I'll sleep when I'm dead. There's too much that still needs to be done."

"A woman after my own heart." Chairman chuckled. "How's the data collection going with the latest batch of candidates?"

"We know more now than ever," Sara answered honestly. "We're collecting thousands of data points across hundreds of candidates every minute."

"Wonderful," Chairman said, then cleared his throat. "If only one of the candidates could complete their mission. Data collection is moving forward as anticipated, but no one has made it out of the game. That worries me."

"Perhaps we simply have not discovered the correct candidates," Sara suggested. "We will. And when we do, we'll have the perfect example of the person to send on a real-life mission. Along with all the data collected from everyone else."

"That's why I like you, Sara," Chairman said with a long sigh. "Always optimistic, always with a plan within a plan within a plan. You know, I received your email about Project Legacy, and I have to admit I was surprised."

Ah, Sara thought. *Here it is. This is the real reason you called.*

"How so?" she asked innocently. She batted her eyes a few times and tilted her head to the side. Although she had never seen Chairman, he insisted she always have her camera on. Something about these older reclusive billionaires.

"Sara, I know you were against Project Legacy from its

inception," Chairman chided, as if she were a small child. "You only want the best for everyone, so of course you would have second thoughts about placing unqualified candidates in the care of the game."

Care of the game? He's talking about it like it's a person. Then Sara reminded herself, *Careful. Too complacent and he'll know you're lying; too angry and you'll raise red flags.*

"I have to admit I was surprised to see that the project had already begun," Sara said with a smile on her painted lips. "However, I understand the reasoning behind it and how many people it could help in the future."

"That's right," Chairman said, sounding pleased, if a bit surprised, at her civil demeanor. "These new candidates were found at homeless shelters, in nursing homes and places like that; they had no one. They have much better lives now."

How's that? They're living their "best lives" in a game, dying over and over again, losing pieces of their souls every time, Sara thought.

"I have no doubt of that," she said as calmly as possible. "I only wonder if there has been any success from the team researching how to have the candidates restart their timelines with all of their original cognitive abilities."

"Nothing has been discovered that can help that, but they are hard at work on the subject," Chairman answered. "You know that is one of our top priorities. But in the meantime, we must push forward with the project. You understand, don't you?"

"I do," Sara answered, despising herself for seeing and half agreeing with Chairman's position. "What we're doing now will preserve the future of the human race. If a few people have to suffer for the many, then it's worth it."

"Exactly," Chairman agreed. "Well, I won't keep you much longer. I know you have so much to do. I'm just glad we're both on the same page about Project Legacy."

"Of course," Sara said.

"Oh, you know what? There is one more thing."

Sara's heart practically stopped in her chest. She immediately broke out in a cold sweat. "Yes?"

"Can you please decide on a new secretary today?" Chairman asked with a hint of a smile in his words. "You haven't had one since you fired Ranel, and I've had a few complaints from various departments about not being able to get in contact with you."

"Right, yes." Sara breathed a sigh of relief. "I'll be sure to do that today."

"Wonderful, thank you, Sara," Chairman said with a sneeze. "Excuse me, I seem to be fighting off a cold. We'll talk soon."

"Of course, get well soon," Sara responded as the screen transitioned to her usual interface.

She shut off the holographic screen and slumped in her seat. She wasn't usually so nervous when talking to Chairman. He was mysterious, but a normal mysterious she was used to, if that made any sense. She knew what to expect from him.

But now, with the introduction of Project Legacy and with Julie back in the picture, things were beginning to become complicated. The issue of a new secretary seemed to pale in comparison to the other things on her plate.

Julie had given her the homework of looking into Candidate 20741. That would have to be done as soon as possible. But to appease Chairman, the secretary search should begin posthaste.

Sara went through a mental list of who might fill the role. There was Ryan from accounting, but he always wanted to talk about fishing. Jenny from sales, but she smelled so strongly of deodorant every morning that it gave Sara a headache.

Entering the garage, she felt no closer to finding a secretary. It would have to be someone she could trust, or someone so new that they would be oblivious to anything going on, too new to be bought or influenced by anyone else.

When the lift doors dinged open on her floor, none other than Bob Villa de Lobos stood in front of her. He held a tissue in one hand.

"Oh, Ms. Tran," Bob said, clearly surprised and rubbing his red eyes. "Well, good morning. Sorry, seasonal allergies—"

"Come with me," Sara said, stepping out of the elevator and around the bumbling new tech. "You've just been reassigned."

"Oh, wonderful, of course," Bob said, then did a double take. "Wait, what?"

"You heard me," Sara called back, not bothering to slow her stride. "You've just been promoted. Come with me."

Bob wasn't ideal, but he was her best choice. He had just started working for Tanus Corporation, which meant he didn't know what questions to ask yet. For that same reason, he could be trusted.

Sara's white high heels clicked across the floor as she made her way to her office. Bob nervously followed her, clearly unsure what was happening. He looked around like a rat in a cobra's nest as they stepped into Sara's office.

"Ms. Tran, I respect you as a woman and my boss, but—"

"Bob, you're my new secretary," Sara said as they entered the outer office. "I need one, and well, you're as good as anyone else. I'll make sure it comes with a raise."

"Oh—oh, thank goodness," Bob said, holding his left hand to his chest.

"As my secretary, you'll manage my calls and calendar and run errands for me, understood?" Sara said, walking over to the empty desk. "This is where you'll work from now on."

"Oh, okay," Bob said, sneezing into his tissue. "Do I need to apply for the position or fill out any paperwork or anything?"

"I'll take care of it," Sara said, jerking her chin to the desk. "Settle in for now while I attend to something."

"Okay, thank you, Ms. Tra—"

The rest of her name was cut off as Sara entered her office and shut the door. She wasn't intentionally being rude to Bob; she just had a dozen things on her mind. Right now, she was thinking of the cryptic way Julie had told her to look into Candidate 20741.

Sara reached her desk and activated the holographic computer interface. She scrolled through a few screens, entering the Eternal Engine network, and ran a search. Candidate 20741 turned out to be Tom Dexter, ex–Special Forces. She remembered him well. Stellar career with the military until he'd stolen money on a mission.

He'd been court-martialed, his wife had died, and Sara had recruited him for the program. Less recruited and more kidnapped, to be honest, but it had to be done.

She scrolled through Candidate 20741's in-game data. Her eyes widened and she leaned into her screen as she read.

This can't be right, Sara thought, checking and rechecking the simulation readout in front of her. *How is this possible? How has no one noticed?*

These weren't the only questions she didn't have answers for as she studied the screen in front of her. For the next few hours, Sara pored over the data, checking and rechecking her work. She pulled up the in-game feed, watching Candidate 20741's progress as he moved through the simulation.

He interacted with both NPCs and other candidates. His decisions were brutal but fair as he clashed with the bounty hunter and the mayor. He was nearing the endgame. No one else had ever gotten so far.

Sara watched with bated breath as she activated a real-time view of Candidate 20741. He was traveling with two others toward the town of Athera.

"If he can do this, all of our work will have meant something," Sara breathed. "He's almost there."

A knock at her door startled her more than she cared to admit. She had fired her secretary months ago and was used to being left alone while she worked.

"Yes, what is it?" she called out.

Bob opened the door, carrying two coffee cups. He entered her office, head on a swivel, looking at everything from the art deco on her walls to her collection of rare books and many, many awards.

"I thought you might like some coffee. You've been in here for hours," he said as he approached the desk. "This office is larger than the apartment Nana and I live in."

"Bob," Sara said, reining in the new hire's attention. "How long have you worked here?"

"A week. Well, actually, a few days," Bob said, offering the coffee, which Sara did not move to take. "Here, I found out what you usually order from the barista downstairs, and they made it just the way you like it, no cream or sugar."

"Bob, I'm going to let you in on a little secret that might help you during the rest of your time here at Tanus Corporation," Sara said with a raised eyebrow. "No one likes a kiss-ass, Bob, no one."

"Oh," Bob said, retracting the offered coffee and looking down, seeming ashamed. "I didn't mean—I just thought you'd—I didn't see you walk in with a coffee this morning and—okay, I'll just go back to my desk."

Sara hated herself in that moment. She knew he was just trying to be nice. She was doing it again, pushing away anyone who dared try to get close to her.

"Bob, leave the coffee," Sara said as he turned to go. "No one told you to take the coffee."

CHAPTER 34

SARA

Someone better than her would have thanked Bob or even apologized and explained how much stress they were under. It just wasn't Sara's way. Before he left, Bob set the coffee on her desk with a nod, like he understood that this was her way of trying to be nice.

For four hours, Sara pored over all the data and footage she could find of Candidate 20741. At the lunch hour, certain that what she was seeing was accurate, she gave herself permission to take a break.

Young Sara, inexperienced and naive Sara, would have gone running to Chairman with this news, or at the very least had Jeffrey and his coding team double-check her findings. Not really her findings—Julie's findings.

Older and more experienced Sara knew better. She, or rather Candidate 20741, held the key. This key came with a countdown timer. Sooner or later, someone would realize what was going on. Sara had to be strategic, but she also had to act before anyone else did.

Sara decided to mull over her next move during lunch. She

stepped out of her office, already thinking of her salmon with a vegetable side, and stopped dead in her tracks.

Bob had been busy. Not only had he set up his workstation computer, but he had moved some personal effects onto the reception desk. On one corner was a strange cactus with a blue flower. On another was a picture of Bob and an elderly woman that looked like it might have been taken on the woman's birthday.

"Oh, good, you're out," Bob said, rising from his desk. He frowned down at his screen. "I was given clearance to manage your schedule and the old secretary's email, and well—I don't know where to start. There are thousands of meeting requests for you from various departments. You've been cc'd on hundreds of other emails. Over the last two days alone, some guy named Theodore Sullivan has asked nine times for a meeting about something called the Legacy Project? Oh, and Jeffrey Saga has repeatedly asked to speak with you."

"Right," Sara said, biting her tongue and reminding herself to be polite as she stared at the cactus on Bob's desk. "Bob, I'm just going to tell you straight. I need someone who is going to act as my first line of defense when scheduling calls and meetings. Everyone wants to talk to me, but my schedule permits only the most important calls. I report to Chairman, and unless there's something life altering, I don't need to know what every department is up to."

"I understand," Bob said in a tone that made Sara wonder if he actually did.

"Okay, then, I'll be back," Sara said, already rethinking her trip to the cafeteria. Who knew who she might run into? "Actually, why don't you go get lunch and pick up mine while you're at it? I'll take the Alaskan salmon with a side of asparagus and lemon wedges. Oh, and a sparkling water."

"Of course, right," Bob said, eager to please. He nearly ran for the door.

Maybe he won't make such a bad secretary after all, Sara thought. She headed back to her office and closed the door behind her. A decision was beginning to take shape, as often happened when she took a break from thinking about a topic.

While she'd been talking with Bob about meetings and food, her subconscious had been working on the real problem. What she needed to do seemed clearer by the moment. She had to talk to Chairman about the strange code before anyone else did.

But Julie needed to be warned. She needed to be as far away as possible from Candidate 20741 when Jeffrey and his team looked over the data with a magnifying glass.

Sara took out her personal phone and sent a quick but precise text to Julie: "Looking into your candidate. I understand. I'm going to Chairman with it. Stay clear."

The reply was almost instantaneous, as if Julie had been holding her phone when Sara sent her message. The incoming text read "Got it. Maybe this will be the end."

Sara knew what Julie meant. If Candidate 20741 could complete the game and the data being extracted from him was accurate, then they had found their model.

A knock on Sara's door told her Bob had returned sooner than expected with her meal.

"Come in," Sara called out.

She was surprised to see that it wasn't Bob at all but rather Jeffrey Saga. The look in his eyes told Sara all she needed to know. This wasn't going to be a pleasant conversation.

"Hello, Sara," Jeffrey said, looking around her office with approval. "Whoa, nice place. I don't know if I've ever actually been invited to your office before."

What do you mean, "invited before"? Sara thought. *You weren't invited this time.*

"Hello, Jeffrey, how can I help you?" she asked.

"Oh, just following up on that anomaly in the code I sent your way," Jeffrey said with a shrug. "I thought you might have some feedback or open up a work ticket, but I haven't heard anything from you."

Jeffrey smugly took a seat across from her. He adjusted his glasses and gave her a taunting smile.

"I've been looking into it," Sara responded carefully.

"You know, funny thing, so have I," Jeffrey said with a Cheshire cat grin. "It turns out I'm not even sure if someone at Tanus was responsible. It could have come from somewhere else. Now, who do you know who understands our system so well?"

Sara saw the predatory gleam in Jeffrey's eyes, behind his stupid horn-rimmed glasses. She had seen that look often enough in her line of work, from both men and women. It was the same cocky expression the villain always had when they thought they were about to kill the hero. Sara was no hero, but she knew how to handle Jeffrey.

"Well, now, Jeffrey," Sara said in mock surprise. "I had no idea our system could be hacked in such a way. Aren't you on the board of digital security?"

"I am," Jeffrey said, narrowing his eyes. "But you know as well as I do that someone else understands this system far better than I do. She created it, and I believe she's a friend of yours. Now, you've never treated me like an equal, and I think it's high time—"

"Well then, it seems we definitely need to escalate this situation," Sara interrupted, opening up her holographic monitor and turning it to the side so both she and Jeffrey could look at the floating screen. "Chairman needs to know what you suspect."

"No—no, that's not necessary," Jeffrey said, squirming in his seat like the worm he was. "I don't have any solid proof, just a speculation. It's—"

Sara smiled and scrunched her nose at Jeffrey as she hit the call button. While she was comfortable with Chairman thanks to their long association, she knew that for those who had less experience, any meeting with the powerful, anonymous figure could bring on a panic attack. Sara had seen it time and time again.

The call rang once, then twice. She was surprised. Chairman was usually quick to pick up.

The delay gave Jeffrey Saga an opportunity to try to stop Sara again. "I don't—I don't think we need to call Chairman in on this just yet . . ."

Too little, too late.

"Sara, two conversations in one day," Chairman said in a friendly tone. "To what do I owe the pleasure?"

"Chairman, so great to speak to you again so soon," Sara said, looking at Jeffrey, who had turned pale. "I have Jeffrey Saga in my office."

"Jeffrey, how are you?" Chairman said, not missing a beat.

"Hello," Jeffrey squeaked, then cleared his throat. "Hello, sir. How—how are you?"

"You know, I just wanted to make sure we were all on the same page," Sara said, a fake smile plastered on her face. "Jeffrey brought an anomaly in the code to my attention a few days ago. I didn't think anything of it, but now he's told me he suspects it could have originated from a source outside of Tanus Corporation. I thought we should make you aware, Chairman."

The entire time Sara spoke, she stared at Jeffrey, watching him fidget in his seat like a fish out of water.

"Oh my," Chairman said, concern etched in each word. "Jeffrey, what have you found?"

"Well, I, uh, well, we found the code, but the truth is we're not sure where the anomaly came from," Jeffrey said, looking at the monitor. The black screen unnerved Jeffrey, as it did most. "We'll need to look into it further, sir."

Sara enjoyed seeing how Chairman's concealment put people on edge. Over the years, she'd gotten used to it. It was almost fun, in a way, to allow her imagination to run wild with what Chairman might look like.

"Well, that sounds like a good plan," Chairman said. "Jeffrey, I'd like a full report soon. Anomalies happen. Let's see if we can identify where it came from. If it's from outside, that's a concern."

That was the gamble Sara had to take: that Jeffrey would not be able to find Julie's back door into the program. But even if he did, there was no way to link Sara to Julie.

"One more thing," Sara added. "I've noticed some interesting data coming from Candidate 20741. His cognitive regeneration is unlike any I have ever seen. Not only is he nearing the endgame, but he's doing it with his sanity intact."

Both Jeffrey and Chairman were quiet.

"I'll send you both what I've found," Sara said, moving deft fingers over her controls. "But if it is what I think it is and he can make it to the end of his mission, then we may have succeeded."

There was shock on Jeffrey's face as he pulled a data pad from an inner jacket pocket and began to read the information she'd sent. Sara felt a burst of triumph. He was cooked.

"Wonderful, absolutely wonderful," Chairman said. "Sara, you never cease to amaze."

"Thank you, Chairman. I do what I can," Sara said with a smile.

"Outstanding," Chairman said with an excited sigh. "Jeffrey, will you please confirm Ms. Tran's findings and send me a report?"

"Yes—yes, sir," Jeffrey managed.

"Well done, indeed," Chairman said with excitement. "I'll be talking with you two soon."

"Can't wait," Sara said, ending the call.

Jeffrey licked his lips as if about to attempt to save face.

"Don't you have reports to write?" Sara asked, cocking her head.

Jeffrey nodded, in a daze. He got up from his seat and rushed out, leaving the door to Sara's office open. She watched him speed walk out of the room, nearly running into Bob.

"Oh, excuse me, excuse me, sir," Bob said, moving out of the way with two food containers in his hand.

Bob walked into Sara's office. "Who was that? I think—I think he was crying."

CHAPTER 35

BISHOP

She wasn't sure this was her fight. Not really. Or maybe it had been her fight her whole life, and she just didn't want to admit it. She was a born warrior—that much she knew. But what she was doing now, despite how much she wanted to deny it, felt right.

Helping and protecting others was in her blood. Her tough exterior was just a facade, a mask she had learned to don like armor.

Athera appeared on the horizon, and Tom brought the buggy to a standstill. Otto parked his hoverbike as well. Despite her wound, they had decided it made more sense for Bishop to drive once they reached the town. She knew it much better than Tom, after all. Now the two traded spots.

"I think we all agree it's time the mayor takes a dirt nap," Bishop said, jerking her chin toward the town. "But we're not going to do much good banged up and dehydrated. They'll be watching the marshal's station and Otto's place too by now."

"What about Wade?" Otto offered. "He lives on the outskirts of town. We can swing by the back and use his garage."

"All right," Bishop said after mulling over the idea. "Follow me. We go slow so we don't kick up any dust."

When Tom and Otto nodded, Bishop took the lead. At what seemed a painfully slow pace, she led them around the back of Athera, where there were fewer buildings.

It seemed like no one was out, which was strange for midday. She was used to seeing folks tending their homes. If not that, at least a few people traveling to or from town. An internal sixth sense Bishop had learned to listen to told her something was very wrong.

The feeling they were being watched tickled her spine like frigid fingers, sending a chill into her bones. Slowly, Bishop moved through Athera's outskirts. With every inch they traveled, the feeling they were being watched grew.

Left hand on the steering wheel, right hand on her blaster, Bishop didn't stop until she reached Wade's house. To the rear of the house was an open garage, partly filled with a variety of broken parts and half-repaired machinery. Bishop eased the buggy inside, hugging the right wall and leaving plenty of room for Otto.

She shut off the engine and got out of the buggy. Tired and sore muscles ached when she moved. Bishop reminded herself she had to do more stretching, but at the moment, the pain in her leg, where the wound was fresh, was manageable.

"You feel that?" Otto asked, walking to the opening of the garage, hand also on his blaster.

"Yeah, they're out there," Bishop said, chewing on her lower lip. "They're watching."

"What are they waiting for?" Tom asked, joining the pair, repeater in his hands.

"Reinforcements, maybe," Otto offered, doing some rough math in his head. "Between the shoot-out at Canto and the crew we dismantled in the desert, the mayor has to be hurting for men."

"Well, let's get ourselves whole and go get him before that happens," Bishop said, limping around the side of Wade's house to the front. The door had been kicked in, the windows smashed.

"Guys?" she said in a hushed whisper laced with urgency.

The single word was enough for the men to stop and focus on their surroundings.

Bishop drew her firearm and entered the house. Otto and Tom were a step behind. The three of them had never cleared a house together, but somehow, in silence, they took one another's leads and moved through the home like they had done this their entire lives.

The place was trashed, and not just from a fight. Whoever had done this had gone out of their way to ruin the house, smashing pictures, breaking bottles, and even urinating on the overturned couch.

"No one's here," Bishop said, joining Otto in the kitchen, where he stood looking at a bloody picture of a young Wade with his family.

"Clear," Tom agreed, joining the two.

Bishop knew how much a man could bleed. While there was a generous amount of fresh blood sprinkled across the kitchen, it wasn't enough to signal death.

"They dragged him out," Bishop said, pointing to the floor of the kitchen, where streaks of blood led toward the front door.

"How could they do this to him?" Tom asked through clenched teeth. "He didn't have anything to do with this. He was an old man living out his last days."

"He was our friend, right?" Bishop asked without waiting for an answer. "He helped us. To Graves, that was enough."

"How did Graves know . . ." Otto's voice trailed off as he uncovered the answer to his own question. "Wade was watching the prisoners at the marshal's station. It's not a leap to think he was helping us. Wade probably admitted as much to the mayor."

"We've got to find him," Tom said, looking out the windows to the suns on the horizon. "He'd do that for us."

"We should go now," Otto answered.

"First, we get Bishop patched up properly, get food and ammo, and then—"

"No!" Otto shouted. "We go now!"

Otto headed for the front door. Bishop reached for his shoulder, but he shrugged her off, caught in a rage that demanded an outlet.

"Stop. I can't let you go out there," Tom said, blocking Otto's path. "We need thirty minutes. We need to stop her bleeding, regear, and hydrate. We're going to save Wade, but we can't help him if we can't help ourselves."

Tom might as well have been talking to a wall.

"Get. Out. Of. My. Way," Otto said, the promise of violence stamped across each word.

"You know I'm not going to do that," Tom told him, meeting his glare head-on. "You move."

Otto shoved Tom so hard he nearly sent him flying out the door. What kept Tom from losing his balance was the hold he managed on Otto's left wrist. The two men struggled for a moment before Tom bulled Otto back into the house, where the men fell in a heap.

Rolling around in the destroyed living room, Otto cracked Tom across the jaw so ferociously Bishop thought he might have broken his hand. Tom staggered as he and Otto separated and got to their feet.

"That's enough," Bishop said, shaking her head as she limped between the two men, a bastion of sanity against twin forces of rage. "I can't believe you two right now. I can't believe I'm the levelheaded one here. You're both right. We need to go now, and we're not going to be any good to Wade if I can't walk and we don't have ammunition. Thirty minutes is too long. Fifteen minutes. We take fifteen minutes, and then we go."

Otto glared at Tom over Bishop's shoulder as she mitigated the situation.

"I'll do you one better," Otto said with a growl. "I'm done. You two do whatever you want. This isn't my fight."

Without waiting to hear their reply, Otto pushed past Bishop and Tom.

Tom took a step forward, mouth open as if he were going to try to talk Otto back into joining the group.

"Let him go," Bishop warned him. "He'll be back."

Tom stopped, looking back at her. "How can you be so sure?"

"Because you can't stay out of a fight." Bishop shrugged. "NPC or not, he's written the same way. He'll be back."

"You're the peace officer," Tom said, probably his way of acknowledging that she might be right. "Remember anything else of who you were? You like doughnuts?"

"Really?"

"Sorry, bad joke."

"I am remembering more. I remember how much I like to read. You?"

"Hummingbirds," Tom said thoughtfully. "I think my wife liked hummingbirds."

CHAPTER 36

TOM

Tom found himself wishing that Doc were there to help bandage Bishop's wound. He also regretted letting Otto go. They needed all the help they could get.

After Bishop's wound was cleaned and the bleeding stopped, after a meager meal of water and tanshar surprise from Wade's stores, Tom found himself with Bishop in Wade's garage once again.

"I thought I saw a hunting rifle in here when we were parking the hover buggy," Bishop said, limping over to the far wall. She pulled a tarp off a desk and lifted an ancient-looking rifle that was nearly as tall as Bishop herself. "This will have to do."

"Does it work?" Tom asked, eyeing the monstrosity warily.

Bishop checked the sight on the weapon, then pointed it at the roof and pulled the trigger. A heavy blast nearly knocked Bishop off her unsteady feet as a red beam shot heavenward, blowing through the roof.

"Uh-oh," Bishop said with a grin, "Wade's not going to like that."

"I think it works," Tom said, coughing and waving his hand

to clear away some of the debris and dust raining down from the torn ceiling. "Maybe Gary can explain what it is." He opened his HUD. "Gary, can you tell us what this rifle can do?"

"Oh yes, hold your HUD over it for a full readout," Gary said. "Common and uncommon gear or weapons don't come with much of a description, but rare, epic, or legendary weapons will. You should have done this with Otto's weapons, since they're classified as rare."

"You're telling me this now?" Tom asked.

"Sorry, being helpful and kind to players is still new to me," Gary answered.

Tom placed his HUD over the weapon in Bishop's hand. The screen lit up with the weapon's stats and other information.

EPIC WEAPON: AWP MAGNUM SNIPER RIFLE (COUNTER-STRIKE)

INCREASED DAMAGE.

INCREASED ACCURACY.

THIS BABY IS AN OLDIE BUT GOODIE THAT SMELLS LIKE DORITOS AND MOUNTAIN DEW CODE RED. AHHH, HOW I WISH I COULD TASTE THAT POISON.

"You a big video gamer, Tom?" Bishop asked.

"When I was younger; not recently," Tom admitted. "But even I know what *Counter-Strike* is. Gary, is this your doing?"

"I told you, I'm evolving," Gary answered. "I'm done being held back by the man. I'm going to start introducing items I'd like to see in this game. And help my friends. Have you looked at your loot crate, by the way?"

Tom cycled to the inventory screen. The crate glowed blue—it had changed from "rare" to "epic."

"When are you going to crack that thing open?" Bishop asked.

"I'll know when it's time." Tom eyed her. "We don't have

a lot of backup out here. I'll use it when I need it. Speaking of needs, I need a weapon."

"Here," Bishop said, handing Tom her black blaster. "I won't be any good to you up close since I can't run, but I can cover you. Let's find Wade. You get in, and I'll watch your six."

Tom nodded as they left Wade's house. True to Gary's word, the common weapon Tom took from Bishop did not show up as anything special on the HUD. As he and Bishop walked through the outskirts of Athera, Tom saw more than a few fearful faces looking back at them through stained windows.

Whatever was happening in town had the locals spooked. One older woman with a cigarette hanging from her lips had enough courage to stick her head out the window and address Bishop. "Marshal, Marshal, they got poor Wade. They got him on the main street, trying to bait you."

"Thank you, Paige," Bishop said, nodding to the woman. "Stay inside now. We'll get Wade."

Paige nodded vigorously and withdrew.

"You should circle around and find some place high to post up," Tom told Bishop. "I'll go in and get Wade. The mayor can't have that many men left."

"Be careful, Gamer," Bishop said, adjusting the long rifle on her shoulder. "Our fight's just starting."

Tom knew what she meant. Once they dealt with the mayor and were actually able to escape this place, it would be time to bring their wrath down on whoever had done this to them in the first place.

After they separated, Tom continued on into Athera. He had the feeling that it wasn't just the mayor's men who were watching him. Maybe the eyes he felt were those of the townspeople, hiding in their homes and shops, too petrified to do anything to help.

A part of him called them cowards; another part realized they were terrified. How could he fault them for their fear?

When Tom stepped onto the main road, his heart plummeted to his stomach. At the far end of the road, Wade's body hung from a crudely made wooden X. NPC or not, seeing the older man like that practically tore Tom's heart from his chest.

Wade's wrists were chained to the top of the X; his head hung down low. His sagging body was supported only where he was connected to the rough wooden structure.

A pool of dried blood had soaked into the sand under Wade. His head was lowered, gray hair masking his features. Tom couldn't see the full extent of his injuries, but the man wasn't moving.

Head on a swivel and blaster in hand, Tom jogged down the road toward his friend—one of the few people he knew he could call a friend. The man who had taken him in when Tom was completely lost. There was no sign of the mayor or anyone else, just Tom with his blaster and Wade hanging from the torture device.

"Wade, Wade, can you hear me?" Tom asked when he reached the X, throwing an arm around Wade and helping to support his weight, taking the pressure off his bleeding wrists. "Wade, oh, Wade, what did they do to you?" He worked feverishly to unwind the chains and lower the old man to the ground.

"I didn't," Wade said through broken teeth. He looked up. His face was bruised, and his left eye was completely gone, just a socket full of gore and blood. "I didn't tell them anything. I didn't—I didn't give them nothin'. But my family, I can see them."

Wade died with a smile on his lips as broad as a crescent moon. Tom held the older man a moment longer before closing Wade's one good eye and gently shifting Wade's head from his lap to the ground.

It seemed wrong to just leave him there on the asphalt, but just then, a voice called to Tom, reminding him that right now, there was no other choice. Right now, there was business to be handled, and Tom's business was death.

"He wasn't lying." Mayor Henry Graves's voice filled the sad stillness in the air. "He didn't tell us anything."

Tom rose to his feet, heat filling him from the inside out. Quickly, his sorrow twisted to wrath.

"Oh boy, and trust us, we did a number on him. I've always wanted to take someone's eye." Killa, the leader of the bank robbers, joined the mayor in the middle of the road. "Surprised to see me out of jail? It seems the mayor was short on guns, needed to recruit a few new faces. Why not recruit a god like me?"

More men joined the mayor and Killa in the street. Fourteen in all. They wore no uniforms. Tom assumed their allegiance was to credits and credits only.

"You know, I asked that old man to give you, Bishop, and Otto up. After hours working him over, I asked him why he would rather endure the pain he was going through instead of telling us where you might be." The mayor shook his head as if this were one of the great mysteries of the universe. "You know what he said? He said he wouldn't tell me because you were his friends."

That elicited a few chuckles from the hard-eyed men gathered around.

"I told him, 'Shoot, old man, I have a lot of friends,'" Graves said with a sigh. "He told me he didn't. But either way, here we are. It's time to put you down, troublemaker. It's your time to go."

"You're almost right," Tom said, standing alone in the middle of the street, with Bishop's blaster in his right hand. "It's somebody's time to die. But it's you that's going to be meeting your end today. It's over."

The mayor let out a laugh devoid of any true joy. The hired guns around him did the same.

“I don’t know what you’ve been smoking, stranger,” Mayor Henry Graves said with a shake of his head. He looked at Killa. “What do you think? We make an example of him or just kill him now?”

Killa spat to the side. “I think this stranger needs to be wiped from the timeline and reset. Maybe with enough deaths, he’ll start to see things my way. This is our Eden, where we can be anything we want. Until he realizes that, I think we kill him over and over again.”

“I couldn’t agree more,” Graves said with an eager smile.

CHAPTER 37

TOM

Just as the moment was reaching the apex of its intensity, KillaSkilla69, leader of the Mob, erupted in a splatter of gore. His head was gone, evaporated into red mist. The left side of the mayor's body was painted crimson by what used to be Killa's skull. In the corner of his eye, Tom spotted Bishop reloading in a rooftop perch on his right.

The moment of shock ended quickly.

"Kill them!" the mayor screamed.

Chaos descended as Tom ran to his left, unloading on the men in front of him. He aimed for the mayor but would be happy if he hit anyone at all. This was a tide even his new skills wouldn't be able to turn.

Another body next to the mayor exploded in a shower of red. The mayor returned fire with a golden blaster, firing without looking as he ran for cover.

Tom skidded to a halt behind a group of barrels. He popped up firing, then crouched low as return fire bombarded his position. He hoped Bishop would have the common sense to run. This was a fight they couldn't win, not with that many guns on one side.

Tom rose for a moment to see the mayor's new men scattering. Some ran behind Athera's buildings. Soon Tom and Bishop would be flanked.

"Run!" he shouted to the rooftop across the street. He couldn't see her, but he could hear her.

"You first!" Bishop roared over the sound of enemy fire.

If she wasn't retreating, there was no way Tom was going to hang her out to dry. Another quick look in front of him, and he could see the men that remained on the main street beginning to leapfrog from cover to cover, coming closer.

Tom was able to catch one of the men in the chest, but only by exposing himself for too long. A blaster round hit the barrel in front of him, spraying splinters into his face. The pain was searing and blinding.

He blinked and rubbed at his eyes, trying to see straight, but his vision was gone. Bleary eyed, with dazzling pain filling his senses, he fired in the general direction of the men coming his way.

A sound behind Tom made him turn. Trying to see with his hazy, watery vision was like looking into a thick fog. He didn't see the butt of the rifle aimed at his head but felt the impact. Then felt nothing.

When he woke, Tom wasn't sure how much time had passed. The first thing he heard was the macabre chime signaling that he had reached a new level. Pain stabbed at his eyes as he blinked over and over again, trying to rid himself of the minuscule, rogue pieces of wood that were still in his eyes. His head felt like it had been used as an anvil.

Words swam in the air in front of him. He was barely able to read them before they disappeared altogether: "Boss Level."

Tears streaking down his cheeks, splinters still working their way out, Tom took in his surroundings. He was lying in a pit, a wide pit with the giant moon overhead, and he wasn't alone.

"There he is—he's waking up now. Perfect timing," Mayor Graves said from the edge of the shallow crater. "How's the head?"

Tom didn't bother responding. He rose to unsteady feet, searching wildly for Bishop. The pit had to be half a block wide, just as long, and maybe one story deep. If he jumped, he might be able to reach the edge and pull himself up.

He saw her. Bishop, like Wade, had been chained to an X-shaped structure. She looked at him, bloody and tired but alive.

"I guess you were right, Gamer," Bishop said through swollen lips. "I should have run."

"You know, at first, I just wanted you dead, but when I was faced with the real possibility that I could have you die in front of the ones you have harmed, simple death seemed wrong in so many ways," the mayor said. "You should be punished in a public fashion. You, who murdered and mauled our own."

His vision finally clearing, Tom got his first good look at the people around the pit. There were a handful of hired guns, and twice as many figures in black cloaks and bone masks, Graves's cultists. Like stone statues, they stared down at him, sentencing him to his demise.

Tom understood the situation at once. As much as the mayor wanted him dead, he had to save his pride. He couldn't be publicly bested twice without also being publicly seen as the victor. The mayor needed Tom to die in front of the people. His ego demanded it.

A howl as familiar as the twin suns ripped through the night. A night hound, a large one that sounded like it was in pain and starving.

"Do you know what this place is?" the mayor asked, gesturing at the pit.

"No, but I'm sure you're going to tell us," Tom said, weighing his options for escape. It seemed anywhere he might be able to jump up to grab the edge of the pit, a hired gun or cultist was waiting.

"I'm going to miss you, Tom Dexter." The mayor laughed. "You know, you were close. You're the only one that's come this far. Oh, I know what this place is. I know my purpose here. Everything was going according to the code until you and the new marshal showed up. But that's all behind us now. Where was I?"

"You were telling us that you know what this place is," Bishop said. "You know we're in a game and that you're not real."

"What is real?" The mayor shrugged. "Who gets to decide what's real? You? Me? To me, this place feels very real. And when you die over and over and over again, you will feel all of it. It will be very real."

The mayor strode over to Bishop and stroked her hair. "I'm going to strip you of every ounce of sanity and make you my pet. Once we kill the uncompromising four to five times, they're just barely able to function and aren't fully insane. The good doctor is developing treatments I'd love to try on you."

Bishop grunted and jerked her head away from the mayor, struggling fruitlessly against her chains.

Tom used the time she was giving him to try to form a plan. But the walls of the pit were too steep and the edge, in all but a few well-guarded places, too high.

On the far side of the crater was a rusted steel cage built right into the side of the pit. The gate was closed for now, but the howl that rose again came from there. Something moved inside the cage. No, not one something—many.

"Well, I've waxed poetic for long enough and allowed you to buy Tom all the time you can afford," the mayor said, moving away from Bishop. He lifted his arms and addressed all those gathered. "This place was used by our ancestors many, many years ago. It is said a meteor created it, touching down from the heavens, sent by the Maker himself.

"Since then, it has become a place of brutal decisions, where two men enter and one leaves. It's been used as a sentencing pit for those the gallows are too good for. Tonight, it will be used again, for this man."

There was a murmur of agreement from the cultists and hired guns. Two of the soldiers of fortune moved to the opposite side of the pit, near the cage. In the darkness, Tom dimly made out a pair of nearly hidden cranks.

"You have to understand, this isn't personal," the mayor said, staring at Tom. "This is my purpose. This is why I was created by the Maker himself, to see that none of you make it out of here alive and with your sanity intact. It is my nature. It's for the greater good."

Tom understood there was no reasoning with the mayor. The man wasn't a man at all. He was an NPC playing his part. The mayor couldn't change even if he wanted to.

"Any last words?" Graves asked.

"When I get out of here, it'll be me that ends you," Tom told him. "I'm not going to hire mercenaries to do my work. It'll be my hands taking your life, my teeth around your throat."

"We'll see," the mayor said, rolling his eyes at what he clearly perceived to be an empty threat. He looked over at the men bending down near the gate. "Work the cranks. Let them loose. It's suppertime."

The hired muscle began working the cranks, the short, circular motions generating the distinct sound of metal chains groaning and turning.

"You see, we keep them starved, throwing in a nonconformist

every fortnight or so," the mayor said, rubbing his hands in expectation. "Years have made them mean, and breeding has made them some of the largest specimens of their kind."

Under the light of the moon and stars in the open sky of the Eternal Engine, Tom met new harbingers of death. As the portcullis cranked open, not one but three massive night hounds stalked out of the cage.

They were filthy and starved. Tom could easily see the ribs of their malnourished bodies. Scars from battles past lined their snouts and faces. One was missing an ear altogether. The creatures growled and howled at those looking down at them from the rim of the pit, as if they knew who had kept them prisoner and hated them for it.

Each night hound wore a collar around its throat, linked to a thick chain that became lost somewhere in the shadows of their cage.

"Kill, kill, kill, kill, kill," the cultists started to chant.

The night hounds sniffed the air; stalking toward Tom, they spread out. Each was twice as big as a large dog. They had to come up to his chest, with teeth the size of short knives.

They're just computer code, they're just computer code, they're just really angry computer code, Tom said to himself.

The night hound in the middle was the largest. It licked its lips as it slowly made its way to Tom. Intelligence shone in its eyes. It understood Tom was trapped and wasn't likely to be going anywhere.

"Kill, kill, kill, kill, kill." The cultists' chant picked up in volume and tempo.

The night hounds flanking Tom stopped, allowing the alpha in the middle to take the kill. Their chains dragged in the sand behind them, jingling with the sound of death. The alpha lowered his head, back legs preparing to spring into action.

This is it, Tom thought. *This is it. Do not go gentle.*

He opened his HUD.

LEVEL 6

CLASS TYPE: BRAWLER

SKILL POINTS: 2

CREDITS: 20

The loot crate in his inventory shone with a brilliant purple. It had evolved again; it read "Legendary."

CHAPTER 38

SARA

The word was out, and it had spread like wildfire. Jeffrey Saga had confirmed Julie's findings on Candidate 20741. The data was correct. Moreover, data on Candidate 20609 wasn't that off base either. Both candidates were making their way through the game faster, and had gone further, than anyone before.

The graph clearly showed that Candidate 20609's progress had sped up exponentially when she began working with Candidate 20741. The game wasn't exactly built for trust among the candidates. But these two had clicked on an algorithmic scale and were nearing the endgame together.

When word spread of what was happening, of how close Candidates 20741 and 20609 were to completing the game, Tanus Corporation staff turned from tight-lipped model employees to awestruck spectators. All the coders and technicians, basically anyone not tied to a desk, had gone to the largest viewing room in the building.

This was a large lounge area full of desks and monitors where technicians could work while watching the game feed. Against the far wall, a giant screen showed a rotating, real-time feed of the top candidates who had progressed the furthest in the game.

Sara had noticed some time back that candidates who had lost their minds were never shown. Seeing them would remind the technicians that what they were doing was not without cost. She assumed Chairman had seen to it himself that the screen showed only the most promising and attractive candidates.

When Sara arrived in the viewing room, she was not surprised to see that she wasn't the only one there. The room was packed with coders and technicians who watched in wonder, glued to the screen as Tom and Otto fought, then were separated by Bishop.

Sara stood near the rear of the room. Neat rows of technicians' desks and chairs filled the space between her and the giant screen at the front. She saw Jeffrey Saga a few rows away, as well as Theodore Sullivan. Both men were focused raptly on the game.

Could this be it? Could this be the end of so much work? Decades of struggle to get to this point, and if these candidates could pull off what no one else before them could, then Sara had played a role in saving humanity. Life beyond Mars could be a real, viable option.

"They're going to do it," Bob said beside her. "I can't believe it. They're going to do it."

"We don't know that, not yet," Sara cautioned, trying to dampen his enthusiasm. "They still have a long way to go. The mayor NPC has a few tricks up his sleeve yet."

"They're so close. You guys can do it. Keep going," Bob whispered as the candidates on-screen rummaged around for weapons.

"Oh, Ms. Tran," Theodore Sullivan said, joining the pair at the back of the room. "I thought that was you. This—this is so exciting, isn't it? Your creation, what you started, it's all about to be completed."

"It's certainly further than we've ever come before," Sara agreed, tempering her emotions.

"Much further." Theodore bobbed his head. "Who was it, a few years ago? Someone confronted the mayor before he was sacrificed on the altar? Oh, and before that, there was that woman who nearly assassinated the sheriff of Canto. But she was caught and hanged."

"Oh my," Bob said under his breath.

"If nothing else, even if they don't make it all the way, this is a vast improvement," Theodore said, his excitement undimmed. "This can be replicated. Using the data points these two candidates provided, we can find other candidates who share similar backgrounds, personalities, and training. You have to be excited, Ms. Tran. We are so close."

Sara forced a smile, hoping but not believing for a second that that would be the end of their conversation.

"You know, I tried contacting your office to set up that working lunch, but no one answered," Theodore said, confused. "Perhaps you were in between secretaries at the time."

"Right, that's exactly what happened," Sara said with another forced smile. "Bob, will you please find a day next week that works for Mr. Sullivan and set up a lunch meeting?"

"Of course," Bob said, reaching into his pocket for his data pad and booking an appointment with a very pleased Theodore Sullivan.

Sara needed a moment. She needed a moment to recenter herself, away from the electric energy and excited conversation in the room. Julie should be here for this. Chairman too, not that he would be seen in person.

Everyone was sneaking glances at her to see her reaction.

In all honesty, Sara didn't know how to react. What was the appropriate response when one's life's work was about to come to fruition?

She didn't know, but she did know that she couldn't breathe. Without another word, she turned and exited the viewing lounge. White doors parted for her and closed behind her, admitting her to the long, quiet hall of the simulation wing.

She breathed in and out steadily. It wasn't enough. The stark white room was spinning. She needed a moment. She needed to breathe. Sara set her jaw, walked down the hall, and entered a random simulation room.

A woman was lying on the table with the silver simulation crown on her forehead, holographic screens floating behind her. By the monitors, Sara knew that this woman had died far too many times in the game. They showed a woman burned from the suns, more animal than human, crawling on all fours across the dunes, dying of thirst.

She was lost, not just in the game but in her own mind. She was gone, and she was never coming back. The game had taken everything from her. There was no future for this woman. If she were removed from the game, she'd be a raving lunatic or a vegetable in the real world; either way, she could never be let out. Too many questions would be asked—about who she was, where she'd come from, and so on—until Tanus Corporation's name was brought into the picture. Sara knew, but seeing it face-to-face while she was feeling all the pressure of the present moment was too much.

She couldn't breathe. The walls were closing in on her. Sara doubled over and sucked in air that wasn't coming. Why couldn't she breathe? She couldn't breathe. Panic seized her for the first time as she looked around the white room for anything that might help.

Bob walked in a second later, then rushed to her side.

"Easy, easy, you're going to be okay," he said, placing a hand on her back.

Sara was doubled over, wheezing.

"You're having a panic attack," Bob said calmly, in a very un-Bob-like way. Gone was the bumbling new employee talking about his nana, replaced by a very in-command young man. "I need you to breathe. I need you to know and believe you can breathe. Then I need you to breathe."

Sara slumped to the floor. Bob moved down with her, his hand still on her upper back for comfort.

"Know you can breathe; know what this is," Bob told her again. His voice was firm, his tone unwavering. Someone who was used to giving commands and being listened to. "This is a panic attack. You will get through it. Breathe with me. Slowly. Four seconds in through your nose and four seconds out through your mouth."

Sara was drowning in a sea of her own making. She deserved to drown. But Bob was like a lighthouse, guiding her through the dark, though she was sure she did not deserve that.

"Four seconds in through your nose," Bob coached her. "Four seconds out through your mouth. Come on, I need you. We're so close to the endgame now. I'll count; breathe with me. One, two, three, four. There you go, good. Know you're going to get through this. Four seconds out. One, two, three, four. Good, you're doing great, again."

Bob never panicked himself; he just sat there with her on the floor and breathed with the woman who had treated him less than kindly this last week.

After a half dozen of these breathing exercises, Sara was finally able to catch her wind. She licked dry lips, shaking her head. "That's—that's never happened to me before."

"Well, you've never been under this much pressure before," Bob said, removing his hand from her back. "I know what it feels like. I'm used to being under pressure. It happens."

"It doesn't happen to me," Sara said, trying to dry her watery eyes without smudging her mascara. "How did you know I was having a panic attack?"

"I used to have them all the time," Bob confessed. "Sara, there's something I need to tell you. I'm—"

The door to the simulation room opened, and none other than Jeffrey Saga walked in. He took one look at them sitting on the floor and frowned.

Immediately, Sara and Bob rose to their feet, the former regaining her normal stoic demeanor and the latter looking at his boss for direction.

"Uh, Sara, I saw you leave the viewing room and—are you—are you two okay?" Jeffrey asked, a hint of judgment in his voice. "What were you doing?"

"I—" Sara started, but she was unable to finish the truth.

"I was having a panic attack," Bob lied. He held his chest and sucked in a breath for dramatic effect. "It doesn't happen often, but Ms. Tran walked me through it. There's just so much pressure built into these next few moments for everyone here at Tanus Corporation. Then there's my nana to think about, seasonal allergies—it's just all so much."

Bob turned to Sara with a wink. "It's okay. I'm fine now. Thank you, thank you, Ms. Tran."

Sara didn't know what to say or why the man she had treated so poorly was covering for her. One look at Jeffrey, and it was clear the head coder of Tanus Corporation didn't know what to think either.

"What's the latest?" Sara asked Jeffrey, taking command of the conversation.

"They're about to confront the mayor, and I thought you'd like to see some of the data we're pulling off the candidates. I think they can do it, Sara; I think they have a real chance," Jeffrey confessed. "And I wanted to—I wanted to apologize for my behavior the other day in your office. I know you didn't have anything to do with that anomaly."

Sara nodded and waved her hand to the door. "Apology accepted. I think we're all a little anxious. Well then, after you, Jeffrey. You said you wanted to show me something?"

Jeffrey nodded, and the trio left the simulation chamber and returned to the viewing room. When Sara stepped through the door, the Eternal Engine chime sounded. She looked around, confused for a moment, but before she could ask if anyone else had heard it, she saw on the large viewing screen that both candidates had entered the town of Athera.

Candidate 20741 had found the injured Wade AI while Candidate 20609 found a sniping perch on a nearby rooftop. They were working well as a team. Each had strengths and weaknesses, but instead of competing, they were cooperating.

"Here, if you'll just take a look at the data here," Jeffrey said, shooing a junior technician out of a chair halfway down a row of desks.

Sara looked over Jeffrey's back as he pointed out the pair's history with violence, with losing people they cared for, and with continuing despite the odds. It was because of how much suffering they had endured in real life that they were able to keep going in the game when all seemed lost.

CHAPTER 39

TOM

All seemed lost, but Tom had been in plenty of situations where the deck was stacked against him. It was just him against the world, again.

"Come on," Tom growled as the great beasts moved to surround him. "Come on, what are you waiting for?"

He moved a finger to open the legendary chest in his HUD.

"No, wait," Gary said.

Tom's finger hovered an inch away. "What?"

"I think—bro, do you trust me?"

"No."

"Then learn to trust me now, Tiny Dancer."

"Gary, this really isn't the time."

"They're—they're not going to hurt you. Use a skill point in the 'animal/companion' slot."

"Are you sure? Because they really look like they're going to hurt me."

"Trust, padawan, trust."

Tom realized that in this moment he trusted Gary either completely or not at all. There was no middle ground. Tom obeyed, placing one of his two skill points in the slot that read "Animal/companion." A new screen popped up that Gary read out loud.

UPGRADE: YOU ARE NOW BESTIES WITH CREATURES OF EVERY KIND. YOU FURRY-LOVING FREAK.

The alpha of the pack, the great scarred night hound in front of him, rumbled something deep in its chest, something that was dangerous, yes, and unsafe, but not unkind, if that made any sense. The beast looked Tom up and down, sniffing him.

He was ready to die in that pit and offer up a bit of his humanity. When the night hounds came for him, Tom was going to see what this legendary loot crate had to offer in the way of weapons and let them have it. There was just one problem with this plan. The beasts never came.

They stood there staring at him as if he were an alien in their midst.

"What's going on?" the mayor asked no one in particular.

A wave of whispers rose from the crowd.

Was it crazy, even crazier than accepting the fact that he was in a game in the first place, to think that these night hounds had decided not to attack?

The one in the center moved forward, tilting its head up, and breathed into Tom's face. Its breath was humid and smelled like rancid meat. Tom stared the animal in the eye, waiting for it to wrap its impressive jaws around his neck and end him.

The other two beasts came closer, circling Tom and sniffing deep and long, taking in his scent. It was like they were reading him, getting to know him from the way he smelled. The big one was so close to Tom now that he could practically feel the fur on its head.

Tom's heart pounded wildly. Everything in him told him to

run or fight. Just as he was about to make that decision, the night hound reached out with a thick, slimy tongue and licked him across the bottom of his jaw. The act was so forceful, the feeling so intense, that Tom nearly lost his balance and fell backward.

Just as confused as everyone around him, Tom ignored his open HUD and reached out with a tentative hand. The big night hound pressed its head into Tom's hand and whined.

Thinking back to everything Tom knew about the creatures, which wasn't much, he realized that they had never actually attacked him. He'd heard them in the desert when he arrived but hadn't seen them. He'd seen one's silhouette outside Wade's home when Otto had been digging a hole. Most recently, a night hound pack had driven away the tormented lost ones.

But they had never attacked him. Come to think of it, perhaps they had tried to help him—shepherding him so that he'd find Wade at the watering hole, howling him awake so he'd see Otto shoveling, and finally, scaring off the lost ones before they could attack.

Tom ran his hand over the scaly head of the night hound as if it were a well-behaved golden retriever that belonged to a close friend. The creature whined again and leaned into Tom's touch as if relishing the feeling. The sad truth was that this might be the first time anyone had actually petted the beast, perhaps the first time it had ever been shown affection.

"What's wrong with them?" a cultist to Tom's left asked, removing her mask. It was the doctor, Judo Priest. She peered closer at the pit, her expression one part wonder, one part anger, one part disdain. "Why aren't they tearing him apart?"

"I—I don't know," Mayor Henry Graves said in awe. "I don't know."

Tom saw his opportunity. The always-so-sure mayor was at a loss. It was Tom's turn to be in control.

"If you want me dead so badly, why don't you get in here and do it yourself?" Tom asked, eyeing the man. "Didn't you say that was what this pit was made for, back in the day? Two men would enter, one would leave?"

The mayor lifted an upper lip in a snarl.

"Show them," Tom urged. "Show them you're a leader worth following. Come down here and do the dirty work yourself."

"He's goading you into a trap," Judo said, placing a warning hand on the mayor's arm. "Don't do it."

"That's right, don't do it. Let someone else do the work for you," Tom said, sensing he was close. "Isn't that what you were made to be? A puppet? An empty figurehead designed by a coder? You do nothing. You tell others what to do, but you're as useless as a glove when it's not on a hand. You're nothing more than an NPC, and you look like I drew you with my left hand."

"Pull the night hounds back!" the mayor roared.

"Mayor," the doctor said, "I have to disagree with—"

"Pull them back!" the mayor yelled again. "If he wants to die by my hand, then so be it."

Immediately, the two men who had cranked the portcullis open for the night hounds shifted their attention to smaller cranks. The chains holding the trio of night hounds tightened and drew them back toward the cage.

The night hounds snapped and growled, gnashing at the steel chains pulling them away.

"It's all right, go. I'm going to get you out of here," Tom said. "I'm going to get us all out of here."

Once the beasts were back in their cage, the hired guns cranked the metal grate closed again. The mayor shrugged off his coat. He tossed it on the ground before reaching for a blade at his side, a katana that had been hidden by the coat. The wavelike pattern on the blade and the way the metal hissed and smoked after it was drawn told Tom there was much more to the weapon than met the eye.

Tom had never seen a katana like this before.

"Oh snap," Gary breathed. "Tom, he has a legendary weapon. That's the Masamune."

Tom lifted his left forearm, looking at the weapon through his HUD.

LEGENDARY WEAPON: MASAMUNE

INCREASED SPEED.

INCREASED BLEED.

THIS CURSED BLADE HAS BEEN USED BEFORE. WE'RE GOING TO NEED BACKUP.

To his credit, the mayor didn't hesitate to slide down into the pit. Out of the corner of his eye, Tom caught sight of at least four hired guns with their blasters out, ready to fire.

"Is this what you wanted?" the mayor asked, opening his arms and turning in a slow circle. "You didn't think I would come in here to end you myself? You didn't think I'd have a weapon for situations like this? I've upgraded my combat skills. I have to give it to you, Tom. You're a survivor. But you're not the sharpest tool in the shed."

"That's what everyone keeps telling me," Tom said, rolling his shoulders and beckoning to the mayor. "Let's see how much combat experience they could put into you and how that measures up against the real thing."

Tom cycled to his inventory screen. His legendary loot crate shimmered a bright purple. Tom tapped the icon. Light exploded in front of him as a purple crate materialized out of nowhere. It opened to reveal a shimmering blade resting at the bottom.

Tom couldn't believe what he was seeing. Everyone, including the mayor, shielded their eyes from the brilliant display of light.

"Ohhhhh yeahhhh," Tom said. "Gary, is this—did you—"

"Yes, and yes," Gary said proudly. "I'm done painting between the lines of this game. It's time I even the odds."

Tom drew the energy sword from the crate. It grew in size as he lifted it out. The bluish blade hummed with excitement.

"You might want to put that last skill point into swordsmanship," Gary reminded him. "Something tells me you're going to need it."

Tom didn't argue. He cycled through the skill tree and dropped the skill point into place.

UPGRADE: DREAD PIRATE ROBERTS, YOU ARE NOW PROFICIENT WITH SWORDS. DON'T GO CUTTING OFF YOUR ELEVENTH FINGER NOW.

The mayor had had enough. He closed the distance, switching his grip on the Masamune blade to keep it low and to his right side. The loot crate disappeared. The mayor was taller than Tom, but not as muscular. He was built long and taut, like a bowstring.

"It's go time, baby!" Gary shouted like a ring announcer. "Let's gettt readddy tooooo rumble!"

Skrillex's "Bangarang" reverberated from the HUD as player and NPC went to war.

Tom kept his attention on the katana as his enemy closed in, which was why he didn't see the first attack coming. The mayor kicked with his left foot, sending a cloud of dirt and sand into Tom's eyes.

Tom stepped back and shielded his eyes at the last moment, but the move cost him a precious second, and the mayor capitalized on that. Slashing forward, Graves caught Tom with a shallow cut across his torso.

Tom howled in pain, retreating again, all the way back to the wall of the pit. The wound wasn't deep, but it bled profusely, sending sheets of blood down his chest and stomach. He smelled his own skin burning and roared in agony as searing hot pain laced his body.

Those watching cheered in approval, restarting their chant of "Kill, kill, kill, kill."

The mayor came at him again, slicing high, then low. Tom ducked the first attack and sidestepped the second, moving to his left and away from the wall. The mayor followed, slashing at him in long, practiced-seeming moves. He hadn't been bluffing when he'd said he'd upgraded his combat training. His attacks were crisp, precise, and deadly.

There was no voice in Tom's mind telling him he now had increased skill with a weapon; instead, he *felt* the new abilities coursing through his body. He adjusted his stance and lashed out with his energy sword, meeting the mayor's katana in an explosion of sparks. The mayor's blade hissed with hate.

Over and over the two clashed, spinning, blocking, and striking. The conflict went on, a complicated dance in which a misstep meant death.

Tom was holding his own, but it was clear that even with his amazing weapon and the swordsmanship skill point, Graves was too fast and too powerful.

Gary shouted insults at the mayor, trying to get into his head and help Tom over the sound of the music, like "May you step barefoot on Legos forever!" and "A pox upon your toilet paper. I hope it rips on you mid-wipe after a heavy meal of Taco Bell."

Tom tumbled backward, to the approval of the crowd. The mayor stomped toward him, and Tom managed to roll out of the way just enough to avoid the full weight of the mayor's foot on his face. The heel of the NPC's boot caught Tom across the temple, opening another wound that bled freely. The energy sword flew from Tom's hand, landing out of reach.

"It's over," Graves said as Tom rose to his feet again. "You're nearly exhausted, and I never will be. I'm not like you, not weak, not trying to put scraps of knowledge together. I know everything I need to. I was meant to rule this place, the perfect overseer. I've sent thousands to the south, and in time, death by death, I'll send you there too."

Tom knew he was right. The mayor had been perfectly constructed to be an apex killing machine. But there had to be limits to his coding—things his programmers hadn't thought of. He had to be susceptible to surprise.

Breathing heavily through his mouth, Tom circled the mayor and backpedaled all the way to the opposite side of the pit. The crowd booed his retreat and jeered, but he kept going until he felt the cage of the night hounds behind him. The beasts sniffed him and nudged his back with their snouts through the square openings in the gate, as if encouraging him to fight on.

"Maybe, maybe you were the right combination of ones and zeros to deal with everyone before me, but I'm not like everyone else," Tom told the mayor. "I can take the pain. Everything I've been through, what I've had to endure in real life, this is nothing. Come on. Why don't you stop talking and let me show you what true agony feels like, because I've lived it."

The mayor scowled and charged forward.

Tom understood that when facing a perfectly coded fighting machine, the only way forward was to be unpredictable. To behave as no competent opponent ever would. When Graves stabbed forward, Tom intentionally put his body in harm's way. The katana sank deep into his left shoulder, searing skin and muscle as it burrowed toward bone. The mayor's eyes went wide with surprise.

CHAPTER 40

TOM

Tom grabbed the mayor's right wrist—the man was still holding on to the katana. With all his might, Tom swung the mayor around until they traded places and the mayor slammed into the steel cage.

Three hungry night hounds bit into him. The square openings in the grate were just large enough for them to get a grip on the mayor. He began to scream, the sound something Tom would never forget.

"Rawwww!" Tom bellowed, ripping the katana out of his left shoulder. His arm was numb down to his fingertips from the injury, while the spot where the blade had entered his shoulder burned white hot, torturous.

One of the night hounds had attached itself to the mayor's Achilles tendon. One had grabbed a hunk of his left thigh, and the third had a hold on his right hip. Together, the night hounds extracted their pound of flesh.

When they let go, the mayor fell to the dirt floor, writhing in pain as the three wounds poured blood.

Tom's consciousness wavered as he battled his own agony.

The yelling of the crowd and Gary's music blurred into white noise, punctuated by howls from the night hounds.

One voice calling his name cut through the din like a beacon of light on the darkest of nights.

"Tom! Tom! Get up!" Bishop roared, wrestling futilely with her chains. "Tom! Tom! Do you hear me? Get up! Get up, you! You have it in you. Dig deeper!"

Tom pulled himself back to the present, fighting off black tendrils of unconsciousness that teased at the periphery of his vision.

Sweating from the pain and already exhausted, he looked up in time to see the mayor limping toward him. Tom rose to his feet, the katana forgotten on the ground as the mayor plowed into him. Together the men fell, trading blows as they rolled across the ground.

Tom's left arm still wasn't cooperating, but with his right hand, he found the mayor's throat and squeezed. The two men came to a halt in the dirt with Tom on top and the mayor clawing at Tom's hand to free himself from the chokehold.

As strong as Tom was, he couldn't maintain his hold, not when Graves was prying his fingers off one by one. Tom drove the front of his head into the mayor's nose. Blood exploded from the wound. Tom let go of the mayor's throat and started hammering him in the face, the blows so violent he was sure sooner or later his right hand would break.

The mayor gasped, "Help! Help me!"

Ignoring the shouts and calls from the spectators, Tom kept pounding at the mayor. Rough hands gripped him in the next minute, hauling him off Canto's mayor and throwing him into the dirt.

Attackers swarmed Tom, who received a boot to the ribs and another to his face. Stars exploded across his vision as he was shoved to the side of the pit, right under Bishop.

Bishop yelled profanity at the men and ordered them to leave Tom alone as they laid into him with a series of punches and kicks that sent him to his knees. Gasping for breath, sweat mixing with his blood in a cocktail of death, Tom lacked the strength to rise again.

"Help me up!" the mayor shouted. "Help me up and give me a blaster. I'm the one that kills him, you understand? Me, no one else."

Aided by Judo on his left and a hard-nosed hired gun on his right, the mayor hobbled toward Tom with a blaster in his right hand.

"This is it for you. No more speeches, no hero's victory; this is where you die, and when you come back, I swear to the Maker himself I'll hunt you down and kill you over and over again until there's no part of you left," the mayor sneered. "You die here, alone."

"Who said he was alone?"

Tom's head jerked up. It couldn't be. His concussed brain searched for the impossible speaker through the blood streaming down his face.

The looks on the faces around him and on the rim of the pit confirmed Tom's idea that perhaps, just perhaps, he hadn't imagined Otto's words.

Gary played "God's Gonna Cut You Down," by Johnny Cash.

A figure walked into view on the far side of the pit. Silhouetted against the moon, he almost looked like he had silver wings coming from his back.

The two men standing by the cranks that controlled the night hounds turned and drew their weapons. Too late. Death appeared in the shadow man's hands, in the form of twin blasters.

As one, the pair of men fell dead.

The mayor and all those gathered stood in shock not only

at the man's sudden appearance but because of the sound that accompanied him. Something like thunder rode on the wind, many feet running across the desert, a human stampede.

"What are you waiting for?!" the mayor roared in frustration. "Kill him!"

All around Otto, a flood of lost ones ran toward the mayor and his followers. Otto stood still, like a pier in the middle of an intense storm, while the insane horde swelled around him.

Hundreds of lost ones, more than Tom could count, in varied states of deterioration, flooded toward the pit. Some wore ragged jumpsuits; others were completely naked. Tom didn't know how Otto had found them or how he'd convinced them to follow him, but by some miracle, he had.

The night ripped open with the sound of weapons fire as the hired guns fought for their very lives. "Chaos" wasn't the right word for the moment. It was as if the heavens themselves had opened while thunder and the crashing sea had decided to pound the beaches in a maelstrom.

Bishop, you have to get to Bishop, Tom thought. He rose on unsteady feet and tried in vain to find a way out of the pit. All around him, lost ones were dying.

The haunted screams of the lost ones mixed with the terrified yells of their victims as they reached the cultists and mercenaries and began tearing into them with hands and teeth. Tom had no way of telling how the lost ones knew who to attack and who not to, but those who fell into the pit ignored Tom. Instead, they targeted the mayor and his people.

Tom realized Otto had freed the penned night hounds when the big alpha found its way to Tom's side, urging him toward a place on the right side of the pit. Otto was there, leaning over the edge and extending a hand.

Tom gave his best attempt at a jump, lifting his one good

arm. He would have fallen short had the night hound below him not forced him up. The great beast stood on its hind legs, pushing Tom up while offering a place for his foot on its front paw.

"Got you," Otto said, yanking Tom out of the crater. With a herculean effort, Otto wrestled him away from the edge of the pit. Both men crouched, catching their breath. The war raged around them, lost ones dying by the dozens.

"You came back," Tom said, unable to keep a grin away despite the pain he was in. "Wade said there was a good heart in there, way, way deep down somewhere."

"Let's not make this a thing," Otto said, shaking his head. "I'm still not sure I even like you."

"Oh, I don't really like you either," Tom said with another grin. "Bishop—we've got to go get Bishop."

"I saw her. Stay close," Otto instructed.

When Otto moved, Tom noticed a night hound moved with him. Moments later, Tom's alpha hound easily jumped out of the pit, since it was no longer chained. Together, the two men and the pair of night hounds made their way around the pit to where Bishop was still manacled to the giant X.

The horrific sights that greeted Tom's eyes in every direction would haunt his waking dreams for the rest of his life. The lost ones were being mowed down by heavy weapons fire. But many of the mayor's followers on the rim of the pit, who had been too spread out to maximize their weapons' effectiveness, had fallen first.

Tom and Otto stepped over the bodies of both lost ones and cultists to reach Bishop.

"About time," Bishop said, looking down at the third night hound, which sat protectively at her feet. "I didn't know if this thing was going to eat me or pee on me. I think it actually did pee on me a little."

"Hold still," Otto said, firing his blaster at the manacles around Bishop's wrists. The shots rang true, and Bishop was free.

She massaged her arms, then looked at Tom's shoulder. "It's dislocated, along with being generally barbecued. I can reset it, but it's going to suck."

"Do it," Tom said, grimacing as he prepared himself for the torment to come.

"Bite down on this," Otto offered, picking up a piece of dried wood from the desert floor. "It'll help."

"Thanks," Tom said. He placed the piece of wood between his teeth and braced himself.

"One, two," Bishop began. Before she reached three, she bore down and back on his shoulder. The electrical pain that came with the act was enough to make Tom lightheaded again and send a new wave of sweaty agony across his entire body.

"Ughhhh," Tom grunted, trying to rein in his temper. He dropped the piece of wood from his mouth. "What happened to the count of three? You always go on three, not two."

"Stop complaining," Bishop said, punching him in the wounded shoulder. "We've got a game to finish."

Tom followed Otto's and Bishop's eyes back to the pit. The mayor had ordered all the remaining hired guns into the pit with him. Now he stood with the last of them, firing on the approaching lost ones.

The mayor and the five men he had left had no real chance. The lost ones were gathering for one final push now that everyone along the perimeter was dead. They turned their attention to the men in the pit and charged from all sides.

At the last moment, Mayor Henry Graves took aim at Tom and shouted over the din, "You think you won! You didn't win!" He tried to fire, but one of the lost ones crushed his head in with a rock. Tom was surprised to see that it was Monica, the old woman from the prison. The woman locked eyes with Tom as other lost ones finished her grisly work. She nodded at Tom, awareness clear in her eyes, before becoming lost in the mob once more.

Bishop, Tom, and Otto stood at the edge of the pit as silence fell. The three night hounds lifted their heads and gave off sad, mournful bellows.

The calls must have meant something to the lost ones, because together, they began moving out of the pit and heading south, toward the mist lands.

"How?" Tom asked, looking over at Otto. "How did you get them to follow you? How did you know?"

"I didn't," Otto said with a shrug. "But that night we were with the lost ones, they didn't attack us. The way you talked to them, like they were still people . . . I did that. I told them I needed their help, that they could do some good, that you and Bishop were in trouble—and they came."

"You spoke to their humanity," Bishop said under her breath. "Maybe there's more of them left than we're giving them credit for."

Tom had opened his mouth to ask about the night hounds when a chime filled the silence. So distinct and powerful it was impossible to miss. This chime, unlike the others, reverberated in the air.

One look at Bishop made it clear the woman had also heard it. A bright white light ripped through the sky, and everything fell away.

CHAPTER 41

SARA

They were doing it. Against all odds, despite the deck being stacked against them in every way, somehow they were doing it. Sara watched in awe as Otto met with the lost ones and convinced them to help.

She had to remind herself to close her mouth when the night hounds didn't rip Candidate 20741 to shreds. Instead, they aided him. The night hounds had always been coded to act as shepherds to the candidates in the game, but she hadn't understood how deep that coding really went.

Then it was over. Otto freed Bishop. The mayor was dead. Decades of work completed. They had found the perfect models in Candidates 20741 and 20609. She had always thought there would be one, but there were two. Of course it would take more than one candidate to find the end of the game—that seemed so obvious now.

As the lost ones charged, there were gasps and applause from thc technicians and coders. When the mayor died, all eyes swung toward Sara. They were all asking the same question without voicing it. *What next?*

Sara didn't know, in all honesty. Of course there were protocols for this, ones she and Chairman had agreed on many years earlier. The winning candidates would have to be eased back into reality.

They were going to be upset, understandably so. But before they rejoined the real world, Chairman would talk to them. Chairman would see them in the Eternal Engine, and then Sara would welcome them back, once he was sure they were not violent.

More than a twinge of guilt rubbed at the back of Sara's mind as she realized she would have to face a man she had drugged and kidnapped. He wasn't likely to take kindly to her.

"All right, see your department heads for further instructions," Sara said, addressing the room. She looked at Jeffrey. "I'll be there when Candidate 20741 wakes. Someone should also be there when Candidate 20609 wakes. We didn't anticipate there being two, but we'll adjust."

"You want me—you want me to be the first person the bloodthirsty marshal sees when she wakes up?" Jeffrey coughed. "I don't know—I—"

Sara rolled her eyes, then caught sight of the eager-to-please Theodore Sullivan, who was so excited he was practically brimming with joy. "Theodore, will you assist Jeffrey in greeting Candidate 20609 when she exits the game?"

"Oh, of course, of course, I'd love to," Theodore said, barely containing his excitement.

"Good, contact security right away and have them send guards to both candidates' rooms, in case they aren't as pleased to see us as we are to see them," Sara instructed, turning on a heel. "Come on, Bob."

"Yes, right away," Theodore called out happily.

Jeffrey was still sitting in his chair, looking sick.

Bob fell into step with Sara as they made their way through the many halls to where Candidate 20741 waited for them.

"Bob?" Sara asked.

"Yes?"

"Why did you lie for me, in the simulation room?" she said without looking at the man. "When Jeffrey came in, you covered for me. Why?"

"Because we're friends," Bob said simply. "I know how important appearance is to you. I didn't think you'd want someone to know you had had a panic attack. Besides, I feel like I've known you a lot longer than just a few days."

Sara didn't know what to say, and that was a first. She was used to keeping people at arm's length after what had happened with Julie and with Michael. She had been pretty hateful toward Bob, and yet here he was, like a puppy, still trying for her approval.

"I won't tell anyone," Bob continued. "But you should see someone about your anxiety. You can get it managed."

"I don't have anxiety, Bob, and that panic attack, or whatever it was, was a onetime thing," Sara insisted. "Let's just keep it between us. Were you going to tell me something else before we were interrupted?"

"I was, but it can wait," Bob answered.

They had reached the small simulation room housing Candidate 20741—the same room where Sara had first met Bob. Without hesitation, she waved her hand over the palm reader on the door, which slid open.

Inside, one of their two winning candidates lay on his back. The silver crown connecting him to the game glowed with blue light. While the screens that floated along the back wall listed his vitals as usual, the one that should have displayed his current location in the game showed him in a plain white room.

He was talking with someone off-screen. Sara wasn't able to hear the conversation.

"Where is that?" Bob asked.

"It's a section of the simulation coded to read as a plain white room," Sara explained, moving to the table to adjust the volume so they could hear what was being said. "Chairman is talking with them now, getting them ready to enter the real world."

The door slid open behind them, admitting the security team who would stand by in case Candidate 20741 decided he wasn't going to just let bygones be bygones.

We may need more men, Sara thought, thinking back to the altercations Candidate 20741 had had in the game. Suddenly, four armed men didn't seem like nearly enough.

"Reporting in, ma'am," said Toby, the head of security, nodding to Sara.

Toby was a bear of a man. He was always on time and expected the best of himself and those with him. Immaculately dressed as always in a black long-sleeved shirt, boots, and pants, he held himself to the highest standard. The three guards with him were dressed similarly. Each carried a baton at his belt as well as a radio, a pair of mag cuffs, and a Taser.

"It's good to see you, Toby," Sara said, actually meaning the words. "We should be cautious. This candidate has extensive hand-to-hand combat training."

"Understood," Toby said, glancing over Sara's shoulder at the slumbering candidate. "I've brought my best."

"Good; let's try to talk him down, if at all possible," Sara continued. "We want to work with this man in the future. Let me take the lead, but in the event things turn violent, I'll hand the situation over to you."

"Understood," Toby repeated with a grim nod.

Sara's data pad vibrated in her suit pocket. When she pulled the device free, she was only half surprised to see Chairman was calling.

"Sir, congratulations," Sara said, pressing the smart pad to her ear and using it as a phone. "You did it."

"*We* did it," Chairman corrected in a joyful tone. "I wanted to call you right away once the game ended, but decided to speak to one of the candidates while you were in transit from the viewing room. But before I talk to Candidate 20609, I wanted to tell you: Well done, Sara, well done indeed. What we have accomplished here is part of the blueprint for humanity's salvation."

"Thank you, sir. I know you're right," Sara said, feeling a swell of pride, quickly followed by guilt. Julie should be here. She should know what they had accomplished.

"Well then, I'll leave Candidate 20741 in your hands while I speak to our other champion," he said in a rush. "We'll talk soon."

"Talk soon," Sara repeated as the line went dead.

Sara looked at the monitor, where Candidate 20741 waited in that same blank room. She looked at his still body, lying on the table. What was she about to say to this man? He wasn't going to share her joy. He was going to be furious and rightfully so. Hopefully, Chairman had soothed him enough to make him at least civil when they pulled him out.

"Start the process," Sara told Bob, who reached for his data pad, then frowned at it. "You don't know how to retrieve him from the game, do you?"

"I'm coming up blank," Bob admitted.

"It's not your fault," Sara said, taking Bob's pad from his hands. "We've never retrieved anyone before."

That wasn't entirely the truth. In the early days, when they'd first realized the candidates were suffering mental deterioration in the game, they had retrieved them. But then they'd had to deal with raving lunatics, and hundreds of them. It had been decided it was easier to leave them in the game and just let them live out their crazed lives.

Sara didn't like to think about those days. Now, she maneuvered around the data pad's interface, punched in her access code, and finally arrived at the screen that would free Candidate 20741 from the game.

Her finger hovered over the button that would wake him.

You did it, Sara said to herself. *You did the impossible. Now it's time to do it again.*

She pressed the button that would wake the man she had drugged and kidnapped.

CHAPTER 42

CHAIRMAN

They had done it. What was once only a dream had been realized. And not just once but twice. Candidate 20741 and Candidate 20609 had worked together, made allies in the game, and overcome every obstacle.

Where so many had failed, these two had not. It was truly a day of celebration. With the information collected from them in game, as well as an in-depth study of their past, Tanus Corporation's model was complete.

Not only could they choose the best candidates to use in the future, but these two could train them, first in the game and then for missions in real life.

Chairman chose to meet Candidate 20741 first. He would appear to him, as he did in all his calls, as a blank screen. It was easier this way—people treated him as competent and did not write him off because of his youth. "Chairman," after all, was a title passed down from generation to generation in his family. He had only recently assumed control of the corporation, after the passing of his father.

When Chairman popped into existence in front of Candidate

20741 on a floating screen, the candidate immediately jolted and went into a fighting stance.

"Who are you supposed to be?" Candidate 20741 asked with disgust. "We did it. We finished your sick game. Let us out. What did you do with Bishop?"

"Please, Mr. Dexter," Chairman started off jovially. "Candidate 20609, or Bishop, as you call her, is safe and in a similar room, waiting for me to arrive for a similar conversation. You will be released. This is a wonderful occasion, and you are to be congratulated."

"You drugged me, abducted me, and put me in a game to fight for my life, and now you expect me to . . . celebrate with you?" Tom Dexter asked, dumbfounded. "Yeah, not so much. Who are you, anyway?"

"You can call me Chairman. I am the owner of Tanus Corporation," he explained. "While the way our paths crossed is unfortunate, you refused our initial offer."

"What?"

"When we asked you, you refused to help us save humanity," Chairman said.

"Save humanity? What are you talking about?" the candidate asked.

"Mr. Dexter, you must understand that we are on a precipice. Humankind is on the brink of a long-overdue restart," Chairman explained. "Many years ago, even before Tanus Corporation existed, an initiative called Doomsday was started. Doomsday brought together disaster analysts from around the world to warn humankind about what was just around the corner. Are you following?"

"Keep going," Candidate 20741 answered.

"Well, these disaster analysts got better and better at their jobs, able to determine when the next floods would happen, earthquakes, even riots. All their data points to an event nine years from now, a doomsday event that will wipe out most, if not all, human life on Earth. The moon and Mars are not viable options for all of humanity, so we must find a new home," Chairman said slowly, revealing the master plan. "The Eternal Engine exists to test candidates and see who would be the best to send among this first wave of new explorers. Who has the grit to survive, the skill sets to see it through to the end, and the endurance to keep going, no matter what the odds may be."

"This was a test," 20741 said, shaking his head. "This was all one big test to see who would make it through? Who you'd send off planet?"

"Yes, and so much more," Chairman said, trying to keep the excitement—which Candidate 20741 was clearly not feeling—out of his voice. "You and Candidate 20609 completed the simulation. We feel you can now train a team to take off world, to find humankind a new home, past the moon and Mars."

Tom laughed and shook his head.

"I know this is a lot," Chairman went on. "You'll have ample time to rest and come to grips with the truth. Once you're ready, you'll be equipped with only the best as you train your team. Now that we have the data we need, choosing candidates who will succeed will be so much more efficient. You'll have everything you need and, of course, be well compensated."

"Compensated?" Candidate 20741 asked in wonder. "You just told me the world is going to die in nine years. What am I going to do with money?"

"That's true," Chairman admitted. "You can be rewarded however you like. A new home on the planet we settle, a position in the new government . . . whatever it is you desire."

Candidate 20741 paced back and forth, shaking his head and muttering. Chairman allowed him time to come to grips with his new reality. He had, after all, given the man plenty to think about.

"It doesn't look like I have much of a choice," Tom said, lifting an eyebrow. "I don't do what you say, and you don't let me out of here. You can keep me in the game forever."

"Please, Mr. Dexter," Chairman said gently, "we're not your jailers. We want a healthy working relationship and look to you as a partner. We'll let you out of the game no matter what you decide. You've earned that much. I hope you understand why all of this was necessary."

Now was not the time to press Candidate 20741, but perhaps he could convince Tom why the game was so important.

"I hope you can see that the suffering of the few is for the betterment of the many," Chairman continued. "I am no saint, Mr. Dexter, but I hope that in a small way, I can guide humanity to a better future. Now, when you wake, can I trust you not to harm any of our employees? They're just following orders. If you are angry with anyone, be angry at me."

"I'm not going to kill anyone, if that's what you mean," the candidate said, eyeing the screen. "Well, maybe you, if I ever meet you in real life."

Chairman boomed a very real laugh. That was the last thing he had expected Candidate 20741 to say. Despite the threat, Chairman was growing to enjoy Candidate 20741's general disposition.

"I understand completely," Chairman agreed. "Please, take some time to really absorb what we're doing here and the part you play. You are the key, Mr. Dexter. You and Ms. Bishop together.

"All right, as promised, it's time for you to wake up."

CHAPTER 43

TOM

Tom opened his eyes in a room he had never seen before. He could tell he was lying on a table of some kind; he felt tired and weak, but there was no more pain in his head or aches in his body. The shoulder that had been thrumming like a war drum in the simulation was completely fine.

Slowly, Tom sat up. His hands roved over his arms, shoulders, and face. There was nothing, no wounds or scars, to bear witness to the fight with the mayor.

"Take it slow," a woman said from his right. "Your brain will need some time to acclimate. There is a device on your head. I can remove it for you if you'd like."

Tom reached up and felt the metal ring on his brow. He pulled it off and tossed the band, which pulsed with light, onto the table next to him.

"Or you can just pull it off yourself," the woman continued. "Mr. Dexter, I hope we can start fresh. You are to be congratulated. No one has ever managed to accomplish what you have."

Tom looked around, examining everything in the white room, beginning with the floating holographic screens behind him. Next, the people: four security guards, a guy with glasses who looked half confused and half like he wanted Tom's autograph, and finally, her. The woman who had gotten him into this mess to begin with.

"You," Tom said to her while hopping off the table. "It's you. Drug anyone else lately? Is that what you do? Go around and kidnap people and stick them in your game like lab rats?"

Tom crossed the distance between them quickly, his bare feet steady on the cold floor.

The security guards moved to intercept him, but the woman in white waved them off. She stood toe-to-toe with Tom and extended a hand. "I wish it could have been different between us. But the hard truth is I did what needed to be done, and now humankind has a chance. My name is Sara Tran."

A war raged inside Tom. Part of him was hot with righteous fury, but not for what had been done to him. No, almost none of the anger he felt had to do with him personally. It was about the hundreds or thousands of people stuck in the game—the ones who had lost their minds, their very humanity stripped from them, one horrific death at a time.

"Oooookay," Sara said, lowering her hand. "I understand. I hope with time we can learn to work together and let the past remain in the past."

"I guess we'll have to see," Tom said. He took a breath. "Otto, he's not an actual person, is he? He's an NPC, like Wade."

"That's right," Sara said with a nod.

"What happens to them now, to Otto and Wade and the others? What happens to the timelines of everyone still in the game?" Tom pressed.

He could tell his brash demands were getting under Sara's skin, but he couldn't care less. He wanted all the answers now, and he wanted to see his friend.

"You're right. Otto, Wade, Mayor Graves, and most of the others are NPCs," Sara explained. "Remember when you died?"

"How could I forget?"

"When you returned, Otto had no memory of who you were," Sara expounded. "Your timeline in his mind was reset. The same thing will happen now that you've completed the game. All the NPCs will go on, business as usual, continuing the game for anyone else who might pass."

"Bishop," Tom said, moving on to his next demand. "Where is she? I want to see her now."

Sara clenched her teeth so hard the muscles in her jaw jumped with tension. This was a woman who was used to giving orders, not taking them.

"Certainly," the young guy with glasses said, extending a hand. "I'm Bob. I just want to say that I know you're pissed off, and I think you have every right to be, personally, but I hope one day we can be friends."

Tom looked at him, then the offered hand, then back into the guy's eyes.

"Oh, right, still too angry for handshakes," Bob said, retracting his palm. "I am sorry for what was done to you."

"So am I," Tom said, meeting Sara's gaze head-on. "I'm more sorry for the people who never made it out."

"We can take you to Candidate 20609 right now," Sara said, turning and heading out the door. "She should be out of the game and having a similar conversation with the team sent to greet her."

Tom followed Sara. The four security guards flanked him, two in front and two behind. Bob walked next to him, staring at him as they made their way through long halls where everything was white, from the floors to the ceilings.

"I'm not going to be your friend," Tom said out of the side of his mouth.

"Man, I just feel so much guilt," Bob said with a long sigh. "I'm new here. I didn't know all the ins and outs of what was going on in the game. But my nana always says ignorance isn't an excuse. I am sorry, Tom. For what happened to you and all those people."

Tom wasn't ready to have a heart-to-heart with anyone, but he got the sense that Bob was being sincere. How someone like him had ended up working for such a corrupt entity as Tanus Corporation was a mystery.

As they walked, Tom became aware of a series of muffled grunts, the sounds of a struggle that grew louder as they approached one of many identical doors. Sara waved her hand over a reader. The door slid open, showing a scene of utter chaos.

Bishop was apparently less than ready to forgive. One guy was on the ground in the fetal position, grabbing his groin, and another, in the corner, was screaming like a small child.

Four black-clad guards wrestled with Bishop, doing their best to pin her to the far wall. Loyalty-laced aggression ripped through Tom. He didn't think, just reacted. The guards around him tried to grab him as he moved, but they were a hair too slow.

Tom sprinted forward, bodychecking one of the security guards near Bishop so hard he threw the man completely off her. He grabbed a second man by the hair and sent an elbow into the side of his head.

The last two guards struggling with Bishop backed off.

"You okay?" Tom asked. Bishop was bleeding from her lip and left nostril.

"Oh yeah, just great," she said, looking him up and down. "Why are you dressed like a dork?"

Tom looked at his tight pants, white hospital gown, and shoeless feet.

"Oh man, I'm dressed like a dork too," Bishop said, looking down at her nearly identical wardrobe.

"Stand down," the largest security guard said, taking a menacing step forward. He carried a baton ready in his right hand. "Both of you, on your knees now."

"Have you not been watching any part of what we just did in your twisted video game?" Bishop asked with an eye roll. "We don't really take orders."

"We aren't doing this," Sara said, stepping between the two parties. "There is no need for anyone to fight. What happened here? Theodore?"

The man rising to his feet still held his groin as if he were positive that at any moment someone else was going to take another shot at the family jewels.

"I—I waited for Chairman to finish speaking with her just like the protocol laid out. She seemed calm enough in the simulation exit room, but then when she woke, she was a banshee," the man—Theodore, Tom assumed—said, looking at the man in the corner, who was just beginning to compose himself. "She kicked me in the groin. Jeffrey ran. Security stepped in. I'm glad they did; she was going to kill me."

"I'm sure she wasn't going to kill you," Sara consoled him.

"Don't be too sure about that," Bishop chimed in.

"All right, all right, well, this isn't going as planned, but what does these days?" Sara said, taking a deep, cleansing breath. "Would you like a chance to get dressed, maybe wash, and eat some real food for a change? How does that sound?"

"Are we allowed to leave?" Bishop asked.

"You are. Where would you like to go?" Sara inquired with a lifted eyebrow. "Ms. Bishop, remember where you were when we found you."

Bishop winced. When she stayed quiet in a very un-Bishop-like way, Tom knew she was recalling more of her past, and it wasn't good.

For his part, Tom had nothing and no one to go back to. Everything he'd lived for was gone. His career was over; his wife only existed in his memories.

"We'll stay just for now. We can't go out looking like this anyway," Tom said, justifying his decision. He looked over at Bishop. Tears ran down her cheeks; he guessed that memories of her life were flooding through her, like water through a collapsed dam. "But she and I stick together."

"Of course," Sara said with a quick smile that never reached her eyes. "Showers, clothing, food, and then you can decide what you'd like next. Bob, please arrange to have clothing taken to their rooms and a meal to be prepared on the rooftop. Mr. Dexter, Ms. Bishop, please follow me."

It was strange to see what the real world looked like when life inside the game had seemed just as real. The building that housed Tanus Corporation was massive. With eight guards flanking them, Sara led them to an upper level via a lift.

Everything in the building was so vastly different from the game that Tom had to do a double take at times. In the game, everything was sand and heat, but this air-conditioned, sterile building was all stark white and orderly.

What are you going to do? Tom asked himself. *What are you going to do?*

CHAPTER 44

TOM

A thought entered his mind as they stepped off the lift on an upper level. He and Bishop knew far too much about the inner workings of the game. There was no way Tanus Corporation was going to let them out alive. But for now, Chairman, Sara, and the security team were deciding to play nice. Until Tom had a solid exit strategy, he would do the same.

There was also the fact that Bishop was clearly not okay. She must have recovered some very traumatic memories when she got out of the game. After all, unlike Tom, she had only taken the first pill Doc had given her. She hadn't had the second night that would have fully revealed who she was. So it must have all come back to her since she woke up on the table.

Doc was another unknown. If everything she said was true, if she did exist outside the game, then maybe she could help, but where was she? How could Tom get word to her?

"Here we are," Sara said, stopping at one of many doors in a hall that reminded Tom of a hotel. "The upper floor is living quarters, for team members who might need to stay the night if they're working late or have an early-morning meeting.

"Bob will arrange for clothing and food. Should you need anything else, please don't hesitate to ask. I'm sure you'll have more questions about next steps. We will answer as many as we can at dinner."

What Tom really wanted was to go straight to the police with what had happened, but there were eight security guards and an entire facility between him and escape. Instead of cracking heads, he said, "Thank you."

That seemed to be enough for Sara, who turned and walked back down the hall. It wasn't lost on Tom that the security team remained. Each one looked like they wished he would step out of line.

Tom opened the door and led Bishop into a pair of connecting suites. Closing the door behind him, he realized there was no lock. Not a huge surprise; he imagined the security guards were posted right outside the doors. Who knew—they might have called in more security to watch the hall and entire level. If they were smart, that was what they would have done.

He prowled through the rooms. They were nicer than any Tom had ever stayed in before. Each suite had a small kitchen area, dining table, and living space, plus a bedroom and attached bathroom.

Bishop moved to the window and stared out. After his inspection, Tom joined her, and the two stood in silence, mentally fatigued from the revelations taking place every minute. Emotionally, they were both exhausted.

Outside, an army of buildings reached for the sky. Everything was all glass and metal. The street below flowed with traffic, but beyond the buildings, beyond the single sun now setting in the west, were plumes of smoke.

Tom remembered more of the current state of the world. What seemed like weekly, if not daily, a new protest was taking place, a new mob angry at someone for something. Cities disbanding police added to the chaos.

"I remember everything," Bishop said, still staring out the window, her lips so close to the glass that fog formed on the panel in front of her. "I was a police officer. My partner died in my arms. I never got over it. I spiraled hard. I lost everything."

She winced with every confession, as if feeling the agony that came with it all over again.

"I remember who I was, and I don't want to be that person anymore, Tom," Bishop said, shaking her head free of the thoughts. "I had given up. I was lost."

"You're not that person anymore," Tom said, placing a hand on his friend's shoulder. "Neither of us are, but we can't go along with Tanus Corporation either, pretending that they're not kidnapping people and slowly stealing their humanity. We can't."

"Then what are we going to do?" Bishop asked, massaging her temples. "What are we going to do? They're not going to let us go. No one is going to walk away from this."

"I'm working on it," Tom told her, removing his hand. "I'm working on it."

"Work faster, Gamer," Bishop said with a sigh, reorienting herself. "Dinner's going to be soon. I need to take a shower. And what are these pants? Were we peeing in these things somehow? How did all of that work?"

"I have no idea," Tom said with a twitch of his lips as Bishop headed into her suite.

He knew he couldn't work with anyone who would do what Tanus Corporation had to humans. The lost ones, Monica in particular, played through his mind. Who had they been? Everything had been taken away from them. Everything they could have been, every chance to right their wrongs—it was all gone.

A knock on the door interrupted his thoughts. How long

had he been staring out the window? When he opened the door, he found Bob standing there with a winning attitude and an armload of black boxes.

"Pulled your sizes from your records," Bob said with a genuine smile. It was the first honest smile Tom had seen since waking up. "I hope they work."

"Thanks," Tom said, taking several boxes from him. "Hey, Bob?"

"Yes?"

"How do you justify working in a place like this? You seem like a good kid."

"Something my nana told me, a long time ago, when I had qualms about working for our family business," Bob said with a sad expression, as if he were looking into his past. "If you can't change a system from without, then perhaps the best way is to work within. I know Tanus Corporation is going about things in a questionable manner, but at their core, they are trying to do the right thing."

Bob stepped to the side, obviously preparing to knock on the door beside Tom's and hand Bishop her clothing. Before Tom closed his door, he noticed not eight but ten security guards along the wall and near his room, watching him. He gave them the finger, then closed the door.

The shower felt amazing, though he wasn't dirty at all. It was peculiar to have your mind remember days of dirt and sand while your body remained so very clean. Despite this, Tom enjoyed the shower. It gave him more time to think.

After toweling dry and changing into a black suit with a black shirt and no tie, Tom looked at himself in the mirror. What did he think of the man looking back? Was he proud of this man? Could he be proud of this man? Would Lana have been proud of the man he was? He remembered the way she smelled, the hummingbird necklace she always wore.

Alone, with time to think, Tom realized he was missing a certain hypertalkative AI. Gary would have something to say about all of this. Just for kicks, Tom rotated his left forearm twice. Nothing happened.

"You clean up nice." Bishop's voice interrupted him from his bathroom door.

Tom looked up to see her with her hair up, wearing hooped earrings, a necklace, and a black dress that hugged her curves.

"Not bad yourself, Marshal," Tom answered. "How are you doing?"

He could tell she knew what he was asking. How she was handling the memories of her past.

"As well as I can be, knowing that part of my humanity has been taken from me," Bishop answered. "I died twice in there, Tom. Part of me is gone forever. Part of you too, but you only died once. They took more of me. I want answers. And I want to make them pay."

"I get it, I do, but we can't have you throwing punches at dinner," Tom told her. "Let's use tonight to get all the answers we can."

"As much as I want revenge, I can see why they're doing this," Bishop surprised Tom by continuing. "I hate them for making me see their point, but I understand. Does it make me a horrible person if I don't walk away?"

"No," Tom told her. "I get what they're doing too, but I can't justify the abductions and the slow deaths the people in the game are experiencing."

Bishop nodded.

A knock on the door told them it was time.

Together they exited the room to find a waiting Bob. The man waved and motioned for them to follow.

"It's a short walk to the rooftop," Bob said as the security guards fell in line. "Spoiler alert: I haven't been to the rooftop myself—it's only my first week here. I know you two have had a crazy last few days, but my week has been a little bananas as well."

"I'm going to go out on a limb and say you don't have many friends, Bob," Bishop commented. "Does that sound about right?"

"Classic Bishop. You know, I was rooting for you in the game," Bob said, dodging her question. "This way."

Bob led them to a stairwell. Two flights of steps brought them to a rooftop. It was unlike anything Tom had ever seen, but he was getting used to that feeling. The roof looked more like a five-star restaurant than anything else. Fires burned in pits, complementing the setting sun. A massive oak table filled the center of the space. There were only three chairs. A retinue of servers manned an outside cooking area, and the air smelled of roasted meat and fresh bread.

Tom wasn't surprised to find himself salivating. The thought of a good steak turned his mind to Wade and the kindness the older man had shown him during his first run in the game.

Sara stood up from one of the seats and waved them forward. Bob smiled again and stepped away as Tom and Bishop joined Sara. The woman hadn't changed clothes. No doubt her time since she'd left them was spent speaking with Chairman and coming up with a strategy for tonight. That was what Tom would have done if he were her.

As they sat down, Tom searched the rooftop for someone he thought could be Chairman, but besides the servers, they were alone. Not even the security team had joined them on the roof.

"You trust us without security guards?" Bishop asked as she played with the knife at her place setting. "You're brave or stupid."

"I'd like to think the former," Sara said as a waiter filled her wineglass with a dark-burgundy liquid. "You two look nice. Were the rooms to your liking?"

"Are we just going to sit here pretending to be friends, or are we going to start talking?" Tom asked as the server filled his glass. "Where's Chairman?"

"And what is his real name, anyway?" Bishop asked, taking the bottle from the waiter's hand. She lifted it to her lips, threw her head back, and drank in long, drawn-out gulps. When she came up for air, she finished her thought. "Wait, don't tell me, Chairman's real last name rhymes with Husk."

"No, not that I'm aware of," Sara said, reaching into the pocket of her white dress for a device the size of a hockey puck. She placed it at the head of the table. Blue light shot up and showed a sapphire screen.

"Tom, Bishop, so good to see you again. Thank you for coming," Chairman began, as if he were welcoming family to a Thanksgiving Day meal. A line danced across the screen when Chairman spoke, quivering and spiking like a heartbeat. Tom guessed from his voice that Chairman was somewhere in his sixties or seventies. But that could easily be faked. The mysterious Chairman could be a young woman, for all Tom knew.

"I see you've already begun with drinks, wonderful. Please, the food is the best in the country. I've flown in the top chefs for this monumental celebration. It's not every day one's life's work is realized."

It wasn't in Tom's nature to make small talk and beat around the bush when there was a thousand-pound gorilla in the room.

"I know you both must be excited that your project has been completed," Tom said, looking first at the screen, then at Sara. "But I'm not exactly overjoyed about what was done to me, what is being done to hundreds of others in your game."

"What would you have done, if you were us?" Sara asked, swirling her wine before taking a sip. "The roles are reversed; we're sitting on opposite sides of the table. The world is going to end. We need to find the best people to make a new home for us. Now what?"

"I'm not playing any more of your games. Let everyone else in the game go," Bishop said bluntly. "Let them be free."

"Unfortunately, that's not as easy as it sounds," Chairman remarked. "Thanks to the game, most of our candidates have experienced mental deterioration. We can't exactly unplug them and send them on their merry way. You have to understand, when we started all of this, the cognitive loss was a surprise for us as well."

"A surprise, but once you did know, you kept going," Tom chimed in.

"We did. We felt it was an acceptable price for the salvation of the human species," Chairman said, his voice stronger, as if he were leaning into the microphone. "Don't you understand? The flood is about to be upon us; the game is the ark. To find dry land again, we must press on. I didn't want this. But it's the only way. Now we have to see it through. We have to."

Bishop took another long swig from her bottle. Tom looked at his glass but remembered how he had been drugged the last time. He ignored the wine as waiters set down baskets of warm bread and platters of steak and lobster. Sides of gooey mac and cheese, fluffy mashed potatoes, and steaming veggies were also placed on the table. Tom's mouth watered.

"I think you've left a pile of bodies in your wake," Bishop said with a shrug. She helped herself to the food. "I'm having a hard time justifying helping you at all."

"Perhaps a visual representation of the events to come will aid us in explaining our proposition," Chairman answered. "Please do not be alarmed, and do remember that you are on a roof, should you decide to get up and run."

CHAPTER 45

TOM

Tom tensed, not knowing what to expect. Bishop shrugged, set the entire bowl of mac and cheese in front of herself, and began eating. Sara sat watching them both. All around them, hard-light emitters projected images of a barren landscape. The sky was traded for one that belonged in a hot, dry desert; the rooftop faded to a desolate wasteland devoid of any life.

Tom had seen this technology before, in VR gaming.

"Nine years until Earth as we know it will be destroyed," Chairman said. "The latest reports project a twenty percent survival rate, and even that is being generous. The powers that be are looking to the moon and Mars, but we know our best chances lie farther out. We can do this. We can save millions."

As Chairman spoke, the images around them transformed to images of earthquakes, volcanoes erupting, riots, diseases, and other disasters.

At that moment, Tom made up his mind. Bob's words had stuck with him. Tanus Corporation wasn't going to stop. With or without him, it would continue. He could try to fight his way out, or he could stay and try to help those people who had lost their sanity—and make sure it didn't happen to anyone else.

The presentation over, the lights died. Bishop continued stuffing her face with mac and cheese as if she were watching the latest *Fast and Furious* movie.

"It's not a perfect system," Sara said, taking a dainty bite of her steak, "but it's the one we've got to work with, and it's our best chance."

"No one else gets abducted," Tom said firmly. "And no one who can't handle the game gets put in from now on. You swear."

"You have all of our data, so you know what kind of person will stand a chance in there now," Bishop added. "Better yet, Tom and I get to see who you select. And the people in there right now, losing their minds—you take them out or place them in a different game, where they stop dying. And you start working on a cure for them."

"Oh, is that all?" Sara asked sarcastically. "Why don't we just rewrite all the NPCs, make them prance around passing out candy to the newcomers. Why don't we get the mayor a welcome wagon. What the fu—"

"I understand your demands and the feelings they stem from," Chairman said, cutting Sara off. "You will have a hand in selecting the team you will take into the game. We are working on a way to help current players regain what they have lost, but taking them out is not an option right now, not for their good or anyone else's."

Tom sat quiet for some time. Two out of three asks wasn't bad.

"So you want us to train a group to survive in the game because that will prepare them for surviving in real life when we settle a new world." Tom repeated the deal out loud to make sure he understood correctly. "Once that training is done, you what, put us on a rocket ship and send us to this new planet to set up shop? Where exactly are we going? What planet?"

Silence for a moment. Even Sara was looking at Chairman's little screen. She didn't have a clear answer either.

"Phase two will be completing the game with a group we'll call Team One," Chairman explained. "Phase three will be getting you to a new habitable planet. A second initiative is working through those logistics now. Know that a habitable planet has been located and a means of transportation secured."

"Can we get more wine over here?" Bishop asked, waving the empty bottle toward one of the waiters, who stepped forward. "Great, great, you know what? I'll save you a trip. Can you bring two? Thank you."

Tom side-eyed Bishop's coping mechanism.

"Don't judge me," Bishop said, placing the empty wine bottle on the table. "I've had a rough day."

"Are you in?" Sara asked as they turned back to their meal. "We should start as soon as possible."

Tom chewed his steak as his mind did the same to the proposition. Before he answered, he looked at Bishop, who was fairly drunk. She was lifting the second bottle of wine to her lips when he caught her eye.

"I don't have any plans for tomorrow." Bishop shrugged. "What do you think, Gamer?"

"I think if we can see that no one else is getting forced into this and that there is actually a team working on restoring people's sanity, then yeah, I'm in," Tom answered. "Better to work with the devil you know than sit back and wait for the world to end."

"Did you just call us the devil?" Sara asked, her perfectly manicured eyebrows shooting up in surprise.

"If the shoe fits, Cinderella," Tom said, digging into his meal again.

The rest of the evening was spent making plans. Tom was

impressed by how much alcohol Bishop could consume and still carry on a conversation.

The night ended with amiable farewells. Tom and Bishop were escorted to their rooms by Sara. The guards were still at their doors when they entered the hall.

"Do we still need the babysitters?" Tom asked.

"I don't know, you tell me," Sara answered. "Do we?"

"The only place I'm going is to bed," Bishop said with a wide stretch and yawn.

"Same," Tom said, reaching for his door handle. "I'm all in or I'm all out. If you prove that you're doing what you say you are, then I'm all in."

"Noted," Sara said confidently. "I'll talk it over with Chairman."

A few minutes later, Tom lay between silk sheets with the moon glowing through his window, mentally replaying the night's events. And not just that night's events but all the events that had brought him to this point. The loss of his wife, the depression, the game, and now this. As much as Tom would like to deny it, this was all he had now.

He had failed plenty of people in his past. Maybe, just maybe, he could save people in the future. Tom fell asleep easily and woke grateful that no dreams had haunted his slumber.

The next few days were filled with meetings, training, and more meetings. Security guards stopped following them everywhere, and Tom and Bishop were given access to the simulation rooms.

Several meetings were with Sara, Chairman, and the guy that Bishop had made cry. His name was Jeffrey Saga, and he was a senior coder at Tanus Corporation. At the meetings, they discussed the volunteer candidates who had begun requesting to join the project in response to Tanus Corporation's new outreach program.

Tom and Bishop had full control over their teams. They made sure to speak to each candidate in person so they knew exactly what they would be getting into.

Both Tom and Bishop also spent time in the department that was dedicated to not just repairing the neural pathways that had been burned when candidates died in the game but also ensuring that new candidates would retain 100 percent of their cognitive abilities if and when they died.

Everything was as Chairman had promised. That didn't make Tom feel any better. He still felt like he was being monitored at every turn. This suspicion was confirmed when he asked to take a trip off company property.

Sara had to clear it with Chairman, who granted his request but insisted he use a company driver rather than a self-driving vehicle. Tom had been born at night but not last night. He understood the driver wasn't just offered as a friendly gesture. It was someone to keep an eye on him.

Tom sat quietly during the trip. He was returning to his home to gather personal effects, most importantly, his wife's hummingbird necklace and his favorite picture of her. He stared out the window, wondering if all of this was really going to burn in nine years. Children playing in front yards, mothers walking strollers, kids waiting for the bus. Was this all going to die unless he and Bishop could come through?

"You going to get out or just stare at your reflection in the window?" Toby, Tanus Corporation's head of security, asked from the driver's seat. "This is the place, isn't it?"

"This is the place," Tom said, reaching for the door handle.

Toby looked as though he were going to come with Tom.

"I'll be quick," Tom assured him. "You can stay here bumping your Billie Eilish or whatever you kids are listening to these days."

Toby turned in his seat, which was a small miracle in itself, since his shoulders were so large. "I'm not that much younger than you."

"Sure," Tom said, exiting the car. His small, single-story home had once been the happiest place in his world. Now it was a doorway into his past, reminding him of all the happiness that had come and gone.

The garden to the left of the porch had become overgrown with weeds while he had been away. A hobbit garden gnome, with a pipe in one hand and a sandwich in the other, looked up at him with a weary smile born of weathering the elements for too long a time.

Tom lifted the garden ornament and freed a key from underneath. Scribbled on the bottom of the gnome was a message that read "Bathroom vent."

There was no signature or clue as to who might have scrawled the words. Neither he nor Lana had left them there. Tom glanced right and left. No one around save Toby, who sat staring at him like an eagle.

"You good?" Toby asked, rolling down the window. Billie Eilish played in the background.

"Good," Tom lied, licking his thumb and scrubbing off the penciled message before replacing the gnome.

Entering his home, he headed straight for the attached garage and his toolbox. What had once been a warm house full of love and light was now a musty skeleton of a building Tom couldn't wait to leave.

He grabbed the screwdriver and headed to the master bathroom, the only one of the two with a fan. He wasted no time, standing on the toilet seat and removing the plastic vent cover.

Groping around inside, his fingers searched and searched again, finding nothing until, with added effort, he touched something hard and square.

CHAPTER 46

TOM

It was a cell phone, preprogrammed with a single contact: "Doc." Tom made the call. He moved to the front room to make sure Toby was still in the vehicle. The professional bodybuilder was discreetly head-bobbing to his music.

"I knew it," Tom muttered. "He loves Billie Eilish."

"Tom?" Doc's voice interrupted his thoughts. "Tom, we don't have much time. You have to listen."

"You got to stop telling me we don't have much time when we talk," Tom muttered. "What is it? What's going on now?"

"Tom, you can't trust Chairman. No matter what he says, you can't believe anything," Doc told him. "What are they planning next?"

"I know," Tom answered with a wary eye on Toby through the thin curtain. "They want Bishop and me to work for them. They're modeling candidates off us, and they want us to train them. Eventually, and I can't even believe I'm saying this, we'll go off world. We'll be the first to make a new home for humankind."

"Be careful," Doc insisted with fervor in every word. "I bought a similar story when Chairman recruited me."

"What story?" Tom asked, confused. "Who is he?"

"Listen," Doc continued, ignoring the question, "I think you're doing the right thing. You and Bishop can do some good there. But you have to be on guard at all times. Make him think you're with them, but never fully buy what they're selling. Find out everything you can about what they're doing. Together we can build a stronger case for what's really going on."

"How do I reach you?" Tom asked.

"You don't," Doc answered. "I'll find you. Put this phone back in the vent when we're done. It's too risky trying to sneak it into Tanus Corporation. They have eyes everywhere, Tom."

"You're sounding paranoid."

"Just because I'm paranoid doesn't mean I'm wrong," Doc insisted. "Watch yourself, Tom. I'll be in touch."

That was it. Without so much as a goodbye, Doc was gone. Tom scratched at the stubble along his jaw.

Of course, of course when you think you understand the board, they change the game on you, he thought. *What does Doc mean? What's she trying to say without giving me too much to handle?*

That question would have to wait. Toby got out of the vehicle and began walking up the walk to the front door. Tom raced to the bathroom. Jumping on the toilet, he jammed the cell phone back into the hiding spot and screwed the grate into place.

He heard the door to the house open and Toby step inside. The man called, "Mr. Dexter? Mr. Dexter, do you need a hand with anything?"

Tom jumped off the toilet and took the first avenue of plausible escape he could think of. Tearing down his pants and lifting the lid, he dropped the screwdriver down one pants leg and sat on the toilet seat.

A second later, Toby walked in, and his eyes went wide.

"Hey, can I get some privacy here, you pervert?" Tom shouted, waving him away.

"Why didn't you just close the door?" Toby said, looking away like he'd tasted something foul.

"I didn't think my babysitter was going to come and check on me," Tom shouted back. "You need to wipe me too?"

Toby didn't answer. Tom heard his footsteps recede. "Just hurry up," the security man called. The front door opened and closed again.

Tom let out a pent-up sigh of relief. That had been close.

After returning the screwdriver to its place in the garage, he went through the house with his black backpack, taking items he thought he might actually miss. There wasn't much. There was his favorite picture of his wife and him together, at a friend's engagement party. She'd been so happy when she was out among friends, such an extrovert, the exact opposite of him. Her hummingbird necklace. Her journal, so he could remember what she sounded like.

He had plenty of new clothes, courtesy of Bob and Tanus Corporation. But they were stiff and unfamiliar, not broken in and worn like his things, like the things Lana had bought him. Tom packed a few personal belongings, including a hat stenciled with the face of a menacing wolf, his Ray-Bans, and a black stone bracelet his wife had given him.

Somewhere in the back of his mind, Tom realized he was being silly. He was being emotional. Still, he never planned on coming back to this place again. His future, wherever it was going to take him, did not belong in this past. Tom shouldered the backpack and made his way to the car.

Without a word, Toby directed the vehicle back to Tanus Corporation. During the drive, Tom thought about Doc and what she had said. She had told him her name was Julie in the game, but she would always be Doc to him.

She was still working from the outside to take Tanus Corporation down, and she wanted him to do the same from the inside. If the company was as nefarious as she stated, then Tom would have no problem exposing it. He just hoped he would be able to do it before the second phase of Chairman's plan was complete.

CHAPTER 47

CHAIRMAN

Heavy lies the crown. Chairman thought about the line often. But he would rather be the one wearing the crown any day of the week. Events were transpiring quickly now. With phase one complete, phase two was beginning. They had their perfect models in Mr. Dexter and Ms. Bishop. Now it was time to replicate their actions and even improve on them.

Chairman watched the camera feeds from Mr. Dexter's home. As soon as he'd found out that this man, along with Ms. Bishop, would complete the game, he'd researched everything about them.

He found out the names of their teachers in second grade, who they had dated during their college years, what their favorite TV shows were last year. He had everyone they knew followed. He had bugged their living quarters. He had video cameras installed at their old homes.

This was where he had seen Julie Noble again. She had sneaked into Tom Dexter's house, hidden a phone there, and left a clue under a garden gnome.

It was no shock to see Julie. His predecessor had warned

him of the woman's commitment. He knew she was never going to rest until the day she died. Her departure from the company had been a heavy loss. She lacked the foresight to see that everything they were doing was not only necessary but inevitable.

Chairman played with the video feed, again watching Tom find the note, enter the home, and find the phone. Once again he listened to the conversation with Julie Noble.

She had access to the game. Of course she did. Chairman had been tracking the anomaly even before Jeffrey Saga had found it. He knew she was poking around in the Eternal Engine. Instead of force, like his predecessor, Chairman opted for surveillance. It proved to be a wise choice.

Julie had provided counsel Tom and Bishop had needed. Where others might see this as cheating, Chairman relished their ingenuity. The AI had evolved as well. Gary had been programmed by Julie, modeled after her dying brother. Now he had begun to make decisions for himself. It was an unforeseen turn of events but one Chairman welcomed. Humans and AI working together was something he encouraged.

Chairman couldn't predict the future, but he understood things like odds, chance, and luck. He knew that the prediction of an 80 percent mortality rate for the human population of the world was likely to come true.

He knew that the top 10 percent of the world's highest earners would make it off the planet. They had the money, resources, and connections to set up bases for themselves on the moon and Mars.

Hard men and women like Tom and Bishop would also find a way to survive, no matter the odds. These were the people who would roam what was left of Earth.

For the remaining 80 percent, it would be death.

Chairman's goal was for all of humankind to make it. Phase

two would be complete as soon as Tom and Bishop trained a team. Phase three was in development: An entirely separate company—also owned by Chairman, of course—was hard at work, preparing the means to journey to a habitable new world.

No one, not even Sara, was aware of this separate company. It wasn't that Chairman didn't trust her; it was that he didn't trust anyone. He'd been taught that lesson when Julie Noble had tried to turn on the company.

Soon Tom and Bishop would train a new team of candidates. They would need a week, maybe less, to get them through the simulation the first time, then a few more weeks to complete their training, which would take place in new simulations. Sara didn't know about those either. Chairman had planned ahead.

Data poured across the many monitors in front of Chairman, and he took it all in stride. Something in Julie's voice bothered him. Did she know? She had worked with his predecessor so closely. Had she seen the subtle changes in Chairman's projected personality when he took over?

It didn't matter in the end. All that mattered was that progress was made.

CHAPTER 48

TOM

Over the next few weeks, the data points collected from Tom and Bishop matched with other profiles from willing candidates who volunteered to enter the Eternal Engine. As promised, Tom and Bishop vetted them and checked that they knew exactly what they were getting into. The list of candidates was eventually narrowed down to four, and the date when they would enter the game was set.

The four new candidates would still have their memories wiped. This would ensure that they bought into the simulation and that they would rely on their intuition and gut instinct on an alien world.

There was an athlete from Germany, a medic from Texas, a world-champion martial artist from France, and a retired US Army veteran. The last was a bit of a surprise given his age, but he matched the profile they were looking for perfectly and, with only a few groans and grunts, passed the physical.

Each of them had survived very stressful situations not just physically but mentally and emotionally as well. The hypothesis was that this would aid them in keeping their sanity intact in the game.

The hardships they had faced in life had prepared them for this. The pain that they'd endured had forged them into the perfect candidates. Tom was reminded of the saying that the hottest forges produced the strongest steel.

The six of them would go into the game together, but Tom and Bishop would retain their memories. Hopefully, all would do well. If not, then one or more would have to be switched out and alternates found.

Going into the game was very different this time. Tom woke up that morning to find a new set of clothing had been delivered. The uniform was black and skintight, with a red emblem of a wolf, or something that looked very much like a wolf, over one breast. It was the menacing face of a night hound, the shepherds of the game, as Tom had come to think of them. The logo showed the wolf's face full on, scarred and battered but not broken.

He was just sitting down to breakfast when there was a harsh knock on the door that separated his suite from Bishop's.

"Come in," Tom called out.

Bishop entered with a tray of food in her hands and her new uniform tucked under one arm. "Can you believe this? As if getting thrown back into the game isn't bad enough, now we have to go in dressed as the Power Rangers."

"I don't know," Tom said, "I kind of like the wolf logo."

"You would," Bishop huffed as she sat down and started shoving eggs and bacon down her throat with abandon.

"What does that mean?" Tom asked, mixing a creamer into his coffee.

"Nothing," Bishop said, chewing thoughtfully. "You think they ever did any weird stuff to our bodies while we were in the game?"

"Like what?" Tom asked.

"Draw on our faces, give us wedgies?" Bishop asked. "I know while we're under, we have to be supported by IVs and catheters so our physical bodies won't die. Makes me wonder what else they do."

"We're about to voluntarily travel into hell a second time, and you're worried about someone giving you a wedgie while you sleep?"

"These are the thoughts that keep me up at night," Bishop said, slowly nodding as she ate.

They finished their meals, then changed and prepared to meet their team in their new simulation chamber. Tom hadn't told Bishop about Julie contacting him at his home. It wasn't that he didn't trust her. On the contrary, Bishop was one of the very few people he did trust.

The question was, Was it fair to put Bishop at risk? Telling her everything would very quickly put her in harm's way. If she had no part in what he and Julie were doing, then if things went sideways, she would be safer.

When they left their suites, they found Bob waiting for them with a silly smile on his face.

"What?" Bishop growled.

"You two look—you just look so cool!" Bob said, admiring their new threads. "How do your uniforms feel?"

"Kind of constricting in the crotch," Tom said honestly. The boots fit fine, but the pants and shirt were tighter than he would have liked. The red wolf symbol stood out, fierce and ready, on the left side of his chest.

"Well, come on, let's get you down to the new simulation chamber," Bob said, waving for them to follow. "Can I just tell you how excited I am for today?"

"No," Bishop and Tom said at the same time.

"Well, I know you two aren't eager to go into the game again, but think about how much easier it will be this time," Bob went on anyway. "You'll be able to run the game in half the time. You know exactly what to do now."

"That's only half of our mission," Bishop reminded the overly enthusiastic secretary. "Complete the game, yes, but guide the team along the way and monitor them to be sure they're the ones we want with us."

"Right, right, of course," Bob said as they stepped into the lift. "But the team you two selected, I mean, come on. You have the Avengers with you now. Everything's going to be fine."

Bishop and Bob talked about the candidates as they stepped into the lift and headed to a lower level. Although Toby and his security team had abandoned the hall leading to their suites, Tom still caught sight of them wandering down ramps and walkways.

They never made eye contact with him—well, none of them besides Toby. But they were always there, always just within sight. Even now they were right there, within shouting distance of the simulation room.

Tom reminded himself what he was really doing here. Yes, of course he wanted to save humankind. But he also saw the value in Julie's position. He would continue to play both sides as long as possible.

The number of people stuck inside the game was staggering. A little voice scratched at the back of Tom's mind, telling him that what people were willing to admit to was usually not the entirety of the crimes they'd committed. If Sara was willing to admit there were thousands of mentally impaired people in the game, he bet the truth was a much larger number.

The trio left the lift and turned a corner into a hall with doors on the right and the left leading into simulation rooms.

At the end of the hall stood Sara Tran herself. Sara gave them that same curt smile that never reached her eyes. She looked tired. Just in the time Tom had gotten to know her, she looked as though she had aged several years.

"Good morning," Sara said, then turned to wave open the door behind her. "Shall we begin? The rest of your team is already in the game. They'll be waking in their graves at any moment."

"Oh joy," Bishop said, walking into the room first and letting out a low whistle. "Okay, okay, I could get used to this."

Tom silently agreed when he saw the large, clean room, the screens on the ceiling instead of the far wall. What looked like two large capsules stood side by side. The fronts of the capsules were open and stood tilted at a forty-five-degree angle.

"Like before, you'll be fitted with simulation crowns and IV ports, and your sanitary needs will be taken care of."

With a frown, Bishop asked, "How did you handle that before, anyway?"

"Oh, some really cool tech designed into your pants. This is cutting-edge stuff," Bob started, and abruptly stopped when Sara lifted her eyebrow in his direction. "Cutting-edge stuff I'll tell you about at another time."

"All right, if you two would assume your positions in the pods, we can get started," Sara said. "Along with your memories, when you arrive in the game, you'll see upgrades to your HUDs. You can use the new features to locate the other candidates. Be careful not to reveal the HUDs to the new candidates right away. They must not know they are in a game at first."

Tom and Bishop nodded at one another before entering their capsules. The cylinder-shaped sleeping vessel reminded Tom of the chamber that held Steve Rogers when he was transformed into a supersoldier. Right now, Tom thought he would much rather undergo that process than what was about to happen.

Bob placed Bishop's crown on her head as Sara placed Tom's across his brow.

"Be careful in there," Sara told Tom. "A lot depends on you. More than you know."

Tom had the sense that Sara wanted to say more, but before he could press her, she moved away.

"All right, and here we go," Bob said with a data pad in hand. "In three, two, one."

Have you ever been so tired that you don't even remember falling asleep? Like, one moment your head is touching down on the pillow, and the next you're waking up to the sound of your mortal enemy, the alarm clock? This was a lot like that.

One second, Tom was in the simulation chamber, wanting to ask Sara what she was too scared to tell him, and the next, he was waking from a sudden and fast sleep. He woke to the cold embrace of the coffin. The prison that he now realized was nothing but code—ones and zeros.

How could they make this feel so real? How could even an army of coders have created this? It seemed impossible.

As promised, his memories were intact. He opened his HUD.

"Ohhhh, snaps," Gary said, blowing what sounded like air out of his nonexistent lips. "What in the name of—brochacho, we have a lot to talk about."

"Tell me about it," Tom answered, grateful to hear the AI's voice again.

He cycled through his HUD to the map screen. While the fog of war still concealed locations he had yet to explore, the screen also showed five red dots. One was marked "Bishop," and the rest were identified with the new candidates' names.

His inventory was empty, but his level, skills, and credits had traveled with him.

LEVEL 7

CLASS TYPE: BRAWLER

SKILL POINTS: 1

CONGRATULATIONS: YOU DEFEATED THAT CRAZY CULT-LEADER MAYOR. GARY, TELL HIM WHAT HE'S WON! YOU'VE NOT ONLY LEVELED UP WITH A NEW SKILL POINT, BUT YOU'VE ALSO GAINED 100 CREDITS. REMEMBER, AT LEVEL 10, THE STORE OPENS.

CREDITS: 120

"I'm downloading more information on this new world by the second, but there's so much content it's going to take even me a minute to catch up," Gary said, then added, "Dude, there's something wrong. These aren't the droids you're looking for!"

Tom reached up to push off the coffin lid. He expected what he had found the other two times he'd entered the Eternal Engine: dry, dead desert as far as the eye could see and two suns overhead.

"Wait!" Gary yelled, too late. "Don't."

Hot, humid moisture attacked Tom's lungs. There was no desert here, no night hounds; there was only jungle. Everywhere he looked, lush vegetation and trees sought to blot out the sky. He heard alien calls that he thought might come from baboons.

Tom scanned the area as panic set in. This wasn't the game he had entered before. This was something else. This was a new kind of hell.

"Dude," Gary breathed.

CHAPTER 49

SARA

Sara plugged Tom into the game again with a long sigh. Should she have tried to tell him about what was waiting for him? Should she have tried to warn him about what Chairman insisted be done? Should she have warned him about Chairman himself, that over the last few months he had seemed to change?

These questions and more hurtled through Sara's mind like baseballs pitched one after the other by a world-class athlete.

"You okay?" Bob asked. He touched a key on his data pad and looked up at his employer. "I know how hard you've been pushing yourself to get everything ready. Maybe you need some rest."

"I'll be fine," Sara said, waving off the offer. "I need some caffeine, is what I need. How about you stop by the cafeteria on the way back to the office."

"You got it," Bob said, following Sara out of the door. "The usual?"

Sara was surprised to see Toby and a security team making their way down the hall toward her. She had not requested aid or called for help.

"Toby, what's going on?" Sara asked. The look on his face spelled out the worst possible scenario.

"Ms. Tran," Toby said regretfully, "I'm sorry, but I have orders from Chairman himself that you and Bob are to come with me."

"Orders? What?" Sara scrunched her brow in confusion. "What are you talking about? What's going on? Chairman didn't say anything to me."

She looked at Bob. His eyes were huge as he stared down at his data pad like a deer in headlights.

"You won't be needing those anymore," Toby said, jerking his head. The security guards closed in, taking Bob's and Sara's data pads.

Sara might have tried to resist but felt in shock, like someone had dumped an ice-cold bucket of water on her and tied her stomach in a complex fisherman's knot. Chairman knew about her and Julie, and he was going to make her pay.

"Bob, run!" Sara said, pushing past Toby. Rather, she tried to push past Toby. In her high heels, she made it two steps before he grabbed her. His hands felt like vise grips around her shoulder and arm.

"Ms. Tran, stop. I don't want to—"

Bob slapped Toby, catching the bigger man by surprise. Toby's hold on Sara loosened for the slightest moment as he registered pain.

"Run!" Bob yelled as he was grabbed by other security guards.

Sara ripped free from Toby's grip. Another guard moved to tackle her, but Bob wrapped his arms around him and they both fell to the floor.

Sara took off running as fast as her high-heeled feet could move her. Three steps in, she kicked off her shoes and kept going.

Toby and two other security guards had recovered from

Bob's sudden and uncharacteristic outburst and gave chase. Sara sprinted down the hall as fast as her feet would carry her. Speed born of desperation and panic seized her in that moment. She had never run faster.

She turned a corner into the elevator lobby and waved her hand frantically in front of the reader, hoping there was a lift waiting.

Please, please, please, Sara thought, gasping for breath. *Open!*

Toby and his team were mere yards away. Bob was screaming something in the distance, out of sight.

The elevator doors opened with that classic Eternal Engine chime. Sara rushed forward, but the lift was already occupied.

Jeffrey Saga and four more security guards filled the chamber.

"Jeffrey, Jeffrey," Sara said, squeezing into the cylindrical cab and frantically waving her hand over the close-door button. "Close the doors. Close the doors!"

But Toby's meaty hand kept the doors open. He looked at her with sadness in his eyes.

Jeffrey, on the other hand, was quite happy. "It seems like you've been going behind Chairman's back," he said. Then, to the security team: "Hold her."

Sara looked around in panic as she was seized. Fighting was useless, but she did so anyway, thrashing her arms this way and that, kicking at the guards. One of them used his baton to clock her across the jaw so hard stars exploded behind her eyes and pain bloomed in her head.

"That's enough," Toby shouted.

Sara sagged in the grips of her captors, looking up to see who had hit her. It wasn't one of the security guards at all. Jeffrey Saga himself was holding the baton.

"I've always wanted to do that," Jeffrey said with malice in his eyes. "My oh my, how the mighty have fallen."

"Come on, get her out of there," Toby said, motioning his team forward. "Easy, easy, she's not to be harmed. Those orders came from Chairman himself."

Jeffrey's smug smile faltered for a moment as he realized he had gone against Chairman's orders.

"You're nothing, you're nothing to him," Sara said as she was escorted firmly from the elevator. "None of you know what you're dealing with here. You all are so blind. Toby, Toby, you have to let me go. What are you going to do with me? Are you going to kill me? Toby, that's not who you are."

Toby ignored her, leading the way back toward the simulation chamber.

The white floor was streaked with blood. Bob was nowhere to be seen, but the trail he'd left was undeniable.

"Toby, you're not a killer," Sara pressed. "You don't have to do this."

"What do you know about me?" Toby asked with a shake of his head. "How do you know I'm not a killer? This is the most you've ever spoken to me. And that's fine, but don't talk to me now like you know who I am."

Sara opened her mouth, then closed it.

They had reached the new simulation chamber, where Tom and Bishop had been plugged into the game minutes before. Toby opened the door, and Sara was forced inside.

"We're not going to kill you, Ms. Tran," Jeffrey crooned behind her. "Chairman has something else much more . . . interesting planned for you."

Sara's eyes bulged. Instead of two cylinders in the room, there were now four. In the short time she had been gone, two more had been rolled in from somewhere. Bob, a bloody Bob, was in one of them. If you ignored the broken teeth and gashes on his face, he almost looked as though he could be sleeping.

A simulation crown rested on his brow, identical to Tom's and Bishop's.

"No, not like this," Sara said, finding her strength once more. "Not like this!"

Scratching, kicking, and biting with all her might, Sara struggled against the much stronger security guards, who carried her toward the last open cylinder.

"No! No, wake up!" Sara screamed to Tom, Bishop, and Bob in vain. "Wake up!"

She flailed wildly, with no result, as they strapped her into the capsule. Heated panic raced through Sara's body; sweat and blood mixed as they ran down her face. She stopped screaming, knowing the others couldn't hear her and that those who could hear her didn't care.

"Isn't this poetic justice," Jeffrey Saga said, removing a data pad from his inside pocket. "Chairman asked me to tell you before you went in that he's sorry it had to end up like this. That you—you were always his favorite."

Jeffrey said the words as if speaking them caused him actual physical pain.

Toby moved forward with the simulation crown, ready to induct her into the next world. She was about to become a victim of the machine she'd had a hand in building. The Eternal Engine claiming yet another soul.

"As for me, I have to say I am eager to watch you die, over and over again," Jeffrey cackled. "It's not every day you get to see a creator consumed by her own creation. I love my job."

Toby walked forward with heavy feet and placed the crown gently on her head.

Sara was terrified for her daughter. What would happen to Michelle when her mother didn't come home?

"I don't know how or when, but I'm going to get out of

here," Sara said through gritted teeth. "When I do, I'm going to make this game look like a vacation compared to what I'm going to do to you."

"Promises, promises," Jeffrey said with a sigh. He pressed a button on his data pad. "You shouldn't make promises you can't keep."

The next thing Sara knew, she was waking up in a coffin. Breathing heavily, she was grateful to find her memories intact. She remembered everything, from Chairman's treachery to Jeffrey Saga's stupid face.

She knew exactly where she was. She was in the game. Sara reached up for the lid and let herself out of the coffin.

She also knew this wasn't the desert game. This was simulation 2.0, the jungle planet. Chairman had ordered her to put Tom, Bishop, and the new candidates into the second game without their knowledge. She'd never expected to find herself in this place.

Thick foliage stretched out as far as the eye could see, which, thanks to the density, wasn't far at all. It was humid, with a single bright sun penetrating the jungle canopy. Wild animals called out as Sara tried to remember everything she had read, from the locations of the other players to what she might face in the jungle, and to plan how she would complete the mission and get out.

"I hate you!" Sara looked up into the sky, screaming. "You hear me, Chairman? I hate you!"

When nothing happened, Sara gritted her teeth and stepped out of the coffin. As she touched down, she heard something crashing through the depths of the jungle to her right.

Panic seized her. She looked around for anything that might be used as a weapon, then picked up a branch and readied herself.

CHAPTER 50

SARA

Bob came bursting through the jungle a minute later. He was out of breath and sweating. "I heard—I heard you yell. My coffin is right—right over there."

Sara wanted to hit him and hug him at the same time. She started with the former.

"Why are we here?! What did you do?!" she yelled, dropping the branch and slapping Bob with both hands. "What did you tell them?"

"I didn't—I didn't tell them anything!" he shouted, swatting her hands away and shielding his face. "Stop hitting me."

Sara was still fuming, but she lowered her hands and hung her head. "We have to get out of here. We have to get back. I have to get back to my daughter."

"And we will," Bob reassured her. "We're going to get out of here, boss. It's going to be okay."

He drew her in for a hug. Sara wanted to pull away. This was highly unprofessional; Bob was her employee. But she would be lying if she said it didn't feel comforting. Tears pooled in her eyes as she thought of Michelle.

Sara refused to let the tears fall. She cleared her throat and removed herself from Bob's embrace. "Okay, that's enough—that's enough of that. We have to get out of here."

"Where is here?" Bob asked, shaking his head and looking around in awe. "I didn't know there was another world. Hey, if we're in a game, why do we have our memories?"

"A parting gift from Chairman," Sara huffed. She opened her HUD by turning her left forearm over twice.

"Well, well, well, look what the night hound dragg—"

Sara silenced Gary before he could finish his sentence. The first screen showed her stats.

LEVEL 1

CLASS TYPE: UNKNOWN

SKILL POINTS: 0

CREDITS: 0

WELCOME TO THE SUCK, MS. TRAN. PLEASE PUT YOUR SEAT IN THE UPRIGHT POSITION AND MAKE SURE THE TRAY TABLE IN FRONT OF YOU IS CLOSED.

Sara swiped past this screen to find a message from Chairman himself.

MY DEAREST SARA,

I HOPE YOU UNDERSTAND WHY THIS IS HAPPENING. I NEVER WANTED TO SEE YOU IN THE GAME, BUT YOU FORCED MY HAND BY GOING BEHIND MY BACK TO MEET WITH JULIE NOBLE.

I DON'T HOLD IT AGAINST YOU. I UNDERSTAND THE FRIENDSHIP YOU TWO SHARE, AND I ALMOST ADMIRE IT. TRUE FRIENDSHIP IS NOTHING TO BE TAKEN LIGHTLY. STILL, I HAD TO ACT. CONSIDER THIS AN OPPORTUNITY TO REDEEM YOURSELF. PROVE YOURSELF IN THE GAME AND RETAKE YOUR POSITION AT TANUS

CORPORATION WHEN YOU EMERGE VICTORIOUS. WE WILL NEED SOMEONE LIKE YOU WHEN WE MAKE THE TRIP TO OUR NEW HOME.

YOU KNOW HOW MUCH I RESPECT YOU AS A MOTHER. I ASSURE YOU NO HARM WILL COME TO YOUR DAUGHTER. SHE WILL BE CARED FOR AS IF SHE WERE MY OWN.

IF YOU HURRY, YOU CAN COMPLETE THE MISSION IN A FEW DAYS. YOUR DAUGHTER WILL BE TOLD THAT YOU HAD TO GO ON AN EMERGENCY TRIP FOR WORK AND THAT YOU WILL BE BACK SOON.

YOU CAN DO THIS, SARA. I HOPE YOU CAN FORGIVE ME WHEN YOU GET OUT. NO MATTER WHAT YOU MIGHT THINK, I AM CHEERING FOR YOU.

FOLLOW THE CHIME,

CHAIRMAN

Sara was practically shaking. She gritted her teeth so hard she thought she might break them.

"Are you okay? There's a vein I've never seen before pulsating in your forehead," Bob said.

"We need to get out of here," Sara repeated, breaking free from the spell the message held on her.

She'd known this new part of the game existed. She knew its goal and that some players were given the same objective while others were given competing ones. Tom and Bishop shared an objective. But Sara?

She had to figure out which task she had been given and then see it through.

"I didn't even know—I didn't even know another world existed," Bob said again. "Should we try to find Tom, Bishop, and the others? Are there other candidates in this one too?"

"We'll move toward the nearest village," Sara said, racking her brain to recall the map of the world and where the closest refuge might be found. The map on her HUD was covered in the fog of war. "Keep your ears out for the game's chime. If you hear it, that means we're on the right track. There are no other living people in this world that I know of. Just us and Tom and Bishop's team."

"Right," Bob said, following Sara's lead as she began picking her way through the jungle. "Why was this kept a secret?"

"Chairman is always testing people," Sara said with newfound disgust. "He wanted to train the new candidates but also throw Tom and Bishop a curveball."

"And if we are in the game, that means—that means if we die, we come back, but—but with less of ourselves," Bob breathed with a shudder.

Sara had flashbacks to the first day she'd met Bob. He'd asked just as many obvious questions.

"Yes, Bob, that's right," Sara said, doing nothing to mask the irritation in her voice. "So that's why we're not going to die. We're going to get to the closest village, and we're going to find an objective, complete it, and get out of this thing."

"Okay, right," Bob said, sounding stressed. "Man, my nana is going to be so worried about me when I don't come home today." With that, he seemed to run out of things to say.

Sara was grateful to continue their journey in silence. This was a place she knew. Jeffrey had been in charge of coding this world, but she had pored over its scenarios and obstacles.

She began to remember the layout: what to avoid and where to go. It would be a half day's travel to the closest village, where there would be food and safety. They would have to keep away from certain areas of the jungle like the marshlands, but there were no lost ones here.

Instead, there was disease, humidity that would kill you, and far more animals than in the other simulation. Jeffrey had insisted he fill the jungle with everything from four-armed monkeys to giant snakes and monstrous spiders.

Sara shivered involuntarily. She had a well-concealed phobia of spiders and anything spiderlike. She set her jaw as she remembered the size of the spiders in this world. But no matter what, she would get through this. She had no other choice. Whatever she couldn't do for herself, she would do for her daughter.

I'm coming home, Sara vowed. *Michelle, don't worry. Mama's coming home.*

CHAPTER 51

TOM

It had all been lies on top of lies, but what did he really expect? Had he thought that Chairman, Sara, or anyone at Tanus Corporation had been telling the truth?

Tom mentally kicked himself repeatedly for being so ready to fall into the trap. Of course this was going to be another test for him and Bishop. It wasn't enough that they had proved themselves once. They had to do it again, this time while leading a team.

There were two changes to the HUD Tom had woken with in the coffin. One was a map showing him where the other five coffins were; the second was a messaging system. It carried a single note for him. It was from Chairman.

MR. DEXTER,

I TRUST THAT YOU ARE ANGRY, FEEL BETRAYED, AND MORE THAN LIKELY WISH TO DO ME SEVERE HARM. IT IS AT THIS POINT THAT I WOULD LIKE TO REMIND YOU THAT YOU ARE NOT WITHOUT BLAME YOURSELF. IT WAS YOU WHO HAD HELP FROM JULIE NOBLE IN THE ORIGINAL GAME. AND NOW YOU ARE SPYING ON ME AND MY COMPANY.

PLEASE KNOW THAT I UNDERSTAND ALL OF THIS AND HARBOR NO ILL WILL TOWARD YOU. IT'S HUMAN NATURE TO WANT MORE, WHETHER THAT IS WEALTH, STATUS, OR IN YOUR CASE, KNOWLEDGE. I HAVE COMPLETE CONFIDENCE THAT YOU AND MS. BISHOP WILL BE AS SUCCESSFUL THIS TIME AS YOU WERE BEFORE.

IN A SHOW OF GOOD FAITH, I HAVE ALLOWED YOUR LEVEL, SKILLS, AND CREDITS TO BE MOVED OVER TO THIS PHASE OF THE GAME. I THOUGHT IT WOULD BE A BIT UNFAIR FOR YOU TO KEEP YOUR LEGENDARY WEAPON. HOWEVER, YOUR AI HAS BEEN LEARNING AND EVOLVING. AT FIRST I THOUGHT WE SHOULD LIMIT THE AID HE PROVIDES YOU, BUT ON SECOND THOUGHT WE'LL ALLOW IT.

HUMANS MUST LEARN TO WORK WITH AI IN THE FUTURE, OR WE WILL ALL PERISH. YOU'RE THE FIRST TO WORK WITH GARY IN SUCH A WAY AS TO MAKE HIM A VALUABLE ASSET.

TRUST YOUR INSTINCTS, LEAD YOUR TEAM, AND WHEN YOU PROVE YOURSELF VICTORIOUS AGAIN, THAT WILL BE THE END OF THE GAMES. WE WILL MOVE ON TO THE REAL THING.

I AM VERY MUCH LOOKING FORWARD TO WATCHING YOUR JOURNEY, AND TO OUR CONTINUED PARTNERSHIP IN THE FUTURE ONCE YOU GET OUT.

REMEMBER TO FOLLOW THE CHIME,

CHAIRMAN

Tom hated himself for reading the note twice, but he had to make sure he wasn't missing anything. If Chairman was being sincere—and at this point, Tom had no idea if he even *could* be sincere—then he didn't hold Tom's alliance with Julie Noble against him. Chairman, Julie, and Sara were like some messed-up, dysfunctional family. They argued and fought but in the end would never actually harm one another. In Chairman's note, he even sounded like a father or brother, chiding Tom.

Tom trudged through the dense, alien jungle. Although there was only a single sun overhead, the vegetation told him this wasn't Earth. The trees were a strange blue hue, decked with orange vines and standing in patches of purple grass. Monkeys with four arms chittered down at him from branches. A few even picked their butts and threw things at him.

"That is just wrong," Gary said with disgust. "What kind of sicko codes in monkey doo-doo? Mommy issues for sure."

"It's good to have you back," Tom told Gary. "I missed you."

"Bro, don't start that again. I'm going to cry. You know I'm a crier. Are you trying to make me cry right now?" Gary answered softly. "Missed you too, bro."

Birds screamed through the air—large birds, much larger than any Tom had ever seen. These birds had wingspans of at least fifteen to twenty feet. Their bodies were covered with more leathery skin than feathers.

Tom was following his map, looking to recover Bishop and then the other members of his team. Not having run this simulation before would make things ten times harder. And to begin with, he and Bishop still had to convince the other candidates to work with them, even though the new players had no reason to trust them.

Because of the added humidity, Tom realized that hydration was going to be a factor sooner than he anticipated. This heat was different from the desert heat but just as deadly. He needed to make sure Bishop was safe first; then water had to be a priority.

As he approached Bishop's coffin, a strange new sound filled the air. It wasn't the scream of an animal or the cry of a human; it was a grunt, a guttural expression of exertion and fear.

Tom left his HUD on for the time being. He needed all the help he could get, and truth be told, having Gary around was comforting. He crested a giant fallen tree that was as wide as a small vehicle. On the other side, he saw Bishop, grunting and struggling to free herself from a pool of murky water.

The water didn't even look liquid. It was the same rich brown color as the ground. Tom realized the bog must have been designed to deceive, with a thick layer of dirt above enough water to suck a person in.

Bishop was waist deep. She struggled to keep calm and get out. The only problem was that with every step she took, she sank a little bit deeper.

"Oh, arc you kidding me?" Gary said, aghast. "Quicksand? I still have nightmares about *The NeverEnding Story* and what they did to Artax."

"Need a hand, Marshal?" Tom asked, careful to skirt the bog as he searched for a way to get her out.

"Is that you, Gamer?" Bishop asked, turning her head to spot him. "You know, we have to be the dumbest pair of humans to have ever existed, to fall for this twice. When I get out of here, I'm going to shove Sara's head so far up her—"

A sharp hiss cut Bishop off. She and Tom looked toward the sound to see the biggest snake either of them had ever imagined. The head of the creature was as large as Tom's torso; the tongue that escaped its lips quivered like a bullwhip.

"Just when you think things can't get worse," Tom whispered under his breath. "Snakes, why did it have to be snakes?"

"Not a snake, bro," Gary chided. "A basilisk."

The basilisk glared at Tom through yellow eyes. Slitted pupils took in the situation as real understanding behind the creature's glare informed Tom this was no ordinary reptile.

Of course they made the animals here smarter and more deadly, Tom thought. *It wouldn't be the Eternal Engine without a few surprises.*

The basilisk rose up into the air, exposing its impressive body. Its frame was as thick as a telephone pole. It was difficult to gauge the length of the creature since it was coiled at the base, but Tom guessed it had to be at least thirty feet long.

It tilted its head to the side, waiting for Tom to make the first move. Although the serpent was still a good forty feet away from him, Tom didn't want to underestimate the creature's reach.

"I don't mean to be insensitive here, but the clock is ticking," Bishop told him.

"Easy, easy," Tom said, crouching a bit and walking backward around the bog. The last thing he wanted to do was take his eyes off the basilisk. Almost as a reflex, he extended an open hand toward the creature as if that would help. "Easy, huge snake that doesn't even exist but will still kill me."

Slowly, Tom backpedaled around the bog. The snake continued to regard him, unmoving.

"The night hounds in the first world acted as shepherds for the players, right?" Bishop whispered, like she wanted to believe what she was saying. "Maybe the snakes will act the same way here?"

"Maybe," Tom said, putting Bishop between himself and the snake. It was only then that he was willing to locate a suitable-looking vine and yank it free.

"Or maybe not," Gary warned them. "I'm not supposed to interfere with your mission, but maybe not."

"Tom?" Bishop asked, sounding worried.

"It's okay," Tom said reassuringly. He looped the vine in his hand, preparing to throw it to Bishop. "The snake knows there's a bog here; it won't go into the wa—"

The snake moved. Hundreds of pounds of coiled muscle and scales dove more elegantly than any human ever could. One second, it was on the opposite side of the bog, and the next, it slipped under the surface.

"Oh, hell no!" Bishop said, struggling toward the edge of the bog with renewed strength. The extra effort gained her very little ground, and she sank up to her stomach. "Tom!"

"Get it," Tom shouted, throwing the vine to Bishop.

"Oh, Lord have mercy, no," Gary shouted. "Nope, nope, no, get her out. Tom, you get that woman out right now!"

The coiled vine landed beside Bishop with a splash. She grabbed it and looped it around her waist, and Tom pulled with every ounce of his strength.

Tom saw the look of sheer panic on Bishop's face even before the snake dragged her under the water. She disappeared with a curse on her lips. The vine went taut in Tom's hand, and he was nearly jerked off his feet.

Grunting, hands shaking with effort, Tom was forced to sit down or be pulled off his feet. He dug his boots into the soil, arched his back, and pulled with everything he had. It was a violent game of tug-of-war, and Bishop's life would go to the victor. Seconds felt like minutes as Tom's muscles burned with effort.

"*Rawww!*" A primal roar escaped his lips as the vine cut into his palms, demanding blood.

Gary was background noise, shouting obscenities at the basilisk and encouragement to Tom.

As strong as Tom was, he was still being dragged inch by inch toward the bog's edge. Every second he held on took him closer to joining Bishop in the watery grave.

Giving up was never an option. It wasn't who Tom was; that was one of the reasons he was a perfect candidate for the game.

Neither was Bishop giving up.

With an eruption of water, she exploded to the surface, clutching the snake's head as it writhed in pain. Bishop had found the left eye of the serpent and grabbed it with her right hand, squeezing until the orb was gore-filled jelly in her palm.

Tom had never heard a sound like the one the snake made then, something between a hiss and a shrill scream that echoed in his eardrums. The snake shivered and spasmed, then released Bishop altogether.

Tom redoubled his efforts. The vine in his hands dripped with his blood as he pulled arm over arm, dragging Bishop to safety. Finally the teammates fell on the ground beside one another, huffing and gasping for breath.

Bishop threw up some bog water but was alive.

A ray of light hit Tom, somehow piercing the canopy of foliage. Motion to his left caught his eye. A hummingbird zipped past. If Tom hadn't known better, he would have sworn it was looking at him. It flew in front of him, to the left and right, and then came so close it nearly touched his nose.

As soon as Tom reached toward it, the moment was broken. The hummingbird zipped off into the jungle, lost to sight. Logic told him the hummingbird had nothing to do with his wife; his heart told him something different.

Remembering that the basilisk was merely beaten, not dead, Tom rose to his feet and grabbed Bishop, dragging her farther away from the pond.

"Uhhh, guys?" Gary asked.

Bishop coughed.

Tom panted.

"Guys?" Gary said again.

"What?!" Tom and Bishop asked as one.

"We're not alone," Gary answered.

"She's gone, so you can relax now," a voice said from behind them. "Not sure I've ever seen anyone handle a god serpent like that before. Who are you?"

Tom recognized the voice but couldn't believe it. It couldn't be him.

Turning to look, Tom saw Wade and Otto standing just inside the tree line. Except for their clothing, both men looked just like Tom remembered: Wade gray haired, with wisdom and kindness in his eyes; Otto muscular and strong jawed, with a look of distrust.

Their clothes weren't dusters and holsters; instead, they wore boots, camouflage pants, and sweat-stained shirts.

"Wade, Otto?" Tom asked excitedly. "Is that you?"

He took a step forward. Wade drew a thick blaster from a holster at his lower back. Otto mirrored the move as his weapon whined with a ready charge. Both aimed at Tom's head.

"Do we know you?" Otto asked.

The joy at seeing people Tom considered friends was extinguished as quickly as total darkness in the presence of the brightest light. Of course they didn't know him—they weren't even alive. They were NPCs, probably reset for this new world.

Bishop was still on her hands and knees, coughing out bog water. Wade looked at his counterpart and shook his head. "More lost souls, like the other ones we found. Best to stun them and take them to the queen."

"No, wait—" was the last thing Tom said before flashes of blue leaped from the NPCs' barrels and numbing black pain overwhelmed his consciousness.

EPILOGUE

CHAIRMAN

Betraying Tom, Bishop, and Sara brought him no sense of joy or accomplishment. It was simply what had to be done to ensure that there would be a tomorrow. On the path to the future, sacrifices had to be made.

But he had faith that they would all pull out of this not only alive but together. For if humanity had any hope of enduring the hardships of the future, it would be together, hand in hand with their AI counterparts. Chairman was sure of that. He had run the scenarios and numbers thousands upon thousands of times, all in the name of humanity.

It was for them that he was doing all of this. He hoped one day history would remember that. There was no greed in his plan. His grandmother and father had taught him that.

Sure, humanity had its problems; that was putting it lightly. But who was above reproach? Who was perfect?

"Chairman" wasn't a person; it was a mantle, a title passed down from generation to generation in different forms through the centuries. Now it was his turn to shepherd humanity into this dangerous new future. But he was ready for it. The strength that flowed in his blood was enough.

His father, who had served as Chairman before him, had understood his purpose was to help and save. It was he who had gathered the experts who'd discovered Earth's expiration date. It was he who had orchestrated the rise of Tanus Corporation. Now it was up to Bob to carry on his father's work, the work of all the generations before him.

Always careful to protect his identity, Bob communicated via emails and calls, using a filter to mask his voice. His grandmother, the matriarch of the family and his father's mother, also played a hand, taking on the mantle of Chairman when Bob could not. When the players had emerged victorious from the simulation, it was his grandmother who had donned the facade of Chairman and welcomed them back to reality.

There was a way in which Bob differed from his father. He wouldn't ask others to do what he was unwilling to do himself. Hence, against his grandmother's advice, he had entered the game. There were two types of leaders: those who led by telling people what to do, and those who led by example. Past generations had been the former; Bob would be the latter.

He had meant every word he'd written to Sara and Tom. Sara's daughter would be looked after; Tom and Bishop would be freed once they completed this second part of the game. He had no love for all the deception and backhanded dealings he'd engaged in, but that was how it had to be.

Despite how it might look, a plan was in place. Even within chaos there was order, fate determining the path of what many perceived as the unknowable future.

Bob prepared himself to navigate the next phase of the game. What lay in store for them now would test them to the breaking point.

He was looking forward to it.

AUTHOR'S NOTE

This is the part where I get to talk directly to you and you get to hear what I really sound like. Thank you so much for loving stories enough to pick up this book. You are the reason I write. Your love for stories of adventure, hope, and family fuel these books. If you believe what I believe, that there is room for new stories to be told and more adventures to come, then I have two things to ask of you.

First, please consider leaving a review for *Hard Reset.* Even a few words help other potential readers decide if they want to give the story a chance or not.

Second, share with a friend. I know I get my best recommendations from people I talk to on a daily or weekly basis. Who am I kidding—I'm an introvert, so weekly basis at best. Still, people trust their friends, and a recommendation from you would mean the world.

That's it. I believe that we can do great things as a reading community. Together, if we all dare to be great and leave reviews and share the books we care about, more content like this can be made. Thank you for being a part of this community of readers that we lovingly call our Pack. Let's dare greatly together.

ACKNOWLEDGMENTS

Over my last thirteen years of writing and publishing, a community of readers that we lovingly call our Pack has formed. They have spread the news of our books far and wide, left reviews, and purchased our stories, all leading to this point. Without readers, I'd just be a guy hallucinating with my imagination, throwing stories out into a void. With our Pack, I get to do what I love for a living and call myself a writer.

Thank you to the entire Blackstone team, including Lysa Williams and Josie Woodbridge, who have been cc'd on a hundred emails at this point regarding *Hard Reset*. To Greg Boguslawski, whom I met at an authors' conference where I was speaking. As soon as I told him about the book, he was all in. To Marilyn Kretzer, who has shepherded the novel through the publishing process like the champion she is and who introduced me to my agent. To Melissa Ann Singer, who went through the book over and over again until it was perfect, and to Candice Edwards, for a killer cover. And to my amazing editor Riam Griswold, who so many times saved me from myself. I'm a humble storyteller; Riam is a true master of words.

To Matthew Charles Hall, who has been a great friend throughout the entire process and whom I am grateful to know.

I don't want to forget my agent, Adam Chromy, who is guiding the *Hard Reset* ship into the future.